STRAPPING SUZETTE

Brunhilde, nude, save for black leather thigh boots, with spiked heels, emerged from the hallway, bearing an English school cane, perched on the stiffened nipples of her jutting bare breasts.

'You are invited to take a bare-bum thrashing,' the master purred, 'in front of these friendly witnesses.'

'What?' Suze gasped, clutching her face. 'Oh, no ... please! Fiona! What is this?'

Fiona had removed her skirtlet, and, nude, was bending over, fiddling at her right thigh. Her bottom melons shone in the shafts of sunlight streaking the shadow, illumining bright red canewelts.

'Oh, no, Fiona,' Suze moaned, 'a sub ... *you*?'

STRAPPING
SUZETTE

Yolanda Celbridge

This book is a work of fiction.
In real life, make sure you practise safe sex.

First published in 2003 by
Nexus
Thames Wharf Studios
Rainville Road
London W6 9HA

www.nexus-books.co.uk

Typeset by TW Typesetting, Plymouth, Devon

Printed and bound by Clays Ltd, St Ives PLC

ISBN 0 352 33783 4

Contents

1

Thighs Asunder

It was a dark and moonless night. There was a storm. The rain slashed down in steel-grey sheets, drenching the boat, and rendering the river Maroni invisible. The howls of monkeys and macaws were drenched to silence. Suzette Shard shivered in her cabin, and turned the air-conditioning unit off. Lightning flared, followed, seconds later, by crashing thunder, and the lights flickered. Geckos, immobile on the walls and ceiling, stared at Suzette with their big ball eyes. The yacht shuddered, and the mirror, occupying the whole length of her aft bulkhead, trembled slightly, altering her reflection, as though some cosmic hand had nudged her breasts, to make them quiver. Rain-soaked twilight descended once more, and the hissing rain thumped the cabin cruiser's hull with its machine-gun spatter.

Sweat beaded Suzette's brow, and the upper portion of her breasts, which were bared by her towelling robe, as the humid heat wrestled with the washed cold air from the air-conditioning unit. She looked down, frowning at a glistening rivulet that streaked her upper left thigh, below her robe's hem. The sweat inched its way towards her knee and, when Suzette flexed her leg, dropped onto the cork floor. Another rivulet advanced, this one on her right thigh, and she wiped it away, rubbing her finger on the white fluffy towelling. Her clock, poised in eminent domain over the pyramid of oils and lotions on her toilette table, gave the time as seven-thirty: half an hour for Suzette to

1

dress for dinner, although, of course, that meant nothing – dinner began when Suzette Shard chose to arrive for it, even in the wilds of French Guiana.

Suzette wriggled, as a further drop of sweat slipped into the cleavage of her breasts, to tickle the bare skin. Sighing, she shucked off her robe, and let it drop to the floor, then wiped the sweat from her breasts. She made a face at her fingernails, manicured to slivers, and devoid of polish or colour, like her toenails. Her naked body gleamed wet in the mirror, as she reached for a cigarette, lit it, and stood to inspect herself, legs akimbo and hands on hips, with the long white fumable dangling at the corner of her mouth, its ember poised over her upturned right nipple. There was no smile on her lips, as she gazed with steely approbation into her own eyes, then down the curves of her body: the perfect breasts, with the big strawberry domes of her nipples, flickering to tenseness, as she scrutinised herself, in a 'bod check': flat, muscled belly, long coltish legs, and between them, the massive golden thatch of her pubis, unable to disguise the abnormally large and ripe swelling of the hillock, nor the fat folds of the girl-slice beneath, red and moist even under the drooping and untrimmed tangle of curly blond hairs, that dangled way beneath the indenture of her thighs, and below the firm crescent moons of the buttocks, visible in her thigh gap, and peeping behind the vulval flesh.

Most models shaved their pubis entirely, or trimmed it to some pathetic wisp of hair, a bikini line, but Suze Shard sported the biggest, richest forest of any girl anywhere: wild at bush, wild at heart. To the world, she was simply 'Suze', or, 'The Bottom', no surname needed. She touched her breasts, plumping them like pillows; patted the thighs and wide hip bones; checked the dimples at her collarbones and navel, then raked a fingernail across her extruded belly-button. Suze drew hard on her cigarette, and turned abruptly, thrusting out her croup, with her eyes fixed on the twin orbs, gleaming a uniform tan in the looking-glass. Her hands clasped her waist, the fingertips almost touching. She expelled the smoke in a long sigh, through her

2

nose, as her fingers crept to the satin fesses, and danced, hesitantly, on the golden mounds of her bare buttocks. She put her hands behind her nape, and swivelled rapidly, from one pose to another, pouting and leering at the mirror, with her buttocks thrust out and up, or open at the crack, *daring* the watcher to touch . . .

An inch of tobacco ash fell onto her nipple, then cascaded over her belly, wet with sweat. Suze ignored it, continuing to pout and pirouette before the mirror, with the ripe golden croup winking at its likeness, clenching and squirming and trembling in teasing paroxysms. She twirled, to thrust her crotch grossly forward at the mirror, parting the swollen lips, and she grinned briefly and icily, seeing a film of moisture smearing the folds at the opening to her pouch. Her breathing came in low, deliberate gasps, like a big cat's, and she wiped a finger across her slimed pubic entrance, holding it to the light, to let the fluid sparkle, before smearing it on a paper tissue. She mouthed a kiss to herself in the glass, without smiling, but in cold approval. Then, she thrust her bare buttocks very close, and blew a thick plume of smoke at the glass, so that her head was obscured in the cloud, and only the likeness of her naked arse peach was preserved, taut, muscled and rippling soft, creamy smooth, yet hard, its – *massiveness* of the most pristine, porcelain daintiness.

The flawless fault line that was the crack of her bum, rippled like a silken hair snapped tight between two perfect skin mountains. Beneath the twin globes of the peach, the skin receded tantalisingly into the smooth hard backs of her thighs, a little mystery of bum flesh tucked underneath the fesses. Not a mark, not a pock or scar or blemish, on that glorious arse-perfection . . . she was 'The Bottom' to the tabloids, that is, Suze *had* the bottom, 'the ten million dollar tush' to the Americans, '*cul de fantaisie*' to the French, '*die blonde Po-Prinzessin*' to the Germans, 'Britbum rules the waves' to the gutter British rags. The broadsheets splashed her silk-swathed moons, to illustrate what, astonishingly, obsessed the readers of tabloids; the thinking journals explained the sociology of Suze, an ice maiden with a toff accent, a bum to die for, rather, to worship, to pray for the smallest wiggle or twitch of those goddess's orbs, a sign of indulgence to her teased and adoring faithful.

Her haughty cheekbones and wide, full lips rarely condescended to a smile, hinting, like her muscled, athletic body, at ancient English firmness, the meat and muscle of a hardy island people, whose ancestors could have *swum* across the North Sea to Albion. Suze was more than a goddess: a keeper of sacred mysteries, an oracle, her sacred orbs familiars, rather than appurtenances, with her public scanning blurred photos for assurance that those forty inch globes wiggled and teased as normal, in augury that all was right with the world, and her slaves could go on enjoying their enslavement. American talk shows marvelled at an English rose's croup insured for ten million dollars . . . can we have a peek? Please, pretty please? Just a little tiny wiggle? *Ooh!* And now, the logical culmination, her own fragrance and clothing line, thongs and jeans and stockings and panties, everything to adorn and embellish the female bottom: called simply 'Suze', designed and marketed in Paris, by Laindoux, the *top* fashion house, and a photo and video shoot in French Guiana, really exotic jungle stuff, and touted to the max, 'Will Suze Bare All?'

Her breath came in gasps, and her smoke burned down to the stub. Suze opened the porthole to throw the butt away, and the glow fizzled out, as soon as it entered the hissing grey curtain of rain. A blast of warm air washed her conditioned cabin, and she opened the glass to its widest, relishing her damp bare skin, before returning to her inspection. She knelt on the floor, parting her thighs fully, and lowered her head, with her back-length blond tresses cascading, and her palm scooping them off the cork floor. She looked at her naked buttocks from between her thighs, the tangle of pubic hairs a great slash before the now swollen lips of her vulva, and the bum pucker crinkled jauntily like a sassy young prune, winking from in the crevasse of her perineum. Droplets of rain blew in, and spattered her fesses and crack, beading the skin of the

4

perineum, and the folds of the vulva. Suzette watched, panting very slightly, as a thick drop of girl come emerged from her quivering slice, and plopped onto the cork board, to be absorbed, leaving a dark stain.

She swallowed, and wiped her brow, then somersaulted to her feet. On her bunk was an array of clothing – jeans and T-shirts, mostly – but she passed it, and climbed up the narrow deck beneath the porthole. Outside, the river Maroni hissed, as the rainstorm lashed its waters. Behind, towed by the cruiser, rolled the barge, with masts and rigging, where the photo shoots took place, every day there was sun, with girls draped half nude over rusted bulkheads, barrels or stanchions, 'for *réalisme*'. Cordovan the photographer infuriated Suze, and her people – Fiona, her PA, and Dr Teidt, her manager and masseuse, and even Cordovan's own people, his girlfriend Soubise making a classic *moue*, at his assurances, throughout the dreary voyage upriver, that they were 'nearly there', wherever 'there' was. Cordovan claimed to feel it in the light and shade, and the whispering of the rainforest . . . genius must not be hurried.

Only Didier, the grizzled skipper, smiled, while the barefoot creole girls, who cleaned and tended the yacht, seemed indifferent. It was their country, after all. They sent convicts here in the old days, which the French would, the beasts, and the snaps of pampered European models, in comfortless poses recalling unnamable penalties and hardships, was supposed to evoke that *réalité*. They were supposed to get to the last village in civilisation, with some weird name, beyond which you weren't allowed to go, but maybe Cordovan had connections to get them further, into the true jungle. The sweat on Suze's bared flesh would be of real fear, as the arrows swished past her, or so he hinted. Why were the best photographers always bastards? Especially the French ones. What could Soubise see in Cordovan? He was smaller than her, thin and wiry, like the monkeys that screamed from the trees alongside the river.

Suze stood for several minutes, gazing at the rain, her big eyes wide and misted. Her lips pursed, and she shut her eyes briefly. Suze poked her breasts through the porthole, and stood, panting harshly, as the rain whipped her naked skin. She swallowed and gasped repeatedly, until she withdrew the wet teats, clambered higher, and placed her buttocks in the ring of the aperture. With a push, she thrust her bottom out of the porthole, until her doubled-over body was wedged at the hips, and her arse crack was opened fully. The rain scourged her bare arse skin, and Suze's teats shook violently, their nipples fully erect, like huge plums, as a low mewling moan escaped her lips. The crack of the rain on her naked buttocks rose sharply above the lashing of the water, like hard, plopping strokes of a watery whip. Water flooded the entire crack of her bottom, washing over her vaginal lips, and into the oily pouch between them. Clenching and unclenching with her sphincter muscle, Suze wrinkled her pouch and her anal pucker, so that both orifices opened, to admit a sluice of water. Her fingers crept between her legs, and began to rub the extruded swelling at the top of her fleshy pouch lips, through the wet tangle of hairs. Her breath came faster and faster, as her breasts and belly heaved, and her bare buttocks wriggled outside the porthole, like orchids brought to life by the rains. Her panting grew to a staccato yelp, as she rubbed herself between the legs, with firmer and faster strokes, and her yelp turned to a long, grunting moan, as her eyelids fluttered, and Suze stared at her flushed, drooling face in the looking-glass, and smiled.

'Suze?' said a girl's voice, outside her door. 'You ready?'

'Moment, Fiona.'

Suze panted, and slipped her bottom from the rain's caress. She dropped to the cork, picking up her robe, and draping it round her, in the same fluid movement as she unlocked the door. Fiona Leatherhead stood bare-legged, and barefoot, in the hatchway, wearing a loose, and very thin, cotton dress, that had once been a flour sack of the *Compagnie de Farine Guianaise, SA*. There was nothing under the flour sack except her skin. As tall as Suze, she was a lush-maned brunette, her billowing hair artlessly secured by a single golden barrette, and the tresses

6

cascading over her naked shoulders. The sack dress clung to her by nothing more than the powerful jutting of her large, upthrust breasts, whose big gooseberry nipples were starkly outlined against the thin fabric. Like Suze's, her skin was a uniform tan, though slightly darker. The breasts were conic, only a little smaller than Suze's, but firm, almost to rigidity, and her long legs swept down from a massive croup hanging from wide hip bones, that were a mare's rather than a colt's. She lowered her gaze, to inspect the droplets of water plopping from Suze's bottom.

'Yah, that's what I do, shower out the window, or the porthole, or whatever the beastly thing's called,' she said, as Suze stepped aside to let her enter. 'You have to wet each bit of yourself at a time. I do mostly my titties, 'cos that's absolutely the best fun. With you, I suppose it's your bum, darling. Be careful –' she whispered in Suze's ear '– there are *arse piranhas* in that river, who'd *love* to bite those forty inch, ten million dollar melons.'

Fiona spoke, or rather drawled, as though a dozen Chelsea romeos awaited her in the King's Road, but she preferred to joke with the girls. Suze's lips creased in a phantom smile.

'My *bum* is your bread and butter, Fiona,' she said. 'Don't knock it.'

'What a charming figure of speech,' Fiona exclaimed. 'Stop trying to stand on your dignity, Suze, you know it doesn't become you. Old school chums may stand on each other, but never on their dignity.'

Suze groped in her assortment of casual clothing, without allowing her towelling robe to fall, until Fiona took hold of its lapel, and firmly stripped it from Suze's body. Suze automatically put her hands to cover her bare pubis and breasts, until Fiona burst out laughing, and Suze laughed too.

'Where would a virginal St Ursulan be without reflexes?' said Fiona, patting Suze's bare bottom, and slithering her fingers through the wet cleft. 'Hurry up and sling some rags on, then we can go and get pissed, while those ghastly Frenchmen show off, correction, I can get pissed, and you can top up with frog water, poor darling. Your cooze is wet. I suppose you've been diddling? Nothing much else to do in this hole. I've been at it like a fourth-former, my clit must look like a balloon. Haven't decided which of the men to bed, you see. Cordovan is tolerable, I suppose, making up in ego what he lacks in looks, and I could replace that Soubise of his without much trouble, as no frog can resist horny English toff pussy, but Didier intrigues me – rough trade, aura of mystery, that foreign legion stuff . . .'

'Fiona, he's so ugly, and he must be forty years old,' Suze exclaimed, flicking through skimpy bikini panties, thongs and loinstrings.

'Yah,' Fiona said, licking her teeth. 'That's the amusement. You going to bother with *knickers*?'

'Well, they ogle me to see if I'm wearing any, and if I'm not, they ogle more,' Suze replied.

'*Were* you diddling?' Fiona demanded.

'Damn it, Fiona –'

'I can always tell,' said Fiona. 'You can't have forgotten the dorm, after lights out, at St Ursula's. Thighs asunder, wanking to the rafters! I'll take silence as a yes, Miss Prim. And you know what a slut's penalty for diddling was. You, of all people, the dorm frigging champion.'

'Oh, don't,' Suze protested. 'All right, I wanked off a lot, but so did every girl. I think I was victimised. Surely, I didn't masturbate more than the others? You, for example. I'm not proud of myself, you know. I hated all the punishments for so-called beastliness – so unfair – and hated what they called me. I never liked girls being called sluts, and mucky pups, and the like, just for not having won school colours. But I'm not prim. OK, I *was* diddling. It's not something I hope to live down, my reputation, and it's not something any girl can easily train herself to do without. It's been such a long time since I had – *you* know, with a fellow – and I don't know when I'll get back to civilisation.'

'Didier said we should reach Maripasoula tonight. That's the last outpost of civilisation, or the last ATM, if you need some euros. You're not allowed to go further upriver without police permission. Maybe we can get laid by some hunky local studs.'

'Fiona, I'm not like you. I mean, it's not that I don't – it's just that –'

'You mean, you can live more than twenty-four hours without cock. Instead, you stick your bum out the window, in the rain, and have a good wank.'

'Damn it again, Fiona. I'm sorry, I didn't mean to –'

Fiona put a finger at the top of Suze's bottom cleft.

'Isn't it as well I don't work for money,' she said. 'That would be too, too vulgar, and you could threaten to sack me for immorality and things, which would be frightfully *pas devant*.'

'Your expenses are immoral.'

'Then maybe I should have a percentage of you instead – a percentage of your bum, naturally. Let's see, which bit should I take? This bit, or here –' she slid her finger down the crack of Suze's buttocks, while prising the melons gently open '– or this bit? That looks nice. It reminds me of the sixth form, when a crowd of us used to go skinny-dipping in the river. And we would walk around in the nude, picking flowers in the meadow. All those bare bums, and yours was always the sweetest.'

'It was a lovely time,' said Suze. 'Naked in the meadow, with the flowers, and the river. So innocent.'

'And then we had a contest, to see who could keep a posy of flowers clenched between her bum cheeks the longest, and you cheated, you stuck the stems right up your bumhole.'

She prodded Suze's anal pucker with her fingernail, making it writhe.

'Oh, you! I did not. Fiona, stop. That makes me feel all funny.'

'All right, Miss Prim,' said Fiona, withdrawing her finger, 'but I bet that's not what you say to Dr Teidt, when she gives you your morning massage. I know what she does. It's quite exquisitely wicked. I'm sure the trollop dyes her hair blond.'

9

'I assure you, she doesn't, and she's not a trollop. She's a fully qualified chiropractor from Rostock University.'

'How would you know? About the hair.'

'I see her . . . down there. She massages me in the nude. Both of us. It's for the healing aura. As for hurting, well, that's the point. It keeps my posture upright, and my thighs apart.'

'I imagine it would.'

Suze slipped on a T-shirt, and began to roll a generous, but high cut, pair of bikini panties, in frilly pink lace, over her thighs. She smiled.

'I believe you're jealous.'

'Courtiers are supposed to be rivals,' Fiona answered. 'That's what my laptop thingy has been feeding the editors back in London. I've already got us all in a love triangle, no, a love quadrangle, really, only you are always the ice maiden of St Ursula's, the pure, undefiled bottom of Britannia, and it is me and the German slugging it out for Didier's twelve inches . . . don't tell me you hadn't noticed. Or maybe you've been drooling over that young cookboy, Hyacinthe, a good thumb bigger than Didier? I got some lovely snaps of *la* Teidt's derriere, with just the hint of el flabbo. "Buns of the Huns" I captioned it. I make a point of peeking at girls' bums, for, as you know from school, the bum cannot lie. That's the point of this cruise up the arsehole of nowhere. The British public loves an eccentric expedition, Stanley and Dr Livingstone, Col Fawcett of the Amazon, the jolly good chap who went awol not far from here, in search of lost cities of silver – our angle is, will The Bottom make it back in one piece, or I should say, two pieces? And is she going to *bare* . . . ?'

'Am I? I'm not sure . . .'

'Yes, you are. It's the media climax, darling. After so much teasing and stroking, there must be a sigh of patriotic satisfaction. I've made your bum the national bum, by convincing my tame media chaps that the British male worships girls with big bottoms, but is too polite to insist on the point in mixed company. Our true national sport, which unites the classes, is spanking bottoms, *le vice*

10

anglais, which we adore more than anything. So does everyone else, but only we British manage the triumphant pretence that it isn't sensuous. How do you think I keep my media chaps tame?'

'You're make me nervous when you talk like that,' Suze said, fastening her white chinos over her croup, with the thin fabric showing her pink panties underneath. 'As if St Ursula's wasn't bad enough. Don't tell me you spank men's bottoms, Fiona.'

'You didn't know the half of St Ursula's,' Fiona said. 'You were lucky I was your dorm prefect. Anyway, first step of male-taming is, the fuck of the century, no footling about, pants off and thighs asunder, over the office desk. Nothing original about that. But many girls tease first, and when the deed's done, they've nothing left in the arsenal. You get away with your tease because it's *you* – you really are the ice maiden . . .'

'Oh, Fiona, stop it. You know my career comes first, a long way ahead of boyfriends. I won't be a *trophy.*'

'. . . but I get the squelching over with, *then* tease. I make them want more by not needing them. Men love disdain. And if they are really soppy, it's a brisk lathering on the bare bum, over my knee. Always in charge, no crushes or attachments or emotional blackmail, or whispers to wifey in Woking. Englishmen will do anything for a haughty girl who allows *them* to get soppy, and spanks them for being naughty little brats. So, your nates could be notorious all by themselves, but I ensure, via the beastly little oiks who feed the British public their news, that they are the *only* nates notorious. You're the toff with the toffee apples.'

'Fiona, I wish you'd stop talking about spanking. It's so gross.'

'Don't tell me you're unaware of how *monsieur le capitaine* keeps these sulky little creole maidens in line.'

'Didier? He doesn't.'

'He bally well does. It's a big boat, oops, yacht, with plenty of soundproof bulkheads. Spanks them on the bare bum, for each and every infraction of his penal code.'

'I don't believe you, Fiona. *You're* the tease.'

'Dare say he'd be glad to demonstrate,' Fiona said. 'You ought to know – how else do you keep a girl obedient? Quick, no nonsense what for, on her wriggling juicy bare. Only language women understand.'

She cupped Suze's arse peach with her palm, tracing the clinging panty fabric at the base of the cleft, then pressed a forefinger into Suze's softly yielding perineum, between the trembling meaty fesses. Suze shivered.

'Now, hurry up, Shard, you mucky little pup. It's time for dinner.'

'Yes, miss,' said Suze.

Soubise glowered, in her permanent moue, as the girls took their seats at table. She was creole, her sultry brown skin a satin mask of silent disdain for all around her, including Cordovan, whom she tended like a slave, with a slave's hatred trembling at the rictus of her ruby lips. Where Fiona was undressed, Soumise was dressed, in a midnight blue silken gown, low-cut, to leave most of her heavy titties uncovered, save where colliers of precious stones draped her creamy dark skin. Like Fiona, she was nude beneath her robe, and the skirts were slit up to past her thigh, revealing the expanse of satin flesh unencumbered by panties, yet, adorned by silken hose: stockings of matching blue, with frilly tops, extending to a garter belt, which held them by taut straps made of braided gold cords.

Her stockinged feet splayed on teetering six inch stiletto heels, the shoes of red patent leather. Also perched on such heels were the girls called fillers, backing models in Suze's photoshoots. They served at table, piquantly dressed, at Cordovan's whim, in perky little French maid's uniforms, with high frilled skirts, black nylon stockings over black heels, and dripping with perspiration into their tight white cotton blouses, open low at the breasts, to leave their teats, trussed in uplift bras, well on show. Beside Soubise sat Dr Teidt, her blond hair pinned up, and her breasts, almost as large as Suze's, restrained in a tight beige linen business suit, whose skirt revealed six inches of thigh flesh above her knees, encased in shiny bronze nylons.

12

The table was lit by candles, and laid with sparkling silver upon crisp linen. Fans whirred, and a battery of blue lights fizzled, as they sucked and devoured their insect prey. Cordovan stood, as the girls took their seats, and lifted their glasses of champagne. Fiona had one poured at once, and sipped heartily, while Suze toyed with her glass of bubbly water. Grunts and laughter echoed faintly from the galley below, where the proletariat, as Cordovan called the servants, assistants, and deckhands, took their meals. The meal was served quickly: soup, salad, and fried fish, with grissini to nibble, and real French baguettes with Normandy butter. Wines were a choice of muscadet or moselle, and Fiona had both. Suze ate sparingly, merely toying with the buttery fish, until Fiona ordered her to finish her plate, or expect a telling-off. Grimacing, Suze obeyed, and soon her plate was clean.

'And your greens. You're a growing girl,' Fiona admonished, emptying her glass.

'I'm twenty-one, Fiona,' Suze retorted, 'just like you. I've grown.'

Cordovan laughed.

'It would be a delight, and a wonder, to observe that heavenly *cul* grow still more,' he said. 'You English are so miserly with your secrets. How does your rainy island produce such vigorous flowers of female beauty? Perhaps it is indeed something to do with greens. You will be pleased to hear that I am most satisfied with our progress on the shoot. The ambience is taking hold . . . far from civilisation, even the outposts of Cayenne, or St Laurent du Maroni, my models ooze a loose tropical languor, or lasciviousness, a casual display of the moist, sweating female body, that slowly becomes that of a jungle animal, drooling and heartless as it displays its naked power, oblivious of all but its prey, and its fascination.'

'Prey,' said Suze. 'Meaning . . .'

'The vast and ignorant public, consumers of the image, the god that rules our age of the late decadence. Let Homer or Shakespeare sing your praises, Miss Shard, and the public is deaf. Let them glimpse a single image by

13

Cordovan, one alone, culled from thousands, and they are your slaves.'

'They are the slaves of her bottom,' said Fiona. 'Paying slaves, we hope.'

'Is not the bottom, as you quaintly put it, the very essence of the female soul?' murmured Cordovan. 'Think what those two divine orbs of flesh can do – they can tantalise, command, reduce a beholder to submission, or part, to reveal still deeper, innermost fleshy secrets; they can squash and suffocate, or themselves be the organ of submissive punishment, wriggling and reddening under chastising spanks – should a girl be naughty, as girls will, and demand correction! – on perfect expression of female obedience. In the Platonic sense, it can be argued that all female bottoms are imperfect replicas of the one, divine, and ultimate bottom. Until yours was created, Miss Shard. Yours, the absolute bottom, to spank which, as it were, would be the ultimate spirituality.'

'I don't care what you do in your spare time,' Suze replied, 'but the bottom is not up for any spirituality.'

Soubise shifted on her haunches, and her face wore a sullen moue.

'Why, mademoiselle,' Cordovan exclaimed, as a maid poured more wine, 'what you think I do in my precious spare time?'

'I didn't mean –'

The maids hovered at table, each attentive to the diners, and filling the glasses of both Dr Teidt and Fiona with regularity. They walked in stiff postures, their legs well parted at the crotch, and rigid beneath them, with their torsos bent, and their croups thrust in the air, like wading birds. Their angle meant that each girl's scalloped uplift bra revealed a generous portion of her teat flesh. Cordovan placed a finger on each of two maids' arse clefts, and both girls stood immobile at his touch. He jabbed one finger deep between the arse cheeks of a sulky brunette, wrenching her panties, and she squealed, tipping wine onto the linen napery. Didier and Fiona laughed; Dr Teidt smiled icily; Soubise glowered, and looked at the girl in disgust.

'What does anything mean, here on the savage river, so far from human ken? What keeps us human, except duty, and discipline? There are many forms of discipline. One is truthfulness – out here, each dependent on one another, no one may be permitted the luxury of vainglory.'

'Suze's truth is her bottom,' said Fiona. 'She reveals herself in it.'

'Agreed. But lesser females, not so honest, must be taught a lesson against false modesty. Otherwise, female pride afflicts us all, and civilisation breaks down – for example, if a maid spills wine, what arrogance is next? Do you know, Michelle?'

He addressed the errant maid, with his finger still tickling between her fesses. Swallowing, Michelle shook her head.

'I think you do. Attend me in my cabin at once, after dinner, maid.'

'Wait,' said Suze. 'Yes, we should be honest and everything, so it's only fair you explain, Cordovan. What do you propose to do with Michelle?'

Cordovan smiled.

'Don't you know, Miss Suzette?' said Dr Teidt. 'The girl shall have a lesson in manners. Not a painless lesson, but one which shall leave no imperfections on her attractive croup, and which, as a doctor, I recommend, for healthy circulation, and to stimulate the gluteal nerve ends, which govern the entire female nervous system. We have been voyaging for a week, and I think have all come to know each other sufficiently, for a certain openness. If nothing else, the lascivious poses of the girls, the way they shamelessly extrude their buttocks for the eye of the camera, have revealed to me their innermost natures. Even yours, Miss Suzette.'

Her finger joined Cordovan's, in stroking the girl's panties, and kneading the quivering nates beneath. The girl gasped, with a sobbing chuckle in her throat, but said nothing. Dr Teidt crossed her thighs, with a slither of nylon, briefly revealing blond pubic tufts, extruded beyond her sliver of powder blue panties, swollen and glistening at her crotch, before she smoothed down her tight linen skirt.

'Gluteal, doctor?' Suze said.

'She means your bum,' answered Fiona.

'You don't mean . . .'

'Say it, Suze,' said Fiona.

All eyes watched Suze's face, with Soubise's lips curled in a sneer, and Suze blushed.

'Anybody would think you meant . . . spanking,' she blurted. 'But you're joking, Cordovan. Aren't you?'

'Didier is captain of the ship,' Cordovan said, 'and I am master. Both of us agree on traditional methods of keeping order. There is nothing to hide. On the contrary, I am sure Michelle will give permission for her discipline to be witnessed. It shall make a pleasant postprandial diversion, with coffee and liqueurs. But let us ask Michelle's colleagues. How many of you maids consider Michelle to have . . . let the side down?'

Each maid raised her hand.

'Why, this is like something from St Ursula's!' Suze cried.

'And you, Michelle?'

Eyes downcast, Michelle nodded.

'Yes, master,' she whispered.

'Soubise,' Suze exclaimed, 'how can you go along with this kind of thing?'

'Soubise is responsible for administering the lessons,' Cordovan said. 'She is, if you like, my first mate, and, frankly, needs my presence to restrain her enthusiasm for disciplining the other ranks. She does not approve of disobedient girls, nor think that any but herself should call me "master", and her lessons reflect that point of view. She tends to lay it on hard. There is no jealousy like that of one slave for another. Am I right, Soubise?'

The haughty creole tossed her mane in disgust. Cordovan removed his finger from Michelle's arse, and flicked it with his thumb, against Soubise's massive titty-swelling. The fingernail snapped on her bare flesh.

'Right, Soubise?' Cordovan drawled.

'*Oui, maître*,' hissed Soubise.

16

2

Slut's Bot Whopped

Michelle Cowley was a sturdy Essex rose, a year Suze's junior, from Southend-on-Sea. A narrow waist, corset-slender, though uncorseted, widened into firm, jutting breasts, and a large posterior, the buttocks strongly muscled, with a delicate layer of puppy fat over the solid pear-shaped fesses beneath. There was a noticable space between her thighs, giving her long legs a coltish aspect, with the ripe slice of the vulva clearly visible, hanging low amid the muscled thigh skin. As she bent over Soubise's thighs, both large breasts, tan from deckside sunning, popped naked from her straining uplift bra, with a squirting sound, and dangled over Soubise's robe. Soubise made a moue of distaste, and deftly tucked the flopping breasts under Michelle's ribcage. Soubise slapped her frilly maid's skirt up, and wrenched down the thong of her panties, stringing it across her knees, and leaving the ripe satin buttocks quivering bare beneath her raised palm. The girl trimmed her pubis, to a bikini-thin sliver, but neglected her arse cleft, from which peeped a generous tuft of brown curly hairs. Soubise selected a long strand, and tugged it between forefinger and thumb. Michelle squealed, her bottom wriggled, and the company laughed, as her un-spanked buttocks clenched.

Michelle's croup was a golden tan, yet slightly paler than the small of her back, with a bikini line faintly visible, not entirely eradicated by the naked sunbathing, that the models practised together on the yacht's deck. The smooth

17

bare buttocks were framed by her pink garter belt and straps, and the frilly stocking tops, beneath which her shiny nylon legs draped awkwardly over Soubise's thigh. Soubise lifted her leg, and slapped it against Michelle's calves, trapping her feet, and straightening her posture for the spanking. The girl's pink panties drooped like a rope bridge between her quivering thighs, with the gusset stained dark. Her head twisted round, to look at Cordovan, who stood with a cigar and brandy glass, overlooking the seated spanker and her subject. Michelle's face was sullen, yet her eyes were wide and pleading.

'Just a spanking, master, yes?' she murmured.

'We'll see,' Cordovan said. 'I had in mind the strap.'

'Oh, no, master. Please,' blurted the girl.

'I was going to add, unless you have any objections,' he purred. 'Obviously, you do, so we must content ourselves with the pretty spectacle of your bottom spanked.'

'It's not my role to object, master,' said Michelle, through gritted teeth. 'I worry that strapping leaves marks, and might spoil my bum for your photographs.'

Cordovan exhaled a plume of smoke.

'We humans have penetrated deeply into the wilderness,' he said, 'and cannot remain unchanged. Photography must reflect the savagery that is gradually unleashing itself in us, even in The Bottom herself.'

He bowed to Suze, sitting beside Fiona and Didier on Cordovan's leather couch. His stateroom was luxuriously furnished, and softly lit, as if he was at home in Paris, the lounge leading to a bathroom, and separate sleeping chamber. Dr Teidt perched on a leather armchair, her breasts poking forward, and eyes bright, as she scrutinised the girl's naked buttocks.

'Here in the jungle, The Bottom becomes more than an empress, she is a goddess, her orbs objects of the most devout and repulsive worship, attended by slaves, subject to whiplashes at her slightest whim. In my photography, The Bottom herself is pristine and sacred, but the fesses of her servants may – must – show the degradation these abject wenches will endure, for the privilege of adoring the world's most glorious fesses. Watchers will feast their eyes on the weals borne by naked slave girls, and they shall long to be in those girls' place, the object of their goddess's vengeance. In a word, from now on, the naked buttocks of my models will show the "Suze" range of bodily adornments in all their awful perfection: the embellishment of scarred and suffering girlflesh, beautiful in its humiliance. People will flock to buy the fabrics and scents of that humiliance, hoping that, by adorning themselves, they may touch the tiniest part of The Bottom.'

'I say, Cordovan,' blurted Suze, 'isn't that laying it on a bit thick? The poor girl only spilled a little wine. I thought she was just going to get a bit of a playful spanking, in fun ... I mean. It's only a photo shoot.'

Her voice ebbed, and she gulped, as her eyes fixed on the firm tan melons of the subdued girl's arse, trembling as it rose, bare and straining, towards the hand of the spanker. Her fingers pressed her lips, and stroked them, as she glanced at Cordovan's thunderous visage.

'I *intend* to lay it on a bit thick,' hissed Cordovan. 'Only a photo shoot, Miss Shard? You and I, the world's perfect female bottom, and the world's greatest portrayer, indeed, priest, of that organ's mysteries? Michelle's croup shall tomorrow bear the fruits of her impetuosity – and shall assume the role of first filler, beside you, Miss Shard. The pristine, creamy purity of your pantied nates, beside the scarred and wretched insolence of your bondsmaiden's naked ones. With Michelle's agreement, of course.'

'Really, master?' Michelle exclaimed. 'Oh, yes! Thank you.'

'A simple spanking, then,' said Cordovan, with a leering grimace at Suze, 'to warm those nates to a pretty pink. Then, when Michelle's bottom is hot and red and squirming nicely, and – delicious subtlety – she is begging me to let her change her mind, then, the awful solemnity of the twin-thonged rubber strap. Nature has provided the disciplinarian with a wealth of implements for chastising errant bottoms – the leather whip, the bamboo, the wooden paddle, or the cane, beloved of you English. The rubber quirt has the advantage of flexibility and lightness, yet extreme severity of weal. A broad thong leaves vivid marks on the punished bottom, yet they do not disfigure for as long as cane or whip weals. She will not know how many lashes she is to receive, for I shall decide that on the basis of her composure under spanking. Girlish squeals and undisciplined wriggling shall attract a harsher chastisement. The spanking itself is at *Mademoiselle* Soubise's discretion, and at least a hundred smacks are usually given.'

'Usually?' Suze cried. 'Wait a minute, Cordovan, this has gone far enough. I think you should explain –'

'Permission to address Miss Shard, master?' blurted Michelle.

'Permission granted, girl,' Cordovan replied.

Eyes moist Michelle turned, to look at Suze.

'Please, Miss Shard, try to understand. To you, the girls are just extras – props, furnishings, whatever. But we've had to fight to get on this shoot. There were contests, run-offs, and only the very best girls, with the very best bottoms, got to work with you. All along, it was made clear, and demonstrated fully, that shipboard discipline would be tough, that it meant spanking, and more, as part of the job of promoting *you*, miss. I didn't endure all those smarting bottoms and tears, for nothing. And the funny thing is, any of us will tell you, after a while, a girl gets to like her spankings, or her strappings, or worse – even to crave the warm throbbing glow, after a really sound thrashing on the bare. It has to be on the bare, I don't know why. It's more shaming, I suppose, or more liberating, when a girl is spanked with no knickers, though it may come as a surprise to you. So please don't spoil things. Don't worry, Miss Shard – *your* pristine million dollar bottom will never have to endure spanking.'

'Why, you cheeky –' Suze gasped, rising to her feet, to be restrained by Fiona. 'OK, Cordovan, lay into her. Let the bitch squirm, if that's what she wants. I want to see that bare bum red and trembling, and tears on her cheeky face. And strap her hard, so she has the welts to show for it . . .'

20

Trembling, Suze slumped into her seat, and looked aghast at Fiona.

'I'm sorry, Fiona,' she mumbled. 'I don't know – it's not like me –'

'Oh, sure,' Fiona said, stroking Suze's thigh. 'You were just surprised at what Michelle said, about being spanked on the bare. Right, Suze? As if you don't remember SBWs at St Ursula's – slut's bot whopped – and the miscreant girl had to cry out "willing and able" before her strapping began?'

'Let the chastisement begin,' said Cordovan.

Michelle smiled, a small smile of satisfaction, and closed her eyes tight. Soubise pursed her lips, and restrained Michelle with one hand holding down her nape, while her other arm stretched high and straight, with the fingers flexing, before assuming a rigid shape, with the fingers spaced slightly apart. Her arm fell, the hand right above the pressed tight flesh of Michelle's bum cleft, and there was a whistle of air through Soubise's spaced fingers, before her hand met the naked skin of Michelle's bottom. *Crack!* Michelle's bum jerked, and a livid pink palm print appeared instantly, across the golden skin, now clenching and slightly trembling.

'Uhh,' gasped Michelle.

Crack!

'Uhh . . .'

Crack!

'Oh . . .'

As her bare nates reddened under the spanks, Michelle's breath assumed a rapid, shallow panting, but, though her bum writhed in more and more distress, with the buttocks squirming and clenching, as though to escape from Soubise's grip at ankles and neck, nevertheless she did not squeal. Her legs jerked rigid at each spank, slamming her ankles against Soubise's imprisoning calf, and the spank's force drove her unpantied labia against Soubise's thigh. *Crack! Crack! Crack!*

'Oh . . . oh . . .' Michelle moaned, her face red, under her jerking mane of hair, and its skin matched by the darkening crimson of her bare spanked bottom.

21

Soubise shifted, drawing up her robe, so that Michelle's naked pubis now rested on her own bare thigh; Soubise's skin shone with a film of moisture, where Michelle's hairy gash pressed against her. *Crack! Crack! Crack!* The creole girl's arm rose and fell, like a metronome, and the lights in the stateroom dimmed to a golden glow, suffused by the lazy smoke from Cordovan's cigar.

'Michelle is right, of course,' he purred. 'For the spanking to be spiritually, and not just physically, effective, it must be taken on the full bare. Observe her exquisite squirming of those juicy naked fesses – she is morally naked and helpless, her bottom has no place to hide. You, Miss Shard, have never known such submissive ecstasy.'

'Certainly not!' Suze blurted. 'Ecstasy . . . ?'

Crack! Crack! Crack!

'Uhh . . . uhh . . .'

'Observe her face,' Cordovan said.

Michelle's head jerked back, tossing her mane, at each of Soubise's spanks, which the creole girl placed squarely upon the imprint of the last, without diffusing the chastisement evenly over the bare bottom. The nates were pale at the circumference, but glowed savagely in the central cleft, where repeated spanks had raised a pattern of finger-shaped welts, puffed and rising from the skin's surface. The girl's face was flushed hot, her eyes closed, and her mouth slack and drooling.

'Does she not look like a female on heat?'

Suze swallowed, and shifted her thighs, as she stared at the writhing bare croup. *Crack! Crack! Crack!* the spanking was past fifty slaps, as Soubise's ferocity grew. The spanker's mouth was twisted in a sneer, and her eyes were wide, fixed on the imprint of her fingers, flaming on the girl's naked buttocks.

'That's . . . that's not a fair comparison,' Suze mumbled.

'Isn't it?' said Fiona. 'I'd have thought it rather hit the spot.'

Dr Teidt was perched at the edge of her chair, her thighs pressed together, and sliding against each other, with a slithering squeak of her nylon stockings. Her eyes and lips were bright, her teeth exposed, gleaming in a rictus of pleasure, as she watched the helpless girl writhe.

'How many, Soubise?' she said. 'Eighty, I think.'

Crack! Crack!

'Eighty-five . . . eighty-six . . .' Soubise hissed.

Crack! Crack!

Eighty-seven . . . eighty-eight . . .'

Crack! Crack! Crack! Michelle's naked cunt basin shudded, slamming on Soubise's bare thigh with a wet, sticky slap.

'Uhh! Uhh!' bleated the squirming girl. 'Ooh . . . !'

Soubise's leg, imprisoning Michelle's ankles, shifted suddenly, plunging between her thighs. Her bare foot slid up Michelle's calves, to lodge at the dangling panties string, forcing the thighs slightly apart. Her bare foot spreading Michelle's thighs, so as to expose the wet, tangled hairs at her anus, and the fat slice of the vulva, squashed against Soubise's own thigh, Soubise directed her spanks between the folds of the girl's bare arse cheeks. *Crack! Crack! Crack!*

'Ooh!'

Her fingers slapped right on the tender skin of the perineum, and the wrinkled plum of the anus bud, which wriggled frantically, as the girl's naked arsehole received spanks. The spanks encompassed the lower portion of each buttock, as well as the stretched arse cleft between, and Soubise's slapping fingernails raked the wet fold of Michelle's gash. The girl's squirming became a paroxysm; Soubise's bare foot was wedged between the thighs, and her leg, bent almost double, suppressed all motion of Michelle's left leg, leaving the right leg to thresh helplessly, drumming the floor with her high stilettos.

'That's a bit cheap, Michelle,' drawled Cordovan. 'All that girly squirming and flailing, I mean.'

'I can't help it, master,' Michelle gasped. 'My bum's on fire, really. It's the hardest spanking I've ever taken.'

Her face was wet with tears. Cordovan laughed.

'That cuts no ice, miss. I'll strap you all the harder for your weakness, and you won't have Miss Soubise to hold you. Pity you didn't go to a proper school, one of your

English boarding schools, like Miss Shard. She wouldn't blub under a spanking, or . . . or wet herself.'

'Oh!' wailed Michelle. 'That's not fair, master.'

Crack! Crack! Crack!

Michelle's pubis was sliding wetly on Soubise's wet thigh, the liquid plainly seeping from Michelle's gash, as she was spanked.

'You *know* I get wet, master . . .' Michelle sobbed.

'I suppose you'll masturbate, as soon as you retire?' said Cordovan, casually. 'You are disgustingly wet.'

Crack! Crack! Crack!

'Ooh . . .'

'Don't deny it.'

'Yes, master, I'll have to masturbate, to get to sleep,' sobbed the spanked girl.

'Repulsive,' murmured Cordovan. 'Take her to a hundred and fifty, Soubise, then I'll strap her the same number. No pause.'

Michelle burst into a new flood of tears, as her bottom flamed dark and crusted with welts, under Soubise's palm, yet the seep of juice from her quim continued to slick over the satin, creamy dark skin of her spanker's thighs. Soubise paused, to hoist her skirt higher, away from the lake of come from the girl's gash, and revealing her own pantiless crotch, a velvet channel between her muscled, quivering thighs; Suze stared at the briefly-revealed vulva of the spanker, for the creole's cunt flesh glistened with a film of her own oozed come. Suze stared at her, then at Fiona, whose face was slightly flushed, and mouth hanging slack.

'Fiona . . . they're wet! Both of them!' she hissed.

'Aren't you?' replied Fiona, without taking her eyes from the spanked bottom. 'I know I'll need a good wank or three after this show.'

Opposite, Dr Teidt was mostly in shadow, but Suze could see her thighs pressed tightly, and with one hand between the nylons, under her skirt.

'Dr Teidt is . . . diddling,' she whispered.

Fiona turned to face her, and licked her teeth, curving her lips into a snarl.

'You haven't answered my question,' she rapped. You wanted the girl spanked hard, and you've got it, princess. Aren't *you* wet?'

Suze shifted in her pants, staring down at the wide dark stain seeping out from her cunt. Trembling, she touched herself, at the clitoris, and jerked, as she felt the hard nubbin tense and flood her belly with electricity.

'Oh . . .' she moaned.

Dr Teidt smiled at Suze. Her tight linen skirt was up, over her sleekly muscled thighs, rippling in their nylon stockings; her hand, in the shadows, moved blatantly, in a rubbing motion, up and down her parted gash, where the pressure of her palm pressed her powder blue thong deep into her pink slice, and the forest of blond curls wetly framing it.

Crack!

'One hundred and fifty,' said Soubise.

Cordovan held his heavy rubber strap, three feet in length, by a pleated handle. Its single flat tongue, four inches wide, forked, two thirds down down the shaft, into two smaller tongues a foot long, and two inches wide. He lashed the air, making the twin tongues whistle, a hair's breadth from Michelle's spank-blushed bottom, below Soubise's trembling bare teat skin.

'Aren't you?' Fiona insisted. 'Just like at St Ursula's, picking flowers in the meadow, and watching all those bare bottoms, ripe for spanking?'

'Oh, Fiona!' Suze blurted. 'Yes, damn you, yes.'

'Say it, mucky pup.'

'I'm wet, I'm wet *down there*, so wet. Oh . . .'

Suze sobbed, her eyes riveted on Michelle's naked bottom, now displayed for whipping, as she bent over the sofa. The girl stood spread-legged, so that the group could see her buttocks, bending over the couch's seat, with the edge of the sofa back biting her gash. Her thighs were fully spread, with her ankles three feet apart, revealing, from the rear, the full portion of her naked quim and arse furrow, with its dainty foliage of dangling wet cunt hairs. Michelle's left hand wiped once, two, three times, between her legs, her palm coming out pooled with liquid each time; a fourth time, she let her fingers delve, squeezing the swollen lips of her gash, and kneading the erect pink thimble of her stiffened clitoris.

'Oh ... oh ...' she mewled, 'do me, master. Strap me, make my bum hurt. Whip me on the bare, the full bare, till I scream. Oh ...'

Her fingers plunged right inside her gash, and she began to finger-frig, with her thumb squashing the clitty. A hiss from Soubise caused her to withdraw her fist from her cunt, with a sticky, plopping sound. The masturbating girl steadied herself, with both arms straddling the sofa back, her head hanging low, framed by her sweat-dripping mane, and her bare bum spread high and naked for the strap. Yet, her quim pressed on the leather upholstery, and her hips writhed, in a light, swivelling motion, as she frotted her gash flaps and clit on the hard chair back, which soon glistened with a trickle of come from her cunt. The sofa's leather, under her grip, was slimy with her quim juice. Her blouse was a translucent rag of sweat-soaked cloth, clinging to her wobbling bare body, with the naked breasts popping free from their scanty brassiere, and her gash squelching against the sofa back, while her stocking tops were soaked in oily come, to halfway down her thighs. Drool oozed from her slack lips, reamed by her tongue. The remains of her frilly chiffon maid's skirt lay plastered against the small of her back, bouncing, like the feathers of an exhausted bird, at each twitch of her buttocks, jerking as she masturbated. Suze's palm was oily, where she caressed the crotch of her pants, and she moaned softly to herself.

'You repulsive beast,' said Cordovan to Michelle. 'A girl who masturbates, blatantly, while others watch, is no better than an exhibitionist animal. Which means, all girls.'

'Oh, master,' Michelle whined, 'spanking's made me so hot. You know what a smarting bum does to girls. Please let me wank off, oh, please, let me come.'

'You disgust me,' said Cordovan, mildly. 'But that is what sluts are for.'

26

Cigar drooping at the corner of his mouth, he raised the twin rubber thongs, over the English girl's spanked bare buttocks. *Thwap! Thwap!* Her legs jerked rigid, and her buttocks clenched tight, as the rubber thongs left their imprint atop the glowing red welts of her spanking. Michelle gasped several times. *Thwap! Thwap!* Her breath came as a low, choked hiss, and her whole body began to tremble. Each stroke of the rubber quirt left a double weal on her bottom, framing the fingerprints of Soubise's spanking with raw, dark ridges. *Thwap! Thwap!*

'Ohh . . .' Michelle moaned, as her bare nates twisted and squirmed; her knuckles were white, where she gripped the sofa back, and each lash of the rubber thongs slammed her cunt against the leather, with a wet, slapping thud.

Thwap! Thwap! Thwap!

'Ooh,' she gasped.

The welts on her bare bum were already raw and livid.

'Cordovan,' blurted Suze, her fingers clutching her cunt folds, as though to stem their moisture, 'you can't give her a hundred and fifty, with *that*.'

Cordovan did not answer, but continued to whip the exposed bare arse, quivering beneath his strap. Suze gasped, as her fingers began to move up and down the swollen hillock of her gash lips, making her jump, when they stroked her clitoris under the sodden fabric. *Thwap! Thwap!*

'Ahh,' Michelle groaned.

'Cordovan, stop,' said Suze, feebly.

Cordovan's response was to switch the angle of his strokes, so that the thongs lashed Michelle right in the arse cleft, and with their tips stinging her anus bud, and swollen, hanging gash flaps. *Thwap! Thwap!* Two stingers caught her right on the cunt.

'Oh! Oh!' she squealed.

'Generally, no disciplinarian for the female fesses is as harsh as another female,' he mused. 'Most men are shy of really hurting a girl.'

'*Most* men . . .' murmured Soubise, through sullen lips, and without irony.

Thwap! Thwap!

'Ooh!' Michelle gasped, her flogged bare bum dancing in spasm. 'Enough, master, really. Honestly, that's enough.'

Cordovan leered at Suze, making her blush. He pointed to the vivid welts on the girl's bare bum, now puffed in angry dark ridges, well in relief, like mole tracks, from the bottom's smooth surface.

'I imagined that Michelle's welts would be short-lived,' he said. 'There, I admit, I was wrong. Quite wrong.'

Thwap! Thwap! Thwap!

'Ahh!'

Dr Teidt's fingers moved incessantly at her crotch, where a dark stain wetted the crisp linen of her skirt. She was openly masturbating; Soubise, standing behind the whipped girl, had her foot perched on the sofa arm, and her own hand played beneath the high slit of her robe, where her pantiless cunt bulged beneath the clinging fabric – and the outline of her knuckles showed, creeping, where she masturbated her gash. Fiona's hands were occupied with a cigarette and glass of brandy, and Suze averted her suspicious gaze; yet, her own fingers emulated those of Dr Teidt, and the burning spasms of pleasure, that shook her body, at each touch to her throbbing clitoris, removed all thought of shame. The darkened room was the sacred chamber of some oracle or seer, whose mystic rites belonged not to the real world, and would be forgotten on the morrow. *Thwap! Thwap!* The beating went on, rhythmically and implacably. Who was keeping count? The flogged girl drooled and whined and pleaded, as her naked bum darkened with welts, and performed its squirming dance of pain, yet she made no move to break from position. Her legs and arms clutched the sofa, every limb trembling and rigid, while the thud of the strap slammed her bare titties into a frenzied wobble, at each lash. The pubic hairs, dangling from her anus and perineum, below the clearly swollen gash flaps, dripped come onto the leather fabric. *Thwap! Thwap!*

'Ahh . . .'

Cordovan alternated strokes across the nates, with vertical slices in the arse cleft, stinging the cunt lips and anus plum at each stroke, with both tongues of the rubber strap. At those strokes, the girl's body jerked stiff, and her face tightened in a rictus of agony, with a gurgling, choking moan, deep in her throat. Yet come oozed faster and more copiously from her swollen vulva, the harder she was beaten, and the more puffy the ridges of her welts grew. Dr Teidt masturbated openly, and Suze no longer tried to dissemble her own masturbation. Soubise's nostrils flared, and her eyes were slits, as she rubbed herself beneath her dress, yet with no indication of sensuous pleasure, as though her frottage was a necessary mystic rite. *Thwap! Thwap!* Two vicious strokes lashed Michelle straight on the cunt flaps, and the thongs seemed to linger, caressing the wealed gash flesh.

'Ohh! Master, I can't take any more. Please,' she cried, the cheeks of her arse clenching with quickfire speed, writhing against each other, like two crimson polyps.

When her whipper withdrew the thongs from the twitching gash flaps, the rubber was slicked with oily come. *Thwap! Thwap!*

'Ohh . . .'

There was a hiss, as a stream of golden piss spurted from Michelle's pussy, washing the sofa in an acrid, steaming pool of pee.

'Oh, no . . .' she sobbed, her head hanging low. 'See what you've made me do, master. I've wet myself.'

She raised her head, swivelling, to address Dr Teidt, Fiona, Suze and Didier.

'The master's made me foul myself. He made me! I begged him to stop. I am the victim. It wasn't my fault.'

Thwap! Thwap! Thwap! Cordovan's rubber quirt lashed her across the piss-soaked gash flaps.

'*AHH!*'

Hsss . . .

A second squirt of piss leapt from the twitching, soaked cunt mouth, to splash into the pool beneath her bottom. Her hand flew to her pubis.

'I have to come . . .' she moaned, drooling. 'I'm in shame, total shame. You've hurt me and humiliated me . . .

ahh, yes ... I have to wank off, master, and you can't stop me. Ahh, yes, that's good, so good. It's not my fault – look at my bum, all wealed. It hurts so, you've no idea. I have to come, you've strapped me so hard, I'm so hot ...'

Her fingers twitched and pounded on the swollen nubbin of her clitoris, while her knuckles squelched and ground the wet juicy cunt lips, gaping open, with the mass of wet pink flesh within, glistening and undulating, as the girl's cunt basin writhed.

Thwap! Thwap! The rubber strap sliced her hard across the central bare fesses, right in her weals of spanking.

'Yes ... yes ...'

Thwap! Thwap! Michelle's masturbation was frenzied.

'Oh! Yes!' she gasped.

Suze masturbated harder, her breath heaving in short, harsh gasps, and through blurred moist eyes, she saw Dr Teidt and Soubise frotting with equal vigour. Dr Teidt's skirt was pulled right up, the powder blue panties pushed aside, and her fingers plunged to the knuckles inside her pouch, framed by the tendrils of her luxuriant cunt mane. Soubise did not reveal her naked cunt, but her slit dress hung open almost to the gash, and her fingers made no secret of their deep penetration of her slit, nor her thrusting, as she fingerfucked herself. *Thwap! Thwap!*

'Ah! Yes ... yes ... so good ... oh! Oh! Oh!'

Michelle's arse wriggled frantically; come spurted from her frotted gash; her fingers were a blur on the naked, piss-wet cunt, as she masturbated herself to climax, with her spine and belly heaving.

'Uhh ... uhh ...' she moaned, gasping, as her spasm flowed and ebbed, and then it was Dr Teidt who emitted small, staccato yelps, as she came, followed by Soubise, her mouth tight shut, breathing hard through her flared nostrils, with a tremor of her flat, muscled belly, and squirted come soaking the crotch of her robe.

Soubise applied green liquid, from a plastic mineral water bottle, to the welts of Michelle's arse, and Michelle moaned.

'Ouch. That hurts.'

Didier laughed.

'The best medicine,' he said. 'Eau de cologne from the Suze range . . .'

Her eyes darting from Michelle's hot bum weals, sizzling under the astringent liquid, to the grinding loins of the creole girl, Suze plunged her hands under her clothing, to grasp and pinch her naked stiff nipples, throbbing in erection. She flicked her clitoris hard, kneading her bare nips, until she writhed in her own spasm, closing her eyes, as the pleasure flooded her, and gasping, her lips slack and drooling, with little strangled mewls whimpering from her throat. She opened her eyes, and blinked at the whole company gazing upon her parted thighs, and the wide damp patch where her come had dribbled through her panties, soaking her crotch and arse cleft. Michelle stood, hands on her hips, skirt up, and her thong knickers still drooped at her knees, with her wet pube jungle pointing straight at Suze's face.

She curtsied, and twirled, poking up her scarred bare bum, and looking over her shoulder at Suze, with a sullen, defiant rictus on her tear-stained lips. She spread her buttocks fully, and put her hands at her cunt, parting the heavy lips, to show Suze the pink glistening flesh inside. She probed her gash with her fingers, and withdrew them, smeared with her come, which she applied to each of her bum welts. As she caressed her weals, rubbing and kneading the ridges of puffy skin, the whipped girl's mouth creased in a sneer. No one spoke, and she stole attention from the cringing Suze; all eyes went to Michelle's bum and wet crotch, as she turned again, and began to masturbate anew, with one foot on the sofa, and the other draped over its back, parting her thighs almost in the splits, and spreading the juicy fat lips of her dripping quim.

'Thank you, master, for what I deserved,' she hissed, as her fingers thumbed her erect clitty. 'I hope you had some lovely wanks, watching my bum striped. As for me, when I'm thrashed hard, one wank is never enough. We're all the same, us girls, only some of us are superstars and some of us are skivvies.'

31

Suze paled at the insult, and whispered to Fiona that she wanted to go. Fiona waved her down, indicating her enjoyment of the frotting spectacle, and that that they should leave as soon as it was over.

'I've been punished and shamed,' Michelle blurted, 'and a whipped girl may do what she wants, and say anything. Right, master?'

'Yes,' said Cordovan.

'Spanking and whipping get a girl's bum hot,' panted Michelle, as she masturbated, 'and getting a whopping is the next best thing to fantasising about one. But I can still fantasise about another girl's arse getting beaten ... the world's biggest, most sumptuous, most beautiful, arse, all bare and roped to the deck, and its owner getting flogged with rubber whips, or caned, or beaten with leather thongs, and darkening with weals, just like mine. Yes, oh yes, look how wet I am, just thinking about it. Come's pouring out of my pussy, can't you see? And aren't you all excited at *that* prospect? All us models are. Not just watching any slut's bum whopped, but *her* arse ... deep in the jungle, naked and helpless and alone as slaves of brutal whipmasters, every girl's dream – oh, yes, I'm going to come.'

Dr Teidt nodded.

'The slut is a submissive exhibitionist, like most females,' she murmured. 'Quite normal.'

Michelle thrust her gaping cunt forward, slopping her frotting fingers in the copious cunt slime oozing from the fluttering gash flaps. As she masturbated, she rubbed and caressed the welts on her bare bum, poking into the inflamed flesh with little grunts of pain, yet smiling, as she did so.

'Yes, the master knows how to thrash ...' she moaned.

She pinched her clitty between thumb and forefinger, and rubbed it, pressing and pounding the erect nubbin, until her come gushed in a torrent ... Dr Teidt's fingers were busy anew at her own gash, while Soubise desisted from masturbating, her face hard and sullen. Suze swallowed and, crimson with anger and embarrassment, whispered to Fiona that she hoped they would reach

Maripasoula soon, for she wanted some fresh air, and a rest from the ship's confinement.

'I meant to tell you,' Fiona whispered back, 'we couldn't dock at Maripasoula, because of the storm. We passed it an hour ago. I forgot to mention it, because I was so peeved myself. I needed batteries for my laptop, so now I'm cut off from the world. Bother and double bother!'

'Ah . . . ah . . . yes . . .'

Michelle brought herself off again, with a series of deep, throaty wails.

'Ah . . . Ah! Ah! And the great thing, in my fantasy, watching that slut's bot getting whopped, is the price tag. Ten million dollars squirm just like the rest of us.'

3

Gothic Massage

'Up further,' said Dr Teidt. 'And spread wider.'

The doctor's nude body dripped with sweat, as she stood behind Suze, kneeling, also nude, with her spine and croup facing the doctor, on her massage table. Suze squatted, with the fingers of each hand on her buttocks, gingerly prising the cheeks apart, to reveal her pubic tufts wreathing her anus bud.

'We agreed that your posture training must enter a new, and more fulfilling stage,' said Dr Teidt. 'You have mastered the art of deportment, walking, sitting and bending, with the stem of a flower clenched between your naked buttocks. You perform admirably, neither moistening nor damaging the fragile wand clasped by your cheeks. Today, we progress. Yet you seem distraught. You shouldn't be, after your massage.'

'No? I ache everywhere,' Suze retorted. 'You're heavier than you think – walking up my spine and on my bum, and bending my legs, then sitting on me . . . I mean, it's painful. Also, it tickles my bum, when you do your massage with your hairs . . . down there, you know. But your bone's very sharp.'

'That's why I massage in the nude. The *Gotische massage* – Gothic massage, with the bare pubis, is supremely stimulating to the gluteal muscles, while the oil, exuded of necessity from the masseuse's vulval pouch, is a nourishing lubricant to the skin. There must be some reason for your nervousness. What's bothering you?' Did you dung before your massage, as you are supposed to?'

'I ... I tried. Nothing would come out. Maybe after breakfast ...'

'You are distraught. Try again, at once, Suzette.'

She helped the groaning girl down from the massage table, and into the tiny toilet cubicle, where she made Suze squat atop the seat, not sit down upon it, with her back and arse facing the doctor.

'This feels silly,' Suze said, aware of Dr Teidt's eyes on her extruded cunt mound, and her anus pucker.

'It's for your posture. Back straight, and hands on your knees. Don't strain – relax your belly, and, most important, your sphincter. Feel anything?'

'Yes ... something's coming. I think it's a big one, it hurts my bumhole. I feel like some schoolgirl, doctor.'

A tiny tip of dung peeped from Suze's spread pucker. Dr Teidt bent forward, and inspected the offering, then agreed that an adequate cylinder was on its way. She told Suze to take her time, and not force its ejection.

'But you may care to tell me why you seem upset,' she said, as the swarthy dung emerged from Suze's strained anus.

'Well, can't you guess?' Suze exclaimed. 'Last night ... it was a bit much.'

'You think so? Perhaps Cordovan is right, and the wilderness is loosening our bonds of civilised restraint, or prejudice against our true natures. From now on, the gloves of deceit are off. I have suspected that Cordovan and Didier practised corporal punishment on the other maids. Why else their sullen docility?'

'It's not that ... !'

'What, then?'

'Well ... the diddling. That girl, Michelle, wanking off, as she was beaten.'

'And you?' retorted the doctor. 'I masturbated at the spectacle, I freely admit. All of us females masturbate, so why not enjoy it, when our fantasy is made real, by an obliging master? An ecstatic spirit can take hold of a crowd, especially of females, and suspend normal prudery. Your panties were wet, Suzette. Don't deny.'

Suze gasped, as her dung protruded by a rapid two inches.

'Sure, I diddle myself, like every girl in the world, Dr Teidt,' she said, 'but last night was spooky, I don't know what came over me. Cordovan may be that Michelle's master, and Soubise's, but he's certainly not mine. He's just some cheesy photographer. Ah!'

The water plopped, as a large brown dung dropped. Dr Teidt ordered her to remain squatting, and poked the hosepipe into her anus, pushing it a good three inches into the shaft, before opening the tap, and sluicing Suze with cold water, which squirted out in a fountain, drenching her buttocks and heels.

'Ooh,' Suze gasped, 'that feels funny. It's almost a . . . you know.'

'A colonic irrigation,' said Dr Teidt. 'I think your bottom is ripe for that hygienic attention, too. We shall see how you fare with the progressive Gothic massage.'

Suze stood, dripping, and made her way back to the massage table, where she resumed her position, with her arse cheeks spread. At the doctor's urging, she spread her buttocks until the perineum was stretched pale, and the anus pucker widened to a mouth. Dr Teidt took a long, thick cylinder of smooth balsa wood, and began to anoint it with jelly. Suze looked behind her, and gasped.

'Wait! I didn't know . . . that's enormous! I'm not sure about any of this, doctor. That looks like one of those toys they sell in sleazy shops. What do you mean to do?'

Dr Teidt laughed.

'You delightful British! In Germany, prophylactic establishments are not considered sleazy. Come, Suzette, we have been together a long time. Do you think I am suddenly going to ravish your person, just because you observed me masturbate – like yourself – at the exquisite humiliance of that young trollop, last night? This device lets a female exercise her sphincter and gluteal muscles. It fits snugly in the anus. I have never delved into your private life, but I would not have expected prudery to be part of it.'

'I'm no prude!' Suze retorted. 'I'm a bit peeved that we aren't going to stop in Maripasoula, that's all. And I'm scared of that beastly thing.'

'Why?'

'It's just that having something big and hard up my bum, it seems unnatural. Even for therapy. To have my hole . . . *down there* filled, it's scary. It makes me shiver.'

'You must relax.'

'I am relaxed.'

'I mean your sphincter. You'll find that the tool enters you smoothly, for a couple of inches, then meets some resistance from your anal wall, and sticks. Do not try to work on the tube, to suck it inside you; rather, loosen your bumhole, as I apply pressure, and, soon, it shall obey your *will*.'

'Please, doctor, no, I'm so scared of what that thing will do to me . . .' Suze whimpered. 'I've never . . . I mean, not like this . . . oh, please don't.'

The doctor placed the tip of the tube at Suze's anal pucker, which tensed, and shuddered. The cylinder entered Suze's anus to about an inch.

'Uhh . . .' Suze gasped, long and slowly, then breathed in and out very deeply. 'Uhh . . .'

Her buttocks clenched, writhing, over the intruding tool.

'There, now,' said Dr Teidt. 'Not so bad after all, is it?'

'Oh! It does feel funny,' Suze panted. 'Sort of like a dung. I suppose I can take it, but I'm still a bit scared – it's so big.'

'It's no bigger than the splendid dung you just accommodated. The will to power is everything, Suzette, and first of all, mastery of one's own body. That explains our fascination – mine *and* yours – for corporal chastisement, as evidenced last night: we admire a girl who can dominate her revulsion from the pain of bare bum chastisement, and turn it into enjoyment, or, even craving. You must squeeze the tube with your sphincter, and by your own willpower, hold it inside you.'

The cylinder stuck, about three inches inside Suzette's anal shaft.

'Ooh! It's uncomfortable, it hurts, yet tickles at the same time. I can't see myself learning to crave this. How bizarre!'

'Yet, some girls do. You have heard of anal intercourse? Many girls enjoy, or crave, the male organ pleasuring them in the anus.'

'Certainly not! I would never –'

'I meant, do you know of it? I wouldn't dream of asking personal details.'

'You must have known that I'd *heard* of it, when I arrived at the clinic. The other girls probably mentioned it in my hearing, as a horrid joke. As for *doing* something so beastly – *ooh!*'

Suze gasped, as the cylinder suddenly disappeared, almost to its whole twelve inches, right to the root of her anus.

'Wow, you were right. It just suddenly slid right inside, as if it knew where to go. But that's silly.'

'Not at all,' said Dr Teidt.

Suze swallowed, and began to wriggle her buttocks, opening and closing her bumhole on the intruding shaft of hardwood. Only a quarter inch of the tube still showed, between her churning anus lips.

'Like this?' she said faintly. 'It feels so strange. I'm scared it might burst me.'

'Squeeze as hard as you can, but you must neither let it escape, nor enter you completely. Remember, it is for beauty of buttocks, and the tone of the arse muscles.'

'Oh, it hurts,' Suze blurted. 'You say some girls actually crave this . . . this kind of thing?'

'Many do. I am sure Fiona would back me up.'

'I don't need Fiona to run my life,' Suze cried. 'Ohh! What . . . ?'

The tube disappeared between her buttocks, and was engulfed entirely by her squirming anus. Dr Teidt climbed on top of Suze's body. She placed one bare foot on each of Suze's buttocks, and began to run on the spot, her full weight pounding the girl's squashed, writhing croup. The buttocks clenched in a rapid rhythm, faster and faster, as Suze squeezed the cylinder, now buried inside her anal shaft.

'Ooh,' Suze gasped. 'It hurts awfully, doctor. That thing is right inside my hole.'

'Not unusual. You are doing well,' Dr Teidt replied, her soles slamming the jerking arse muscles. 'Twenty minutes, then shower, and breakfast.'

Below Suze's churning crotch, a seep of clear, oily fluid oozed from her pussy lips, as they rubbed against the massage table.

'Uhh . . .' she groaned. 'I can't imagine wanting *this*. I mean, a man doing it to me with his *sex organ*. Oh, it hurts so!'

'Then it is doing you good,' said the doctor, as her soles pounded Suze's buttocks.

Her fingers crept between her legs, and she began to rub her hairy wet slit, in time with the slaps of her feet on the girl's arse. Clear, oily come oozed down the rippling muscles of her thighs.

'Gothic massage is supposed to hurt,' she panted.

The doctor casually masturbated, as she looked down at Suze's naked arse, churning under her soles.

'You're crushing me,' Suze moaned.

Dr Teidt thumbed her extruded clitoris, and stifled a gasp.

'I think it wise to follow Cordovan's instructions, regarding the photo shoots today and henceforth. Michelle's strapping last night was no accident, I think. We are past Maripasoula and civilisation, and must be prepared for the true animal in you to emerge, Suzette. There will be images of cruelty, pain and restraint, girls tied with real ropes, and – who knows? – spanked on the bare with real wands. Fiona assures me your advertising campaign has become a news item in itself. How far will The Bottom go? I hope, all the way. It is for your success.'

'I don't want to be spanked,' Suze cried. 'That's frightful.'

'Yet you masturbated,' replied Dr Teidt, 'watching bare bottom chastisement, so the spectacle cannot be repugnant to you.'

'It was. It is.'

'That is *why* you masturbated.'

Oily come seeped from the doctor's cooze, to glisten on her pumping thigh muscles. Her fingers delved deep in her wet cunt meat, reaming the pink, shiny walls of the pulsing slit.

'You were transferring the image of Michelle's flogged buttocks to yourself. You imagined *your* arse was drubbed.'

'No,' blurted Suze, her buttocks threshing under the woman's feet, and the arse cleft parted by the intruding tool, deep in her rectum. 'I could never . . .'

'Come, come, Suzette. Fiona has told me about your enchanting English boarding school. The bare bottom canings, the spanking masturbation games, in your communal sleeping quarters. Such training leaves its mark, in every way.'

'I don't know. You and Fiona say such awful things . . . I'm so confused.'

Drops of come fell from Dr Teidt's squirming wet cunt lips onto Suze's buttock cleft, smearing the churning arse cheeks with its oily sheen. Suze gasped, and started, as the hot drops of come plopped onto her bare arse, and her cunt basin slid on the table, in a pool of her own seeped come. Her buttocks churned harder, and she groaned that the inhuman tool was hurting her anus root. Dr Teidt dropped to a squat, and delved between Suze's buttocks, her fingers forcing apart the anal pucker, and gaining entrance to the shaft. She clasped the plunged tool, and withdrew it, with a rapid plop, from Suze's bumhole. Suze gasped in protest, and the doctor ordered her to turn over, and lie on her back. Suze obeyed, flushed and panting, and squeaked, as her bare arse slipped in the pool of her own seeped come. Dr Teidt smiled, and indicated Suze's dripping cunt, as wet as the doctor's own, on which Suze's eyes were fixed.

'*You* . . . you were diddling,' she gasped.

Dr Teidt nodded, and squatted, so that her buttocks touched Suze's and their cunts and bumholes faced each other. She inserted the tool in her own anus, and Suze watched, as her sphincter muscle sucked the tube fully into

40

her rectum, expelled it, and sucked it in again. She repeated the operation, until the tool slid in and out of her anus, like a piston. Leaning back on her elbows, she squashed her cunt on Suze's, and Suze yelped, as the tool reentered her own anus, propelled by the doctor's arse muscle. Both females reclined on their elbows, with Suze almost prone, and the doctor raised above her. Dr Teidt's cunt basin writhed, as she tooled Suze's arse with the giant shaft, darting between both their bumholes, and shiny with their arse grease. Dr Teidt placed her hands at her cunt, and recommenced masturbating, her thighs and vulva gaping wide, for Suze's eyes.

Suze turned her face away, until Dr Teidt ordered her to observe the masturbation, and pleasure her own dripping cunt. Moaning, Suze let her hands creep down her belly, to her extruded stiff clitty, and she squealed, as her fingers brushed the stiff nubbin. The tool slammed harder and harder into Suze's anus, with the doctor's buttock muscles rippling, as she buggered the trembling girl. Suze's fingers crept between her pouch flaps, ingressed the wet slit, and began to churn inside the cunt, emerging slimy with come, at each vulval thrust. She got three, then four fingers inside the come-soaked cooze, and began to gamahuche herself, with her thumb pressing her engorged clitoris, as she emitted little sobs and yelps from her thoat. Her face rose, and she gazed at Dr Teidt, both masturbating females licking their teeth and lips, with Suze bright red in the face. At last, Suze smiled.

'Oh, yes . . .' she groaned, as Dr Teidt's buttocks slapped noisily against her own and, beneath their writhing cunts, a pool of mingled cunt slime soaked the table cloth. 'That's so good. So good . . . Oh!'

Dr Teidt's fingers were a blur, as she frigged her cunt, drooling slimy come over Suze's squirming bare perineum.

'All about power,' she hissed. 'Massage, spanking, diddling, fucking. Sometimes, Suzette, power over yourself is in others' power over you.'

'Oh . . . oh . . . don't stop. Fuck me, fuck me . . .' Suze whimpered.

'Are you going to climax?' asked Dr Teidt.

'I don't know. Oh . . . oh . . . yes, I'm coming. Ooh . . .'

Suze masturbated as hard as her gamahucher, and her buttocks clamped the impaling wooden shaft, as her belly tensed, then fluttered, and began to heave in orgasm. Come spurted between her fingers, as she sobbed, moaning, in staccato yelps. Dr Teidt smiled in a rictus, and took her clitoris between her thumb and forefinger. She wrenched the swollen organ, pinching it with her nails, until her breath came in sharp pants, and her writhing wet cunt, and slab-muscled belly, twitched in climax. She emitted shrill, grunting yelps, as her cunt gushed come. As her climax ebbed, she thrust hard with her arse cheeks, slapping her slimed skin against Suze's cunt and lower buttocks; the massage tool squirted into Suze's anus with such force, that the girl's sphincter greedily embraced it, and sucked it into her bumhole, until the cylinder was once more embedded fully in her anal passage. Dr Teidt climbed off the massage table, and ordered Suze into the shower.

'Aren't you going to pull that thing out of my bumhole, doctor?' Suze whimpered. 'It hurts so . . .'

'You masturbated to orgasm, at your own pain, rather than the witnessed pain of a whipped girl,' Dr Teidt replied drily.

Suze took a few hobbling steps, towards the bathroom.

'Oww! I'm bow-legged,' she gasped.

'It is good for the posture, forcing you to walk with your thighs apart, and back straight, to minimise the discomfort. So we shall leave it in,' said Dr Teidt. 'Let us see if any of our friends guess your secret.'

Suze whirled, and stared angrily at Dr Teidt.

'What do you mean by that, doctor?' she blurted.

'Why, the secret of your upright posture,' said the doctor, wiping come from her dripping thighs and labia. 'Unless you have others.'

'No . . . no . . .'

Her face pale, Suze turned on the shower, and strutted, legs apart and rigid, beneath the spray.

* * *

42

'Spread wider, Miss Suzette,' Cordovan said. 'I want to see the thong, right between your cheeks. And hold your whip higher.'

Suze squatted on the deck, wearing a pair of 'Suze' running shoes, in garish and aggressive purple: 'Power Shoes,' the line was called. Her upper body carried a wispy white bikini top, matching her panties: a tiny triangle of translucent fabric sheathed her nipples, yet clung to the buds, showing their every contour. Each breast covering was fastened behind her neck, by an arc of threads, presenting the firm, unsupported titties as two separate sacs. At her loins, she wore one of the more daring thongs from her clothing line, its tiny string a disdainful sop to modesty, and allowing bushy tufts of pubic fleece to bulge on either side of the labia shield. 'Fuck me panties,' Fiona called them. Sweat beaded her bare skin, aided by dabs of gel, made to look like sweat. She carried the same rubber quirt which had flogged Michelle on the bare, the evening before. Michelle's striped bottom was now presented, thrust towards her for further punishment, with the naked girl strapped to the mast of the barge, towed behind Cordovan's yacht. Suze shifted on her haunches, spreading her near-nude arse cheeks a crack more, and raising the rubber quirt menacingly, towards Michelle's bare bum. Cordovan's camera clicked, and Fiona's video whirred: filming the entire shoot for a video promo, an advertisement for the advertisements.

Michelle had her promise – she was the star extra in the scene. Suze's running shoes gave it extra, ironic menace: she was a slavemistress, deep in the jungle, taking a break from her chastisement of errant bondmaidens, but ready to spring into action once more, whip at the ready. Michelle's face wore an expression of mingled dread and resignation. Suze breathed deeply, her quirt twitching in her grasp, as she eyed the full bare moons of the trussed captive, and the line of ten lesser girls, nervousness on their faces, as they awaited their turn to be strapped to the mast. The late afternoon sun was creamy crimson on their bared limbs, sheathed in a set of 'Suze' knickers and bra, basque, or petticoat. They were roped together by a cord, looping around their bare ankles.

Soubise played Suze's second in command. She wore a pair of cream-coloured 'Suze' jeans, cut away at mid thigh, and apart from that, only a scalloped pink bra, which thrust her creamy brown teats up and out. The fabric of the jeans was tissue-thin, clearly outlining Soubise's panties, in a high bikini cut. The bra was smudged and ripped, like her cut-offs: Cordovan's doctrine of minimalism, that the image of the imperfect article would attract buyers of the perfect. She, too, brandished an instrument of discipline: a cane, over three feet long, yellow in colour, and very springy, which, Suze imagined, would hurt more than the twin tongues of the rubber quirt. Cordovan's breath was on her nearly-naked teats, as he crouched beside her, lens focussed on her nipples, then her flat, muscled belly, then her open crotch. He bent further, until his face was almost at her pubis, getting his close-ups of the sliver of white gusset amid the jungle of her pubic mane. Suze shifted on her haunches, unable to rub her thighs together, to smear away the seep of come from her swelling cunt flaps, and unwilling to move, as every gesture increased the tickling discomfort of the tool nestled in her bumhole, and seeming to fill her.

'I feel like a slave at market,' she murmured to Fiona.

'But you're the boss,' Fiona replied. 'You could whip these girls for real, if you wanted. Cordovan might approve.'

'Whew,' Suze gasped. 'Fiona, don't.'

Dr Teidt, in her linen business suit, its narrow short skirt high over her bronze-nyloned thighs, sat observing the proceedings. A long cheroot dangled from the corner of her mouth, wreathing her head in blue plumes of smoke. She smiled at Suze, when she made that remark, and crossed her legs, with a rasping slither of nylon, revealing, for a split second, the befurred triangle of her naked gash. The doctor wore no panties this day.

'They are the slaves, Miss Suzette,' she said, 'you their mistress. Do not forget your role. The Bottom chastising

44

other bottoms, for daring to mimic hers – for daring to be bottoms at all.'

'Yes,' enthused Cordovan, 'these sluts have no hope of escape from cruel chastisement. No repentance can save them from the whip. Their juicy bottoms demand your revenge, Miss Shard.'

'I suggest a little more realism,' said Fiona. 'Why doesn't Suze give a real lathering? The maid has shown she can take it.'

'Fiona!' Suze gasped, her bottom twitching, as a spurt of come moistened the thin string, biting between her cunt lips.

'A St Ursula's girl has no right to be shy,' added Fiona.

Michelle twisted her head, and sneered at Suze.

'Sure, I can take it,' she sneered. 'She's only a girl.'

Suze paled, memories of Michelle's taunts, the night before, overwhelming her. As if the bitch wanted to be flogged. No fourth-former at St Ursula's would get away with such cheek . . .

'Cordovan?' drawled Dr Teidt.

Cordovan shrugged, leering, while Didier, holding the rope that tethered the ten maids, grinned lopsidedly. The maids were Wendy Cozens, Sandra Gorge, Yvonne Atras, Heather Yonge, Giorgia Provone, Marcia Subovic, Truud Nijmegen, Pierrette Dupuis, Nadia Colsemi, and Danielle Paresse. United by their tethering rope, European origin, and fullness of breast and buttock, they looked apprehensive and sullen.

'Corporal punishment?' said Truud Nijmegen, a heavy-titted blond Dutch girl. 'Is that in our contract?'

Cordovan laughed; Didier jerked their ankle rope.

'May we remind you of your selection process,' said Dr Teidt. 'Your contracts allow for *full modelling*. Of course, you may disembark at any time.'

She waved, smiling, to encompass the jungle, on either side of the darkly glinting stream. Fiona and Didier chuckled.

'Master,' hissed Michelle. 'You promised me the prominence.'

Cordovan shrugged again.

'Miss Shard,' he said, 'would you please – if you approve – give Michelle a real whipping? The strokes and severity at your discretion, of course.'

'No bitch can break me,' whispered Michelle, theatrically, to Heather Yonge.

Suze leapt to her feet.

'What did you say?' she spat.

'Nothing to you, miss,' answered Michelle.

Lips maliciously pursed, the entire ship's company looked expectantly at Suze, who, after a moment's hesitation, threw away her rubber quirt, and turned to Soubise.

'Mademoiselle Soubise,' she said, 'may I take your cane? I think the maximum realism is required.'

After obtaining a nod of approval from Cordovan, the creole girl sullenly surrendered her long yellow cane to Suze, taking the quirt in return. Suze flexed the rod, and made a practise stroke, stumbling, as its whistle cleaved the still air. Michelle's eyes widened in fear.

'Now, wait a minute,' she began, a drip of drool appearing at the corner of her lips.

Swish! Suze lashed the air, inches from her bare buttocks, which clenched, unwhipped. The roped maids giggled at Michelle's pale face.

'You said no bitch could break you, eh? Unhappily for you, miss, I'm not a bitch. I don't mind teaching your vile tongue a lesson, you *mucky pup*.'

She retreated a few steps, and lifted the cane high above her head.

'No, wait,' bleated Michelle, 'I'm sorry, I didn't mean . . .'

Suze sprang forward on her power shoes, and ran the few steps to the bare arse, slicing the cane down, in the momentum of her runup. *Vap!*

'Ah!' Michelle shrieked.

Michelle's ripe, pear-shaped buttocks pouted out and up, thrust cheekily towards the cane, despite the girl's whimpering, as if begging to be kissed by the rod. The cane lashed the full flesh of the middle fesses, its springy wood curling around the entire buttocks, in a clinging embrace, before sliding off the naked skin, leaving a trembling pink welt. The bare arse clenched and quivered, the clutching cheeks squeezing the arse crack, then springing wide, to reveal the moist wet gash and anus bud.

'Oh . . . Oh . . .' cried Michelle, in a choking sob.

Suze retreated, and ran at her again. *Vap!*

'Ah . . . No, please, no . . .'

The power shoes thudded on the deck. *Vap! Vap!* a forehand, and a backhand slice, took the girl in the same weal.

'Ooh . . . Ahh . . .' she whimpered.

The firm melons of the girl's bare, writhing buttocks, shuddered like jellies under the cane, striping the naked skin to ruby welts. Panting, Suze sloped further back, and took another runup. *Vap! Vap!* A low, choking gurgle escaped the flogged girl's lips, as Michelle's buttocks jerked fantically, and raw stripes appeared on their clenched bare flesh. Suze remained, towering over the writhing nates, and delivered two more strokes from a standing position. *Vap! Vap!* Sobbing, Michelle found her voice.

'Ooh . . . ! That's too much! You're hurting me, miss!'

'Dare say they didn't have the cane at your school,' Suze spat.

'No . . .' Michelle sobbed.

'Filthy little tykes like you don't diddle their clits when they are *caned.*'

Vap! Vap!

'Ahh!'

'Nor a real strap, not some namby-pamby rubber thing, but –' Suze's panting voice faltered '– a proper strap, two thongs of thick studded leather. A real English girl can take fifty strokes with that, on the bare, without whimpering.'

'Yah, right,' Fiona murmured.

Suze's hand darted briefly to her thong, and her fingers came away, slimed with come. She gasped, and swallowed, wiping sweat from her eyes, as she raised the cane to the vertical, then took a few steps back, for her runup. Her feet pounded the deck, as she flew at the helpless bum. *Vap!*

47

Vap! Vap! She sliced Michelle straight in the buttock cleft, lashing the anus.

'*Oh! Ahh!* That's not fair, miss,' sobbed the squirming girl.

Michelle's wriggling body strained at her rope bonds, which held her helplessly to the mast. Fiona's video whirred, like Cordovan's clicking camera, focussing alternately on the flogged bare bottom of the shuddering girl, and on Suze's heaving breasts, which bounced in their separate sacs like ripe bare udders, threatening to pop from her scanty bra. She flogged the girl's clenched arse once more in the cleft, forcing the clamped buttocks to open, writhing, in order to clench again, and followed her stroke with two rapid stingers while the cleft was still open, catching Michelle squarely on her anus bud and her drooling, swollen cunt lips, which, like her whipper's, oozed come slime.

'AHH!' Michelle screamed, and her body drooped, hanging from her cords.

Suze continued the caning; her half-insensate victim jerked, mouth and cunt flaps bubbling with drool, as the wood wealed her crimson bare bum-flesh, the bruises puffy and ridged, darkening to purple. Suze's thighs were spread wide, each exertion of the flogging sending the tool dancing inside her anus, ramming the root of her arse; she was insensible of the stream of come gushing from her cunt, and gave no sign of noticing both cameras focussing on her rippling thighs, slimed with her own juice. Soubise stood akimbo, with the rubber quirt dangling before her vulva. Her lips were slack, and her face flushed, as her eyes fixed on Michelle's squirming bare bottom. *Vap! Vap! Vap!* The caning proceeded past the thirtieth stroke, and Soubise's quirt pressed into the folds of her vulva. *Vap! Vap! Vap!* Michelle's welted bare arse globes danced.

Soubise began to rub her thighs together, and slide the quirt handle up and down between them, touching her cunt, through the thin cream fabric of her cutoffs, which moistened rapidly, with an oily dark stain of seeped come. Her caress turned to overt masturbation, and her eyes fluttered, while a trickle of drool oozed from the corner of her mouth. Soubise's thighs pumped, as the rubber quirt handle stabbed her clitoris, and the leg tubes of her cutoff jeans began to slither, as they were soaked in her come. The roped girls, eyes bright, licked their lips, as they stared at the naked bottom flogged inches from their eyes. All the girls rubbed their thighs together; Heather Yonge, Marcia Subovic, and Yvonne Atras moved their roped wrists between their legs, and blatantly stroked their cunts through their knickers or slip. Nadia Colsemi, wearing only a frilly, skimpy petticoat, of lace-trimmed powder blue satin, was bare-cunted beneath, and thrust her fist under the satin, to stroke her naked quim. Suze's power shoes began to squelch with her dripped come, as she balled her feet and tensed, then hurtled at her victim, to deliver each stroke with maximum impact. *Vap! Vap! Vap!*

'Oh! Enough! Stop, please stop!' bleated the sweat-soaked girl, her body jerking and writhing in her ropes.

Vap! Vap! The cane lashed bare flesh, its crack echoing above the howls and chirps of the dark jungle, sliding past. *Vap! Vap!*

'Ooh . . . no!' whimpered Michelle.

Soubise's breath came in short gasps, as she frotted her swollen cunt; her thighs pumped, slithering, as her come-soaked jeans legs rubbed together. The roped girls all masturbated, none discreetly, and Dr Teidt placidly stroked her own pantiless cunt, beneath her ridden-up linen skirt. All the masturbatresses pouted and posed for the cameras, their juicing loins thrusting for spectacle. Only Soubise's face was withdrawn, her masturbation a private ceremony. Cordovan trained his lens on her, and frowned. Soubise did not smile; her teeth were a defiant rictus, as if she struggled against frigged pleasure. Suze continued to cane, until Didier drily predicted the flogged girl would piss herself soon. *Vap! Vap! Vap!* The fiftieth stroke was past, and Suze, panting hoarsely, mustered her sweating body to deliver harder and faster strokes. Her knickers and bra were translucent with sweat, and her power shoes squelched at each runup, for they were filling with her seeped come, trickling in shiny rivulets down her bare thighs and calves.

'Oh ... Oh ... Oh ...' sobbed Michelle.

Vap! Vap! Two more strokes took her in the unprotected arse cleft.

'Ahh!' she yelped.

There was a hiss, and a stream of steaming golden liquid splashed the deck.

'Oh, no ...'

It was Suze who wailed, having pissed herself. Soubise's teeth widened in a smile, as she stared alternately at Michelle's flogged bum, Suze's crimson face of dismay, and the sluice of piss that cascaded down her come-streaked legs, from her swollen cunt. Soubise began to gasp, in little staccato yelps, as her fingers danced on her cunt, bringing herself off. The other frotting girls, and Dr Teidt, were in no hurry to come: their masturbation was slow, and pleasure-prolonging. Sighing, and trembling, Suze flung down her cane. Cordovan announced that the day's session was complete, and stood over the frigging Soubise, his face grim.

'Masturbating, mademoiselle?' he said. 'And without my permission? You shall attend me in my quarters this evening, after supper.'

'Cordovan, everybody is masturbating,' Suze blurted.

Cordovan turned to her, furiously.

'Did I ask for your opinion, Miss Shard? Did I?'

'No, but ...'

He picked the quirt from Soubise's grasp, and wiped his fingers along its slimy surface, where come had seeped through her jeans and panties, to anoint the rubber. He dabbled the thongs in the pool of Suze's piss, and let the dripping rubber dangle at her cunt mound; piss dripped over her thong, wetting her tousled pubic fleece. Then, he wiped the thongs slowly across the trembling bare melons of her croup.

'This is a matter of shipboard discipline, you understand, Miss Shard. The ship's master is the law, and must punish disorder.'

He lashed the air with the quirt, the thongs whistling inches from Suze's piss-wet cunt, and smiled grimly at her.

'From *whatever* quarter . . .'

4

Pale Pink Blush

Fiona accompanied Suze back to her cabin. The two girls said nothing, but eyed each other; Suze blushed.

'You know what I'm thinking,' she murmured. 'Oh, I'm so embarrassed. I'm . . . I'm awfully hot.'

'I feel the same way,' Fiona replied, 'minus the embarrassment.'

'Shall we?' Suze blurted. 'Just like the old days, at school. A girl never really grows out of her school, does she?'

Fiona bared her teeth, and nodded assent.

'The cane at St Ursula's, giving or taking, meant one thing,' she purred, 'girls wanking off.'

Suze blushed.

'Such a crude term,' she sighed, 'but you're right, Fiona. You're always right.'

Hurriedly, the two girls stripped naked, and squatted on Suze's bunk, with their thighs spread, each girl displaying her wet swollen gash, and each clitoris, already erect and glistening with oozed come. Without touching each other, but each with her eyes fixed on the other's cunt, the girls began to masturbate.

'Ahh . . .' Suze sighed. 'I need this. I'm so hot, after doing that to Michelle. 'And –' she blushed '– awfully wet, *down there*.'

'Me too. I could hardly resist joining the doctor, and the skivvies, in a frig – but you see what hot water it got Soubise into. I don't envy her bum tonight. Or, maybe I do . . .'

'That's awful! Fiona, you don't think she – I mean, I can't imagine that haughty Soubise willingly baring up for corporal punishment. But I'm so confused, not least about my own motives. I flogged Michelle, and enjoyed it! But I feel guilty. This isn't the simple photo shoot I imagined.'

Fiona shrugged.

'You don't think the Essex slut enjoyed it? I'd like to be a fly on the wall, when Cordovan's alone with Soubise. Maybe she spanks *him* – though I doubt it. I've peeked at her bare arse. She's a taker, all right. Let's concentrate on our wanks.'

Fiona led, curling her fingers around her open, swollen cunt flaps, and teasing the folds of flesh, until come drooled over her fingers. Suze did likewise, following Fiona's lead, in brushing, then stroking, and finally ramming hard on her clitty with her thumb. The two girls delved into their pouches, thrusting two, then three, and four fingers into themelves, while maintaining the rolling rhythm of the clitty-thumbing. They began to frig vigorously, straightened fingers jabbing deeply into their cunts, while their bellies fluttered, at the thumbing of the erect red nubbins. Both masturbating hands were soaked in the come, that seeped more and more copiously from their wanked slits. Their cunts were inches away, and their knuckles touched, as they frigged, with each girl's eyes lowered to her friends's wet gash lips.

'I'm so ashamed, about beating Michelle,' Suze panted, 'I mean. I . . . I wet myself. I really let the school down, didn't I, after all my fine words. And I feel sort of guilty for getting wet, down there, as I caned her. Should I?'

'You did fine, Suze,' Fiona said. 'You have an idea of school . . . gymslips, and hockey, and cream teas and all that. Mine is different. Naughty bare bums under those gymslips, all waiting for my cane, and lots of lovely wanks afterwards.'

She licked her lips.

'That's what I think of, when I frig. Mm, this is good. I can see Michelle's lovely big melons, all red and naked and helpless, as they squirmed under your

53

cane. Lovely technique – the runup, faster and faster, then the crack on the bare. Anyone would think you *had* been a prefect at school. Oh, I'm so wet just recalling it. Look at me, Suze.'

Each girl stared at the other's sluicing wet cunt.

'Uh ... uh ... yes ...' Fiona gasped. 'Who needs men, except for spanks? By the way, I love your walk. So *empowered*.'

'Oh, no. Does it show?'

'It's rather obvious. You lost your frigging tool inside your bum, I'd imagine. I remember Judy Prosser of the sixth form, playing with herself, the dirty slug, and got a corn cob stuck inside. I had to cane her bare, while two other prefects pinioned her, and held her gymslip up over her back, and it took almost forty strokes until she peed herself, and dunged out the dildo.'

'It's not a dildo,' Suze gasped, and explained about Gothic massage.

After prompting from Fiona, with her own coy blushes, she related her gamahuching, with the tool sliding from Dr Teidt's anus into her own.

'Then you won't mind lending it to me,' said Fiona, masturbating hard, with her eyes closed to narrow slits.

'I can't ...'

'Go on.'

Fiona slid her bum, so that her cheeks touched Suze's.

'Do what the doctor did.'

'Oh! I can't.'

'Suze, you're The Bottom. You can do anything you like.'

Without ceasing to masturbate, Suze squeezed her arse cheeks, and the dark tip of the tool emerged from her stretched anal pucker. Fiona gaped.

'It's enormous. You brave girl.'

The tool touched Fiona's anus bud, which widened, making a mouth to receive it. The wood entered her bumshaft, and Fiona writhed, her anus sucking in the tube, which slid rapidly from Suze's own bumhole, with a loud plopping sound. It was sucked deeper and deeper into

Fiona, with her fingers masturbating faster and faster, as her rectum filled with the giant cylinder, until only a sliver of the tube remained visible. Suze's thighs were spread to the full, and she panted, urging Fiona to give it back the same way. However, with a squelching noise, the dildo plunged fully inside Fiona's bum, its tip vanishing, and the anal pucker closing to a wrinkle over the shaft.

'My, it's good,' she gasped. 'I'm going to come and come . . .'

'Give it back, Fiona!' Suze cried.

'What if I don't? You'll spank me?'

'You know I couldn't.'

'Then maybe I'll have to spank you, *slut*.'

'Fiona, don't. You know how I hate that.'

'Slut, slut, mucky pup. I'll spank that big bare bum all red, and there's something for a photo. The Bottom blotchy! Those melons, wriggling just like Michelle's . . . ooh, Suze, aren't you going to come? Wank harder, let's come together.'

'You're a tease, Fiona,' Suze gasped. 'You always were.'

Fiona's arse globes writhed, as she ground the dildo further up her bumhole.

'It's so good,' she panted.

'Give it back, Fiona,' Suze pleaded.

'Oh . . . yes . . . I'm coming . . .'

Fiona's finger and thumb grasped the raw, extruded nubbin of her clitty, and began to pull and pinch at the distended organ. Come poured from her cunt, wetting Suze's bedlinen. As Fiona's belly heaved, fluttering in her approaching come, Suze grabbed her by the mane, and pulled her head down, across Suze's lap.

'What . . . ?'

She crammed Fiona's face into her pillow, and got her hand between the legs, mashing the wet cunt, as she forked Fiona's squirming body into a position for spanking. *Crack! Crack! Crack!* Her palm slapped the full bare arse melons, which clenched timidly, then faster, as spanks rained harder and harder, in quickfire rapidity, on her naked fesses. *Crack! Crack! Crack!*

'Ooh . . .' gurgled Fiona, from beneath the pillow.

Her hand still masturbated her clitty, but more slowly, with the fluttering of her belly matching the twitching of her spanked buttocks. *Crack! Crack! Crack!*

'Ooh . . . Mmm . . . not fair. I can't spank you back, you slut.'

Crack! Crack! Crack!

'Mm . . .'

Fiona's wriggling bare did not offer a struggle; rather, a choreographed response to the darkening of her spanked bare. Suze spanked her to fifty, then sixty, seventy spanks, no longer needing to hold Fiona's head into the pillow, but masturbating her own cunt, with her free hand, as she spanked. Fiona's frigging was accompanied by her slapping her loins on Suze's thigh, which was soon slippery with Fiona's come; the spanked girl hunched her torso, writhing, so that her left teat poked into Suze's own wet quim pouch. Suze's frotting fingers grasped the nipple and pulled it taut, making Fiona squeal, then used it as a tickler for her throbbing clitoris.

Crack! Crack! Crack!

'Ooh . . .'

Crack! Crack! Crack!

'Ooh . . . yes . . . yes . . .'

'*Ahh* . . .'

Suze's spanking arm drooped, as orgasm flooded her heaving belly, and Fiona writhed simultaneously in her own come. The bed was drenched in the fluids from their twitching gashes; Suze let her head sink onto Fiona's back, and then slide down to her buttocks, where she nestled her nose in the arse cleft and perineum, slimed with Fiona's come.

'Oh!' she exclaimed, then giggled, as Fiona expelled the dildo suddenly from her anus, and squashed Suze's nose.

Laughing also, Fiona rose, and inspected her red bottom in the mirror. Her fingertips brushed the puffy red ridges, blotched with Suze's palm and fingerprints.

'Not bad,' she said. 'A hundred and forty-three spanks, in less than three minutes. Your hockey arm hasn't lost its strength.'

'Oh, Fiona . . . I don't know what possessed me,' Suze blurted, 'but it was a lovely diddle, wasn't it? And the spanking . . . you were willing and able, don't deny it. Your bum was hot for spanks.'

'Yes, it was. But you took advantage of me, and now I should bear a grudge, shouldn't I?' said Fiona. 'A revenge feud, just like at St Ursula's.'

'Fiona?' said Suze, as the girls soaped each other, in the shower.

'Yes?'

'What do you think of Soubise's bum?'

'You mean, is it as pretty as yours? Of course not.'

'That's not really what I meant. I mean, I'm not sure.'

'I know what you meant, *slut*,' said Fiona. 'You want to know if she's striped. Poo! I shan't tell you.'

'Fiona, don't be a beast.'

'You can jolly well peek for yourself. Don't forget Soubise has been summoned by the master, tonight, so you have a fine opportunity for keyholing. That's a skill no St Ursulan forgets.'

Supper was a muted affair, with Michelle once more joining the rest of the models in frilly French maid's attire, and serving in sullen silence. Cordovan was moody, staring into his wine glass, without speaking, for long periods, while Soubise's eyes flashed defiantly, almost in hatred, at all those whose gaze met hers, speculating what would happen during her interview with the master. Even the normally jovial Didier had a hard face, as he scrutinised the maidservants, that of a cruel overseer rather than a genial playmaster. Dr Teidt met no disagreement, when she opined, with bright enthusiasm, that recent events had changed them all, opening a new dimension to their voyage.

'A new reality,' she said. 'As we progress up the river, we enter a primordial, mythopoeic world, where the human elements are no longer disguised by the artifices of so-called civilisation. We revert to type: master and servant, owner and slave, the whippers and the whipped.

We enter strange realms, and this vessel is becoming one of them.'

'Where do you fit in, doctor?' Fiona asked.

'There is room for an observer. I observe each and every one of you.'

'A voyeuse,' Fiona shot back.

'Which of us is not voyeuse or voyeur? Especially when witnessing naked chastisement of another's nates. I made no secret of masturbating at the spectacle of Michelle's deserved chastisement. In the jungle, primitive desires are manifest.'

Fiona wore a loose blouse, sloppily unbuttoned, to show her braless teats, and below, a simple miniskirt, a yard of thin cloth fastened by a single pin at the haunch, and without knickers or stockings. Dr Teidt reached suddenly across Suze's lap, and grabbed Fiona's skirt, pulling it away from her hips, so that her cunt bush was seen, and the portion of bare buttock not covered by the cane chair bottom. Fiona's fesses were vivid with the crimson marks of her spanking, with Suze's handprints discernible. Fiona took the assault with poised indifference, continuing to eat, as the doctor inspected her bare flesh, and even, as she sipped wine, shifting her bum, and lifting the melons inches into the air, to provide a better view. Suze blushed furiously.

'Seen enough?' Fiona said, with a leer.

Dr Teidt let the skirt fall.

'I observed your walk, Fiona,' she said, 'and could tell you had been spanked. But by whom? I inspect – the handprints are known to me.'

She looked at the blushing Suze.

'Oh . . . you know . . . just a girlish prank,' she stammered.

'Quiet, Suze,' Fiona snapped. 'If you want to diddle, Dr Teidt, I'll strip off entirely, and wriggle for you, as I wriggled when Suze spanked me. It was damned hard, as only an English schoolgirl knows how.'

The taunt stung, and Dr Teidt flushed.

'I had you figured as the dominant type, Fiona,' she said icily, 'while Miss Suzette . . . well, evidently, English schoolgirls are eclectic.'

Cordovan's morosity had brightened to a leer, and Didier's face cracked into a lustful smile.

'Ladies,' said Cordovan softly. 'No one objects to, ah, English girlish pranks, but I remind you that shipboard discipline is at the behest of the master alone ... understood, Miss Shard?'

'Yes, Cordovan,' Suze blurted.

'*Parlons d'autre chose*,' Cordovan said curtly.

Soubise's nostrils flared, and she bared her teeth at Suze. Her eyes twinkled, like dark pools in the jungle river outside. The rest of the meal was accompanied by small talk, as though the whippings of late had never happened. Yet, the serving maids trembled, as they waited at table, and blushed, at the lustful looks to their partially-bared croups, the tiny knickers, stocking tops and garter straps shivering. Who was to be next?

Suze regained her cabin, and lay nervously on the bed, in only her bra and knickers, while listening to the hisses and chirps of the jungle night, and the slither of the water, masking the soft throbbing of the yacht's engines. Their vessel never slept; at this time, Didier's crew of creoles, males and females, continued to labour in the bowels of the ship. Shortly after midnight, Suze rose, and wrapped herself in a thin sarong, then padded, barefoot, into the corridor. Shivering, she made her way towards Cordovan's cabin, through the deserted passageways, illumined by sparse nightlights. She arrived at the locked door, and stood, panting, for moments. There was no sound from within.

Suze listened to the squeaks of jungle fauna, the snapping of jaws and the screams of beasts of prey, or those who were prey. She wiped the sweat from her brow; her whole body was moist, in the clammy heat of the ship's interior. Her sarong stuck to her, and she took it off, draping it around her neck. Her scalloped bra and thong panties were drenched too. Suddenly, above the animal screeches of the night, she heard it: a human voice, a woman's, nothing more than a single whimper, and a choked sob. And it came, surely, from within Cordovan's cabin. She stood rigidly still, listening; for a long time there was nothing, and then, she heard it again: a sob, followed by a long, gasping, moan. It could have been a jungle beast, the sound playing tricks on her ears, and still she hesitated to kneel, and apply her eye to the large keyhole, an act of voyeuse's commitment. Then she heard what belonged in no jungle; a rhythmic tap-tap-tap, followed by a stifled scream, and a growl, culminated in a series of sobbing wails. The woman crooned a shrill sob of distress, until the tap-tap-tap, repeated, raised her voice to a muffled shriek. Trembling, with her teats heaving up and down in their skimpy brassiere, Suze squatted, and pressed her eye to the keyhole.

There were the familiar sofa, chairs and coffee table, but moved to one side. In the centre of the room, with her back to the keyhole, Soubise hung by her wrists, roped to a bolt in the ceiling. She was nude, but for her bra. Her legs were splayed wide, the tips of her toes just touching the floor, with her ankles tethered by long ropes, to bolts in each opposite bulkhead. Her arms were tight together, wrenched taut, while her hair was twisted to a rope, and knotted around a second bolt, inches from the one suspending her wrists. Hair and arms took her whole weight. Her jaws yawned open, with a wooden ball wadded between her teeth, and held in place by a rubber strap around her nape. Her naked buttocks flamed with the stripes from a twin-thonged rubber strap, with a long handle, and stiff tongues, a foot in length.

The welts on her bare croup suggested the whipping had lasted some considerable time, for her weals were already puffing to dark, crusted ridges, and formed a crisscross pattern that covered the whole skin of both buttocks, as well as especially dark and swollen ridges on the tender skin of both her haunches. The weals were a livid crimson on her brown flesh, although some had darkened to deep purple. Her nude body wriggled, quivering, and dripped with sweat. Between her parted thighs, the vulva hung down, with pins popped through piercings in the flesh of the cunt flaps, suspending a glass vial beneath her gash, and its weight stretching the cooze flaps to two inches. The vial was half full of fluid, and Suze gasped, seeing copious come, dripping from the bound woman's cunt. Wearing only a black silk robe, Cordovan relaxed on a chair, slightly beneath Soubise's trembling bare buttocks. His cigar pluming the air with blue smoke, he flicked the quirt upwards, lashing the creole girl's bare brown fesses. *Tap! Tap! Tap!*

'Ooh . . .' Soubise groaned, her gasp muffled by the wooden ball-gag.

Tap! Tap! Tap!

'Uhh . . .'

With that flurry of strokes, Cordovan angled the tongues, to strike Soubise right on the gash and anus bud. The come vial jangled, slopping the liquid inside, which was soon augmented by a rapid spurt of come from the oozing cunt. *Tap! Tap! Tap! Tap!* Two strokes sliced each bruised haunch, deepening Soubise's existing welts, striping her flanks like dark tendrils. Her body shuddered, straining at the ropes holding her wrists and hair, whose roots were wrenched taut. *Tap! Tap!* Two strokes took her across mid-buttock, then – *Tap! Tap!* – two to the soft underfesses. Soubise's brown buttocks clenched, squirming, yet the spread of her thighs prevented the melons from fully wriggling.

Suze swallowed several times, stifling her moans, as moisture oozed into her thong string, covering her swelling cunt lips. Her hand crept down her belly, fluttering already, to the tense and throbbing clitoris, swollen and extruded from her wet gash. She gasped, as she pinched the extruded nubbin, and a shock of pleasure shook her spine. Her nipples stood erect, against the thin fabric of her brassiere, and the trembling fingers of her free hand rose to caress the buds, pinching and rubbing the naked nipple plums under the bra cloth, as her fingers masturbated her clitoris, sweeping aside the scanty thong, to plunge through her wet pubic jungle to the gaping, swollen cooze mouth.

Her fingers moved faster and faster on her naked quim, chafing and worrying the swollen clitoris, until wet oily come flooded her cunt basin, and reduced her panties to a sodden string. Her fingers made a squelching noise, as they jabbed repeatedly inside her gushing cunt pouch, reaming the walls, and poking the pulsating wombneck, bathed in hot come. *Tap! Tap! Tap!* Her eyes gazed at the squirming bare buttocks of the hung girl, the beating all the eerier, as it took place in total silence, apart from Soubise's choked screams. From Cordovan there was no sound, as though flogging her, with the deceptively mild-looking hard rubber tongues, was no more than a household task. Suze masturbated harder, unable to divert her eyes from the whipped girl's trembling bare buttocks, their weals growing to raw, vivid slashes, as the flogging progressed.

Soubise's eyes were wide open, closing only briefly, in anguish, at an especially painful cut, on the tender top buttock or haunch; she stared at the ceiling, yet her squirming suggested no protest – rather as if she, too, were participating in a necessary task, or rite. It seemed that she restrained her loins and buttocks from excessive squirming, mindful of the come vial, filling with her dripped fluid. Suze's belly fluttered, and she could no longer restrain her hoarse, rasping pants, as her twitching fingers brought her cunt to more and more copious, squelching spurts of oily come, and her belly heaved, in the onset of orgasm. As she began to growl in her throat, her eyes darted to Cordovan, sprawled, with his black silk robe open. She gasped aloud, seeing a woman, squatting at Cordovan's groin.

Her wrists were roped behind her back, and she was nude, save for garters and suspender belt, and shiny bronze nylon stockings. Her sucking lips enclosed his erect cock, plunged to her throat, so that only his balls were visible. It was Dr Teidt: her head bobbed up and down, like a pigeon's, as she fellated the master. Her own arse was just below Soubise's gaze, and the suspended girl, with an inclination of her head, could observe the fellatio. After each lashing of her bare croup, she jerked her head, to see the bound German woman sucking hard on the master's cock, at which Soubise's eyes closed tightly in anguish. *Tap! Tap! Tap!* The creole's naked arse melons twitched and clenched, as three strokes deepened the pulpy, crusted weals across her mid-fesse, and she gurgled in pain behind her gag.

'Uh . . . Uh . . . Ahh!' gasped Suze, as orgasm flooded her.

She was panting, in the throes of her spasm, with her masturbating hand slopped in her gushed come, when hairy fingers clutched her by the throat. She continued to masturbate, under the fist's pressure, and squealed, as the final sweetness of her climax pulsed through her cunt and belly.

'*Bonsoir, mademoiselle*,' said Didier.

Trembling, Suze rose, and Didier's fist transferred to the back of her neck. He pushed her down the deck, away from Cordovan's door, then to steps, leading down to the bowels of the ship.

'Where are you taking me?' Suze blurted, as she stumbled down the darkened stairway.

'In the foreign legion, spies were unpopular,' Didier purred. 'You English have a saying, about curiosity and the cat.'

'Wait, Didier, I can explain,' Suze gasped, trying to pull up her sodden knickers.

'Your behaviour is explanation enough, Mlle Shard,' he said. 'You are a lustful and curious beast, no better than the other sluts.'

'You can't harm me,' Suze cried. 'I pay for all this. It's my photo shoot.'

'I believe Cordovan has sufficient photos,' said Didier, 'that is, of your *cul* in an unblemished state. You had no hesitation in spanking Miss Fiona, nor in masturbating, as you watched forbidden scenes of Mlle Soubise's chastisement – imagining, no doubt, that such a fate could never befall your own fesses.'

'I can't believe this,' sobbed Suze, as they pushed open the door of the crew's quarters.

'Belief is not necessary,' said Didier. 'Experience is all. Until now, you have played mere games of submission and dominance, for the camera, flaunting your voluptuous *derrière*, like a butterfly fluttering its wings. Soon, your eyes shall open. We enter strange realms, as the doctor said.'

The heat in the crew's quarters was stifling, and, in the half darkness, Suze saw a dozen barely clad girls' bodies reclining on three-tiered bunks. As well as Michelle, and the other models, there were a dozen of Didier's creole crewgirls. At her entrance, the girls propped themselves on elbows, to stare at her, their eyes like fireflies in the gloom. The chamber stank of sweat, perfume, and stale food. Its low ceiling covered a floor of forty by fifteen feet, with another door, at the far end, behind which murmured male voices. In the centre stood a frame, similar to a vaulting horse in the gymnasium at St Ursula's, but constructed of bare metal girders, arranged, in the shape of a pyramid, with rubber straps dangling from the feet of each strut. Didier ripped Suze's sarong and bra from her body, ignoring her squeal of protest, then hooked the waistband of her knickers with his thumb, and tore the thong in half. It dropped to the floor, while Didier spreadeagled Suze's nude body across the metal frame.

'Oh, that hurts,' Suze wailed, as the sharp metal struts bit her belly flesh. 'Let me go. I'll tell on you, just wait.'

'About your frigging, as you watched the master chastise an errant maid?' said Didier, holding Suze by her nape, so that her bum stuck up, its bare melons wobbling wildly, and her legs jerking.

She could not wriggle her torso, for fear of the sharp metal damaging her naked breasts, pressed against the struts.

'Well, well,' sneered a girl's voice. 'Who's the slut now?'

Suze shuddered. It was Michelle. Beds creaked, as bodies rose, and feet thudded on the deck.

'No, wait,' she cried, trembling, as rubber cuffs were fastened around her ankles.

The tight restraints spread her thighs and buttocks wide, exposing her anus and cunt lips, with her legs splayed, one foot at each corner of the frame. She flailed out with her fists, punching the air, and drawing 'oof!' from girls, whose belly or breasts she struck, before her wrists were slapped into the rubber cuffs at the other side of the frame. Didier stepped back, leaving Suze thoroughly trussed, her bottom raised above the toprail of the frame, and both arms and legs spread in vee shapes. Her vulva was right at the pinnacle of the sloping metal, with the girder's sharp edge jammed against her spread gash flaps. Suze sobbed helplessly, shrieking, as her wriggles made the metal bite her bare body.

'May I do her, please, Didier?' said Michelle, in an ingratiating voice.

'No, me, please, please?' said Truud, followed by Nadia and Yvonne, and most of the model girls, now standing in a ring around Suze's body, and with their night attire discarded, leaving them naked and dripping with sweat, in the fetid chamber. Marcia and Pierrette had their fingers at their hairy wet vulvas, blatantly masturbating each other, as Suze squirmed.

'Let me spank!' cried Truud.

'Let me!' shrilled Danielle.

Didier raised his hand.

'You girls are precipitate,' he drawled. 'You have not yet learned of the maid's offence, nor determined a suitable punishment. In this case, the bottom presented is merchandise, indeed, the source of our present good fortune, so that it may perhaps be excused from the obvious chastisement.'

'You can't spank *me*,' Suze cried. 'I mean, please, Didier, I'm sorry. I'll apologise to Cordovan, and Soubise. Please don't spank my bum.'

'For the moment,' Didier added.

'Titty-whipping,' cried Yvonne.

'A cunt-strapping,' growled Michelle.

'Those, too, would leave marks,' Didier said.

'Mark her!' cried the maids.

'You are obdurate ladies,' replied Didier. 'You may relax, Mlle Shard. You shan't be spanked at this juncture. Your crime was not the worst, and if every peeping slut who diddled herself were brought to justice . . . why, we should have no crew at all.'

He stroked his chin, running his leathery hands over the creamy satin smoothness of Suze's arse globes. An index finger dipped into her arse cleft, then to her perineum, where he patted the wrinkled anus pucker, drawing a moan, and a shudder, from Suze. He poked the top of a fingernail into the apex of her cunt flaps, withdrew it moist and shiny, and held it, for the girls to see. Giorgia, Heather and Yvonne were also masturbating now. They made no sound, save for harsh grunting gasps, as, one by one, the whole crew of models began to frig their wet cunts, staring at the English girl's helpless nudity.

'Please . . . don't hurt me,' Suze whimpered. 'I'll do anything . . . anything.'

'Submission, and the fear of thrashing, makes the English girl moist,' Didier said to the masturbating maids. 'Curious, no? She thought this was all a game . . . the photographed pouting, and pretend hurt, and make-believe thrashing. Like her dildo she wore in her anus, for a whore's gait, imagining no one noticed, and that her parted thighs and ungainly strut were no more than the stride of an English girl of her class, addicted to spanking, and the more sensuous pleasure of *enculement*.'

'No,' Suze moaned.

'Do not lie, mademoiselle. English girls are known to like stripes on their bare arses, and stiff cocks in their bumholes. You have never enjoyed such pleasure?'

'No . . . that's beastly. I swear, I never have.'

Suze's voice faltered.

'Are you sure?' Didier asked, snapping his fingers on her wet cunt lips, then, five or six times, hard, on her exposed anus pucker. 'If it is true, then the task of chastising you is much easier. There are subtler punishments, which will make your bottom groan, without leaving a mark on your skin.'

He took off his shirt, and stood, with his muscled hairy torso bared, and his crotch bulging with the enormous snake of his erect cock. Suze twisted to look at him, and gasped, her eyes fixed on the throbbing mound at his groin.

'Oh . . . please, no,' Suze sobbed. 'It's too big for me. You'll split my bumhole.'

'As you say, mademoiselle,' Didier purred.

He accepted a short leather strap, its tip cut into three tongues, from Michelle, and pressed it against the flesh of Suze's bottom, then against her swollen wet cooze. He tickled and stroked her in the perineum and arse cleft, letting the edge of the tongues linger within the mouth of her pouch, and remarked how copiously her come flowed. Yvonne placed a wine glass beneath the rail of Suze's spanking frame, from which the oily fluid dripped rapidly, with little plopping sounds, into the wine glass. Didier continued to brush Suze's naked arse with the strap, pausing to tap it gently against her cunt lips, and her swollen, extruded clitoris. Suze gasped, her breath coming in hoarse pants, as her ooze of oily cunt juice quickened, and the wine glass filled. She kept her head turned, gazing at the rippling cock straining against Didier's uniform. Come flowed from her gaping, swollen cooze mouth. The stubby thongs of the strap were smeared shiny with cunt juice from her own slit.

'No . . .' she moaned. 'It's too big for me, I swear. It won't fit . . . I mean, it'll burst me. Oh, please, please, no. Spank me if you must – anything but that.'

'How would you know, mademoiselle?' Didier snapped. 'How would you know it is too big, unless you were already adept?'

'Oh . . . no!' Suze wailed, bursting into frenzied tears.

'I have reliable information, about your past,' Didier said.

'Surely not from Dr Teidt . . . Fiona wouldn't sneak, she's my best friend! I'm sure I didn't tell either of them about . . . about . . . Oh! I'll do Fiona, the rotten slut, I swear, if she's blabbed on me.'

'Can you be sure of Dr Teidt?' Didier asked. 'You have observed her intimacy with the master. As for Fiona, we shall see.'

Yvonne removed the glass filled with Suze's come, and handed it to the smiling Didier, who sniffed it.

'Admirable,' he said. 'You may have the honour, Mlle Shard, of contributing to your own fragrance.'

Suze's jaw dropped.

'What . . . ?' she blurted, and Didier laughed, followed by giggles from the masturbating models.

'What do you think gives your line of *odeurs* their special something?' he chuckled. 'Perfume is nothing but gut alcohol, with a few oils and spices mixed in. The finest oil is obviously from the female *sexe*, mademoiselle. When not being photographed, my models, and my crew of ripe young creoles, are masturbating below decks, juice spuming from their busy sexes, to provide oils for your scent, and you with your fame and fortune. Small wonder they are eager to see their mistress humbled.'

He parted her anus bud with fingernail and thumb, showing the pink anal passage within, thick with Suze's arse grease. He lifted the leather strap, and brought it smartly across her naked fesses. *Thwap!*

'Oh! No!' Suze shrieked, a spurt of come squirting from her cunt, over Didier's trousers, as a pale pink blush appeared on her clenching bare arse, in the outline of three thongs.

'A ship's captain must maintain discipline, in your case,' he said, 'and for his crew, provide the occasional morale-boosting spectacle, mademoiselle.'

5

Acceptable Crupper

'Let me go, you fucking sluts. You're hurting me,' Fiona snarled, as Pierrette and Nadia hauled her, struggling, into the crew's dormitory.

Her short pyjamas, of frilly red satin and lace, were half pulled from her body. Seeing Suze trussed to the frame, she started, and ceased struggling.

'Suze? What have they done to you?' she blurted, 'that horrid weal on your bum –' then swivelled her head, to gaze furiously at Didier.

'Mlle Shard has been less than forthcoming,' purred Didier. 'Corporal punishment may induce her to yield her secrets – the truth behind that frosty and teasing exterior. That she is a hot, wanton slut, like these others, craving the same delights, the same degradations. I refer, of course, to the English girl's utmost fantasy, of anal sex – in your case, Mlle Fiona, scarcely fantasy. Truth by ordeal, shall we say.'

The crew paused in their masturbation, on Fiona's entrance, but smiled at Didier's insult, and resumed their frottage, pointing their wet gashes cheekily at the squirming Fiona. Their hips swayed together, as they frigged.

'Didier, you bastard, let her go. We cannot harm The Bottom.'

'Not *her* bottom,' Didier replied.

Fiona yelped, as her arms were forced over her head, and her wrists knotted by a coarse hempen string, to a bar in the ceiling, thus suspending her, with her ankles swaying two inches from the floor, and her bottom directly above

Suze's head. A second cord looped Suze's mane, bunching it, and the cord was tied to the same bar, forcing Suze's head up, with her eyes pointed at Fiona's pantied bottom. Nadia ripped down the frilly pyjama panties, knotting them around Fiona's ankles, so that Fiona was securely bound at both hands and feet. She twirled, helpless in suspension, with her unbuttoned pyjama top fluttering around her flapping bare breasts.

'Mlle Shard was caught *in flagrante delicto*, of a serious sexual disorder,' Didier said, 'that of voyeurism. I have discussed Mlle Shard's case with the doctor, who favours a gentle investigative approach, a female method. My own is more robust. As ship's captain, my aim is to discover the origin of this perversion, so that proper chastisement may be applied, to treat her, for the security of my vessel. Frequently, it results from some traumatic event, which the sufferer keeps secret, even from herself. Mlle Shard refuses to divulge the secrets of her past. The ordeal of her best friend may elicit them.'

'No,' Suze gasped. 'You couldn't.'

Standing to one side of Suze's uplifted head, Didier raised the strap over Fiona's nates.

'It's not fair,' wailed Suze. 'I said you could do anything you wanted to punish me. Even . . . that.'

With a grimace, she nodded at Didier's stiff cock, bulging in his uniform.

'Don't hurt Fiona, please,' she begged.

'You have only to confess,' Didier said.

Thwap! The tongues cracked across Fiona's naked buttocks, leaving three raw pink welts. Fiona gurgled, her bum clenching and wriggling, as her bound nude body spun, with the titties quivering violently. *Thwap! Thwap!* The tongues slapped the naked flesh twice more, and Fiona's naked bottom began to clench and squirm. She did not cry out, or make any sound, save a long, gasping exhalation. *Thwap! Thwap! Thwap!*

'Ahh . . .'

The tongues left vivid red welts across the entire expanse of Fiona's bare croup, now wriggling and clenching automatically, even when the tongues were raised. Fiona's eyes were shut, and lifted to the ceiling, with her head hanging back; she breathed harshly, through flared nostrils, with her teeth bared and clamped tight in a rictus. *Thwap! Thwap! Thwap! Thwap!* Two strokes took her on each haunch, raising instant bruises on the tender skin, and Fiona groaned, twisting her hips, and twirling, as she dangled from the cords, biting deeply into her wrist skin. Didier stepped back, and looked down at Suze, whose eyes gaped wide, as the bare fesses writhed above her face. Between Fiona's clenched buttocks shone an ooze of cunt oil.

'Care to stop your friend's pain, Mlle Shard?' he said. 'Enlighten us – what happened to you, the prim English maiden, to turn you into a masturbating, peeping slut? You diddled, watching Michelle flogged, but of course she is from a lower class than your disdainful self. Perhaps Mlle Fiona's chastisement – a bottom flogged, of your own rank – may induce you to speak.'

'No! Stop, Didier. I've never told anybody,' Suze sobbed.

'Don't talk, girl,' Fiona panted 'Remember St Ursula's. School's honour! These brutes can't tame us. Uhh . . .'

She panted, as the thongs took her across the middle of her back, leaving a jagged threefold welt, below her flapping pyjama blouse. Didier nodded, and Pierrette replaced the wine glass beneath Suze's spread vulva, to catch the oily come seeping from her cooze flaps. He threw the strap to Michelle, whose fingers flew from her frigged cunt, to catch it; eyes gleaming, she took Didier's place before Fiona's reddened bare bottom. She lifted the strap to the full length of her arm, and brought it down savagely, across the thin skin of Fiona's top buttocks. *Thwap!* Fiona's bum jerked, and she moaned softly, between her convulsive gasps. *Thwap! Thwap!* The thongs slapped her naked fesses in mid-section, ploughing deeper into the existing welts, and Fiona moaned again, with the seep of come turned to a trickle, smearing the whole backs of her thighs, and dribbling past her knees. With a soft plinking sound, come dropped faster and faster from Suze's own cunt, as she watched her friend's bare bum striped and reddened by the slapping leather tongues.

Thwap! Thwap! Thwap! Michelle panted, as she resumed her masturbation, diddling her extruded stiff clitty with her free hand, and getting her fingers inside her wet pouch, to ream and jab the pink meat of her slit. Come trickled down her thighs, as she flogged Fiona. Suze was silent, while Fiona's whipped body hummed with a low, gurgling moan. Michelle licked her teeth at each stroke to the wriggling bare before her, and the leather tongues kept lashing Fiona, with Didier interrupting at intervals, to invite Suze to talk. Suze sobbed, gasping, that she could not, but her eyes were moist with tears, as she stared at Fiona's bruised bare nates; the trickle of come from Suze's slit half filled the wine glass under her wet gash. Fiona's panties, tied around her ankles, were soaked in her own dripped come; still, she held her gaze upwards, gritting her bared teeth, and panting hoarsely between her moans. Didier ripped off Fiona's pyjama blouse, baring her back, and, at his nod, Michelle began whipping Fiona on the back and shoulders. Michelle's own gash writhed, as the girl masturbated harder. She lashed Fiona's back for several minutes, until it was a lattice of crisscrossed stripes, and then resumed whipping the buttocks, which had not ceased to clench and squirm, even as Fiona's back was flogged.

'Uhh ... Uh ... No, stop, please ...' Suze sobbed; Pierrette replaced her wine glass, full of come, with a fresh one.

Fiona's whipping continued for upwards of forty minutes, with the crew and model girls masturbating to repeated orgasm. Michelle yielded the whip to Truud, then Nadia; Giorgia and Heather took turns, their cunts dripping wet, and breasts trembling, with the points of their nipples stiff, as they flogged the trussed girl on back or croup. When Fiona's back and buttocks were striped purple, and Suze's cunt had filled two glasses with come, Didier repossessed the strap from Michelle, and tersely announced an 'intimate' beating. Fiona's ankles were unbound, and her legs pulled wide, then the ankles refastened in a hobble bar, a four foot plank of wood, with cuffing restraints at each end. Her dripping cunt, perineum and anus bud, all sluicing with come, were fully exposed. Didier swung his strapping arm backwards, not up, and lashed between Fiona's legs, to land a loud slap on her anus and cunt lips. *Thwack! Thwack! Thwack!* The tongues landed with a squelchy thud, as they flogged the girl's bare spread vulva, sending up a spray of come from the whipped cooze. Fiona's body wriggled frantically; her bum, and her striped back jerking, with the lips of her cunt flapping convulsively, as she was whipped on her most intimate area, naked, exposed and helpless. Didier flogged her cunt for six minutes, before Fiona wailed, and pissed herself, a long, steaming jet of acrid golden fluid cascading from her writhing cunt lips, and hissing to the deck beneath her thighs. Suze wrinkled her nose, and turned away her eyes.

'All right, damn you,' she sobbed. 'I'll confess.'

'No, Suze,' hissed Fiona.

'I can't stand you being hurt, and shamed so, to pee yourself,' Suze wailed. 'Not you . . .'

Thwap! The quirt lashed Fiona's buttocks. *Thwap! Thwap!* Fiona grimaced, as her bare nates clenched, writhing anew.

'Her treatment will cease, when I am convinced of your sincerity, Mlle Shard,' said Didier, raising the lash over Fiona's bare bum.

Thwap! Thwap!

'Ooh . . .' Fiona sobbed, a long, slow moan, as the tongues, moving only a short distance, and powered by only a flick of Didier's wrist, raised new puffy welts on her inflamed bare.

'People already ask who funded this whole trip, and I suppose I can't keep it secret forever,' Suze blurted, her voice ripe with bitterness. 'I'm so ashamed . . . it's something I've tried to forget, but I'll blab! Just stop this terrible beating.'

The whip was still.

73

'Please begin, mademoiselle,' Didier said, and Suze spoke.

His name was Grobard Westerham, more properly, Fulke Grobard de Ouistreham, an earl, and, in his twenties, owner of an estate and fortune that descended from the time of William the Conqueror. He boasted of being decadent, but kept his eye on the money markets, from his flat off Cadogan Square. He was louchely handsome, and amused himself in London, Brazil, or the French Riviera, when not on his vast acreage in Northumberland. He liked to recount the pleasures of his ancestor, the first Fulke Grobard de Ouistreham, who dined to the screams of women slaves flogged naked by his table. Northumberland was far from the king's writ, and had not progressed to feudalism: Fulke enjoyed raiding across the border in Scotland, to capture blond or red-headed females as slaves and bedmates. His torture chambers, and the intricacy of their equipment, was legendary, although Fulke's chastisement of choice was the whipping of naked female flesh, specifically, the bare buttocks, with an ingenious array of quirts, scourges, flails and canes.

After the restoration of Charles II, a Grobard de Ouistreham entertained the merry monarch at his house near Egham, where Surrey milkmaids were tied up, spanked and whipped, and nursing mothers were milked, or gave suck, to courtiers, before sound spankings on the bare. Decades later, the infamous Hellfire Club was eclipsed by Fulke Westerham's Abbey of Delight, near Cheltenham, where naked girls were imprisoned in a cage, and encouraged to fight, with no holds barred, until the victrix emerged, to be buggered by every male member of the club, while the losers were fastened in stocks or pillories, to have their naked buttocks whipped or caned raw. Young Grobard Westerham declared himself an admirer of his ancestors, but Suze was ignorant of such details, until later.

They had met at a party in Chelsea, and the languid aristo quickly captivated her, by his lazy indifference to her fabulous bottom. 'Quite a filly,' he said. 'Acceptable

74

crupper.' Suze did not know of Grobard's, or his family's, history, but loved his attentiveness, listening to her blurted complaints of Gilles, her French former boyfriend, a photographer with the morals of a stoat, who had treated her disgracefully. Grobard opined that 'present-day froggies' were 'a rum shower', emphasising that he was a Norman. His charm, his fascination, was partly that he was not eager to get into her panties, yet his lazy smile made it clear he might choose to do so, if he pleased. His control made Suze shiver, and her pouch moisten.

He expressed interest in her dreamed-of photo expedition to South America, of which his knowledge was 'passing fair'. A relative, Capt Foulkes Westerham, of the Guards, had disappeared on a 1923 expedition to the mouth of the Orinoco, in search of Eldorado, 'or some such tommy-rot.' It suited both of them not to be seen alone in public, but dining or partying, always in a group: that way, the tabloids could not link them as an item, which, indeed, they were not, as the nobleman had not bedded her. When Grobard suggested investing in her photo shoot, Suze confessed gratefully that she was in serious money trouble, and that the future of the 'Suze' line was in jeopardy. Gilles, as her manager, had lost, or purloined her money. Suze should spend a few days as Grobard's guest at his 'cottage' in Northumberland, to finalise matters. She was to come alone, and Suze accepted, finding the opportunity for secrecy and solitude quite thrilling. Even on the train to Newcastle, in semi-disguise, she chuckled at the tabloids' fever, 'Where has The Bottom gone?'

The first thing that struck her at Ouistreham Castle was that, apart from some field labourers, stripped to the waist, all Grobard's staff were females: well-formed and muscular, or pert and dainty, but all young, and of Suze's age, none more than twenty-one. They seemed not to know who she was, which pleased Suze, although she sensed their steely politeness was only to her as a new acquisition of their master's, not as an individual. She was amused, though rather nervous, that they addressed her as 'milady'.

The ancient house seemed oddly decrepit, with broken furniture carelessly displayed amid rusting suits of armour, and cobwebbed oil paintings, although the bondsmaidens, as they called themselves, were uniformly crisp, in frilly maids' uniforms, or stern, in costumes of chauffeur's leather, or nurse's skirt, bib and pinny, depending on their function; on arriving at the nearest station, a good thirty miles from the castle, a spiffy new Benz had picked her up, its driver Brunhilde, a stern German girl with blond hair piled high under a black leather peaked cap, and her large teats and croup stiffly encased in a black leather jumpsuit. She had said nothing to Suze, throughout the moorland journey.

Marcia was her escort: a dainty young bondsmaiden, in frilly French maid outfit, displaying large portions of bare breast flesh, and the bottom halves of her full, ripe buttocks, in seamed fishnet stockings. Teetering on her stilettos, she took Suze to her draughty but luxuriously-draped room, with a four-poster bed. Her heels clacked through the windy, stone-slabbed corridors, and up the creaking wooden staircases, to the bedroom, in one of the castle's turrets. Suze averted her gaze from some of the numerous paintings, which depicted men in ancient costume, and the very likeness of Grobard himself, supervising unseemly rituals of bare-bottom spanking, whipping, or even grisly torture with metal apparatus, the victims being all young, female, and in scanty underthings or nude. Particular attention was paid to meticulous depiction, both of the stripes, welts and bruises on the tortured bare flesh, and on every detail of the girls' faces, contorted in agony. Seeing Suze's aversion from the paintings, Marcia explained that their lordships had always been fond of joking. She said it gravely, with a straight face.

Suze broke off her narrative at that point.

'This is very difficult for me,' she said.

Thwap! Thwap! The quirt lashed Fiona's bare buttocks; she trembled, grimacing, and her whole nude body trembled, dangling from her cords.

'Not as difficult as for Fiona,' said Didier.

'Can't I talk somewhere private? These girls ... I mean, they are diddling themselves. It's awful.'

'That is the whole point,' said Didier. 'Please continue.'

Thwap! Thwap! Fiona's buttocks jerked, under the whip, with two fresh weals laid on her mosaic of blotchy bruised skin.

'Uhh ...' she moaned, her slack lips drooling.

Suze swallowed her sobs, and went on. She did not see Grobard until dinner, when Marcia ushered her to the gaunt, vaulted hall, adorned with more of the dusty paintings, from which Suze could no longer, politely, avert her gaze. Before that, Marcia had assisted her at toilette, which meant an old tin bath, filled with jugs of hot water by the maid, while Tania, another bondsmaiden in the same costume, sponged Suze's back, and helped her shampoo. Tania was decorously insistent on shampooing Suze's cunt bush, as well as her top mane. When she returned to the bedchamber, she found that Marcia had laid out her costume, which the master wished her to wear. Suze's fingers flew to her lips, and she exclaimed that it was gorgeous: a low-cut, clinging, frock, in bronze chain mail, the skirt coming down just below her pubis, and accompanied by bronze sheen stockings in real nylon, with a white lacy suspender belt, but no panties. As well, a narrow waspie corset, of beige latex, with strings and eyelets. Her footwear was calfskin slippers, that bared her toes, ankles, heels and most of her upper feet, and perched on impossibly high stiletto heels.

She complained that the suspender belt and stockings were too tight, and Marcia had to help her don the garments, pulling and pinching Suze's skin, until they fitted like gloves. Suze baulked at the corset, saying she would never fit into it, but Marcia assured her it would resize her waist to a healthy seventeen inches. Suze gasped, as both maids pulled the corset around her belly, and Marcia knotted each eyelet as tight as it would go. The corset thrust her teats up, so that, when she donned her chain mail frock, the breasts jutted like towers, under the thin metal. The frock shimmered on Suze's body, clinging tight, and hung by two bronze shoulder ropes. She clasped her waist, in wonderment, and asked if she had really gone to seventeen inches; Marcia gravely assured her it was so. The maid unbuttoned her blouse, and, unsmiling, displayed her own latex corset, which she said took her to eighteen. The smell of latex and metal were strange in Suze's nostrils, as she sat at the end of the long dining table, with Grobard standing at the head, in evening dress, with a broadsword dangling from his waist. He took his place, once Suze was in her chair, allowing his sword to rest on the stone-slabbed floor. There were five frilly maids to serve them dinner: soup, fish, roast boar or venison, and claret to drink. The tightness of her corset, stockings and supender belt made it difficult for her to eat much, and she kept shifting in her chair, feeling the gritty chain mail tickling her naked cunt, and pinching the long, thick hairs of her pubic forest.

'Power is what we have in common,' he said to Suze. 'You, the power of your beautiful hindquarters, and I, the power of my ancestry. These girls here serve me without stipend – does that amaze you? Power satisfies, either by wielding it, or, like my maids, submitting to it. People will do things for power, that they will never do for money. The aura of brute power remains the same, imparting a glow to the flesh of empowered and submissive alike. Your corset is the symbol of my power over you, as my guest, and imparts just such a glow, in your thrilled submission to its bondage.'

Suze laughed nervously at the back-handed compliment, and, blushing, sipped her wine. At that moment, Tania made an error in the serving of pudding – a strawberry fool, in the shape of the castle – and a dollop of cream lodged at her bared upper left breast, just above the nipple.

'Oh,' she gasped, and, without another word, lay across the table, on her belly, with her teats pressed to the wood.

Her bottom bobbed in the air, and she reached down, to raise her sliver of frilly skirt, revealing her bare fesses knickerless. Wiping strawberry fool from his lips, Grobard rose, without haste, and unstrapped his broadsword. He raised the flat of the blade over the girl's trembling bare bottom, while Marcia and another maid held Tania's shoulders flat on the dining table. *Crack!* The impact of the sword, lashing Tania's bare, echoed through the vault. *Crack! Crack! Crack!* The maid wriggled, her face a grimace, and reddening, as her bare bottom reddened. She squirmed and writhed against the polished oak table, while Grobard effortlessly thashed his maid's buttocks, until they were dark puce with bruises, and clenching like bladders. The beating took the girl to over forty strokes, until Grobard resheathed his sword, and sat down again, to resume his pudding, with a gulp of the madeira wine, which the flogged girl hurried to pour for him. Suze blushed, realising she had watched the beating avidly, and that her unpantied cunt was moist with seeped come. Grobard leered at her, in a way she had not seen before.

'Bronze mail is more fitting than iron, since moisture does not rust it,' he purred, and Suze blushed deeper, knowing he had guessed her excitement at the girl's bare-arse thrashing.

'Power and punishment,' he continued, staring into his wine glass. 'My steel is still warm from Tania's crupper. Suze, would you like to thrash Marcia's arse? I am sure she will commit some misdeed in the next minute or so.'

Blushing furiously, Suze was speechless. Grobard laughed.

'I shall take that as a yes,' he said. 'I know about St Ursula's, the school for spankers . . . but you must answer yes, Suze, in your own voice. Go on. Look at Marcia's bum – how sweet and smooth those melons would look, bared for a thrashing, and trembling, under the cuts from a Norman broadsword. This sword has flogged innumerable wenches on the bare, over nine glorious centuries of chastisement. What else has made our island great, Suze my dear, but naked bottoms, trembling under the lash?'

He pulled Tania's skirt up, to reveal the welts on her naked fesses, now puffing into blotchy purple ridges.

'Proud, Tania?' he snapped, and Tania curtsied, trembling, and murmuring that she was.

Marcia stood beside Suze, her head hung, and her hands at her crotch, not looking up, her face pale, and her long legs trembling in their fishnets.

'Do you deserve chastisement, Marcia? Some error, some fault ... milady's bathwater was perhaps tepid.'

'Yes, master, it was, I confess,' Marcia blurted. 'It would be fitting, if milady chose to thrash me on the bare.'

'Doesn't that excite you, Suze? You can thrash her, rack her, do anything. She is only a bondsmaiden, after all. Doesn't your own excellence of croup make you want to chastise the croups of other girls? Say it, Suze. Someone must thrash the wench. Shall Tania do it? Or Brunhilde? She would hurt poor Marcia far worse than you, I wager. You, as an Ursulan, understand what needs to be done ...'

Suze's pussy was wet, as she gazed at the trembling buttocks of Marcia, and knowing they were to be thrashed bare. Sweetly, horribly, she longed to thrash them herself – for the insolence of being so pert and proud and ripe, daring to distact attention from Suze's own bum.

'OK,' she gasped. 'Yes, I'll do it.'

Grobard leered again.

'You choose power,' he said. 'Seize her, maids.'

Suze was taken unawares by the cruel bondsmaidens: pinioned, and prepared for chastisement.

Sobbing, she halted in her story.

'It is too painful,' she gasped. 'You must understand ... this is a memory I have blanked completely. It is traumatic for me to relive a horror I thought forgotten.'

Thwap! Thwap! Didier's whip lashed Fiona's buttocks, and the dangling girl wriggled. Didier smiled at Suze, who groaned, and recommenced her narrative.

The first two days of her subjugation were the worst, she said, because of her uncertainty. What did Grobard want with her? As it became clear that he wanted to break her in, as a castle wench, her doubt cleared, though not her dread. There was a programme of submission, one which all the wenches had willingly undergone, and which they happily imposed on the newcomer. Grobard said that female submissives were a haughty breed, and, since Suze already possessed the haughtiness, it remained to coax her innate submissiveness from her. At that first dinner, Marcia and Tania grabbed the startled Suze, and flung her from her chair, over the table, with her chain mail dress pulled up, to bare her knickerless buttocks, and bag her head in a shroud. Struggling, she was pinned down, and helpless, as two other maids grasped her ankles, and held her legs wide apart. She was whimpering, begging for mercy; all she received was a sound spanking from several girls' hands, and was almost grateful that it was so little, although over two hundred spanks left her bare bum sore, welted and burning. After her spanking, with her head still bagged, she cried out, as Grobard's fist invaded her spread cooze, and the master invited the girls to look at the copious come Suze's spanking had milked from her.

The same girls who had spanked her took turns at masturbating her, until she came, shuddering and wriggling, with her jerking cunt thudding on the table, and her face wet with tears of shame. Tania and Marcia stripped her of her dress, leaving her shoes, corset, stockings and suspenders, then hogtied her, with her roped wrists and ankles suspending her from a pole, and carried her upstairs to her chamber. Her wrists were roped to the header and footer of her bedframe, stretching her arms straight, on either side of her torso, so that she was unable to climb onto the bed, nor lie down on the floor. The least uncomfortable position for sleep was to kneel at the bedside, with her head on the coverlet, arms stretched, and bare buttocks exposed, as in prayer, or for spanking – or worse, Suze whispered, trembling. It was worse. She was gagged with her own panties she had worn on her journey, the soiled garment wadded into her mouth, and secured around her neck, with a rubber cord. Tania and Marcia accomplished those tasks, and departed, without a word of answer to Suze's anguished queries, before her gagging. She begged them to show mercy, demanded an explanation, why decent girls should be slaves of a pervert's beastly lusts, but got no answer, only a frosty silence.

81

About midnight, just when she had drifted into a doze, her door opened, and Grobard entered, accompanied by Tania and Marcia, and a young, bare-chested labourer, introduced curtly as Jed, with rippling muscles and an insolent leer. Grobard, still in evening dress, carried a cane, with a crook handle, such as Suze recognised from the headmistress's study, at St Ursula's, the kind kept under lock and key, in a wired glass cabinet. It was a three-foot-long ashplant, tough and springy, and capable of dreadful bruising to unprotected bare flesh. Grobard swished the air with his cane, sending eddies of air across Suze's naked buttocks. He wore spurred boots over his dress trousers, and used them to rake Suze's naked flanks, while the two girls each secured one of Suze's ankles by squatting on it, preventing her legs from moving.

'Acceptable crupper,' Grobard said, while lifting his cane high.

Suze squealed through her gag, and wriggled, but the ropes trussing her were too tight for her to shift. *Vip!* She howled through her gag, as the cane lashed her bare nates, still red from the bruises of her spanking. It was the worst pain she had ever endured, far worse than anything from a girl's hand, at St Ursula's. Grobard was strong, and put every ounce of strength into his flogging. *Vip! Vip! Vip!* The strokes came fast, searing Suze's bare bum like lances of white-hot steel. She squealed through her panties, gasped and sobbed and wriggled, her voice a broken, muffled yelp, as the wood stroked her naked bum flesh, and her proud arse melons darkened in puffy, smarting welts.

Vip! Vip! Vip! The cruel cane whistled and lashed, again and again, and, after the twentieth cut, she lost count, scarcely noticing when she pissed herself loudly and copiously, not long afterwards. The strokes kept slicing her bruised, flaming bare, as she pressed her face to the bed, wet with her tears. She was near fainting at the pain, when the beating stopped. Grobard pushed his hand inside her wet cunt, and said that the mare was winking, and hot for it. He withdrew his hand, and once more she felt flesh between her legs: not the master's hand, but the tip of Jed's naked, and monstrously engorged cock. The cock reamed her pouch, and Jed grunted, then transferred his organ to her spread bum pucker, wiping his hand in her soaking cunt: he smeared her anus bud with the come that had dripped from her gash, throughout her caning. Tania and Marcia simpered approval, as the naked male mounted Suze, taking her in the bumhole. She almost choked in horror, pain and shame, at this dreadful invasion of her body.

'Enjoy her, my boy, she's an arse virgin,' Grobard said, and Jed grunted, as he plunged his giant tool right to the root of her anus, its progress eased by the copious come lubricating his cock, and by Suze's abundant arse grease.

Suze cried out at the excruciating pain of the monstrous hard cock, that she thought would split her bumhole and belly. Ignoring her cries, and the frantic wriggling of her impaled arse, Jed began a vigorous bum-fucking. Suze's body jerked up and down like a rag doll, at the force of his buggery. Despite her shame, she found that her buttocks began to rise to meet his cock, and her anus widened to allow the shaft entrance, and access to her deepest bumhole. She told herself, in her agony, that her feigned compliance was only to ease her distress, yet her bucking arse seemed to have taken on a life of its own, widening and squeezing, to milk the thrusting cock, as eagerly as any cunt. Her arse grease seeped strongly, sliming the cock, as it rammed her root. The pain of buggery melted her loins to hot wax, until her entire cunt basin seemed a searing cauldron of agony. The brutal farmhand buggered her for several minutes, while his master smoked a cheroot, blowing blue plumes over her dancing bum, as the massive cock, shining with her arse grease and come, hammered the squirming girl's anal root.

Suze used her sphincter to squeeze the cock's tip hard, hoping to bring the male to orgasm; after an age, she felt the cockmeat tense and stiffen further, then one or two hot droplets of spunk bathing her rectum; she squeezed mightily, and the cock bucked, flooding her bumhole with

83

hot, creamy sperm, so copiously, that she felt it spurt from the lips of her anus, and dribble onto her thighs, to mix with her own hot flood of come from her cunt. Her belly fluttered.

'No ... no ...' she moaned.

Yet, as the cock spurted its creamy load into her anus, Suze's cunt squirted ever more copious floods of come, and her spine tingled with electric pleasure. The whipped heat of her buttocks, and the agony of her pierced bumhole, turned to a vast, melting pleasure of orgasm. Whipped and buggered, like an animal, or common trollop, Suze experienced one of the most intense climaxes she had ever known. She was released from her gag and wrist ropes, permitting her to lie, sobbing, on her bed, with one restraining rope fixing her ankle to the top of the fourposter. The others left, Jed thanking his master, and agreeing that Suze indeed had an acceptable crupper. Suze fell into guilty sleep, dreading what she knew awaited her as a castle wench, yet longing for it.

6

The Wet Bare

Every evening, Suze dined with her master, sometimes wearing the bronze mail dress, sometimes in ripped and stained knickers and bra, sometimes nude; she was roped to the table leg, beneath Grobard's chair, where she ate scraps that he threw down to her, and drank her claret from a saucer, like a dog. Sometimes, her rope was fastened around her waist, wrists, or ankles; sometimes, it looped through clothes pegs, painfully pinning her nipples, or cunt lips. At nights, her master would visit her bedchamber, with the smirking Tania and Marcia, and a lustful young male, who would bugger her, while Grobard watched and smoked. She was never fucked in the cunt; always in her anus, which never stopped throbbing with the pain of her impalements. Neither did her buttocks cease to smart, from daytime lashings with horsewhip or riding crop, in the fresh air, where she had to labour in the nude, in the damp and cold. When Grobard planned a formal caning on the bare, trussed to one of his many flogging frames, he would give her a few hours' notice, so that she had time to shudder in dread. Before every buggery, Tania and Marcia would frig her clit, then tongue the erect nubbin, their skilful gamahuche bringing her to the brink of orgasm, until she was desperate to climax. Then, she would orgasm after a few minutes of hard bumfucking, when she felt hot sperm spurt at her arse root.

She was beaten before every frig or buggery, so that she could not help associating orgasm with the smarting of the rod on her naked fesses, shameful masturbation by the tongues and fingers of unabashed tribadists, and the agony of a hard cock ramming her anus. All those sensations merged into one – the most intense, and craved, being the release of orgasm, which grew more powerful as the days passed, and whose pleasure seemed to obliterate her shame, pain and degradation, so that she came to crave all of her humiliance. Caning on the bare, buggery, and her masturbated excitement from Tania and Marcia, fused into one, along with the ropes which always trussed her, when she was due treatment, so that she could no longer imagine pleasure without restraint, or orgasm without pain.

In the day, she went naked. Everything conspired to make her an animal. She had to piss or dung, into a tiny chamberpot, in full view of the assembled castle wenches, who laughed. Hygiene was a hosing with icy water, in the stable, by one of the farmhands who had buggered her – she knew the males only by their size of cock, each equally painful, as it cleaved her bottom. Her breakfast was a bowl of oatmeal, also eaten in the stable, and, after her hosing and dunging, she was harnessed to a small, rapid cart, like a chariot. Grobard supervised her trussing with reins, bit, bridle, and halter, just like one of his ponies, and her feet were encumbered with heavy iron horseshoes. She was not alone: any wench, erring beyond a simple bare-bum caning, was sentenced to a day under bridle, which included any number of strokes from the riding crop to her naked fesses, pumping, as she struggled to pull the cart at the trot. Grobard rode his cart, standing close to the crupper of his steed, within range of his long whalebone riding crop, plaited with studded leather strips. It hurt abominably, as he lashed his pony wenches on, over rocky hills and fields, driving them up to their titties through icy streams, and finally awarding the slowest mare with a public thrashing.

There were usually two or three other girls sentenced to the bridle, which, for Suze, was every day. Sneering, they conspired to lame or hobble her in some way, so that it was usually Suze's bottom which received the fearful public caning, as she was bent over her own cart, with her companions in humiliance holding her down by wrists and ankles, to take her punishment from the master's cane. Sometimes, Grobard added to her shame, by allowing the other girls to cane her: naked like herself, they competed to see who could raise the deepest weals on her bare. During these thrashings, she learned to stifle her squeals, as Grobard rewarded weakness with further thrashing. Caning was rarely less than fifty strokes. At first, Suze thought she would faint with the pain, having known nothing like it at St Ursula's, where a caning of thirty strokes was deemed normal – but the castle wenches considered fifty only a dusting. Suze was not allowed a mirror, so that she could not see how horribly her bum was bruised; but, running her hands over her flogged skin, she shuddered, at the deep coruscation of welts and ridges, hardened to the consistency of ribbed leather, or even wood.

Suze learned to fight, or rather, to be shamefully defeated. Wearing horseshoes, two girls would wrestle, no holds barred, in the stinking stable slurry, while Grobard allowed his farmhands to wager on the outcome. The combatants would gouge or kick each other's cunt and titties, something which Suze could not bring herself to do. The ten-minute contests always ended in her defeat, so wagers on her were suspended, although she still had to fight: sure of losing, she would be handicapped with weights suspended from cunt flaps and nipples, or have her hands tied behind her back, or one ankle bent behind her and roped to one wrist, so that she was no more than a punchbag. In one contest, during her second week of captivity, a Derbyshire girl called Doris Norton ground her face, cunt and titties into the muck, walking up and down her spine, and kicking her vulva, between her spread, squirming bum cheeks, while Suze burst into tears, and lay in the muck, sobbing. No number of lashes from Marcia's cane on her muck-sluiced bum could rouse her. She hated Doris Norton.

Grobard ground his cigar on her wet bum cleft, and said she was free meat. Jed was the first to take up the offer;

pushing his mates aside, he dropped his jeans, revealing an already stiff cock. He straddled Suze in the slurry, and forced her fesses apart, then thrust his cock between Suze's buttocks, and into her bumhole. She squirmed, whimpered and wriggled under Jed's buggery for several minutes, before he spermed in her anus. No sooner was his spunk frothing at her anal lips, and drooling on her thighs, than a second male took his place, and Suze's gasps and sobs did not cease, nor her impaled arse stop writhing, until six of the farmhands had buggered her in succession, her buggery lasting over ninety minutes. As she lay motionless and whimpering, Grobard decreed a further whipping, for dumb insolence; four girls stood on each ankle and wrist, while Marcia wielded the riding crop, lashing her wet bare buttocks, and drawing howls from Suze, whose every shudder slimed her further with stable muck, mingled with the come dripping from her winking cooze. After fifty strokes on the wet bare, Tania hauled her up, and, with a sneer, held her cunt open for all to see, with rivulets of come gushing down her browned thighs. Tania applied her thumb to Suze's clitty, and after a few jabs to the distended nubbin, Suze cried out again, in the throes of orgasm, as her belly fluttered, and her cunt gushed oily come.

The second week dragged into the third, and Suze was no more than a naked, whipped and buggered animal: yet, a female animal, brought to orgasm several times in each day, and her female animality honed to crave any shame and any pain, as long as it led to the ecstasy of climax. Grobard himself never fucked her. His ministrations were limited to the whip or cane on bare, never to penetrating her bruised flesh. Her ordeal entered a new phase: Suze endured chastisement from the girls alone, with Tania and Marcia supervising her buggery by the farmhands, and devising tortures for her bare flesh. Sometimes, though, they were sweet, taking her for long walks in the country, to pick flowers and enjoy conversation, although, during these rambles, Suze was kept naked, and led on a rope, tied to a clamp on her nipples, or vulva. Just when Suze felt she was reaching out to the wenches, they became brutes again, without warning. Stripped of clothing, with bruises visible on her bare body, she was stripped of dignity.

The whip lashed her breasts, vulva and belly, with Suze dangling in suspension by knotted wrists. There was no inch of her body unbruised by cane, quirt or crop, including the naked soles of her feet, writhing under the canestrokes of one girl, while Suze, bound by cords, was restrained by the other, sitting bare-bum on her face, with Suze obliged to lick her gash and swallow her come, and often a torrent of acrid piss as well. During suspension, they would weight her nipples and gash flaps with stones, the attaching strings clamped or stapled to her membranes. Her titties would be pinned upwards, with clamps wrenching her nipples, revealing the undermeat of the breasts for caning; or, weighted down, so that the upper teat was stretched to receive strokes. Her nipples would be tightened in a vice, swelling them to bursting, and severe caning applied to the popping teat plums.

Often, she was dowsed with slops or slurry, to take her strokes on the wet bare, for extra pain. Grobard would appear, at Suze's shrieks, and order her released, pretending to be shocked at his minions' abuse; sometimes selecting one of Suze's torturers for a swift punishment on the bare, before Suze's eyes. During the other girl's beating, Suze had her cunt masturbated to orgasm by the spared torturer, as she watched Tania's or Marcia's lashed bare fesses squirming, and purpling with bruises from the master's crop. Either of the girls seemed to derive as much pleasure from watching her friend whipped, and masturbating Suze, as from applying the whip to Suze's own nates. It was a lark, Marcia said – a jape, according to Tania. She came to see Grobard not as her master, but her rescuer. And she wanted to show her gratitude. Masturbation, or being rudely taken in the arse by successive farmhands, was not enough: she wanted to give herself to her master.

One evening, when she was roped naked beneath Grobard's table, she sneaked beneath the linen drapes, and got her head at his crotch. He did not respond, as she clawed open his trousers, releasing his naked cock, but with a few flicks of her tongue, the cock swelled to a hugeness more frightening, even, than Jed's.

'Why do you never bumfuck me, master?' she whispered, her tongue playing around his peehole, and the corona of his glans, after she had pulled his foreskin down, stretching the membrane fully. 'I've such a tight bumhole for you, and it's thirsty for your spunk.'

If she could please her master that way, he would make her into a castle wench, and permit her to wait on him, wearing a frilly maid's uniform. She did not think of release, or escape. Grobard allowed her to fellate him for several minutes; her mouth played on his glans, swooping, to engorge the whole stiff helmet, while her fingertips stroked the tight, massive ball sac; eventually, she dived to the base of his cock, her lips nuzzling the balls, as she sucked and squeezed on his entire huge shaft, plunged to the back of her throat. As she fellated Grobard, her hands were at her cunt, masturbating, her fingers slopped with eager wet come.

'I'm having to diddle myself, master,' she whispered, lips brushing his stiff cockshaft. 'I'd much rather have your cock inside my bum, fucking me hard, then I'd come without diddling, when I felt your cream.'

Her head plunged in a swift motion, and her mouth engorged his cock. Grobard's response was sudden. Without a word, he flung aside the table linen, revealing Suze, with her lips at his balls, and his cock deep in her throat. Tania, Marcia and the other serving wenches gasped in pretend shock.

'This slut is impudent,' Grobard hissed, slapping Suze several times across the cheeks, until she withdrew from her fellatio, rubbing her stinging face. 'She is addicted to vile pleasures, the mucky pup. Take her to the dungeon.'

Suze shrieked, as several wenches grabbed her, then lifted her to shoulder height, and carried her, kicking and screaming, through the castle's labyrinth, to an oaken door, its hinges red with rust. The door creaked open. It was a cell, with a wooden ox yoke, dangling by chains from the ceiling. Suze was hung naked, with the yoke pressing her nape, arms bent back, and her forearms curled over the wooden beam. Her arms were roped to the yoke, which held her suspended; Tania wound the chain, raising her, until her toes just touched the flagstones. Marcia and Doris each took an ankle, and pulled, spreading her legs, until her ankles were inches above the floor, and in line with the edges of her yoke. The girls roped her ankles to the yoke, so that Suze's weight was taken by her shoulders. Marcia wound her hair into a knot, and tied it to another, slender, chain, which Tania lowered from the ceiling. That chain was wound up, wrenching Suze's hair by the roots, and plucking her head high.

'Oh . . . oh . . .' she sobbed. 'It's agony. Please don't.'

The more Suze whimpered and wriggled, the greater the wenches' merriment. A metal corset was fastened around Suze's belly, with pointed studs on the inside, and the corset tightened to seventeen inches. The handle of a pitchfork was inserted into Suze's anus, and the pitchfork propped between her legs. Doris pressed her fingers between Suze's stretched cunt lips, soaking wet from her masturbation while sucking Grobard's cock. She said the bitch was gagging for it. Wenches came to watch, as Doris masturbated Suze's cunt, while jabbing the pitchfork handle in her anus. Soon, Doris gave way to another wench, who knelt before Suze, and began to tongue and chew her wet vulva, biting the stiffened clitty, and tongue-fucking inside Suze's squirming wet slit. The wench flung up her frilly skirtlet, and thrust her fingers inside her panties, to frig herself, as she gamahuched Suze. The others followed suit, diddling themselves, with panties lowered and skirts up, while awaiting their turn to tongue or frot Suze's dripping quim. Marcia placed a chamberpot beneath Suze's gash, and at once, there was a plinking sound, as her come dripped into the vessel.

'Are you going to beat me?' Suze gasped.

'Why, no,' said Marcia. 'We are going to wank you off, bitch. Beating is master's privilege today.'

The pitiless masturbation continued for over two hours, during which Suze was brought to the brink of orgasm, but left, gasping and flapping, unfulfilled. At length, the diddling of her cunt became less intense; a wench would slop at her gash flaps, then spring away, leaving Suze's clit distended, and her belly fluttering, as she begged, mumbling, for more, to bring her off. Drool dribbled from the corners of her slack mouth.

'Please,' she begged, 'Tongue me . . . I so need to get off.'

She could not believe that the supplicant voice was her own.

'If you won't wank me to climax, then thrash my bum. Please! Please!' she sobbed.

Marcia would respond by flicking her nubbin, making Suze squirm, and her cunt drip come into the chamberpot, while Tania or Doris would jab the coarse pitchfork handle into her rectum, making her squeal. They refused to take her to orgasm. Suze begged and wriggled, her belly fluttering, and her cunt gushing come, as the wenches cruelly teased her wracked body, throbbing with the need to climax. She begged for just a few licks or spanks, for the relief of orgasm.

'Think how blokes feel, looking at your arse on the telly,' said Doris. 'Now you know what it's like to be teased, slut. You think you're class, but you aren't, you're just a fucking tease with a plum in her mouth. The master, he's old class . . . *real* class.'

'Then thrash my bum, and punish me, for my teasing,' Suze wailed.

'You are a mucky pup,' said Tania. 'Addicted to beating and wanking and coming. You'll never be a castle wench.'

'No . . .' Suze howled.

Tania removed the pitchfork handle from her anus, and propped the pitchfork with its spikes pronging Suze's erect nipples; Doris lifted the chamberpot, filled with Suze's dripped come, and swirled it, making a sloshing noise, all the time sneering in Suze's tearsoaked face. She upended it, pouring hot come over Suze's naked fesses, and wenches rubbed it into her skin, until her bottom shone, glistening wet.

'There is whipping on the bare, and whipping on the wet bare,' said Marcia, 'Exquisitely painful.'

The door opened, and Grobard entered, wearing a silken robe, with spurred boots, and his studded whalebone crop. Tania lowered Suze, until her bum was waist high with the master, who doffed his robe, and stood nude before Suze's arse, his bare cock monstrously erect. He smiled, staring at her buttocks, shiny with her own come. Without a word, he lifted his crop, and began to lash Suze on the wet bare. Suze screamed, as her skin flamed in red weals, under rapid, vigorous thrashing, and, after a few strokes, her screams turned to gurgling shrieks of ecstasy, as her belly fluttered, and her cunt gushed, in the intensity of her climax. Her beating did not stop; the master flogged her bare wet arse, until, after sixty lashes, she had climaxed, drooling and whimpering, twice more. He handed his crop to Marcia, who whipped Suze on the naked breasts, the crop slapping the pitchfork tines, digging into her nipples.

The yoke was lowered; the master parted her buttocks, to reveal the hairy bum cleft slimed with come, and the winking cunt and arse pucker displayed in the stretched perineum, the skin tight as a drum's. With a grunt, the master plunged his cock into her anus bud, thrust hard for several seconds, then slammed his organ home to her root, with Suze uttering a piercing wail, as the giant tool seemed to burst her rectum. Her body jerked, as Marcia's crop flailed her bare breasts, now streaked with ugly red bruises. Tania held a short, stiff rubber quirt, its four thongs only nine inches long, and flicked those hard against Suze's extruded clit, with the tips of the quirt slapping her swollen wet cunt lips, while the master fucked her anus, from behind. Suze howled, as the pitchfork speared her nipples, her cunt danced under the whipping from the quirt, and her bumhole was impaled by the master's cock.

'No . . . no . . .' she moaned, yet her body writhed to the rhythm of her torture, the cunt thrusting forward to meet the whipping tongues, and the buttocks opening, to embrace Grobard's buggering cock.

Her nates clenched around his tool, squeezing and caressing; each withdrawal made a sucking, plopping sound, as Grobard bared his cock right to the corona of the glans, slimed with Suze's copious arse grease, before slamming it back inside her anal elastic. *Vap! Vap!* The cunt-whipping grew fiercer, and Suze's flogged titties were dark with welts; the wenches masturbated, taking it in turns to grasp the pitchfork, between strokes of the crop, and jab its points into Suze's bruised titties. Suze gasped, and panted, wriggling, and drooling from her lips, tightened in a rictus of agony. A deep gurgling sound issued from her throat, as she felt the droplets of hot cream seep from Grobard's peehole; her anus tightened on the cock, trapping it at her arse root, and then her sphincter began to squeeze powerfully, milking her master of sperm, as he spunked copiously in her anus. The *Vap! Vap!* of the crop on her titties, and the quirt on her bruised cunt flaps, grew louder in her ears, as she shuddered, in her most intense orgasm ever. When Suze was released from bondage, she sank to the floor, at her master's boots, and began to lick them.

'Master,' she whinnied, 'thank you for buggering me, and giving me your spunk. My bumhole is yours. I promise I shall be a good girl. Please let me stay, as a castle wench. Oh, please.'

An envelope fluttered to the floor, by her face.

'What ... ?' Suze groaned, as her fingers fumbled to open it.

Inside were a cheque, and an airline ticket. The master kicked her face with his boots, forcing her away, with a yelp, then raked her breasts with his spurs.

'The cheque is my investment in your expedition to South America,' Grobard drawled, 'and should cover all your costs, on condition that I am sole backer. The airline ticket will take you to Munich, where Dr Teidt will meet you, for a fortnight's skin and buttock therapy, at her clinic. After the clinic, your arse will be even more impressive than before. Now go. Brunhilde is waiting to drive you to the airport.'

'No! please, master!' Suze howled, clutching Grobard's boots.

The wenches carried her to her chamber, bathed her, and applied ointment to her bruises. Tania brought a looking glass, and Suze gaped in horror, at the rutted welts that scarred her whole croup, and the tracery of weals across her thighs, cunt, titties and belly. Marcia said it would be wise to obey the master, and attend the clinic. Numb with grief, and sobbing, Suze allowed herself to be escorted to Brunhilde's waiting Benz.

'Remember, milady,' said Marcia, 'what you have endured is what we have all endured. Imagine an ordeal a thousand times harder and more painful – you haven't even begun to be a castle wench.'

And that was the mysterious disappearance of The Bottom, Suze blurted bitterly. Four weeks of torture, followed by two weeks of recuperation at the *Klinik Gaulbach* in the Bavarian Alps, where Dr Teidt nursed her, until her skin glowed fresh and free of welts, and earned her affection and loyalty. Never again, Suze vowed, would she call any man master. She had put the episode out of her mind, suppressed it completely, until now, she sobbed. Even Dr Teidt did not know the full story.

'I'm sure she didn't. She knew I'd been cruelly disciplined, but I can't believe she knew my whole shame,' Suze gasped.

Thwap! Thwap!

'Ooh . . .'

Fiona gasped, as her squirming bare bum flamed, with a final two slices from Didier's quirt. Didier laid down the instrument.

'Well, Didier,' she gasped, 'are you satisfied? You know most of what I know. You can let me down now. I so need a wank.'

'Fiona,' Suze blurted, 'how do you know? I never told anyone.'

'Why, Grobard told me,' said Fiona nonchalantly. 'Come on, Didier, I'm just aching to wank off. Let me down now.'

Didier waved a fist, and whistled; a bulky figure loomed in the doorway. The male was nude, and his cock was fully erect, its long shadow drawing gasps from the maids, and a quickening of their fingers on their nubbins. It was

Hyacinthe, the creole cook, holding a glass, into which he cracked the yolk of an egg, throwing away the slimy albumen, to splatter on Suze's bottom. Michelle handed him the vessel brimming with Suze's come, and the cook poured her come drop by drop into the egg, whisking it with a fork, until the whole volume of cunt oil was absorbed into a creamy yellow mayonnaise. Michelle, masturbating as she giggled, smeared Hyacinthe's huge dark cock with gobbets of the gel, until his organ was wholly glazed. At Didier's direction, she smeared gel over Suze's croup, until her bare buttocks gleamed wet. The creole positioned himself in front of Suze's face, so that his cock was nuzzling her lips. Didier ordered Suze to suck the entire shaft of Hyacinthe's cock, and lick up the cunt mayonnaise, swallowing every drop. Suze moaned, looking desperately at Fiona, who stared lustfully.

'You lucky girl,' she murmured. 'I'm so randy!'

Suze paled in anger, then squealed 'Ooh! –' Didier had released his own erect tool, and his peehole pressed her anal pucker '– No, please noo . . . urrgh!'

Her words were stifled, as both males thrust their cocks into her at once: Hyacinthe slammed his helmet into her open mouth, filling it, while Didier made a hard, swift plunge, his cock penetrating her anus, halfway into the bumshaft. Hyacinthe's buttocks pumped, as he plunged his cock into Suze's throat, and her head bobbed, as she began a convulsive gobbling of the slimy tool, while gobbets of the cunt mayonnaise drooled from the corners of her lips. Didier thrust again, and his cock disappeared into Suze's anus, right to his balls. He rammed hard against her anal root, making her gag and shriek, her voice muffled by the invading cock. Didier slid his tool from her anus, until only the tip of the glans still stretched her anus bud, then slammed it in again, in one swift plunge ramming it fully into her rectum. Suze gurgled and writhed in her bonds, as her bum wriggled under fierce buggery, and her mouth slopped the sauce from the huge stiff shaft plunged in her throat. Didier's hips slapped her squirming bare, as he drove his cock into her bumhole, making a sucking noise, as he withdrew for each new stroke, and Suze's anal elastic squeezed and embraced the invading organ, shiny and slimed with her arse grease.

'Oh,' Fiona moaned, 'won't somebody wank me off?'

Michelle knelt before Fiona's dripping cunt, prised the fat wet lips open, and began to tongue her clitty. As she gamahuched Fiona, her claws raked the fresh raw welts striping Fiona's bare arse, and Fiona crooned, her bum jerking under the caress. Suze's body shuddered, under the impact of Didier's buggery; her face was bright red, and moist with tears, as she sucked the giant cock, and swallowed the mayonnaise made of her own come. Juice poured from her cunt, splattering the deck. Michelle's lips drooled with Fiona's come, as she tongued the girl's clitty, and buried her nose in the soaked gash, slopping her face with the suspended girl's cunt slime. The watching maids frigged at the spectacle, silent, but for the groans of the tongued Fiona, and Suze's gurgling, as she swallowed her own come.

'Oh ...' cried Fiona, and pissed herself, splashing Michelle's face in a torrent of pee.

'You fucking bitch,' Michelle spluttered.

She opened her jaws, and took Fiona's entire vulva between her teeth, then bit savagely, and began to chew the clitty and gash lips. Fiona cried out, her cry rising to a shriek, as Michelle's claws raked deeper into her tenderest and uncrusted flogging weals.

'Oh! Oh! Don't stop ... yes!' Fiona moaned, as her belly heaved in orgasm, and come poured from her cunt, bubbling over Michelle's face.

Suze's arse globes parted and clenched, in the rhythm of Didier's buggery; her anus embraced his cock, milking it, as her fellatio of Hyacinthe grew deeper, now that she had swallowed the last of the cunt mayonnaise. She trapped his cock tip at the back of her throat, which trembled, as she squeezed his peehole with her uvula. Hyacinthe began to sway, moaning softly, and his buttocks jerked, as his sperm filled Suze's throat, so copiously that frothy bubbles drooled from her lips. Didier grunted, and his buggery quickened, until his sperm frothed at Suze's hole, with his cock impaling her rectum, and spurting in her deep anus. He withdrew his cock with a plop, as Hyacinthe's tool pulled out of Suze's still-bobbing throat.

'Lash the slut,' he rapped to Michelle. 'Her arse is nicely wet, with her own cunt's filth.'

Wiping her mouth of Fiona's piss and come, Michelle took the quirt, and raised it high over Suze's trembling arse, shiny with her own come. *Whap! Whap! Whap!* She whipped the croup with three fast strokes, tracing instant pink weals, that made Suze scream in protest.

'No, no, you can't,' she spluttered, with droplets of Hyacinthe's sperm spraying from her mouth.

Whap! Whap! Whap!

'Ahh!'

Suze shuddered, as the quirt's tongues bit deeply into her bare croup melons, and the maids, masturbating, urged on her whipper.

'Give it to her, Shelley.'

'Make the snotty bitch squirm.'

Whap! Whap! Whap!

'Oh! No, please . . . please, I'll do anything.'

Whap! Whap! Whap! Whap!

Her wet bare buttocks writhed scarlet.

'Ah! Ooh! Please, don't whip me. Please . . .'

Whap! Whap! Whap!

A gush of come spurted from Suze's cunt flaps, as her bare arse reddened, then darkened, under Michelle's whipping.

'Oh . . . oh . . .' Suze moaned. 'Not so hard . . .'

Whap! Whap! Whap!

'Oh . . . it hurts so . . .'

Michelle flogged her haunches and top buttocks, as well as mid-fesses and the underfesses, for over ten minutes, until Suze's naked buttocks were streaked with livid dark welts, puffing to ridges. *Whap! Whap!*

'Uhh . . .'

Suze moaned; her titties and belly heaved, as her legs jerked against their ropes, and her bum convulsed in wriggles, under each kiss of the quirt's tongues. Juice poured from her cunt, sliming her thighs, and the fronds of her cunt bush, sodden in her come, swayed between her gash flaps and arse cheeks. Michelle's whip sliced her bare nates for the sixty-third cut; Suze shrieked and gasped, her belly heaved, and her legs and arse threshed, while her titties shook violently, as orgasm enthralled her.

'Oh! Oh! You promised not to beat me,' she sobbed, as Michelle cut her loose from her bonds.

'Surely you didn't believe us,' said Fiona.

'I promise nothing to sluts,' hissed Didier.

'My bottom is ruined,' Suze wailed. 'And my hole hurts so. You bastard, bastard, bastard.'

'On the contrary, mademoiselle, your bottom is in perfect order. It is the rest of your body we must work on,' Didier said.

Hyacinthe slung her across his shoulder.

'Didier!' Fiona gasped. 'Wait a minute. What – ?'

Didier slapped Fiona hard, across the bare nipples.

'Oh!' she squealed.

'Shut up, bitch,' he snarled. 'Hyacinthe will be back to bugger you, after we dispose of your friend. Don't complain – buggery is what you want, *n'est-ce pas?*'

'Yes, damn it. You *are* a bastard.'

Suze was carried out on deck, and across the gangplank leading to the barge floating behind. There, Didier and Hyacinthe strapped her to the mainmast by her wrists and ankles, nude, and with her bound feet flapping, inches above the deck. Her squeals were stifled by a fouled pair of girl's panties, wadded in her mouth. They drenched her in water, and whipped her back to sixty strokes, with rubber quirts, blushing her virgin back skin raw with welts, while Suze sobbed and wriggled in her bonds. Didier said she would look good for the next day's photo shoot '– your most provocative ever, mademoiselle. You have never looked so stunning. Soon you will be tame.'

They departed, leaving her alone, smarting with weals, under a crescent moon, with the howls of monkeys, and the slithering of reptiles in the river. She sobbed uncontrollably, her back, buttocks, and anus throbbing with pain. After a while, she heard the sounds of cane on bare flesh, and a female voice, unmistakably Fiona's, roused in protest; Fiona's squeals turned to excitement, then pleasure, as her punishment on the bare gave way to buggery by Hyacinthe's cock. Sweat dripped from Suze's scarred body, in the sweltering jungle night, and, towards dawn, she dropped into a fitful slumber. She did not see the girl who crept onto the yacht's deck, and severed the ropes holding the gangplank to the barge. Separate from the thrumming motors of the yacht, the barge drifted behind, as the yacht put space between the vessels. When the dawn woke Suze, shivering, smarting and naked, and tied to the mainmast of the barge, the pink sunbeams were already scorching. Cordovan's yacht was out of sight. Worms and lice crawled over her skin, in the welts of whipping, and inside her gash. She managed to chew through the gagging panties, and screamed long and loud, jerking frantically against her bonds, but only the jungle answered her.

7

Full Forty

The nude blond girl stepped, dripping wet, from her tin bathtub, and allowed her maid to scrub her body briskly, with a tattered dishcloth, parting her thighs wide, so that the girl could dry her arse crack and vulva. The maid wore a bra, made of rags sewn together, and no panties. An apron covered the maid's pubis, but left the buttocks bare, their hard satin pears blotched with dull bruises. She was barefoot, her hair dirty, with her ankles tied together by a two foot length of rope, and around her neck she wore a rubber dog leash, with its strap tucked between her breasts. Her blond mistress picked up her wristwatch from the table, and looked at the cracked dial, then, at herself, in the looking glass propped against the bamboo wall of her hut. She rubbed her fingers up and down her torso, lingering at the full breasts, and brushing the peaks of her nipples several times; then, sliding her hand down the flat muscle of her belly, to the lush tangle of her pubic forest, the same blond as her mane. Her fingers played in the fleece, while she parted her thighs, revealing the red, shiny lips of her quim. Nestling in the fold at the top slit was the extruded bulge of her clitoris. Her fingers hovered over the large red nubbin, until she pursed her lips, and inhaled loudly, in a sharp gasp, then abruptly drew back her fingers, swivelled, and applied her hand to the firm fleshy orbs of her naked buttocks. Her maid did not raise her eyes to observe her mistress's hands.

Dismissing the maid, the blond girl stroked herself on the bare for over a minute, then wrapped her buttocks and

101

haunches in her towel, and padded, breasts swaying bare, through the beaded door of her private chamber, into her office. There, she opened a cupboard, within which gleamed a rack of instruments of discipline: canes, and short whips of several thongs. She rubbed her fingers along the tongues of the whips, and the smooth wood of each cane, before selecting a cane. She checked that no one stood at the beaded front doorway of the hut, then removed her towel, and placed it neatly on her desk. She flexed the cane, let it spring straight, and drew the wood gently over her bare buttocks. She let it linger in her bum cleft for several moments, breathing heavily; her hand crept once more to her naked clitoris, which she brushed three times with her fingertips, panting slightly, with her eyes closed tight.

Her hand withdrew, up her belly, to her nipples, already erect. She played with each nipple, pinching the stiff buds, and shutting her eyes once more, then replaced the cane in its cabinet. She removed the towel from her desk, using it to wipe some patches of dust, but did not bother covering herself, as she padded back to her chamber, and snapped her fingers. The maid reappeared, and took down the girl's selection of panties and bra, helping her mistress to don them, with a fresh uniform skirt and blouse. The maid knelt, to lace the girl's boots, and was again dismissed; uniformed and crisp, the mistress reentered her office. After consulting her watch again, she sat down at her desk, and waited, making small rearrangements of her pencils and papers. After a few minutes, the two guards outside stamped their feet, and slapped their canes against bare thighs. A tall girl stood at attention, inside the doorway of the frond-roofed hut.

'Prisoner Corporal Annique Dutoit presenting herself, *mademoiselle commandante*,' she said, saluting with her left hand, a motion which made her breasts bob in their sackcloth brassiere.

That, and a short skirt were her only garments, both makeshift items a dull khaki, and held together with clumsy stitching of twine. The ragged uniform bared most of her full figure – the long, colt's legs, muscled back and belly and ripe, thrusting breasts – her skin a deep tan. Her mane of long hair had once been a dark chestnut, but was now bleached by the sun, its mass a honey blond, with dazzling yellow streaks. She was no older than twenty, a few years her mistress's junior. She wore soiled tennis shoes, with fluffy ankle socks, both a smudged white. The true blond girl, seated at her desk, smiled, and tossed her head, making the bright bleached streaks in her own hair shimmer, over her military uniform of short skirt, pulled high over her tan bare thighs, and blouse with epaulettes. Like Annique's her face was beaded with sweat, and the bare skin of her upper breasts, revealed by the blouse – open to the third button, and showing her faded cream bra – shone with a dew of perspiration.

'Don't stand on ceremony, Annique,' she said. 'MaBelle will do, same as always. And you may dispense with the "prisoner", as if I need reminding. I consider my hospital matron as more than a mere prisoner. Come in and sit. I'll just be a moment.'

MaBelle tidied her pencils and pencil sharpeners, placing them in a row above her notepad, then slapped her stack of documents on her desktop, to straighten them, before aligning the pile with her row of pencils. She rose from her desk, and joined Annique at a wooden coffee table, where both girls sat in easy chairs made of sacking stuffed with straw. MaBelle was tall, like Annique, with similar coltish legs, but slightly riper of figure: her breasts heavier, yet jutting more sharply, with her acorn nipples poking against the thin brassiere and blouse fabric, but without Annique's titties' conical pertness. Her bottom melons, straining against her clinging khaki skirt, tight across her mid-thigh, revealed the outline of high cut panties. Both girls crossed their legs, automatically smoothing down their skirts, while Annique plucked at her sloppy bra, to hoist it over her breasts. Sunlight, slanting through the beaded doorway, streaked their shiny, shifting limbs. As the visitor crossed her legs, a massive bush of chestnut thatch flickered, between her briefly-glimpsed thighs. MaBelle smiled, making no secret of her quizzical gaze.

'Sometimes I think it would be more comfortable to be a mere prisoner,' she murmured. 'Yet, my responsibility for our camp . . .'

She gestured with a small rotation of her wrist, encompassing her hut, the cluster of buildings visible in the distance, through the door, and the two girls in dark green military uniform, and armed with whips, who stood guard before her hut. Like MaBelle, they wore laced knee boots.

'Your summons was more formal than usual, MaBelle,' the girl said.

'It was?' replied the commandant. 'I must have been distracted by the treat I'm going to offer you – some real Brazilian coffee, just arrived from the frontier. You'll take a cup?'

Annique eagerly signalled her assent. MaBelle snapped her fingers, and her maid reappeared from the beaded curtain at the rear of the hut; MaBelle gave orders, and soon, the maid reappeared, with a tray of coffee things and sweet biscuits. She poured the steaming brew, and both girls sniffed the aroma, then drank, with sighs of satisfaction.

'You have read my report on the captured fugitive, MaBelle?' said Annique.

'Glanced at it,' MaBelle replied. 'I gather she is under guard in your infirmary. Is she healthy?'

'Fundamentally, yes – full details are in my report – but either delirious, or a wicked conniver. She claims to be English, and her French is suitably barbarous. She babbles that she is a fashion mannequin. The stories these escapees come up with!' Annique said, tittering. 'Everyone knows the only girls here are sent from the *prison départmentale* in St Laurent, or else those who have escaped from it. They forget that anyone found in this forbidden zone is automatically delinquent. The slut was found by one of our patrols, on a grounded barge, on the river bank in sector four. She was naked, and bound by her wrists and ankles to the barge's mast. I am afraid we had to apply restraint, once we got her to her hospital bed. She has ankle and wrist hobbles, and a nipple brace, with a double strap across her back, since we had to lie her face down. As you know, we often have to treat girls back from patrol, who have been mistreated by the *indigènes* – I mean, flogged to the bone – so we are used to that, but I have never heard of a girl tied to the mainmast of a barge.'

'The girls know the risks, when they go out on patrol,' snapped MaBelle. 'They are felons, inmates – they accept the task, hoping to gain credit, and an early release date.'

Annique swallowed nervously, and sipped her coffee.

'Well, although she is not one of our girls, her back and buttocks bore the mark of severe corporal punishment, MaBelle. She had been whipped recently, most likely on the bare, and I assume trussing was part of a punishment, by . . . whoever disciplined her.'

'Which doesn't make her sound like the average felon, escaped from the PD,' MaBelle said crisply. 'Corporal punishment is, technically, not part of their regime. Maybe she *is* a mannequin – who knows what those Parisiennes get up to? Yet, just by being here, she is a truant. Send her to me as soon as she is up, and fit for hard labour. We shall have to detain her, pending orders from Cayenne, or Paris.'

Annique smiled ruefully.

'If they ever remember our existence, MaBelle,' she mumured.

'Prisoner Corporal Dutoit,' snapped MaBelle, 'I do things by the book. There is a chain of command, established by the laws of the French Republic, which it is my duty to uphold. The fact that our detention camp was established in 1942, by the *Vichy* Republic, is not my concern. Cayenne knows of us, if grudgingly, and unofficially, which is why the hardest and most vicious female truants are sent here, as I scarcely need to remind *you*, convict Dutoit! Paris, I am afraid, may not know of us at all. Do you think it is easy to control over a hundred vicious sluts, in this infernal heat? Perhaps you would rather return to Mlle Gundersheim's rule.'

Annique paled, and trembled.

'No, MaBelle,' she said. 'All the sluts are grateful to you, for . . . *removing* her. Her rule was rather harsh.'

'You mean, bestial. I firmly believe in corporal punishment as an effective means of discipline, but I mounted my *coup d'état*, perceiving that Gundersheim was inflicting punishment for her own perverted pleasure, to the detriment of discipline. She maintained order by fear, and the promise of gaining early release dates for her favoured girls – that is, those whose bottoms could take the most lashes. I, too, strive for release dates, but I think it better to release a girl with her bottom reasonably bare of stripes. Hence my honour system of delegating discipline to the corporals.'

'There are rumours, MaBelle,' said Annique, 'that Mlle Gundersheim's release dates were not release at all, but sale into a worse form of captivity, to strange realms in the south, where whipping, and sex servitude, were daily, savage, and for the pleasure of the girls' owners. Pure slavery, *mademoiselle commandante*.'

'Every prison thrives on rumours,' said MaBelle, quickly. 'I suppose it is no harm to have the girls take their lashings, knowing that it is the lesser of two evils. Personally, I am not fond of whippings, nor of my occasional duty to witness them, but I believe that is the best way of maintaining order, and morale. I rely on the good judgement of my corporals, even when the cries of whipped girls, writhing in their ropes, are heavy on my heart. You prisoners do not know the cares of high office! However, no whipping is administered without a thorough medical examination to ascertain fitness for punishment, so if an inspector *were* to arrive from Paris, our records are spotless. Which brings me to the reason I sent for you, Annique.'

Annique crossed her legs, her buttocks shifting nervously, her thighs parting insouciantly, for several seconds, to reveal her pubic thatch, its tangled hairs glistening with sweat. MaBelle did not take her eyes from the prisoner's crotch. She reached behind her blouse, and twisted the catch of her brassiere, shifting her breasts, so that they jutted more firmly.

'You are not wearing panties,' she observed.

'It's so hot, MaBelle,' Annique replied. 'I know I'm required to wear them in the hospital, but you know how squishy it gets, down there, when all you have is nylon panties, that make your thighs sweat –'

MaBelle silenced her with a wave of her hand.

'It is as well, Annique,' she said, placing her hand on the girl's bare knee, and stroking the skin of her bare thigh, with her fingertips. 'I'm quite aware of the discomfort of underthings. Count yourself lucky you are not camp commandant, and obliged to keep up appearances, so that I have to wear my stockings for more than ceremonial duties. A crisp uniform is forbidding enough, but proper stockings add that little something, should an inspector from Cayenne ever deign to visit.'

She tapped her bum cleft, where the shape of her own nylon panties was a moist stain on her army skirt, and smoothed the dampness over her thrusting arse hillocks.

'There is an irritating trifle, which we must settle,' she continued, 'and I thought it best to do so between us, as it were.'

'A disciplinary matter?' blurted Annique.

MaBelle nodded.

'Concerning the hospital,' she said.

'We do administer bare-bottom canings, or naked whippings, in hospital,' Annique said cautiously, 'and I do supervise, sometimes wielding the whip or cane myself. We have padded frames, adjustable either for whipping on the back, or caning of the buttocks. But I prefer, when possible, a surgical chastisement, that is, binding in bandages and splints for a period of restraint. Persistent cases are treated with a mixture of both, with corporal punishment administered on the bare buttocks, while the truant is orthopaedically immobilised.'

MaBelle rose, and riffled through a stack of papers on her desk, extracting a single sheet.

'Last week you caned the inmate Mimi Barbure thirty strokes on the bare bottom,' she read, 'while her legs and arms were encased in plaster.'

Annique shuddered.

'Barbure is a particularly hard case,' she stammered. 'Repeated canings have done little to quell her delinquency.'

MaBelle held up her hand.

'I do not question your judgement, Annique,' she said, 'but your security. Barbure complained, after her chastisement, that her lucky rabbit's foot was missing from the clasp around her neck. She alleges that one of your nurses must have taken it.'

Annique flushed.

'That's absurd,' she exclaimed. 'Nurses Castor and Borne administered the beating, under my supervision, and I trust them completely.'

MaBelle opened her desk drawer, took something out, and held up a rabbit's foot.

'Nathalie Delvoix, the scrub slut, found this in nurse Borne's instrument cabinet, this morning,' she said. 'The silly bitch purloined it, and had the stupidity to wear it around her own neck.'

She sighed.

'Scrub sluts are stupider than you can imagine. I had to beat her, of course, and she confessed, after forty on bare, with the strap. Nevertheless, a stolen item in your trusty's possession? Rumours are already all round the camp. I'm afraid it doesn't look good, Annique. If the prisoners cannot trust the hospital, what can they trust?'

Annique bit her lip. The silence in the foetid hut was stifling, and she mopped her brow, while nervously adjusting her rag bra, too tight on her squashed titties. She opened her thighs, allowing her skirt to ride up, plainly showing her hairy bare mons, and, in her agitation, did not bother to smooth it down. MaBelle smoothed her own skirt, pressing out the crinkles over her bottom, and her palms cupping each jutting fesse.

'It's a dreadful shock,' she said. 'I suppose there will have to be a tribunal of enquiry, and the guilty girl will take a whipping, even though the responsibility is mine, ultimately.'

'I'd like to deal with the matter discreetly,' MaBelle murmured. 'We cannot prevent rumours, and, as you say, the responsibility for nurse Borne's conduct is yours – how you deal with her subsequently is your affair. Morale would be stiffened, and an example set, if it were known that the guilty person had taken summary punishment . . .'

'You mean me?' Annique gasped.

The commandant smiled thinly, her hand brushing moisture from her brow, and falling across the damp hillocks where her bra cups thrust under her blouse. She stroked her breasts with gently brushing fingertips, before turning, to present her croup to her guest. At her lower arse cleft, a small dark stain indicated moisture seeped from the gusset of her panties.

'I'm afraid so,' she said, opening her wall cupboard, where canes and three-tongued straps hung on a rack. 'I'm afraid I have decided to cane you, prisoner Dutoit. On the bare.'

Annique gasped, as MaBelle took the longest cane from her rack, a thin, three-foot rattan, and flexed it across her breasts.

'Here, mademoiselle?' she blurted, paling, at the sight of the whippy rattan.

'You are not wearing panties. All you must do is bend over my desk, and lift your skirtlet, so that I may access your naked buttocks. Your caning will be over – well, I can't promise in a jiffy, but soon enough for word to get round by lunchtime, thanks to my loquacious guard maids and scrub slut. Unless you insist on your medical inspection first?'

Annique sighed. She rose, and looked at MaBelle, who stared at her, her face stony and expressionless, giving the girl's pleading eyes no hint of an emollient. Annique's hand crept to the melons of her arse, rubbing the buttocks over her skirtlet, with a frightened look. After swallowing several times, her breasts heaving with heavy gasps, she took position, with her pubis wedged against the desktop. She raised her skirt, revealing her bare buttocks trembling slightly, and parting her legs, so that her massive cunt hairs dangled, in a wet sweaty fleece, below her arse cleft, and the lips of her gash.

'I shan't insist, mademoiselle,' she whispered. 'What choice have I? You know that as chief medical officer, I must pronounce my bottom fit for the cane. There are worse chastisements, I know.'

The prison governess stroked the naked bumflesh of the girl, bending for punishment. Her fingers dangled in Annique's cleft, spreading the cheeks apart, and brushed the sopping wet cunt hairs, and anal fleece, hanging between her thighs. Annique gasped, holding her skirtlet pinned tightly at the small of her back; gooseflesh appeared on her bare bottom. The buttock flesh was a paler tan than the rest of her nut brown skin, showing the fading outline of a long-ago bikini line. Annique's breasts were squashed by her body, pressing them to the desk, so that almost all the naked skin appeared, thrust out of her bra cups; the teat flesh bore no remnant of faded bikini whiteness, but was all of a brown with her arms, belly and shoulders, apart from the wide pink nipples, their saucers half visible under Annique's submissive posture.

'I haven't even told you the number of cuts you're to take,' said MaBelle, lifting her cane over Annique's quivering nates. 'You *are* brave. Keep your cheeks well spread, please, and I warn you that any excessive squirming or clenching will result in a cut repeated. You, as senior staff, must set an example.'

'Even with no witnesses, MaBelle?' gasped Annique bitterly.

'I am a witness, slut,' hissed MaBelle.

Vip! The cane slashed a pink weal across the full midfesses, and Annique's bare bottom wobbled, as the melons clenched. She did not cry out, but grunted, in a sharp exhalation of breath, and bared her teeth in a rictus, while screwing her eyes shut, for several moments.

'Tight?' said MaBelle.

'Y-yes, *mademoiselle commandante.*'

The whipper did not correct her subject's form of address. *Vip! Vip!* Two strokes, a backhand and forehand, lashed Annique's arse in the same weal, darkening it to red, and raising puffy skin at the edges of the long, jagged slash.

'Uhh . . .' Annique groaned. 'Please, how many is it to be?'

'I hope you'll agree to forty,' said MaBelle. 'Same as the thieving scrub slut.'

'Forty?' whimpered the nurse.

Vip! Vip! Vip!

'Ah! It *hurts.*'

Vip! Vip! Vip!

'Oh! Oh!'

'Yes, I expect it does. You'll take the forty?'

'I don't know if I can, MaBelle. You cane awfully hard,' panted Annique.

'Why, thank you, Annique,' said the older girl, her own breath quickened by the caning, and patting her skirt over the cusp of her thighs, where a triangle of seeped moisture spread from her panties' gusset.

Vip! Vip!

'Ohh . . .'

The strokes shifted to Annique's tender haunches, whose skin soon darkened to purple, under heavy lashes. The girl's fesses clenched rhythmically, as her bare bottom squirmed, making her growing stripes writhe in a rainbow of pink, red, and puce. *Vip! Vip!* Two stingers to top buttock made Annique's legs jerk straight from under her, and she whimpered.

'Oh, mademoiselle, how it stings . . . please, not so hard?'

Vip! Vip!

'Ahh!' squealed the flogged girl, her squirming arse darkened with welts.

'Your bum is quite pure,' panted MaBelle. 'You haven't been caned for some time.'

Vip! Vip!

'Oh! Oh! Not since I was a junior nurse, mademoiselle, and Mlle Gundersheim caned me, for dropping a catheter.'

'Is that all?'

Vip! Vip!

'Ooh! Oh . . . No, before that, I received normal canings, from the duty corporal, usually for masturbating, after

111

lights out. All the girls masturbate, it's accepted, and we knew that every evening, one of us would be singled out for a tenner. I wasn't caned any more than the others.'

Vip! Vip!

'Uhh . . .' groaned the flogged girl.

'Go on with your story,' drawled MaBelle. 'It will relieve the monotony of caning.'

'Well, we all masturbated, and we all got thrashed on bare for it, which only made us do it more. But you have to set an example, and we accepted that, in fact, the duty corporal would have been disappointed if we didn't masturbate, to let her catch us. Her thrashings were quick and clean, and afterwards, we were left in peace, to wank off as much as we pleased. It was the only way to get to sleep, in this heat, and I'd be a fool to pretend I don't masturbate myself to sleep, now that I have my own hut, though it isn't as much fun as doing it with a whole dormitory full of wanking girls, all showing each other their spread slits, and frigging hard, to see who can make herself the wettest. If only we had access to men . . . but of course, that is the essential of our punishment, isn't it? With Mlle Gundersheim, it was different. She took pleasure in a caned girl's pain, and did not disguise the fact that she masturbated, while administering the caning. When I dropped the catheter, she had me strapped to a hospital bed, full trussing, she called it, with ropes, and gagged, too.'

'How many?' said MaBelle.

Vip! Vip!

'Ahh!' she gasped. 'That was tight. Sixty on the bare, mademoiselle. It was awful. My bum smarted so! At the time, I thought nothing could ever hurt so much, but you . . .'

Vip! Vip!

'*Ohh* . . . Y-you are harder by far. Oh, please, mademoiselle, don't mark me too much. It took ages for Gundersheim's stripes to fade. My bum was all hard and crinkly, and it hurt to sit down.'

Vip! Vip!

'Uhh . . . Uhh . . .' Annique grunted, her gasps turning to a sob, as her buttocks threshed.

Her knuckles, holding her skirt pinned over her writhing bare bum, were white; from the tangled cunt hairs, swinging beneath her gash, between parted, quivering thighs, dripped a steady flow of oily fluid.

'It is not I who mark you, Annique, but the cane,' murmured MaBelle.

Her fingertips brushed Annique's dangling cunt tuft, and came up shiny with come. She showed her slimy fingers to the beaten girl.

'And it seems your bottom, at least, welcomes the rod's attention,' she said curtly.

Vip! Vip!

'*Ohh!* I can't help it,' she whimpered, blushing.

The commandant paused to undo all the buttons on her blouse, and strip herself of the garment.

'You don't mind if I make myself comfortable,' she said. 'It is a long time since I caned such a satisfying bottom. So pure, and ripe for bruises.'

Vip! Vip!

'*Uhh . . .*'

Annique's bare bum jerked and clenched in maddened rhythm; as the cane whistled, MaBelle's free hand unclasped her bra, and let the cups dangle, so that her heavy bare teats sprang from their confinement, and quivered, at the force of her canestrokes. *Vip! Vip!* Her nipples were risen to stiff plums, and the stain of moisture at her crotch was a large triangle. Sweat dripped from the pinnacles of her swaying breasts. *Vip! Vip!*

'*Ooh!* Oh, mademoiselle, enough, please.'

'We've scarcely begun to warm you up for a full forty,' panted the commandant. 'You have already earned several repeat cuts, with that girly squirming and squealing, so I am just making myself comfortable . . . slut.'

Vip! Vip! She sliced Annique fully in the cleft, the cane slapping her anus bud, and the bloated, slimy lips of her dripping gash.

'Ahh!' Annique shrieked, as a livid red bruise rose across her perineum, and the inside cheeks of her bum crack; her cunt spurted copious shiny come.

MaBelle unpinned her khaki skirt, and let it fall to her ankles, She stepped out of it completely; her bikini-cut knickers were sopping at her quim, and she quickly rolled down the panties, revealing her massive cunt bush, wet with oozed come, and the tops of her thighs bathed in her exuded juice. Nude, she continued the caning, with one hand pressed between her swollen wet gash flaps. *Vip! Vip!* Sunlight, beaming through the beaded doorway, dappled the rod, as it flashed, whistling, in the dust-laden air. The light made rainbows in the droplets of sweat, trickling across the quivering bare fesses, and into Annique's bum crack.

'Your bottom is very beautiful, Annique,' the commandant whispered. 'I wonder if the new arrival's croup is as fine – well whipped, I understand?'

'Caned and whipped, mademoiselle – scourged, I'd say,' gasped Annique.

Vip! Vip!

'Uhh . . . Yes . . .'

Annique's fesses danced, under a sharp stroke to each haunch, and the commandant's own buttocks writhed, in time with the glowing bare orbs of her subject. The strokes slowed in pace, but landed accurately, on each unmarked portion of Annique's bum, until her whole croup was a livid pattern of darkening weals. Her cries stilled, to an unbroken wailing sob, choked with harsh gasps, as the cane striped her; come flowed from the pulsing flaps of her gash. MaBelle's fingers were inside her slit, and her thumb on her swollen, erect clitty, as the caner masturbated.

'So you still wank off,' she panted.

'Yes, mademoiselle. Everyone does. Oh. I didn't mean you,' Annique blurted.

MaBelle's hands dived between Annique's cunt lips, and began to rub her wet slit, with her thumb and forefinger rubbing the girl's nubbin.

'Oh, mademoiselle . . .' Annique moaned. 'Oh, yes . . . oh, that is so firm . . . so good.'

'Does a beating always make you wet?'

'Yes, MaBelle.'

'Your own bum caned, or you caning another girl?'

'Caning other girls, for my own croup hasn't been caned for so long ... there's something about watching another girl's bare arse twitch, and it makes mine wet, to imagine it is my own, sometimes. When I escaped from the departmental prison, I feared they would whip me for it. I dreamed they would whip me! The guards carried long canes, but any thrashing was brief and summary – a few cuts to a surly slut's shoulders. I fantasised of being stripped, and tied down, for a public thrashing, on the bare, in front of the other inmates – to set an example. The cane would lash my bare bum, again and again, and I would writhe and cry out, and all the girls would get hot, just watching my naked buttocks striped to thirty or forty lashes, and afterwards, they would masturbate, thinking of me. It did not happen, of course. I was transferred here, to the penal colony.'

'This foundling,' said MaBelle, 'she says she is English. It is well know that English girls have a propensity for bare bottom discipline; it is not hard to believe her. If she has been recently thrashed – I wonder if this is not some trick of Gunderheim's. A warning, perhaps.'

MaBelle pinched Annique's stiff clitty, and slopped her fingers in the girl's dripping cunt, making a squelching noise.

'Caning makes you want to come?' she demanded.

'Y-yes, MaBelle. Oh, yes, wank me off, it is so good, MaBelle.'

'When you are obliged to administer bare bottom discipline to one of your nurses, do you masturbate, either after, or during, your punishment of the girl?'

'Must I answer that?' Annique gasped.

'Not at all. But think how I may construe your silence. It is natural for a girl to masturbate, especially in this heat, and the more so, when her own, or another girl's, bare bottom is inflamed by caning. I myself attended a school where masturbation was rife, and the punishment for it severe. We were thrashed hard, on the bare, when caught, but that did not deter girls from frigging.'

'The answer to your question is yes,' said Annique. 'I always masturbate, whenever I must cane one of my nurses, and sometimes, if she squirms and reddens with unusual vigour, I wank off while I beat her.'

'The English girl – is her bum juicy enough, that you would like thrashing her? And wanking off, as you made her Anglo-Saxon buttocks squirm?'

She rubbed Annique's throbbing clit, snapping her fingers, to make gurgling noises inside the girl's sopping wet gash.

'Why, yes, *mademoiselle commandante*,' gasped Annique. 'She has the most adorable peach. I asked if she knew her measurements, to save us the trouble of taking them, and the haughty bitch said she was a full forty. She meant English inches – the measurement of her titties, and her bottom. I had to warn my nurses not to diddle her, they were so lustfully excited.'

The commandant ripped the thin skirt from Annique, leaving her entire back and buttocks nude.

'You will oblige me by wanking off, as I beat *you*,' she hissed.

Vip! Vip! Vip! Three cuts took her across the darkly-striped, puffy skin of top buttock.

'Ahh!' Annique screamed, yet her fist was between her legs, pummelling her cunt lips and stiff wet clitty.

She gasped more and more harshly, as the strokes fell on her squirming bare, and her fist went inside her pouch, to jab between the gushing cunt flaps, into her wombneck, withdrawing, for her knuckles to smear her clit with come. MaBelle wanked off with an unceasing caress of her gushing cunt, as she continued the caning, past the thirtieth stroke. Between each cut, she raised the cane tip to her quivering stiff nipples, and caressed them with the hot wood, moaning, as she slapped the cane on her bare teat-flesh. Both girls gasped, the caner's breath harsh, and the subject's choked with sobs, yet both females masturbated vigorously, as Annique's bare bum glowed darker and hotter with welts.

Vip! Vip!

'Oh . . . Oh . . .'

'Uhh . . . !'

Their cries mingled; at the fortieth stroke, the caner placed her foot on Annique's nape, and thrust her wet cunt against the girl's ridged bare bottom, sliming the flogged bumskin with her gushed come. Moaning, MaBelle rubbed her clitty on Annique's welts, while she brought the cane flush with her breasts and began to saw at her nipples with the hot wood, rubbing it back and forth, while her cunt basin writhed on the buttocks. Annique frigged herself, gasping, and her buttocks churning, to meet the caress of her caner's bare wet cunt, while copious come sprayed from her own wanked gash, between her slippery frotting fingers.

'Oh . . . *mademoiselle commandante* . . . I'm coming . . . yes!' Annique whimpered, as her fingers feverishly wanked her clitty.

Vip! Vip! Vip! Vip!

'Ohh! Yes! Ahh . . .'

The girls climaxed, each gasping, in high, staccato wails, while MaBelle's cunt lingered on the whipped bumflesh, to caress the ridges of each welt her instrument had raised on the girl's nates. When it was over, MaBelle quickly slipped into her panties, bra and skirt, while Annique rose, groaning, and rubbing her livid bum. Gingerly, the girl lowered her skirt, wincing, as the cloth touched her smarting fesses. She wiped tears from her scarlet face, and said she would be unable to sit for many hours, or even days, and that MaBelle's caning was far harsher than Mlle Gundersheim's.

'But she was, then, the only one allowed to masturbate,' said MaBelle, with a thin smile, and Annique sobbed agreement. 'You will take me to see the new slut at once, Annique, if you can hobble to the infirmary. She will quickly understand that she is a felon, until orders from Paris decree otherwise. And it has been a long time since we had orders from Paris. I am disturbed she is still in restraint. No girl, however vile, should be deprived of her glorious and exhilarating freedom to wank off – even if it is a crime.'

8

Misprision

'I demand to see the British consul!' blurted the girl, in English, as she wriggled against her straps.

'You demand nothing, mademoiselle,' said MaBelle, answering her in French. 'You are a detainee of the French Republic, and you will speak only French, understand? I am eager to release you from your restraints, but you must cooperate. I have no wish to listen to snivelling lies, nor barbarous foreign grunting.'

'I'm not a convict,' Suze cried, in stumbling French. 'Let me go, you dirty bitches.'

In addition to her restraining ropes, nurses Castor and Borne held the nude girl by her wrists and thighs.

'You are now, slut,' said Annique Dutoit, wearing a crisp white nurse's skirt and bra. 'Cooperation means submitting to the prescribed regime of forced labour, and the penalties for any breach of our code. It seems your French is good enough to insult our nurses, which may already have earned you a whipping, at our commandant's discretion.'

Annique's eyes shone, and her thighs pressed together.

'Yes, I award a whipping on account,' said MaBelle, 'to be added to any future chastisement.'

'Oh, no,' Suze wailed. 'Stop this.'

'I want to know where you got those stripes. Who flogged you, slut?' the commandant demanded.

'I've told you,' Suze moaned. 'I'm Suzette Shard, the model, and we were doing a rather raunchy photo shoot, and things got a bit too playful, that's all. People I thought were my friends turned against me.'

'We are your friends, now,' said Annique, 'the only ones you've got.'

Her fingers brushed Suze's bared buttocks, and the prisoner started. Suze's head, twisted to look at her interlocutors, sank onto her pillow. She was still bound, and lying on her belly, with her bruised bottom in the air. Annique withdrew her hand, and placed it squarely on her vulva, as though to scratch an itch. Her lips and cheeks were flushed, as her hand moved gently at her groin. MaBelle put her fingers in the ridges that striped Suze's bare, and stroked the puffy, welted skin. Suze's bum jerked, clenching, and she gasped.

'Hurt much?' MaBelle said.

'A little, mademoiselle,' Suze replied sullenly.

'But you wouldn't like another whipping, so soon, on your *full forty*.'

MaBelle used the English phrase.

'Certainly not!' Suze retorted.

'Then, I think you *will* cooperate,' MaBelle said. 'Obedient inmates can easily avoid discipline. For fractious girls, discipline is humane, but swift. Corporal punishment is, we find, the most effective way of crushing wayward spirits.'

She laid the palm of her left hand on Suze's left buttock, and cupped the wealed flesh.

'Very firm,' she said. 'If you are indeed English, you are used to corporal punishment – caning on the bare.'

Suze sullenly agreed that ever since her schooldays at St Ursula's, she was no stranger to bare-bottom caning.

'St Ursula's?' drawled MaBelle. 'No doubt a fine school, turning out girls with well-disciplined bottoms. I think this detainee will cooperate. Nurses, you may release her to the discipline corporal, for assignment to an isolation cell for one week, before she joins the general population in dormitory. She shall go to work at the drainage platoon, and shall spend her first week hooded, as is normal.'

'Wait!' Suze cried. 'I've been poked and prodded, had things stuck up my bum, and my titties squeezed in clamps,

119

and my . . . my pouch fingered, and a hundred other horrid things. I've had the nurses waggle their fingers right inside my bumhole, and say I'm too slack to be an arse virgin, and am addicted to cock in the anus – to buggery. That's awful. Now you want to put me in restraint, like some common criminal. It's too much. It's some sick joke. Let me go this instant, you witch.'

'Really,' murmured MaBelle. 'You accuse your camp commandant of misprision? That is a grave breach of discipline, mademoiselle. To the administration, you *are* a common criminal.'

She raised her hand, and took from a shelf a surgical boot, with black rubber soles, five inches thick. *Whap! Whap!* Without preamble, she began to spank Suze's bare melons with the heavy rubber boot. Suze's shrieks were stifled by nurse Castor, whose hand gagged her. *Whap! Whap!* MaBelle beat her coolly and fast, raising broad pink bruises over the existing cane scars. Suze wriggled and sobbed, with tears streaming down her face, as her naked bottom reddened to crimson. MaBelle left no part of her bottom unslapped. The surgical boot thudded on the top buttock, haunches, and fleshy underfesses, always returning to the central buttocks, where Suze's welts coalesced into a mass of blotchy crimson skin.

'That boot is heavy,' Annique said, rubbing her whipped, pantiless bottom through the thin cloth of her skirtlet.

'Wait till she must wear the pair,' replied MaBelle.

The flogged girl's breath came in sharp gasps, and she shook her head wildly against nurse Castor's restraining palm. Her bare bum cheeks clenched and squirmed, jerking at each spank, yet powerless to escape the beating. Gradually, her choking sobs stilled to a low continuous moan, and the buttocks trembled only slightly, as the hard rubber slapped them, each stroke making Suze's bare bum jerk a little, then subside, quivering and flushed dark.

'Ooh . . . Ooh . . .' she whined.

Her body ceased to struggle against the imprisoning nurses, and sagged into her hospital palliasse. After thirty spanks, MaBelle ceased the thrashing; Suze's raw bare bum was crimson. Annique, red in the face, and her lips darting over her drooling lips, continued to rub her soaked groin, churning and mashing her thighs across her cunt lips, swelling under her wet skirt.

'Yes,' said MaBelle, I am sure the slut will cooperate. Add to her first week surgical boots, and an ankle hobble.'

Sobbing and wailing, Suze was released from her bonds, and led by two nurses, across the yard, to the hut of the discipline corporal, Sylvie Pette. MaBelle licked her lips, while Annique kept looking at Suze's nude buttocks, swaying, as she hobbled. The matron turned to the wall, and quickly, surreptitiously, frigged herself through her skirtlet, until she gasped in climax. As she climaxed, her hand dived under the billowing skirtlet, and caressed the naked gash and clitty. MaBelle glanced at her, then smiled, and looked away.

'Yes, wank off, Annique, she's certainly tasty,' she drawled, 'with buttocks that deserve punishment. The arrogant slut didn't recognise me, but I should know her croup anywhere. I am sure – I *know* – I have caned it before . . .'

Cpl Sylvie Pette was elfin, silken-haired, and bony, with her massive, conic breasts and full buttocks jutting from her muscled frame like ripe fruits, that had grown and clung to her. She wore a uniform like MaBelle's, the thin skirt hugging the mounds of her croup, with the thighs well spaced, like a colt's, and the blouse buttoned up to the neck, where she wore a bright yellow tie, draped nonchalantly over the swelling mounds of her titties. Her single right leg was bare, hard with whipcord muscle, and tanned dark; her left leg was a prosthesis, stained the same tan, and with hinges. On her desk lay a long and wide leather strap, its tip forking into two tongues.

'You're not going to give any trouble?' she said, smiling. 'I can see you've been spanked recently, and I dare say you don't want the strap.'

Still smiling, she whipped the strap on her desk, with a loud crack.

'Do you, slut?' she asked.

Numbly, Suze shook her head, hanging low. Cpl Pette nodded to the nurses, who released the prisoner. Suze stood, trembling and sobbing, naked, in front of the crisply-uniformed corporal, who stood, and walked around Suze's body, still rubbing her strap, and with her hinged prosthesis flexing just like a normal flesh leg. Suze's eyes followed the artificial limb, as the corporal paused to inspect Suze's bruised croup, running her fingers along the puffy spankmarks, and the older, ridged weals, from her previous thrashing.

'Find my prosthesis fascinating?' she said.

'Why, no, miss,' Suze blurted.

Whap! Suze gasped, and her bare bum jerked, as the strap laid a pink weal across her mid-fesse.

'Liar,' said Cpl Pette, pleasantly, in a slightly teasing tone. 'You do seem a troublemaker. I suppose you are the kind of whore that takes stripes in her stride, or even craves caning – such flagellomanes mostly like being fucked in the bumhole.'

'That's a lie,' Suze blurted. 'I'm no whore.'

Thwap! The corporal's body did not stir, save for a quiver of her tightly-swathed breasts; her wrist flicked, and the strap lashed Suze's bare bottom.

'Ooh!'

Sobbing, Suze rubbed her fesses.

'You address me as corporal,' said Sylvie, 'and you never –'

Thwap!

'Uh!'

'– accuse a corporal –'

Thwap!

'Ohh!'

'– of lying.'

Thwap! Thwap! Thwap!

'Ahh! Stop, please . . .'

'Squeal in French, pig,' said Cpl Pette.

Thwap! Thwap! The strap wealed dark red on Suze's naked croup.

'*Ah! Ah! Arrêtez, mademoiselle! Ayez pitié,*' Suze screamed.

She rubbed her reddened nates, frantically squirming, as her legs and breasts trembled.

122

'Oh, corporal, please!' she whimpered. 'How much more shame must I take? The commandant thrashed me, for no reason, and now you. I don't deserve this.'

Sylvie laughed.

'Are you sure?' she said. 'Not that it matters. Let's get you kitted for your first week's restraint, whore. After that, when your hobble and mask come off, you won't feel you're in prison at all.'

She brandished her strap.

'Kneel, whore.'

Suze knelt, her head hanging low. *Thwap!* The strap sang again, as Sylvie thrashed her a dozen strokes across the back, unmarked by MaBelle. Suze snuffled and sobbed, her body rocked by the blows, and her titties jolted from side to side. Through tears, she gasped harshly, as the leather cracked across her bare skin.

'Oh ... oh ... oh ...' she sobbed. 'Corporal, please ... I promise to obey.'

'Better,' she said.

Sylvie ceased strapping her. Lifting her skirt, she unfastened her prosthesis. Her naked cunt, massively-lipped beneath her flat belly, gleamed wetly between her furred stump, and the heavily-muscled right thigh.

'Amputee girls are more aware of their pleasure organs,' she said. 'My bum isn't as big as yours, but my cunt is preternaturally big and seductive, so I have been told.'

'Your bum is very attractive, corporal,' Suze gasped. 'And your cooze is very ... well-formed.'

'Enough to wank over?' demanded Cpl Pette. 'That's what we do here.'

She put her fingers to her stiff red clitoris, and began to rub.

'Lick me, slut,' she said.

'What?' Suze blurted.

Cpl Pette lifted her strap.

'Tongue me, bitch.'

Sobbing, Suze began to lick the wet folds of the corporal's cunt, then got her tongue on the distended clitty, and began to slurp the throbbing stiff nubbin.

123

'Swallow my come, bitch,' hissed Cpl Pette.

Suze gulped the copious flow of come, dripping from the corporal's swollen cooze. Pette's hand clutched the back of Suze's head, and moved her to the furry stump. As Suze licked the silky hairs, Pette recommenced masturbating her clit and, pushing Suze's face to her quivering stump, groaned softly, as come flooded from her gash, and her belly fluttered, with her breath exhaled in harsh pants of orgasm.

'Now, what are you, Miss Suzette Shard?' she gasped.

'A whore,' Suze whimpered.

Thwap!

'Ahh!'

The strap lashed Suze full across the naked breasts.

'I didn't hear you, miss,' said Sylvie. 'What are you, English bitch?'

'A whore, corporal! I'm a whore!' Suze shrieked.

Thwap! Thwap! Suze's teats wobbled, as the strap lashed them.

'Ahh!' Suze sobbed. 'I'm a whore, a slut.'

Thwap!

'I . . . I love cock in my bumhole,' she whimpered.

Thwap! Bright red bruises streaked both her stiffened nipples.

'Oh! please . . .' she moaned. 'Yes, I crave cane on the bare.'

Thwap! Thwap! Thwap! Suze shuddered, taken off guard by three vicious cuts to her bare top buttocks.

'What are you, blond bitch?' demanded the corporal.

Thwap! Thwap! Thwap! Suze's quivering melons were bruised crimson.

'Oh! Oh!' she sobbed. 'I'm . . . an English whore.'

'I thought as much,' drawled Cpl Sylvie Pette. 'Cheer up, English whore. With an arse like yours, you shouldn't wait long for your release date.'

'*Have* you taken it much, up the bumhole?' said Mimi Barbure. 'I know Cpl Pette is a brute, but she had reason to ask. If you've a squeezy, virgin anus, you might get an

124

early release date, so I've heard. I've also heard that an uninhibited girl, who can take flogging, and knows how to use her sphincter, to pleasure a master, gets an early release that way. That was the big question with Mlle Gundersheim. She had weird punishments, shameful ones – as well as whipping girls, she would bugger them with a rubber tool, that measured the elasticity of the anus.'

'That's disgusting,' Suze gasped.

'It's reality,' said Mimi. 'Go on, tell me. Friends have no secrets.'

'I don't have to tell you anything,' retorted Suze, 'but, I can use a friend. I can't get over the brutality of that bitch, the corporal. She thrashed me, and made me tongue her, and called me an English whore. That was the most shameful part – I'm proud of being English. And the awful things she made me confess ... wanting sex up the bum, and wanting the cane on my bare, like some pervert! My ... my bumhole's pretty tight. I do exercises. I've never – I mean hardly ever – taken it there, and I loathed it. Having a man's thing, poking you in there, it hurts so much, and it's just disgusting. I couldn't resist, somehow – you know how it is. You get so confused, when a man gets stiff, and is stroking your bare bum and cunny, you just flow, and turn to jelly, and let it happen. Men are vile brutes. As for the beatings – I hate that just as much. I went to an English girls' school where they punished us on the bare, with a cane, and I never liked it. You weren't supposed to like it. I could never get used to bare-bottom caning, and I can't see how girls crave it. Yet I've seen girls that do, who are actually proud of their weals. It hurts so much, and it's so gross and shameful, and just horrid. I can't look at my own bum, even if I had a glass, because it's spoiled utterly, by cruel beatings. Oh, when will I get out of this dreadful place?'

'That's easy,' said Mimi, smiling. 'There are no fences or perimeter guards. Disappear into the jungle, or swim.'

They were hidden from the duty corporal's view, by the drainage trench they were digging. The main focus of hard labour girls was on the ditches, since the camp lay in swampy ground, and needed drainage into the river Maroni. The two girls wielded shovels, but their progress was slow; Suze hobbled, with her ankles barred by a two foot length of wood, and her feet teetering on surgical boots with five inch rubber heels. Her voice was muffled by her hood, a rubber bag strapped to her nape, with its only aperture a pair of eye slits. Otherwise, both girls worked in the nude, save for tight rubber loinstrings, that barely covered the vulva, and showed the buttocks naked, with the tight thong chafing between the cheeks. They constantly shifted, thumbing the waistband or gusset of their loinstrings, to ease their discomfort; prisoners were forbidden to remove the garment, for the ease of full nudity. Sweat dripped from Suze's masked face, onto her breasts. Their naked bodies were slopped in mud, as they frequently slipped and fell, and Mimi's full breasts and buttocks were caked in a carapace of mud that had dried earlier. The mud, crusting her bottom, had moulded to the shape of her numerous and deep arse welts, from past beatings.

'Swim, in these horrid things?' Suze said bitterly.

Ever since her interview with Cpl Pette, she had slept alone, roped to her cot, in a tiny, foetid isolation cell, after ten hours of shovelling mud alone, under the sun, and the cane of the duty corporal. In that time, she had escaped beating, although the wounds inflicted by MaBelle, with the surgical boot Suze now wore, and by Cpl Pette's strap, still showed on her skin. According to MaBelle's programme, this was her first day of labour with another girl.

'They'll be off in a couple of days,' Mimi replied. 'We all have to do that, although you must have pissed off MaBelle to earn spanking, boots and a hobble. It is to break us in. The hood hides your face, so that you forget who you are. Although –' she put down her shovel, and touched Suze's bare bottom '– with this fabulous *cul*, I imagine you'll never forget who you are.'

'Yes,' blurted Suze, 'a caned whore, covered in weals of shame, nothing more.'

'Come, come,' Mimi cooed. 'There are masters who value a well-marked bum, I mean, the masters we may be sold to.'

'*Master?*' Suze cried, shuddering, and dropping her shovel.

'That is the rumour', Mimi added, 'that when we get a release date, it is only to go down river, to the highlands, or all the way to Brazil, where there are slave plantations that make this one look positively nice. I hope it's not true. MaBelle doesn't know half the punishments we endure, at the hands of her corporals. Or, if she does know, she dissembles. Hygienic discipline, indeed. Girls buried alive in the mud for an hour, or whipped on the bare, upside down, with just their heads buried in mud . . . Cpl Pette is the worst, that is why she's corporal in charge of discipline.'

'The bitch thrashed me horribly,' muttered Suze. 'I'll get back at her, I swear.'

Mimi stroked Suze's croup, her fingers lingering in the sweaty cleft, and plucked the thong from Suze's fesses, snapping it back on her skin. Suze shivered.

'She thrashes everyone horribly, Suze,' she said. 'I suppose you had to swallow her come, when you tongued her?'

Suze nodded, grimacing.

'We all do. She does have gorgeously large cunt folds and clit, but be careful of her. She is *unijambiste*, and uses her single leg to acquire sympathy, and excuse her worst barbarities. Some say that she is the real power in this camp, and has MaBelle in thrall; that Cpl Pette assigns girls their release dates. In a few days, you'll be unhooded, and out of solitary. You'll sleep with us in dorm, and we'll have lovely wanks, won't we? That's what we girls do together. It keeps us healthy and sane.'

She patted Suze's bottom, then stroked it with firm, circular motions of her palm, and twanged her cleft string.

'Or, I've heard lucky girls get sent to pleasure palaces,' she added, laughing, 'as pampered whores of the harem, fed on ice cream and champagne, and servicing a whole rake of lustful dark males with huge cocks. They say that Mlle Gundersheim is a slave, or mistress, of one such camp.'

127

'Whatever happened to her?' Suze asked.

'MaBelle fought her, in private, and vanquished her in a dark and terrible way, so rumour has it.'

'Is there nothing here that's not a rumour?'

'No,' said Mimi.

She had her hand under Suze's cleft string, and her fingers prodded the damp tufts of Suze's pubic fleece, tangled round her gash and anus bud.

'You are beautifully hairy,' whispered Mimi. 'I'm so jealous! I say. Let's wank off now. I'm very hot, and that bum of yours ... well, it would make any girl want to wank off. Aren't you hot, Suze? Hot to diddle?'

Suze blushed, and fanned her face with her rubber mask.

'I ... I haven't wanked off, as much as I'd like,' she murmured. 'Normally, yes, I do masturbate a lot, but lately I've been so frightened.'

Mimi's fingers crept to Suze's vulva, and penetrated the thick wet lips.

'Diddling keeps fear away,' she whispered, getting her thumb and forefinger around Suze's clitoris, and stroking the nubbin, which rapidly rose to erection. 'My, you've such a big, juicy clitty, like your bum. Go on, Suze, let's wank off. No one will see.'

'I don't know ...' Suze gasped.

'You're all wet, Suze. Don't pretend you're not wet. It's not lesbian, or anything. We're not lesbians, just hot girls.'

'I'm so tense,' Suze whimpered. 'I don't know if I'm ready ...'

Mimi's fingers were inside her wet pouch, reaming the meat, and jabbing and caressing at the hard ridge of her wombneck, while her deft thumb rubbed Suze's stiff wet clitoris. Sighing, Suze let her fingers be drawn underneath Mimi's string, between the girl's fat cunt lips, which were swollen and slimy with her gushing come.

'See how wet you make me,' Mimi whispered. 'That bum of yours, Suze ... how can a girl keep from worshipping it?'

She knelt, lifted Suze's loinstring away from her cleft, and plunged her nose, then her tongue, into Suze's arse crack. Her nose nuzzled the anus bud, and Suze gasped, pressing her wanked vulva against Mimi's probing fingers, and squeezing on the hand that filled her cunt. Mimi thrust her tongue inside Suze's anus, and poked, until she had the tongue's whole length jabbing and licking the narrow hole. Mimi crouched, her arse high before Suze's titties, and her long dark hair cascading over Suze's cunt basin and thighs. Suze ran her fingers up and down Mimi's spine, making her sigh, then, squatting, she thrust three fingers inside Mimi's gash, and began to fingerfuck the girl. Mimi's pouch was so wet and slimy, that without much struggle, Suze inserted a fourth finger, pummelling the slimy cunt walls and wombneck, while thumbing Mimi's stiff nubbin.

Mimi's come dripped over Suze's wanking wrist. The girls sank down into the muddy trench. Both had their rubber loinstrings pulled halfway down their thighs, as they gamahuched, wriggling in the mud. Suze's mouth found Mimi's cunt flaps, and she bit them, starting to chew, with her fingers still poking the gash. She withdrew her fingers, and replaced them with her tongue, darting to the wombneck, which she licked with flickers of the tongue tip. Her fingers rolled Mimi's erect clitty between them, drawing gurgles of pleasure from the shuddering girl, whose tongue was thrust deep into Suze's anal elastic, while her own fingers squeezed pleasure from Suze's clit, massively extruded above her cunt folds. Their bodies squelched, as naked muddy flesh slapped and writhed, and come gushed from both cunts, to mingle with the mud, forming a slimy ooze. Their bellies fluttered.

'Oh! It's so good,' Mimi gasped. 'It's the best diddle I've ever had. How I'd love to spank your bum, Suze. I'm going to come . . . oh . . .'

'Me too,' Suze panted. 'Yes . . . yes . . . rub my clitty . . . Mimi, stroke the weals on my bum, please? Yes, yes, that's it . . . they smart so, but your fingers are so cool. Oh . . . oh . . . you want to spank me, you slut? Maybe I should spank you, for saying it.'

Mimi's mud-slimed fingers, dripping with come, stroked Suze's bum weals.

'I shouldn't mind,' she gasped. 'Oh, spank me, Suze.'

Suze raised her arm, dripping mud on Mimi's open pink gash, and flipped the girl, so that her face was squashed in the mud. Suze held her down, wriggling. *Smack! Smack!* Her palm slapped Mimi's bare bum.

'Ooh!' squalled Mimi, the mud bubbling round her lips. *Smack! Smack! Smack!*

'Ooh! It hurts. Don't stop.'

As she spanked, Suze squatted on Mimi's face, and the spanked girl's tongue plunged into Suze's pouch, licking and tonguing the clitty, and darting in and out of the gushing wet slit, now slimed with mud and come. Mimi's fingers played at her own cunt, gaping wide and pink and wet, with her thighs spread, and her fingers swirling the heavy black pubic tufts, plastered across her anus and bum cleft. Come flowed from her wanked quim, into the mud. *Smack! Smack! Smack!* Her other hand continued to rake Suze's wealed bare, with sharp fingernails.

'Oh, yes, I'm coming!' she gurgled, her nose and mouth smothered in Suze's clamping cunt basin, and her mouth filled by Suze's erect clit, gash lips, and tresses of wet pubic fleece.

'I'm coming too,' Suze moaned. 'Don't stop . . . tongue me, feel my bum welts. Oh, yes, that hurts. That's so good. Please, harder . . . Oh! Oh! I haven't had such a good wank for so long . . . it's like honey, pulsing through me . . . Oh! Yes . . . ahh . . . ahh . . .'

The girls writhed together in the slime, then lay, panting and with fingers embracing each other's cunt and bum, until twin shadows fell over them.

'You have dropped your shovels, sluts,' said Cpl Pette, her mouth twisted in a thin leer, as she stroked the oiled tongues of her strap. 'Who is to be strapped first? Or perhaps a spell in the sweat box?'

'Come, corporal,' said MaBelle. 'The girls were working so hard, and the mud is so slippery, they must have dropped their shovels, in their zeal. Isn't that what happened, Mimi?'

The girls clambered to their feet, and stood, dripping, heads bowed before the two custodians.

'*Oui, mademoiselle commandante,*' Mimi blurted. 'That's exactly it.'

'And you, Suzette,' said MaBelle. 'Do you agree? I know you would not lie, as you'd get the chastisement in abeyance, already earned.'

'It is as she says, miss,' Suze murmured.

'If you were masturbating,' MaBelle said, 'it would mean public flogging for both of you.'

'*Masturbating,* commandant?' Mimi exclaimed. 'We certainly weren't masturbating.'

'The bitches are lying,' snarled Cpl Pette, slapping her strap against her left thigh, very hard.

MaBelle turned serenely to the corporal.

'According to the *code pénal,* we must give them the benefit of the doubt, corporal,' she said.

Sullenly, Cpl Pette followed the commandant, until they were out of vision, then both girls broke into sly smiles.

'It was a good show, commandant,' said the corporal. 'I got quite wet, watching it.'

'I confess I did, too,' said MaBelle. 'By the way, be careful about letting your cunt juice so shamelessly, in public.'

'Were you not my commandant, I should decree a whipping on bare, for that insolence,' said the corporal.

MaBelle placed her hand on Pette's crotch, squeezed her knicker fabric, and came up with her hand slimed in oozed cunt oil. She placed the corporal's fingers between her own legs, and sighed, at the smaller girl's brutal squeezing of her vulva, to milk the sopping gash of its come.

'Let us pretend I am not the commandant, for twenty minutes,' she whispered.

'Won't Annique be jealous?' said Cpl Pette.

'That is her privilege, until I thrash it from her,' MaBelle said, and both girls laughed, quickening their pace towards MaBelle's hut, the commandant hurrying, to keep up with Cpl Pette's jerky stride.

Two days later, Suze's restraints were removed, and she was given a palliasse next to Mimi Barbure's, in the long

131

shed that served as prisoners' dormitory number three. The prisoners slept in the nude, with a thin rag for covering, although few girls bothered to cover themselves, lying in a pool of sweat, and shifting continuously. Before bedding down, they paraded in the latrine, at the end of the shed, for their final evacuations of the day, and were permitted to sluice their fouled cunt basins, but not to shower. Then, they were sprayed with insect repellent, and locked into the shed. The moment the lights went out, almost every girl in the shed began to masturbate, sighing and groaning, as they essayed to frig themselves to sleep. They frigged for show, that is, with their thighs and cunts spread wide, inviting a partner, and, after several minutes of determined frotting, most of the girls paired off in couples, or even threesomes. Suze did not at once begin to wank off, but propped herself on an elbow, eyes wide, as she watched the pumping bare cunts of the masturbating prisoners. Her cunt rapidly moistened, the oozed come adding to the copious stains on her palliasse. After only a few seconds, she grunted, as a warm, naked body pushed against her. It was Mimi. There were sneering whoops as the naked girl pressed her body to Suze.

'I have no shame,' she said.

Mimi explained that in the prisoner power structure, it was deemed weakness to give way to temptation, and join a wanking girl, for mutual tribadism. The girl wanking off alone, and displaying herself, had power, while an intruder, having given way to uncontrolled lust, risked public rejection. Indeed, one or two or three girls were repulsed by their intended wank partners, to hoots of derision from the other masturbatresses.

'Wait,' said Suze, half giggling, as Mimi pushed her fingers into her already wet pouch. 'I want to watch.'

'Watch, while we diddle,' said Mimi, beginning to wank off Suze's hardening clitty.

Suze gasped at the thrill of electric pleasure that coursed through her spine and belly, as the girl expertly thumbed her clitty, and got her own fingers into Mimi's sopping wet gash, already wanked to a copious flow of come. The two girls frigged each other's swollen quims, with Mimi's fingers exploring Suze's bottom.

'You're smooth,' she said, with a moue of disappointment. 'I was hoping for some lovely crusty welts to scratch.'

'I haven't been beaten,' said Suze, 'not since we last wanked off, and not, in fact, since my horrid thrashing from that beastly Cpl Pette. Look, is it safe to pleasure ourselves so obviously? What if the duty corporal inspects? There is no possibility of pretence, or concealment.'

Mimi's come-slimed finger scratched the pucker of Suze's anus, and she thrust, to get her fingernail a short distance inside the bumhole. Suze squirmed.

'Oh . . .' she said faintly, 'stop that.'

Mimi did not stop. She said that the duty corporal's rounds were part of the game; at one of the two or three inspections, a girl would be selected for whipping, either a bare caning on the spot, or, if she were particularly flagrant in her masturbation, a public flogging the next day. As she spoke, she pushed her finger further into Suze's anal elastic, its progress aided by a copious oiling with Suze's own come, and by Suze's seeped arse grease. Suze gasped, her buttocks clenching, as Mimi widened her hole, and got a second finger inside, and then, with Suze shivering, and her cunt gushing come, a third. Mimi's three fingers thrust suddenly home, as Suze's anal elastic yielded, and they struck her arse root, beginning a vigorous reaming of the rectum. Her other hand thrust deep into Suze's cunt pouch, slamming and pinching the hard wombneck, with Suze's come dripping over Mimi's wrist, onto her soaking palliasse. Suze had her fingers inside Mimi's juicing cunt, and was rubbing the massively extruded clitty; on Mimi's whispered instructions, she balled her fist, and began to punch Mimi inside her pouch. Mimi groaned, and bit Suze's erect nipple.

'That is so good,' she moaned. 'I shall hate you if you wank off, ever, with anyone but me.'

'Ahh . . .' Suze panted, her sweating, come-soaked legs threshing on the palliasse, as many pairs of eyes watched the tribadists. 'I promise . . .'

'No,' said Mimi sharply. 'You mustn't promise something you can't deliver. 'With your bum, every girl will want you for wanking off, and it would be wrong to disappoint them.'

Her two fists jabbed Suze rhythmically, in the cunt and anus, and Suze clung to Mimi's neck, writhing helplessly as her cunt basin shuddered under the girl's assaults. Her own masturbation of Mimi's gash continued, jabbing harder and harder inside the wet pouch, and rubbing the stiff, throbbing clitoris, its slippery pink surface a hard thumb of shuddering pleasure, as each pinch or slice of the clit flesh drew gasps and yelps deep in Mimi's throat.

'You make me sound like a piece of meat,' Suze gasped, whinnying, as Mimi punched her greased arse root. 'Oh, that's good. Don't stop. Mm ... you know, it seems only yesterday, I was an innocent English girl, living among English streams and meadows, and now, where am I, and what am I? Locked up in a jungle prison, naked and wanking off, with a lovely French girl squashing her slippery nude body against mine, in a dormitory full of naked felons, stinking of girls' piss and sweat and come. And people wanting to whip my bottom, and fuck me in the bumhole, and telling me I *want* it. England seems so far away.'

'You do like it in the bumhole,' Mimi panted. 'Admit it, Suze. It is such a lovely hole, like the globes outside; so creamy and smooth and clingy, sucking my fingers. How wonderful it would be to have a cock, and feel that anus suck on me as I buggered you. With that arse, Suze, you are a piece of prime meat. No girl could resist those arse cheeks. Don't tell me you want me to like you for yourself. I do. That splendid arse is your self.'

'Oh ... oh ... I'm coming,' Suze gasped. 'OK, a piece of meat, if that pleases you, Mimi. I've never felt like this before. Perhaps it is true, we are all girl meat, to be wanked and arse-fucked and whipped ... Oh!'

There was a crash, as the door flew open, and a flashlight illumined the two girls, writhing together, in a slippery naked embrace, as they wanked off.

134

Crack! Crack! The corporal's strap lashed twice across Suze's bottom, bruising the skin with ugly pink weals.

'Ah!' Suze yelped.

'I may settle the debate,' drawled Cpl Pette. 'By your own admission, inmate Shard, you are a dirty English whore. You have debauched this French citizen. One of you must be publicly whipped for it tomorrow. No doubt, the girl to whom shame and the pain of whipweals are second nature – who craves the exposure and flogging of her naked flesh.'

Suze and Mimi stared at each other, aghast, and Mimi's face wrinkled in anguish, as her eyes moistened.

'That would be me, corporal,' blurted Suze. 'I'm the guilty one. I'll take the whipping.'

9

Submissive

The guard closed the door of MaBelle's hut, and draped a tarpaulin over the beaded ropes, leaving the room in semi-darkness. The shades were drawn shut over the windows, leaving only a few narrow shafts of sunlight to pierce the shadows.

'Please sit down, Suzette,' said MaBelle.

'Thank you, *mademoiselle commandante*,' Suze replied, her lips tight, and her eyes hooded, as she glanced at the commandant, in her crisp morning uniform, the breasts jutting braless under the blouse, open to the third button, and her body streaked by thin shafts of sunlight.

Suze wore merely a ragged bra, that left most of her breasts uncovered, and a loinstring stuck fast between her arse cleft. Her face, bare legs, and the melons of her arse and teats, were burnt to a tan.

'You know why you're here, I'm afraid,' said MaBelle, without rising.

She spoke in a lightly-accented English.

'You are going to beat me, *mademoiselle commandante*,' Suze answered. 'Because of my fault, last night. My scandalous behaviour.'

'There is no need for melodrama,' said MaBelle. 'You will be lashed, yes, but not here. I want to put you at your ease. You know why I have to lash you.'

'As an example to the others,' Suze blurted.

MaBelle yawned.

'No, *mucky pup –*' she used the phrase in English '–

136

because you like it. You would enjoy a nice cup of English tea? I have my own supply.'

'Yes, miss!' Suze exclaimed, then bit her lip. 'Please,' she added.

'Don't be nervous. It's not a trick,' MaBelle said, smiling. She rose, and rang for her scrub slut.

'Please, miss, I'd rather get my beating over with,' Suze blurted. 'It's the suspense . . . oh, it's awful.'

'I know,' said MaBelle. 'Thinking of your bare bum whipped is almost as bad as the reality, isn't it? Almost, but not quite. I want to have a little chat, and show you I am not the ogre you may have thought. I must be harsh, with new arrivals, you understand. In this case, you have merited a flogging, and indeed asked to take the stripes in place of your co-miscreant, which is noble. There is also the matter of the caning in abeyance, already awarded to you. Would you like to take both chastisements at once? I would recommend you do, as it clears the decks, so to speak. Take your time in deciding, while we enjoy our tea.'

The scrub slut, her breasts bound flat, in tight rubber straps, and her ankles separated by a two-foot wooden hobble, brought in the tea things, and MaBelle joined Suze at the table.

'Milk?' she said, pouring the tea. 'No sugar, I suppose. You will be careful of your weight.'

Suzette accepted milk, and four spoonfuls of sugar. She gulped the steaming brew.

'My punishment in abeyance,' she said. 'May I ask how many?'

'Your tariff is thirty strokes with the cane, on bare,' said MaBelle, moving her bare thigh closer to Suze's. 'Then, for last night's disgrace, a whipping. Fifty strokes. You'll have to be bound in straps, I'm afraid.'

Suze shivered.

'I was afraid of that,' she said. 'I'm not sure I can take it.'

'But it's not the first time, is it?' asked MaBelle, putting her hand on Suze's knee. 'You are apprehensive, naturally, but there is a difference between a girl who is terrified of

137

the unknown, and one who is merely apprehensive of the familiar. When I thrashed you the first time, I knew your bottom was a craver of strokes.'

'No, mademoiselle!' Suze cried. 'It hurt awfully, when you thrashed me with that horrid surgical boot. I could not possibly get pleasure from it. Why does everyone taunt me? Just because my bottom is . . . well . . . big . . .'

'Don't confuse rhabdophilia – love of the rod – with pleasure,' said MaBelle. 'It is the need for shame and submission, for baring the most intimate part, helplessly, in thrall of another's cane. It is the little things, like the way a girl's skin either recoils from her strokes, or else clenches to the beating's rhythm, as if in welcome. The way her buttocks writhe, making a sensuous pattern of her bruises. Almost taunting her chastiser.'

'I am sure I have never done that,' Suze blurted. 'I hate to be beaten. Oh, why won't anyone listen?'

'Why did you volunteer so fast, to take Mimi's stripes?' MaBelle countered. The girl is a shameless masturbatress.'

'I . . . I don't know,' Suze whimpered.

Gently, MaBelle eased her fingers beneath Suze's ragged loinstring, and touched the lips of the girl's vulva. Suze jerked, and tried to close her thighs, but MaBelle's wrist prevented her. The commandant probed Suze's gash with her fingertips, making Suze shudder, as she touched the clitty. The fingers came out gleaming, oily wet, and with a long strand of Suze's pubic fleece adhering to the skin. MaBelle held them in front of Suze's nose; Suze closed her eyes, and turned her face.

'Just talking of your beating makes you wet,' MaBelle said softly. 'There is no point in denying yourself, Suzette. You are a rhabdophile.'

Suze was sobbing quietly.

'I believe you were initiated into the rituals of corporal punishment at your school, St Ursula's,' she said. 'And I believe you came to crave such rituals – the lowering of the panties, bending over, in a posture of submission, and the sting of the cane on your naked buttocks. Didn't you Suzette? And didn't you and the other girls masturbate

138

after your canings, showing off your weals? I'd like you to be frank. The habits of English schoolgirls fascinate me.'

'It wasn't like that!' Suze blurted. 'OK, I was beaten, and yes, we girls used to masturbate together after a thrashing, but it was to ease the pain, not because we enjoyed it. Certainly not because we were submissive. The head-mistress was strict enough, but not unkind, and quite often would let us keep our knickers on for a caning, although we had to pull them up tight, so it was really the same as being bare bum. Or else she would cane us in our nighties, but that was shameful, because you had to walk through school to get to her study, and wearing only your nightie, barefoot, so everybody knew you were for the cane. Then, the nighties showed your bottom underneath their filmy stuff, so you could choose to wear knickers under your nightie, which made all the girls jeer that you were shy, or else come out of the beating in your nightie as normal, without knickers, and everyone would crowd round to count the bruises. But the prefects caned without kindness. There was one, who liked to beat four or five girls at once – she liked to catch us smoking, which was an easy pinch – and would save up their punishments until she had what she called an orchestra. It was awful, having to wait for the strokes, as well as actually receiving them. Girls couldn't eat, for worry. This pre liked to play the xylophone: she lined a squad of girls, bending over a rail, all bare bum, of course, and with our knickers round our ankles. She used to slipper us, which she claimed was playing a tune, although all the slaps sounded the same. That went on for half an hour, slap after slap on each bum in turn, with a gym shoe stuffed with golf balls, which is almost more painful that the cane, while her prefect friends watched and laughed, as we wriggled on the rail, with our bare bums getting all red and crimson with big deep bruises. That was Marchant, the very worst – she loved flogging girls, and I think it was the only thing she did like, with as much pain, and as many tears, as possible, and always on the bare. Her favourite punishment was a caning without tariff, to end only when we began to cry. It was cissy to blub, so we had

139

to take the caning until we really couldn't help bursting into tears, sometimes twenty strokes or more. She liked to beat us in the most shameful postures, bending over a barrel, with our heads in a coal scuttle or even an old horse trough which was outside, in the back courtyard. I took a whole two dozen, once, before she let me go, and all in the same welt. My head was pushed in a coal scuttle, and I couldn't help crying out, she caned me so hard, and my cries sounded like a bull roaring. I was in agony, and my bum was like corrugated leather for days. I'll never forget that beating.'

'You must have masturbated vigorously, afterward,' MaBelle murmured.

'Y– yes, I admit I did. More than once. It was the only way to relieve the . . . the tension,' Suze blurted.

'So, you came to associate the smarting of the cane with the relief of masturbation,' the commandant insisted.

'Not associate,' Suze whimpered. 'Being beaten was so horrid, you wanted something nice, to make up for it. That's all, I swear.'

'I want you to masturbate for me now,' said MaBelle.

'What!' Suze ejaculated.

'Stand, inmate, and remove your loincloth,' ordered MaBelle. 'Part your legs, and perform the act of masturbation. Bring yourself to climax as fast as possible. I wish to ascertain what are your favourite techniques. Be natural.'

Trembling, Suze got to her feet, and obeyed. Her loincloth dropped to the floor, and she parted her thighs, thrusting the gash slightly forward, then applied her fingers to her clitty, which was already extruded from the thick wet folds of her cunt, seeping come.

'Look at me,' ordered the commandant, her face in shadow, but her buttocks facing Suze.

Slowly, MaBelle lifted her khaki uniform skirt, to reveal her bare nates; as Suze fingered her cunt, and thumbed her throbbing clitty, MaBelle's hand crept between her own cunt flaps, and twirled her thick pubic hairs between finger and thumb, before massaging her clitty, and thrusting three fingers inside her pouch. MaBelle's gash oozed come.

Gasping, Suze wanked off, dimly hearing MaBelle's whispered taunts: that Suze should imagine herself caning MaBelle on the bare, making her melons squirm, redden and wriggle, a fantasy all the more juicy, as there was no chance of it happening. Suze grasped the desk for support; her nipples were stiff, and her legs trembling, as her hand slapped her dripping cunt, and her thumb reamed the erect bud of the clitty.

'You *do* want to whip my bum, don't you?' whispered MaBelle. 'You are jealous. You fear my arse is lovelier than your own, and want to disfigure it with bruises. Don't you, slut? The truth.'

'I can't help feeling that way,' Suze panted. 'Your bum is so beautiful and firm . . . of course I'm jealous.'

'Look at my bum globes,' hissed MaBelle. 'Look how ripe they are, yet smooth, and free of weals. Just think, Suzette, your cane is striping me, lashing my naked skin with horrid dark welts, my fesses puffy and purple with bruises, and the whole croup squirming helplessly as you flog me. Isn't that sweet revenge for all the unfair canings from those beastly prefects? Isn't that making you wet? Don't you want to come?'

'Oh . . .' Suze sobbed, rapidly wanking her come-slopped cunt, 'Yes . . .'

MaBelle sighed in satisfaction, and then her sighs turned to rapid, grunting gasps, as her bottom shook, and her flow of come increased to a slimy torrent, dripping from her wanking hand. Suze frigged faster, and, as the commandant's pants softened, Suze herself cried in whimpers, as her belly and vulva fluttered, and come slimed her fingers.

'There is one other thing, distinguishing a female submissive,' MaBelle said. 'That is why my room is in shade. Not content with masturbating, such girls like to stimulate themselves with a mimicry of copulation – but not in the normal channel. They wish a stimulation which is painful, like the cane, and humiliating, beyond any decent girl's nightmares. They like, in a word, to be fucked in the bumhole. Are you such a girl, Suzette?'

Suze's jaw dropped, and she blushed fierily; she began to stammer a reply, but MaBelle held up a come-slimed hand.

'I require this information to complete your dossier. There is only one way to find out, and I propose to spare you the shame of having it done in the public ward of the hospital. Do you know what this is?'

She held up a thick baton of ragged, bulging leather, about fifteen inches long, and a fist thick, with a loop at the end. Numbly, Suze shook her head.

'It is a bull's pizzle,' said the commandant. 'You will please take position as follows, inmate Shard. Bend over my desk, holding the right corner with your right hand. With your left hand, I require you to masturbate once more, until your vulva is sufficiently wet to lubricate the intrument. When you have collected a palmful of come, you will do so.'

Crack! Her palm slashed the air, and landed a single wet slap, very hard, on Suzette's bare croup.

'Oh!' Suze cried, her spanked bum clenching.

'On the double,' snarled MaBelle. 'You submissive slut.'

'*Oui, mademoiselle commandante,*' Suze sobbed.

She gasped, wanking her slime-soaked cunt, until her palm held its fullness of her oily ooze. MaBelle grasped her wrist, and rubbed Suze's hand up and down the gnarled shaft of the bull's pizzle.

'Have you ever had a cock as big as this in your bumhole?' she asked.

'Mademoiselle, please!' Suze cried.

'Answer, slut,' said MaBelle calmly. 'You are due a whipping, my poor girl, so it would be wise to tell the truth. Remember that as an inmate you have no rights. Look at the pizzle. In a little while, it will be inside you. Ever had one like it before?'

Twisting her head, and her jaw slack, Suze gaped at the monstrous leather tube.

'I . . . I'm not sure,' she whimpered. 'Certainly not one so cruel, so knobbly. Oh, mademoiselle, why do you torture me?'

MaBelle thrust the tip of the pizzle into Suze's anal opening.

142

'Oh! Ah!' Suze shrieked.

The commandant wiped her moist brow, and flicked back strands of hair. She applied both hands to the base of the tube, and rammed it the full length into Suze's bumhole, until only the base was visible, stretching the anal pucker to several times its normal width. Suze moaned, her buttocks convulsing, as the shaft filled her anus.

'Hurt much?' panted MaBelle.

'Oh! It's awful,' Suze blurted.

'Worse than the others?'

'Much worse.'

'So there have been others,' MaBelle hissed. 'Just as I thought. You crave buggery as well as bare-bum chastisement. Don't deny it.'

Suze opened her mouth, but could only shriek, as MaBelle began to plunge the leather tool in and out of Suze's anal elastic. Each thrust slammed the root of Suze's anus, and the whimpering girl shuddered, as her rectum was penetrated. Her buttocks began to move, squirming in the rhythm of MaBelle's buggery, and she gripped the sides of the desk, pushing her hips in the direction of the dildo; her anus now squeezing the tube, as her arse globes clenched around the invading instrument, emerging, after each thrust, coated more and more with Suze's copious shiny arse grease. From Suze's shivering cooze dripped clear drops of come, bigger and faster, as the pizzle buggered her. The come drenched her dangling pube hairs, forming them into matted tangles, that swirled and slapped against the lips of her swollen cunt, jerking at each slam of the pizzle in her rectum. She moaned and shuddered, as her hips swayed in time with the older girl's buggering thrusts.

'Ah! Ah! Oh, please, enough . . .' she moaned.

'Are you going to come again?' MaBelle asked. 'Your cunt is wet.'

'No,' Suze cried, then placed a hand at her dripping cooze, and recoiled. 'Oh, no . . .'

MaBelle replaced the girl's fingers at the soaking slit.

'You want to wank off, don't you?' she snapped. 'I know your kind. Then, do so. That is an order.'

143

'Uhh . . .' Suze gasped, as she recommenced masturbation, her thumb and forefinger fastening on her swollen clitty, to press and pinch the distended red organ.

Come gushed from her cunt; MaBelle sweated profusely, as she rammed the pizzle between the squirming buttocks. She, too, masturbated, as she buggered the girl, her hand delving between her cunt lips, and frotting herself in the same rhythm as the pizzle, jabbing Suze's anus. After two minutes' frigging, Suze began to squeal, then pant fast, and again brought herself off; MaBelle ceased her own masturbation, without climax. Suze glanced round, and saw MaBelle's wet fingers emerge from her pouch. MaBelle smiled.

'I save the pleasure of coming, slut, for when I watch your bare bum all red and dancing under my cane,' she said.

She pushed the pizzle, until the entire instrument disappeared inside Suze's anal shaft.

'No, please don't,' Suze wailed.

While Suze clung to the desk, sobbing and gasping, MaBelle took a roll of clear plastic adhesive tape, and began to apply it between the folds of Suze's arse crack. As Suze gasped, MaBelle completed the sealing of Suze's anal orifice, with strands of the plastic tape looped around her waist and inner thighs, until Suze's hips and cunt basin glistened with tape, leaving the buttocks and vulva naked. Suze squirmed, sobbing, with the bull's pizzle trapped inside her anus. MaBelle smartened her uniform, and told Suze to replace her loincloth.

'It is time for your whipping,' she said curtly. 'I take it you can walk to the hospital? Or do you wish the guards to escort you?'

'I can walk, *Mlle Commandante*,' Suze whimpered. 'So you mean I am to be whipped with this dreadful thing inside me?'

'Of course,' said the blond girl, flicking hair from her damp brow. 'It will make your bum-caning all the juicier. Just like the old days, eh, Shard? I know you for what you are: a lustful, submissive slut. Your wanking off under buggery is the proof. Those bruises on your arse, when you arrived here, were no accident. Whoever these companions were, they were there to indulge your lust for caning games. Quite the haughty one, aren't you, miss ten million dollar arse? All you subs are the same – demanding, sulky, and whingeing, when you don't get the thrashing you crave.'

She cleared the doorway, and beckoned Suze to follow her.

'How did you know – the ten million dollars?' Suze gasped, as they stepped into the light.

'You really don't recognise me?' sneered MaBelle, lapsing into English. 'Maybe it's because of my blond hair. You silly cow, I'm Mabel Marchant, prefect of St Ursula's. I've followed your career, Miss Shard. The Bottom, indeed, as if your fesses are superior to mine! I used to masturbate, after I beat your cheeky arse, thinking of those lovely bare fesses, all red and squirming, and ever since I first beat you I've longed to whip your bottom to shreds. And now I have you. Supermodel, eh? I'm going to mark your bum, miss, so that you'll never model again.'

'How do you feel, Suzette?' Mimi whispered.

'I'm scared, Mimi,' replied Suzette, shivering in her bonds. 'I had no idea it was going to be like this.'

Suze hung naked, under the eyes of Cpl Pette, and the nurses Borne and Castor, with half a dozen nude and hobbled prisoners, including Mimi, detailed as punishment witnesses. Annique Dutoit introduced two young, swarthy and muscular males in doctors' smocks, as Drs Morue and Pance, come from Cayenne to evaluate the prisoner. Foul-smelling French cigarettes drooping from their lips, they leered unashamedly at Suze's quivering nudity. Ropes attached Suze's wrists to the ceiling of the hospital ward; her legs were spread wide, and her ankles fastened in hinged metal clamps set in concrete blocks, which fixed her toes just an inch above the floor, so that her body was fully stretched, but with little room for manoeuvre, or squirming, to dissipate the smarting of strokes. She would be beaten, restrained from easing her pain by anything more

145

than a shudder. The buttocks were spread so wide, baring the entire perineum, cunt lips and arse cleft, that there would be little possibility of satisfactorily clenching the cheeks after each stroke.

Her hair was pinned on top of her head, to bare her whole back. The humid ward had little to suggest healing. Apart from a bed, and cabinets of syringes, needles and stethoscopes, the furniture was disciplinarian: a barrel between two sets of floor clamps, a vaulting horse, a stocks and some upturned stools. Cpl Pette stood between the two male doctors, almost touching them, and had left her prosthesis off: her uniform skirt clung tightly to her buttocks, and ended just below her crotch, showing the sheer bronze nylon adorning her whole leg, as well as the white garter strap holding it to her suspender belt; she supported herself on a knobbled walking stick. The khaki skirt itself was no more than a single strip of cloth wrapped around the thighs and buttocks, and secured to her haunches by two safety pins. The silky hairs on her stump were visible beneath her short skirt, and every sensuous wriggle of her haunches drew the males' eyes from the suspended prisoner to the amputee corporal.

'Courage, girl,' said Mimi, touching Suzette's bared bottom. 'It won't last forever, no matter how hard it seems. It is so brave of you, to take the blame for me.'

Suzette told Mimi of the pizzle taped inside her anus; Mimi paled, and said she had never known either MaBelle or Pette impose a punishment so horrid. Suze did not mention her previous acquaintance with Mabel Marchant, now MaBelle, the camp commandant – what would a simple, sultry French girl understand of relationships at an English girls' boarding school?

'Every jolt of your buttocks under cane will be ten times worse,' Mimi said, 'as it presses the pizzle inside you, against your bum root. Is it all the way into your rectum?'

Suze grimaced, and said yes.

'That's awful,' Mimi blurted.

'Mimi, I have to tell you,' Suze blurted. 'I am no stranger to corporal punishment. I've been whipped and caned on the bare, more times than I admit, even to myself. Every time, I hate the pain more, and hate my chastiser, yet still it seems to happen. I wonder, is there something in me that attracts the whip, and even craves it? Why else did I own up so fast? Am I being rightly punished for . . . you know, my big fesses?'

Mimi stroked Suzette's naked buttocks with her fingertips.

'They are too tempting,' she murmured. 'Now, I have to wet your bottom. That's to make the pain worse. I'm sorry, Suzette, those are orders. It is to make me feel guilty.'

'Don't say you are sorry,' Suze gasped. 'I deserve it.'

Mimi began to rub sticky gel on Suze's fesses, while nurses Castor and Borne attached sensors to Suze's nipples, clitoris and cunt flaps, with wires, leading to a machine. Suze jerked, at the touch of the pads on her bare flesh. Fingers stretched her anus bud, through its plastic sheath, and naked wires were poked through the tape, penetrating her anus to a depth of an inch.

'Mlle Dutoit wants to monitor your rate of sexual stimulation under chastisement, whore,' said Borne, leering. 'There are some medical people here, to witness your flogging. They are excited at having a true submissive as subject, for a submissive slut like you will always juice under the cane. Mlle Dutoit wants to measure precisely the swelling of your private parts, and the dilation of your bumhole, with that bull's prick swinging around inside. I bet it hurts.'

Suze gasped that it hurt awfully.

'And you love it,' sneered Castor. 'Dirty submissive slut.'

'Nobody deserves this,' Mimi said, bitterly.

Suze's bare bottom shone with fluid. From her naked cunt flaps, a steady drip of come seeped. Nurse Castor took a roll of adhesive tape, like that closing Suze's anus, and wound the clear tape round and round her bottom and haunches, until her entire nates were encased in a thick translucent film, trapping Suze's oozed cunt juice inside it, in a mosaic of flattened bubbles. The nurse said that Suze would be caned, until the filmy casing was whipped off.

'But ... the commandant said thirty and fifty,' Suze blurted.

'New orders,' drawled the nurse, parting Suze's taped arse. 'No tariff. You'll be whipped raw, slut.'

Suze's thighs and bum squirmed, as a new spurt of come oozed from her gash flaps, and slopped beneath her plastic adhesive panties.

'Oh, Mimi,' she gasped, 'look at my pussy. It's juicing, and I'm so ashamed. What if they are right – what if I really do crave it?'

Mimi touched Suze on the clitoris, beneath her plastic wrapping, and Suze shivered and gasped, with a little mewl, and a flaring of her nostrils. A further spurt of come sloshed beneath the plastic.

'Your pussy looks like a sea anemone,' Mimi murmured. 'A lovely pink mouth, all wet and sloppy, with big squashy lips, and that pubic forest clammy around the gash, like a jungle of seaweed, and the shiny tape like a pool of seawater. I'm getting wet in my pouch, just by looking. I had a boyfriend who liked to strip me bare, then wrap me in glued cling film. He used to wank me off, and sometimes fuck me in the bum, through the cling film. It stretches, you see. Such a lovely squishy feeling. But he never caned me wrapped up, only on my bare skin. He used to cane me a dozen on bare, after he'd wanked me off, and ripped away the cling film, which hurt awfully. So did the caning, but I always climaxed a second time.'

'Silence, sluts,' said Castor, cracking her cane. 'The commandant is ready to commence chastisement.'

Mimi took her place, kneeling among the hobbled prisoners, eyes fixed on Suze's front body. Cpl Pette ordered the girls to look at Suze's face, for evidence of her distress under punishment, and also to scrutinise her cunt lips, for evidence of perverted stimulation.

'It will be a pleasure to whip this submissive bitch in full suspension,' MaBelle said to Annique Dutoit.

148

She eyed the nurse's moist breasts, thrusting under her sweat-sodden tunic, unbuttoned to the third button, and showing the ragged tops of her bra cups.

'If it goes well, I may institute full suspension as my preferred mode of caning.'

Annique shivered, and turned to her monitor screen, showing Suze's body as a series of blips. MaBelle lifted a crook-handled cane, four feet in length, and addressed the male doctors.

'This subject, as I promised, is an example of a full submissive,' she said. 'Although she is in denial, she is that not so rare female specimen, who craves thrashing of the bare fesses, and also the perverted stimulation of anal intercourse. She is English, which may explain such tendencies, notably her rhabdophilia – love of the rod. For her chastisement, I have obtained a cane like those used on English girls in their single sex boarding schools, where perverted practices are rampant.'

The two males leered. MaBelle laid the cane aside, and picked up a rubber flogging quirt, with three tongues, four feet in length.

'As *hors d'oeuvre*, she shall be flogged on the back,' she added, raising the quirt over Suze's quivering bare shoulders.

Crack! The heavy scourge lashed Suze across the back, jolting her against her bonds, and knocking the breath from her lungs. She grunted, her face grimacing, and her eyes briefly screwed tight. *Crack!* The second stroke flailed her in the same pink welts raised by the first, and a low moan escaped Suze's lips. Tears formed at the corners of her eyes. *Crack! Crack! Crack!* The whip descended rhythmically and hard, striping every inch of Suze's naked upper back, until, after a flogging of twenty minutes, her skin was a patchwork of puffy red welts, darkening to crimson. All this time, Suze's body shuddered helplessly in her restraints, while a sobbing wail crooned from her slack and drooling lips. Her head hung low, jerked upwards in a grimace by each stroke of the quirt. MaBelle flogged her for another ten minutes, while the hobbled prisoners, timid under the canes of Castor and Borne, looked ashamed at Suze's anguished face, and with furtive glances at her taped gash, where her come glistened, rolling, at the impact of the whip on her body.

Cpl Pette stood, bright-eyed and with flared nostrils, licking her teeth, as she followed every weal of the thongs on Suze's back. The men pressed her, patting her shoulders and waist, and sharing her smiles. Annique pored over her monitor. When the sweating MaBelle put aside the whip, she reported that after sixty-seven lashes, the prisoner showed signs of definite, though not excessive, stimulation. The nipples were erect, the clitoris semi-rigid, and the flow of come was normal, as for the initial stages of masturbation. MaBelle took up the cane. She lifted it to the full extent of her arms, grasping it with both hands, and swivelled her torso, to swing the cane down across Suze's buttocks. *Vap!*

'Ah!' Suze squealed, her buttocks squirming violently, as the cane scorched a rip in the plastic panties, and left a jagged pink imprint on her skin beneath.

MaBelle swivelled again, this time swinging her body with such force, that her left breast popped from its bra cup, and swayed bare, as the cane landed a second time on Suze's taped nates.

'Ahh! Oh!' Suze yelped, her cries melting into a choking sob, as her bum writhed under the shredded plastic.

Panting, MaBelle lifted her cane, without bothering to replace her naked breast; she frowned, smiled, and freed the second, then prepared to continue her bare-breasted caning. Annique stared at the flashing blips on her monitor, and licked her lips. She looked up at Suze's cunt basin, squirming under her plastic sheathing, and nodded; the caned girl's cooze was seeping come. Cpl Pette whispered and joked with the two males, now openly pawing her, as her shifting skirt revealed more of her stockinged thigh, and naked left stump. *Vap!* MaBelle's naked breasts shook violently.

'Urrgh,' Suze groaned, as the cane lashed her quivering bare.

MaBelle curtly ordered her to be gagged, and nurse Castor placed a rubber ball between Suze's jaws, fastening it with a cord around her nape. *Vap! Vap! Vap!* The caning continued, the strokes on the one second, with Suze wriggling and jerking helplessly in her restraints, while drool seeped from her open mouth, and a low wail gurgled in her throat.

'Uhh . . . uhh . . .' she moaned.

The plastic panties taping her buttocks shredded further with each stroke, until the older girl was caning her direct on bare bumflesh; as her tape casing ripped apart, the taping around her cunt was held only by the strands at her waist. MaBelle lashed Suze across top buttock, bringing a squeal of agony from the bound girl; again, and again, then, deftly slashed the tape binding her waist, slicing it open with three cruel cuts above the buttocks, that had Suze shuddering like a rag doll. She moaned, as her cunt panty filled with golden fluid, spewing from her gash, making the panties bulge at her crotch. The tape casing sprang away, and bared Suze completely, with a flood of mingled come and piss spraying the watching prisoners.

'The filthy slut,' said Cpl Pette, her fingers brushing Dr Morue's crotch, while Dr Pance's hand was stroking her fleecy naked stump.

Vap! Vap!

'Mm! Mm!' Suze's wails were stifled by the ball gag, clamped between her teeth, which bit halfway through the solid rubber.

Dr Morue reached for a cigarette, and Cpl Pette whispered to him. They giggled. The male knelt in front of Cpl Pette's skirt, with his lips at her crotch. The corporal took his cigarette lighter, and parted her skirt, to reveal the massive jungle of cunt hairs bushy and wet, and pantiless under her sussies. She inserted the lighter upside down into her slit, and squeezed her thighs, making her huge cunt lips grimace. A flame sprang from her gash, lighting the doctor's cigarette. He sucked on the fumable, and blew a stinking cloud of purple smoke into Pette's open flaps, before retrieving his still-flaming lighter. Soon, Dr Pance,

151

too, needed a cigarette, and the operation was repeated. Suze writhed, squirming, in her bonds, as her bare bum jerked under the canestrokes, and her cunt spewed come onto the floor. Her nipples stuck up erect; her shiny oily come flowed faster, bathing her cunt flaps and rippling thighs, until Annique looked up from her monitor, and shrugged to the caner; at forty-four strokes of the cane on bare, Suze's blips had gone off the screen. *Vap! Vap! Vap!*

'Urgh! Urgh!' she squealed, having bitten almost through her rubber gag. 'Mmm . . .'

Her belly fluttered, and come cascaded from her cunt. A new jet of strong pee hissed down her thighs, splattering the girls crowded beneath her loins, with their eyes on the erect clitoris, and torrent of cunt juice. Suze's flogged purple buttocks parted, extruding the bull's pizzle, shiny with her arse grease, from her writhing bum pucker. She groaned, as her torrent of pee was strengthened by a flood of her come, and the pizzle slipped completely from her anus, plopping onto MaBelle's left boot. The prisoners blushed, as they witnessed the forty-seventh canestroke, on the naked buttocks, bring the English girl to orgasm.

10

Girl Meat

Panting hoarsely, MaBelle ordered Annique and her nurses to escort the prisoners back to their duties. The girls lined up sulkily, their ankle hobbles clanking, and gleams of seeped come between their naked thighs; MaBelle told the nurses that any caught masturbating were to receive double thrashing. When the last bottom had swayed out of the hospital ward, MaBelle's fingers flew to her erect bare nipples, which she pinched savagely, while her breath came in hoarse gasps. Suze remained sobbing in suspension. Cpl Pette's skirt was undone, and hanging loosely from her waist, while both doctors played with her naked stump and quim, oozing copious come, beneath her tangled pubic thatch. She giggled, whispering to them, and placed a male hand inside her blouse, to feel her bare titties under her bra. Button by button, the blouse was completely opened, and the bra came off, with Pette's firm young breasts snapping to attention, the nipples hard and conically erect. MaBelle, meanwhile, stroked the bottom of the hanging girl, while her own fingers crept to her gash, and she began to masturbate with blatant vigour.

Dr Pance had three fingers in Pette's gash, and was masturbating her cunt and clitty, while Dr Morue had a finger in her arse crack, and Pette squealed as he penetrated her bumhole. They frigged the girl for several minutes, with caresses to her fleecy stump drawing throaty squeals, while Pette pinched and rubbed her nipples. MaBelle gazed at the masturbated corporal, while frotting herself more and more vigorously, with a stream of shiny come trickling down her thigh, past the hem of her uniform skirt, now moistened with her cunt's exudation. Her brow was scarlet, and dripping with perspiration.

'Damn you, Shard,' she hissed.

Snarling, with a rictus of her teeth, she knelt on the floor beneath Suze's suspended body, and began to tongue the hanging girl's cunt. Suze whimpered, as her loins jerked under the tongue's caress of her clitoris, and fresh spurts of come began to wet her thighs, slopping over MaBelle's lips and nose. The commandant's throat wobbled, as she swallowed every drop of Suze's gushed come. The two males ceased their frottage, and grasped Cpl Pette by the armpits and buttocks, throwing her over the barrel in the corner of the ward. Pette's squeals of protest were unaccompanied by any physical resistance; rather, she hung inert and pliant, as the males buckled her ankles and wrists into the blocks mounted on the floor, stretching her body over the barrel, with her naked bum spread wide and angled high.

'Gentlemen,' she cooed, 'whatever are you about?'

Vap!

'Ooh!' trilled the corporal, her thigh stump jerking, as her own strap lashed her on the bare.

Vap! Vap! Vap!

'Ooh! That hurts awfully.'

Her cry was of delighted surprise.

Vap!

'Oh . . .'

Vap!

'Ooh . . .'

Come trickled from the girl's cooze, wetting the top of her barrel, which rolled, at the impact of every heavy stroke from the strap, applied by Dr Morue. Her reddening bare buttocks wriggled energetically, squirming and writhing, so as to rub her clitty on the rough wood.

Vap! Vap!

'Ooh! Mm! Urrgh!'

Cpl Pette's exclamations of distress were stifled, as Dr Pance thrust his erect cock into her throat, and began to fuck her in the mouth.

'Suck, bitch,' snarled Dr Pance.

Her throat shuddered, and her lips puckered on the intruding flesh, as she sucked the cock, its entire shaft impaling her throat, so that her lips pressed the balls. *Vap! Vap!* Dr Morue lashed the squirming bare buttocks with the strap; come flowed from the girl's cooze, as her buttocks were striped with dark red weals, wide, from the strap, and puffing at the edges.

'Mm ... Mm ...' she gurgled, as her bare bum squirmed.

As Cpl Pette sucked Dr Pance's cock, Dr Morue took her thrashing to fifty lashes, after which her bare bum was a mass of crimson and purple bruises. MaBelle sucked the juice from Suze's flowing gash, with one eye on Pette's flogged bum, and her fingers vigorously wanking off at her own cunt, the lips and stiff clit swollen and slimy with come. Pette's cunt banged on the barrel, at each lash of the strap, and, as her wealed buttocks clenched, she rubbed her cunt and clit on the wood, before the next stroke jerked her up, with a squeal, muffled by the engorged cockmeat she sucked vigorously. Her face was red, and eyes popping, as she tongued the massive cock, and she jerked her head up and down, and from side to side, pulling at the organ, before slamming her face down on the balls, and sucking the cock to the back of her throat. Dr Morue threw aside the strap, and bared his own cock, massively erect like his fellated colleague's.

'Bitch. Slut,' he hissed, parting Pette's purple wealed buttocks, and stretching the perineum and anal pucker.

His peehole nuzzled the wrinkled anus bud, and he thrust his helmet inside, to the neck of the glans. Pette gurgled, as the cock rammed into her anal elastic, and her buttocks began to squirm anew, as she squeezed the invading cockshaft. A further thrust, and the cock impaled her to the full length of her anus, with only the balls visible beween her quivering arse cheeks. Her cheeks hollowed and swelled, as she sucked and chewed on Pance's cock, and at the same time, raised her buttocks to meet the thrusts of Morue's buggery. His hips slapped her buttocks;

155

his arse-greased cock slid fully from the anus, only the glans tip remaining inside the anal lips, before he plunged inside her in a new stroke, that rammed the root of her anus, to fill her rectum. Her buttocks and thigh stump quivered, as the doctor's tool impaled the bumhole.

'Mm! Mm!' Pette squealed.

Suze's eyes were wide, gazing at the amputee corporal flogged on her taut young bare, and savagely buggered. Suze's cunt flowed with come, as MaBelle's lips and tongue danced on her clitty, and her nose and chin butted the pink pouch meat, between the gash flaps. MaBelle masturbated, with her cunt lips spread, and her fingers pounding and nipping the engorged clit, while her fist thrust fully to the wombneck, emerging slopped with her gushing come. Dr Pance snatched the strap and, as the squirming amputee sucked his cock, lashed her across the bare back, using backhand and forehand strokes, and striking hard at short range – *Thwap! Thwap! Thwap!* – until the naked skin of her back was a welter of blotchy red bruises. Pette groaned and gurgled, her cunt basin writhing, to rub her clit on the barrel, as Morue slammed her buttocks in buggery; come flowed beneath her squirming loins, and dripped down the curved wood.

Morue gasped, and grunted; a bubbling froth of creamy spunk spurted from the girl's stretched arse pucker, as he spermed inside her anus. Pance groaned, as the girl sucked his bursting stiff cock to spurt; a creamy froth drooled from her sucking lips, and his spunk jetted into her, filling her throat and mouth. Her throat bobbed, as she swallowed the spunk. MaBelle continued her masturbation, fingerfucking her own gash, as her tongue and lips fastened on the whole width of Suze's quim, and her teeth began to chew both the cunt flaps and clit nubbin. Suze howled, behind her gag, biting further into the rubber. MaBelle grunted in the onset of orgasm; as Suze's loins wriggled in the clutching teeth of her gamahucheuse, come spurted from her cunt, drenching MaBelle's face, and drool seeped from the corners of her mouth. Suze's belly fluttered, and she gasped, sobbing, in a new climax. MaBelle moaned, as her own orgasm ebbed, then rose, and wiped her mouth.

'You dirty, submissive slut,' she snarled. 'You masturbating bitch. We can well do without your kind.'

She turned to the two males, now disengaged from the
sweat-drenched body of the coporal, glowing with welts on
her flogged back and bum.

'Do we have a deal, gentlemen?' she asked them. 'The
amputee slut?'

Both smiled, and nodded agreement, as they lit cigarettes, the lighter poked in Pette's dripping cunt, and the
gasping girl obliged once more to make flame. When both
cigarettes were lit, there was a sizzle, as the flame was
extinguished by a new ooze of come from her slit. Cpl Pette
let her head flop, as she licked her lips of the fellated
doctor's drooled come.

'And the other one,' said Morue, indicating Suze.

'She is a demanding submissive,' warned MaBelle,
smoothing her skirt over her slimed cunt, and pushing her
titties back into her bra, but neglecting to button up her
blouse.

The doctors prescribed wine and cake; Nathalie Delvoix,
nude and hobbled, brought the refreshments, and they ate
and drank, holding a glass of wine, for Suze to sip.

Dr Pance looked at the wobbling melons of Nathalie's
bare arse.

'That, one, now . . .' he began, but was stopped by his
colleague.

'Next time,' said Morue. 'We could easily take all of
them, but think of our credibilty as connoisseurs.'

He leered at MaBelle.

'We could take *that* prime cunt, for example.'

MaBelle's nostrils flared, and she paled.

'You disgust me,' she spat. 'If I didn't need your filthy
cash . . . do your business with this slut, take them both,
and be away.'

Dr Pance tut-tutted, as he pushed aside his medical
gown, revealing a newly stiffened cock, bulging and red,
with the purple shiny glans winking at MaBelle. Dr Morue
did the same. They helped MaBelle cut Suze from her
bonds, and draped her over a flogging rail, with her

bottom in the air. Wracked by choking sobs, Suze offered no resistance. Dr Pance thrust his fingers into Suze's cunt, and took them out, slopped with her come. He spread her bum cheeks, and greased her anus with her own fluid. Suze hung on her rail, groaning, and without bonds. As the doctor's fingers lubricated her anus, she jerked, whimpering. Her hair hung low, masking her face, with the shredded rubber ball still between her teeth. The doctor tickled her anus bud with his peehole, churning the glans around her anal crevice, and then she gurgled, as his massive cock, still slimed with spunk and Pette's drool, plunged to her rectum, and began to bugger her with fierce, slapping strokes. Morue, monstrously erect, grabbed MaBelle, and ripped off her skirt.

'What?' she shrieked.

He slapped her across the mouth with the back of his hand, and she began to sob, but did not resist, as he thrust her down across Pette's crouching back, and ordered her to spread her buttocks. She obeyed. Suze faced her, and the two girls' eyes met; each blushed fiery red.

'You'll pay for this – ahh!' MaBelle squealed, as Morue's cock drove into her anus, and he began to arse-fuck her.

'It's what you want, you vixen,' he hissed.

'Oh, no . . .' she whimpered, 'please, be gentle with me.'

Pausing for sips of wine, the two males buggered their victims for over seventeen minutes, with both girls groaning and shuddering under the stiff cocks pounding their arses, and their tears flowing. Come flowed from both cunts; the hospital ward echoed with hand spanks. Suze wriggled and jerked, as the doctor's cock impaled her, but her whimpers of pain softened to a bleating, gasping moan of pleasure. MaBelle cursed her buggering male.

'Oh, it hurts so,' MaBelle shrieked. 'You bastard . . . you'll never get away with this . . . you're splitting me in two . . . oh, it hurts. Don't stop. You bastard! Yes! Ah . . . Ah . . .'

Suze groaned, as Pance's spunk filled her anus, and saw MaBelle grimace, as Morue's cock spurted its cream into her deepest rectum. Morue was up swiftly, and wiped his cock on MaBelle's hair, before dressing. Suze wriggled her cunt basin, spraying drips of her copious come, as a sign that she needed to be wanked off – but already, Pance, too, was wiping his slimed cock on her hair, and getting ready to depart. Both doctors delivered final slaps to the groaning MaBelle's bottom, and her thighs rippled, releasing globules of spunk and arse grease that had trickled from her buggered anus. Morue threw an envelope on the floor.

'The money is correct, slut,' he said. 'Sorry we haven't time to give you the thrashing you really want.'

'Oh!' MaBelle exclaimed, her face beetroot red. 'There will be no next time. I didn't come. You monsters!'

MaBelle's hand scrabbled in her slimed gash, as she frigged herself. The doctors laughed, shrugging. Lifting Cpl Pette and Suze, they bound both girls in ropes and halters, fastened together, and placed Suze's ankles in a hobble bar, with Cpl Pette permitted a crutch. Nude, they were paraded through the camp, down to the boat waiting at the river. Prisoners on work detail pelted them with mud, and Mimi, laughing, from her trench, landed slimy gobbets on Suze's face, titties and cunt. Tears streamed down Suze's face. Behind them, voices floated from the hospital.

'Jealous, Annique? Jealous, you little pervert? I'll give you cause to be jealous.'

Vap! Vap! Vap!

'*Ah! Mlle commandante . . .*' Annique wailed.

The doctors shrugged, and lit cigarettes, from a lighter manipulated by Cpl Pette's slit.

'Always the same,' said Dr Pance.

'Till the next time,' said Dr Morue.

'It would be satisfying to give the perverted cow what she really wants, a thrashing to the bone.'

'If that slut's arse was properly flogged, she would no longer need to gloat over the flogging of others. She would not be hungry and frustrated, and our best supplier of girl meat.'

159

Dr Morue slapped Suze's bare croup, right on her puffiest, darkest weals, then stubbed his cigarette in the slimy crevasse of mud, between her cunt folds.

'You won't be hungry and frustrated, where you are going, slut,' he said.

Suze managed to control her sobbing, a day into the voyage upriver, but still snuffled and sighed, during her workday. Pette and Suze had to keep the thirty-foot boat spotless, and spent most of the day crouching, with buckets, cloths and sponges. The amputee proved adept at propelling herself across a wet floor, reclining on her stump, and using her one leg as both rudder and sail. Sometimes, the doctors deprived them of cleaning things, and made them swab the decks with their bare breasts, then wriggle their loins, to use their cunt fleeces as mops and drying cloths. Their food, which they also had to prepare, was soup with some mushy tuber. Drs Morue and Pance spent most of the time on deck with their fishing rods, drinking wine or pastis, and smoking cigarettes. Their food was grilled fish, which had to be gutted and cooked by the captive girls, who were forbidden to cleanse their skin of the filthy, fish-stinking mess, for several hours, with the Frenchmen laughing that the two cunts smelled like cunts. Both girls spent the entire day roped, or hobbled, or both; there was no time at which they had freedom of movement, but were always fastened to a post, or rail, by their waists, ankles, or necks. They remained naked throughout the sweltering day, but at night were permitted a flour sack, as covering.

When the doctors wanted a break from fishing, they stood over the crouching girls, canes poised over their bare bottoms, with occasional lashes on the bare, to encourage them in their work. There was no objection to their talking, while they slaved, but laziness was punished by a formal caning: each girl received at least one caning of ten on the bare, every day, the punishment being carried out on deck, with some ceremony. She bowed to her chastiser, then assumed the position for caning, with buttocks wide, and hands clinging to the guard rail. As Suze winced under the smarting cuts to her bare – now bruised beyond cosmetic repair, she bitterly supposed – she gazed out at the green, chirping jungle, shimmering in the heat haze, and unchanging, as it flowed serenely past their boat. Cpl Pette was caned lying on her back, with her leg draped over a rail, and her stump waggling in the air, as she took the slices to her buttocks, thighbacks, and, frequently, right in her perineum, or on the lips of her cunt. She became very red in the face, as she was caned, but, unlike Suze, never whimpered.

Suze could not restrain her sobs and squeals, as rods lashed her bare buttocks. After taking her caning, Suze alone was required to make a 'spectacle –' to masturbate in the open air, for the enjoyment of the doctors and Cpl Pette, who seemed at those times to be more their ally than their captive. At night each slept in a doctor's cabin, roped or chained to the foot of his bunk, and with her hands tied behind her back, to prevent her masturbating. A tug on Suze's neck chain was an instruction to join the doctor on his bunk, and, without speaking, which was forbidden, to turn over and spread her buttocks. She received a savage buggery at least twice a night, for both men were virile and voracious: they really were doctors, and, as Suze shortly discovered from Cpl Pette, were doctors of the French Foreign Legion. The doctors swapped girls every night for a week.

'You don't have to be unfriendly,' Pette said. 'Is it because I whipped you? Then I made you abase yourself, by tonguing me. I dare say a girl can't forget that. Taking a whipping from another girl is shameful, yes? From a man, it's different. It is the normal way of things, for a man to whip a girl. Well, I've no authority here, as you can see. I'm to be a sex slave, same as you.'

'A what . . . ?' Suze gasped.

'A service girl, in the legion brothel, at the base upriver, near the border with Brazil. You see how lusty these legionnaires are. Well, of course, they need a brothel full of girls. They are real men, they want a woman for the power of her arse and cunt, and are not seduced by some plastic image of a photo mannequin.'

She spat the last words with contempt, then smiled.

'An amputee is not handicapped, in their view, but is all the sexier for her *unijambisme*. And if I had a second amputation ... anyway, brothel service is the fate of all inmates given a release date. It was so funny, to see the sluts embark, only not to freedom, but to slavery. You see, girl prisoners either graduate to become staff officers, like me, or else are sold into slavery. Every officer in the camp including MaBelle, is a former inmate.'

Suze asked what had caused MaBelle to be imprisoned.

'Prostitution, probably. But all records are destroyed. Once a girl is an inmate, that is all she is, and the past is forgotten. Paris doesn't know about us, even Cayenne doesn't. Brute males are the only power in this land. There is no escape.'

'Oh ...' Suze wailed, bursting into tears.

Pette looked at her in disgust.

'Stop blubbing, bitch,' she snapped. 'You have what you want. Caned on the bare, fucked in the arse and shamed, and put to work as the slave of men.'

'That's not what I want!' Suze cried. 'I wish I was in England, free to walk amongst the flowers and meadows.'

'Are you sure?' said Cpl Pette, smiling. 'It's what I want. That's why I seduced MaBelle, and persuaded her to sell me. I'll always find a buyer, with my hard bum, and my amputation, and my quim, with its big juicy petals, ripe as an orchid's. Didn't you like licking my quim? I know you did. All girls do, as well as males. You thought me dominant, and so I am. I love whipping girls, and seeing them squirm and weep. But it works the other way, too. I can switch to being the submissive, and relish the cane on my own bare. It is the fact of shame and whipping that matter, not whose bottom squirms. I see my own flogged arse from the outside, that's the trick. And when a girl is smarting with welts, and she has cock after cock inside her hole, why, that is the best of all. Imagine your future, slut – whipped, shamed and arse-fucked.'

Cpl Pette licked her lips.

'No!' Suze hissed, her breasts slopping in the suds on the floor. 'I must escape.'

Pette waggled her stump, in the direction of the jungle.

'Feel free,' she sneered. 'That side of the river is Surinam. Swim across the border, if you like, and see how they treat you. Girl meat is just girl meat, anywhere in this wilderness. There is talk of another power, beyond the legion – an overlord, on the frontier with Brazil, a true master, with a fabulous pleasure palace, and a tribe of girl slaves, kept naked and chained, humiliated and beaten almost beyond endurance.'

Her eyes sparkled.

'They say that if a girl tries to escape his regime of constant whipping and buggery, she is amputated, and her humilation increased tenfold.'

Cpl Pette's tongue lolled from her slack lips; her eyes glazed and hooded.

'Corporal,' Suze said, 'what's wrong?'

'Look at my cunt, slut,' panted Pette. 'I'm wet. Oh, wank me off, please.'

Her hand fell to her open, juicing cunt, and the one-legged girl began to masturbate, her stump jerking, as she frotted her clit, and pinched the swollen folds of her wet cooze, exuding shiny pearls of come.

'Please, Suze, wank me off,' she gasped.

Suze stretched out her fingers, and touched the amputee's juicing gash. Pette removed her own hand, and clamped Suze's over the clit, rubbing it there, until Suze took up the rhythm, and frotted Pette's cunt of her own accord. Her free hand crept down her quivering belly, to her cunt; as she masturbated the writhing, drooling amputee, she masturbated her own swelling clit, gasping, as her wrist slimed with rapidly oozed come. Pette grasped her nipples, swollen to stiff cones; she pinched the buds, and slapped them, harder and harder, until she was spanking her own titties. She balled four fingers, and fisted Pette's dripping cunt, driving her knuckles to the wombneck, while thumbing the erect nubbin. Suze's own masturbation was a simple clit-rubbing, but sending such shocks of pleasure through her body, that she gasped as harshly as the wanked amputee, and soon, both girls lay on the deck, wriggling and panting, as Suze's fingers brought them both to shuddering, mewling climax. A shadow fell over the two bodies, soaked in sweat and come.

'Well,' said Dr Morue, 'masturbating, like the sluts you are. That earns you both a whipping. Lucky for you, Miss Suzette, that you have reached journey's end. You, Pette, have further to go, as we can get a better price for you upstream. Your penalty for unauthorised masturbation is a caning of fifty on the bare, as Suzette's punishment, and your own punishment, a cunt-caning, upside down in suspension, with spread bare gash.'

Pette's eyes glazed, and she panted, licking her teeth.

'Is the slut to flog me, and add to my shame?' she gasped.

'Miss Suzette shall not have the pleasure of witnessing your punishment,' said Morue. You are to prepare her body bag at once. If your work is satisfactory, you shall be permitted to masturbate again, for our enjoyment, after your flogging.'

'Yes, master,' murmured Cpl Pette. 'Thank you, master.'

Numbly, Suze allowed the amputee to zip her, without protest, in a heavy canvas sack, perforated for breathing. She was trussed by ropes at her ankles and wrists, the ropes being drawn together by a tight chain painfully pressed between the lips of her cunt. She was gagged with a rubber ball, secured by a cord around her nape. Her squeals, as her body was jolted over the deck, ashore, then over rough stones, were muted by her tight ball gag. There was the sound of Morue's voice, and girls' voices, strangers; then Suze was hoisted, and carried on shoulders, in an ascending path. After two hours' jolting, she was put down on a soft surface, and her bag unzipped. The air was warm, but not sultry. She blinked in the light, and looked around, to see two female faces staring down at her.

One of the females was in a doctor's white smock, over blue skirt and nylons, and blue blouse, stained with sweat, and open to the third button, revealing massively swelling golden breasts, supported by a lacy scalloped bra in pink satin. She wore white calfskin boots, coming up to just below her knees. The other wore nurse's uniform, with a pretty navy bonnet, white skirt and blouse, and stockings and shoes also white. Both women were honey blond, and had skirts clinging tightly to ripe, swelling croups; their skirts were very short, so that the tops of both women's stockings were visible, along with garter straps, the doctor's being pink, and the nurse's, white. The doctor was tall, of Suze's own height, with the nurse an inch taller. Suze was lying on a bed, in what seemed to be a clinic. Her eyes opened wide in fright, as the nurse removed her ball gag and restraints, shifting her, to expose her wealed bare buttocks.

'You speak English?' said the doctor, in a guttural accent; Suze nodded.

'Good,' the doctor said. 'We may use a decent tongue.'

'Those wicked men,' the nurse said. 'Don't worry, I am nurse Aldwine, and this is Dr Fredegund. We shall look after you.'

'A nurse,' Suze croaked. 'No ... please ...'

Dr Fredegund laughed.

'We are real medics,' she said. 'We are concerned only for your health, not for your chastisement.'

Politely, she motioned Suze to lie on her belly, and, when her wealed buttocks were exposed to view, the two medics tut-tutted in sympathy.

'Who did this?' said Dr Fredegund.

'Why, the prison commandant, MaBelle,' stammered Suze, 'and Cpl Pette – she was a prisoner on the same boat – and Drs Morue and Pance ... oh!'

She burst into tears.

'I suppose the males had anal sex with you?' Dr Fredegund said gently.

'Oh, please, don't,' Suze wailed, and the doctor sighed.

'Please lie very still,' she said, and Suze gasped, as Fredegund's rubber-sheathed and greased finger penetrated her anus, filling her rectum, and probed the arse root for a full minute, before withdrawing.

'It is as I feared,' she said. 'You have been the victim of vicious and prolonged buggery, as well as thrashing on the buttocks, and, evidently, whipping on the back.'

'The swine,' said nurse Aldwine. 'How dare they sell us damaged goods.'

'Nurse,' chided the doctor. 'Remember our mission. It is precisely damaged goods, as you inelegantly put it, that we must nurture back to full womanhood.'

'Yes, doctor,' mumbled Aldwine, blushing.

She gave Suze a vessel of water, from which she drank in gulps, and then massaged oils and creams into the whipweals on Suze's body.

'It will take some time for these bruises to fade,' said Dr Fredegund, 'but you have no structural damage – even your anus is remarkably resilient, or, malicious tongues might say, accommodating. You should be fit for work in the community at once.'

'Work? I . . . I don't understand,' Suze blurted. 'What community? Where am I? Please don't send me back to digging muck . . . oh, it was so awful.'

Gasping, she sobbed the story of her ordeals at the prison.

'I've been the victim of so much unfairness,' she concluded, sobbing. 'I don't know why. Every time, I'm hurt more, and the only way I can cope, is to blank the memory of all my pain.'

The faces of her two guardians were grave, but creased into kindly smiles.

'There are no filthy dormitories, full of naked sluts, and no trenches to dig in Lady Saxworfa's,' said Fredegund. 'Our plateau is healthier than the foetid lowlands, and our accommodations comfortable. You will work at embroidery, gardening, flower arrangement, or social administration, perhaps. We are a foundation dedicated to instilling the ladylike arts in our guests. Such disciplinary measures, as regrettably become necessary, are ladylike and tasteful. A mild spanking settles most offences or disputes, we find. Nothing like the horrors you have been used to, under male oppression.'

166

'French oppression,' interjected Aldwine bitterly.

'That is usually, though not always, the case,' said the doctor. 'We must keep an open mind. Brazilian males, too, have their victims, with their fondness for ... anal practices. We have all sorts of girls here.'

'How long must I stay?' asked Suze.

'Until we issue a social-medical aptitude certificate, attesting your fitness to survive, by submissive and ladylike means, in a male world,' Fredegund said. 'Polite accomplishment is the ultimate weapon in the female's arsenal.'

She swooped, to poke with tweezers in Suze's pubic fleece.

'This is very good,' she said. 'You are a natural blond, so dyestuffs will be unnecessary. It is scientifically proven that blond females, especially of generous physical endowment, succeed more than others. Your endowments, especially the buttocks, are more than generous – spectacular, I might say.'

She laughed shyly.

'There are two schools of thought, here at Lady Saxworfa's,' she added. 'Those who consider big breasts as the summit of female enhancement, and those who favour large buttocks. You have both. As medical staff, we do not pronounce on social questions.'

'There are no men here?' Suze asked.

Fredegund and Aldwine exchanged glances.

'No ... not here,' the doctor said. 'You have been in an all-female prison, Miss Suzette, and know that female friendships are inescapable in single-sex institutions. Your dossier says, furthermore, that you attended an all-girls' English boarding school. I dare say corporal punishment, probably bare-bottom caning, was on the curriculum.'

Suze blushed, and agreed that at school, she had become used to chastisement on the bare.

'And masturbation, I expect?' Fredegund continued coolly. 'We know what happens in schools, and prisons. Friendships at Lady Saxworfa's are encouraged, within the bounds of decorum, as long as they do not tend to exclusivity, or threaten the social fabric. Masturbation, the natural concomitant of such friendships, is actively encouraged. A girl need not be furtive in her pursuit of pleasure. I trust I do not shock you.'

'Why, no,' Suze blurted, blushing deeply. 'As a matter of fact . . . I don't know why, but . . . I masturbate quite a lot.'

Fredegund slapped herself on the bottom, and laughed.

'You don't know why?' she said. 'It's because you are a healthy, normal, Anglo-Saxon girl, that's why. Your love of frigging is also in your dossier, and I am glad you confirm it. Tell me the last time you masturbated.'

'Really! I . . .' Suze gasped.

'I am a doctor,' said Fredegund.

Suze admitted that she had frigged only a few hours earlier, and related her episode with the insistent and lustful Cpl Pette.

'You are undoubtedly under tension. I recommend that you masturbate again, and gain a few hours' untroubled sleep.'

Swallowing hard, and blushing, Suze agreed that a frig would relax her.

'Go on, then,' said Dr Fredegund.

Doctor and nurse gave no sign of leaving.

'I . . . I'm used to masturbating in private,' Suze blurted. The doctor smiled.

'I wish to medically observe your psychological and physical composure, under stimulus,' she said, 'so consider masturbation my prescription. It is, in fact, my most common prescription, far more efficacious than man-made chemicals. You must get used to one convention, here at Saxworfa's. Mutual or group masturbation is encouraged, but solitary masturbation, unshared by another girl, is frowned on, as *unfolkish*. Please begin when you are ready.'

Suze's eyes lighted on a row of implements, that looked like cricket bats or pingpong bats, together with several straps and belts, hanging in a row, on the infirmary wall. The straps were mostly buckled, or studded; the wooden implements had round holes bored in their blades. She asked their purpose.

'They are disciplinary tools,' said Fredegund, 'for chastisement of the bottom. The holes are to permit passage of air, and increase the painful impact of the wood on bare skin. Some girls find it difficult to pleasure themelves, without the stimulus of a mild spanking on the bare, administered by nurse Aldwine. Then, there are the frigwenches, who pleasure themselves only too readily, in a rather unladylike fashion, and require real chastisement to temper their ardour. I am sure you are no frigwench, but, if you prefer, before you masturbate . . . ?'

She gestured towards the rack, causing her left breast to thrust from its bra cup, revealing a strawberry nipple, its bud hard and erect.

'No, no . . .' Suze gulped.

Her fingers crept down her quivering belly, and fastened on her clitoris; as she gazed up at the bared breast hillocks of the two blond girls, she got two fingers inside her slimy pouch, and began a slow frigging. Her cunt flaps were already wet.

11

Frigwench

'I admire her prowess,' said Dr Fredegund.

She and her nurse peered at Suze's slit, their noses inches from the clitoris, which Suze's fingers had brought to erection. Come dripped from the squelching flaps of Suze's gash, and her fingers penetrating the inside of her pouch. Suze lay on the hospital bed, gasping as she wanked off, and with her back arched, thighs spread wide, and toes clutching the edge of the bed. Her legs and belly quivered, as her cunt poured shiny come onto the sheet, staining it with a wide damp pool.

'She is a seasoned masturbatress,' said nurse Aldwine.

'Pleasantly shameless,' added the doctor, 'although she must learn to control herself outside medical premises. I particularly like her manipulation of the clitoris, while at the same time thrusting inside the vagina.'

'She juices heavily,' said nurse Aldwine.

'And an exhibitionist,' said Fredegund. 'She is better at the technique of self-pleasuring than any other English girl we have had. Note the rhythmic thrusting of the fingers inside the pouch. Three fingers spanned, so as to stretch the cunt walls, while the nails pound her wombneck. Also, the thumbnail, alternately stroking and slicing the nubbin. That is advanced technique, combining pain and pleasure. I use it myself, sometimes.'

'I have never seen a girl juice so much,' gasped Aldwine.

Suze thrust her buttocks up and down, mimicking the motions of fucking, jabbing her pouch, as she rubbed her clitty. Eyes closed, she moaned, with spirals of drool seeping from both corners of her mouth, tightened in a rictus, to bare her teeth.

'Uhh ... Uhh ...' she panted.

Nurse Aldwine licked her teeth, her face blushing red. She pushed damp strands of hair from her brow.

'How wise you are, doctor,' she murmured. 'The girl obviously needed to masturbate, to relieve the stress of her journey, and that horrid French prison. If we can console just one tortured girl, then our work is not in vain. Look, she loses herself in her own pleasure. I wonder what she sees, as she wanks off.'

'Let's ask her,' said Dr Fredegund, wiping sweat from her face. 'Hypnosis is unnecessary. In her state of erotically altered consciousness, any inhibitors should vanish. Miss Suzette, please describe to us your fantasies, as you masturbate. It is for your medical dossier.'

Suze began to moan, and thresh her head, causing her naked breasts to spill from side to side.

'Mm ... mmm ...' she moaned. 'Girls in an English meadow, flowers and the perfume of the breeze, bare bums splashing in the stream, buttercups and daisies ...'

Her fingers twitched, pounding the swollen wet lips of her cunt, as she masturbated faster.

'The male comes, big brute of male, oh please, no ... , no, don't spank, it hurts me on the bare, my bum is so sore, oh yes, more, cock so hard, split me, oh, yes, big cock, how I need it ... spank my bum, make me squirm, master, whip my bare to ribbons, please fuck me in my hole, burst my bum with your cock ...'

The medics looked at each other, both girls' faces beaded with sweat, and their blond ringlets dancing in the breeze from the whirring ceiling fan.

'Anal fantasies,' murmured Dr Fredegund. 'Together with fantasies of spanking.'

'More than spanking,' added Aldwine, her tight nurse's skirt shifting, as she pressed her thighs together.

'Whip me on the bare, make me wriggle,' Suze gasped, as her cunt basin jerked, and her fingers frotted her

171

dripping gash. 'Whip me hard, oh, so good, hurts so much, bugger me, master, fuck your girl slave in the arse and make her grovel.'

'Grovel?' said nurse Aldwine.

'Shamefully submit,' replied the doctor. 'Do you think she is a frigwench?'

Suze's mouth flapped open and shut.

'Bugger me, while I swallow whore's come, master,' she gurgled. 'Let me lick their cunts and drink their juice. No shame is too great for your dirty slave. Oh, yes, yes . . .'

She grasped her pubic bone, squeezing her cunt, with her thumb pounding the nubbin, and all four fingers reaming inside her slit. Aldwine began to breathe heavily, and lick her lips.

'I don't like the word "dirty",' said Dr Fredegund. 'It implies a negative attitude.'

'Can't you see the slut is a frigwench?' said Aldwine. 'An addicted masturbatress, for sure – that clitoris is engorged by frotting. Go on, lustful frigwench, wank off all you can, for the mistress will lash you, when she catches you at solitary games.'

'Let us not condemn her unfairly,' said Fredegund.

Suze's tongue flapped over her gasping lips.

'Mm . . . Mm . . .' she gasped, 'come all over me, slut, sit on my face, press me with your dirty bumhole . . . stick your cock up my bum, sir, fuck me in the hole, split my arse with your tool and spunk in me, fill me up with all your dirty spunk . . .'

'That word again,' said Dr Fredegund. 'Nurse Aldwine, did you perform your normal masturbation this morning?'

'Why, my roommate Elfina was in a hurry, doctor,' answered Aldwine. 'We normally wank off together, so, in her absence, I omitted the practice.'

Watching Suze's wriggling masturbation, both women blushed red. The doctor pursed her lips. Aldwine rubbed herself between the thighs, where a damp patch stained her skirt. Dr Fredegund nodded, unfastened her skirt, let it slide down her stockinged legs, and stepped out of it. At once, she removed her blouse, and let it too fall. She stood, in bra, panties, stockings and sussies, and whispered to the nurse that she, too, had neglected her morning masturbation. They smiled.

'Strictly therapeutic, doctor?' said Aldwine, and the doctor nodded, rolling down her panties.

Aldwine reached towards the rack of disciplinary instruments, her hand passing over each one, until Fredegund nodded again. Aldwine took down a leather strap, studded along one side.

'The legionnaire's belt? Are you sure, doctor?' she asked, hesitantly. 'What if the mistress were to visit?'

'It is her hour for correction of miscreants,' said Fredegund, 'and she never misses that. This is my surgery, and treatment is strictly therapeutic, remember.'

Without removing her boots, she vaulted onto the bed, and squatted over Suze's face, before lowering her buttocks, so that her cunt and perineum squashed the masturbating girl's mouth and nose.

'Mm ...' Suze moaned, her face trapped under Fredegund's buttocks, as her fingers frotted her cunt faster.

'My, she's adept,' gasped Fredegund. 'She has her tongue right into my anus, good and stiff.'

Aldwine lifted her skirt, and fastened it with a pin stuck through the left cup of her brassiere. She rolled down her white panties, and stepped out of them, squeezing the garment, to wring a few drops of come, before dropping them to the floor. Her clitoris was stiff and extruded amid her bushy cunt mane, with the gash flaps swollen, and oozing juice. She touched her clitoris, and stifled a gasp. Dr Fredegund shifted forward, so that her cunt was directly over Suze's lips, and her bottom raised slightly, to present its entire nudity. Her cunt basin began to writhe, as Suze tongued her clit.

'Oh, yes,' gasped Fredegund. 'She's got her tongue on my nubbin, with her mouth sucking my whole quim lips.'

Aldwine's fingers vigorously masturbated her flowing cooze. She lifted the strap, and brought it, whistling, through the air, to land across Fredegund's bare buttocks. *Whap!*

'Mm!' she grunted, as a wide pink weal appeared on her bare.

Whap!

'Oh, yes . . .' she moaned, wriggling her cunt on Suze's tongue.

Whap! Whap! Two more livid bruises from the nurse's strap appeared on Fredegund's bare buttocks, which clenched, and began to squirm. At the sound of each stroke, Suze's loins and croup jumped, and she moaned, with her fingers pounding her clit and cooze lips. Come dripped from Fredegund's gamahuched quim, sliming the masturbating girl's upturned crimson face. *Whap! Whap!*

'Oh, yes,' gasped Fredegund. 'That really hurts. The strap stings beautifully. Whip me harder, Aldwine. Are you wanking off?'

'Of course, doctor,' panted the nurse, her fingers delving in her come-slopped cunt, and wanking her clitoris with firm, grinding thumbstrokes.

Whap! Whap!

'Ah! Yes . . . good . . .' Fredegund groaned. 'Oh! My bum's on fire, I'll come any minute, with this slut's wicked tongue in my cunt. I've never been so wet! Whip me, nurse, whip me, whip my bare bum raw.'

Whap! Whap!

'Oh! How it hurts! It's super. Please, Aldwine, beat my bum scarlet.'

'Yes, doctor. I think this girl is a true frigwench.'

'That is for a doctor, not a slavey nurse, to decide. Do you want a whipping, you impudent slut?' hissed Fredegund.

'You know I fear pain, doctor,' blurted Aldwine.

Whap! Whap! Fredegund's firm bare nates reddened with puffy flesh, as her spanked arse wriggled on top of Suze's face, shiny with the cunt slime gushing from Fredegund's quim.

'Yet you like spanking girls on the bare,' she gasped.

'It is therapeutic for my patients, doctor,' Aldwine replied.

Whap! Whap!

'*Ooh*,' Fredegund whimpered, as her bare fesses darkened with bruises.

Aldwine wanked off, with her cooze dripping copious shiny come onto her bedraggled panties. *Whap! Whap!* Fredegund's whipped bare nates flamed crimson, with puffy, blotched bruises, darkening to puce. The welts covered the entire surface of her buttocks, which shivered and clenched, as the strap cast its shadow on the striped globes, throwing the ridges of welted skin into stark relief, against the smooth satin of the arse cheeks.

'I'm not your patient, bitch,' said Fredegund. 'I am your superior. I know your own mucky secret. Whip me harder!'

Whap! Whap! Moaning, Suze wanked off, as Fredegund's slimed cunt squashed her face. Her tongue delved into the doctor's wet slit, while with nose and teeth she frotted the clitty pressing on her. Suze's fingers danced inside her own dripping gash, pounding the stiff clitty. *Whap! Whap!*

'Oh,' moaned Fredegund, 'I'm going to come, all over the slut's face.'

Whap! Whap! Her buttocks jumped under the strap.

'Ooh . . . yes . . .'

Nurse Aldwine masturbated hard, as she whipped.

'Have I your permission to come, doctor?' she asked.

Whap! Whap!

'Ah! Oh, yes,' groaned the squirming Fredegund.

'I find it difficult . . . you know . . .'

'What? Whip me, bitch, harder . . . Oh, yes, that. You filthy slut. Wait . . .'

Whap! Whap!

'Ahh . . . ah! Ah!' Fredegund shrieked, her belly heaving, with spurts of come gushing over Suze's face.

Suze gasped, gurgling in the oily girl come that drenched her mouth, and her cunt basin writhed, as she fingered her erect clitty, to bring herself off, in time with the writhing gash atop her face. *Whap! Whap!* Aldwine continued to whip Fredegund on the bare, while she climaxed, and as soon as the doctor's wails of coming had ebbed to sobs, Aldwine crouched on the floor, with her bottom up. Dr

Fredegund slid from Suze's face, and mounted Aldwine, who moaned, and continued to wank off. As the doctor rode her like a pony, a heavy stream of pee hissed from Fredegund's cunt, splashing the nurse's naked buttocks, and soaking her arse cleft and exposed quim.

'Ahh ... yes ...' gasped the nurse, masturbating furiously, as her rider bucked on her bare back. 'Yes ... piss on me ... oh, yes!'

Her legs quivered, and she groaned in little staccato yelps, as she orgasmed, her bum, thighs and cunt dripping with golden piss. When she had finished trembling, her rider dismounted, and curled her lip, while running her fingers over the welts on her bruised bare bottom. The whole expanse of buttock flesh was lividly bruised by the strap; her face was scarlet, and twisted in a grimace. Aldwine turned her face up, and Fredegund squatted over the girl's head, bucking her loins, to send a final dribble of piss cascading over the nurse's face, and into her eager mouth. Suze raised herself on her elbows, wiping her face of Fredegund's come. The doctor smiled at Suze, as she wiped her wet cunt with nurse Aldwine's hair, causing the nurse to whinny in pleasure.

'We each have our therapies, Miss Suzette,' she said. 'I wonder what yours will prove to be?'

Aldwine grinned, licking Fredegund's piss from her lips.

'She is a common tart,' she said, leering. 'A frigwench.'

'Language, ladies, please,' said a female voice.

A tall young woman, carrying a jewelled cane and a parasol, stood in the doorway, her knuckles mimicking a knock, in the manner of a superior not obliged to knock. Her right hand caressed the ornate handle of her cane: in shining yellow gold, the figurine of a naked girl, hands behind her neck, in a model's pose, with her breasts and buttocks thrust out. The woman's honey blond hair was braided, and the braids coiffed up over her head, with strands of hair dancing over her ears, giving a girlish look to her twenty-something years. She wore a narrow one piece dress of cream silk, buttoned up to her neck, the thin fabric of its tube clinging tightly to her heavy buttocks and breasts, and outlining in every detail the apparatus of her high cut bikini panties, garter belt and straps, and her frilled stocking tops. Her gossamer bra clearly showed the large nipple plums, vividly extruded. She wore a waspie corset, pinching her waist to pencil thinness. The breasts swayed slightly as she breathed, making the big nipples roll beneath their filmy covering. Her skirt clung to mid-thigh, beneath which her long coltish legs, swathed in shiny bronze nylons, with chocolate seams, descended to cream shoes, matching her skimpy dress. Dr Fredegund and nurse Aldwine rose, smoothing down their hair and tucking their uniforms over their bottoms, then curtsied.

'Oh, mistress,' said the doctor. 'We were explaining Saxworfa's to the new entrant, Miss Suzette Shard.'

'I know who she is,' said the mistress, smiling, 'but must you begin your explanation with frigwenches? She shall find out about that unfortunate minority in due course. Never mind. What a lovely day! I have just taken Bodwenna for a most refreshing canter around the perimeter. Has this girl had her tea?'

'Not yet, mistress,' said Fredegund. 'I was conducting her medical examination.'

'Well, get the girl her tea, as soon as you can, and then send her to my study, not later than five o'clock,' said the mistress, smiling at Suze. 'She looks a strapping wench. I must chair a closed tribunal – a *vehmgericht* – with two wenches, and I need a fresh face, as disinterested party.'

'Portia and Gabi, mistress?' said nurse Aldwine.

'The same,' sighed the mistress, brushing a honey blond wisp from her brow, and, continuing the gesture, smoothing the sheer silk of her skirtlet over her buttocks. 'It will end in tears, of course, with forfeits for one, or both.'

She approached Suze, and held out her hand. Suze took the cool fingers, pressing hers. The mistress's eyes fell on Suze's striped bare bottom, shiny with come, and she clucked with her tongue, extruded from her teeth.

'Dear me, such bruises,' she murmured. 'I had rather hoped her dossier exaggerated. I see the nurse has applied ointment. May I?'

Without waiting for Suze's reply, she reached down, and began to stroke the naked buttocks, her fingernails resting in the deep ridges of Suze's cane weals. She paddled her fingertips in the skin gleaming with slimy come, and brought them to her nose, then licked them.

'The very best ointment,' she purred, gazing at Suze, who blushed. 'Fredegund has been the best of our doctors.'

She stroked Suze's come-slimed pubic fleece with the handle of her cane.

'A natural blond,' she said. 'I am so sorry that our new entrant is a victim of these beastly French, but hope that her bruises will inspire kindness towards others. Portia's and Gabi's process will surely end in whipping, and I want a merciful witness to the chastisement. I am no longer sure of my own impartiality, when presented with either of those impudent bare bottoms to cane. You wouldn't mind, Miss Suzette? I mean, it is entirely up to you. I'll quite understand, if you are put off at the prospect of witnessing a girl thrashed on the bare. Only, it would be such a help.'

She put her cane to her lips, and licked the golden handle, putting the buttocks of the sculpted girl in her mouth.

'N-no, mistress,' Suze blurted. 'I'll be glad to help.'

'Splendid,' said the honey blond mistress, with a smile.

She stepped to the door, and stood, rubbing her hand lightly over her croup, and turning slightly, so that the girls saw the ripple of her panties and garter belt over her taut bumflesh. She slapped her cane against the doorway, the shaft swishing, before cracking on the wood, and her breasts trembling at the stroke.

'Till five o'clock, then, Miss Suzette,' she said, licking her teeth.

Suze was given into the care of a wench, Warsweide, who took her to her new lodging: a shared room, with its own entrance, in a long hut thatched with leaves. There was no lock on the door, a light wooden panel, with a window at eye level. For the walk, Suze had a grey surgery sheet, to cover her nudity. Warsweide, nineteen years of age, was blond, like all the other wenches, with a long-legged, springy gait, that made her big breasts and buttocks bounce, under her skirtlet and clinging cotton blouse, both brightly patterned in flowery pastel colours. The wench wore no underthings, as the lightly pleated cotton skirtlet lay sheer on her buttocks, with no panty line marring the smooth ripeness of the fesses; at a particularly high step, Warsweide's skirtlet flew up, revealing her bare buttocks, tanned evenly with her legs. Her breasts jutted firm, bouncing tightly as she strode on her long tan legs, with no stockings, and her feet bare.

They passed through clearings, then tracks through dense shrubbery and arbours, before coming to the residence hut, in its own clearing. Birds sang all around, over the chirps and shrieks of the forest. They passed groups of blond girls, Warsweide's age, playing ball games, and wearing fluffy white socks and tennis shoes, but otherwise nude, save for short frilly skirtlets, also in white, bouncing up over their bare bottoms, as they jumped and lunged. Briefly glimpsed, their cunt basins revealed large, untrimmed pubic fleeces, blond like their manes, and the naked buttocks of some wenches shone pink with marks. One group of four competed at hula hoops, their naked breasts whirling, and their bums and quims gyrating furiously. Those girls had bottoms vividly coloured with dark blotches. Several of the wenches at play, sweating generously, with breasts bouncing and faces flushed, waved greetings to Suze and Warsweide.

'Oh . . . it's lovely,' Suze said, as she sat on her new bed, one of two, side by side.

The room was simple, with table and chair, two armoires, wash stand, and a simple metal cot.

'It's just like back at school,' she added, blushing.

Warsweide threw open her armoire, to show an array of simple attire like her own, skirts and tops in flowery patterns. There was one pair of black stiletto shoes, and one of white tennis shoes, together with two pairs of white fluffy ankle socks. From a coathanger hung a bulky sealed package, which, Warsweide said, was her costume for ceremonial occasions.

'No underclothes,' she said. 'Wenches don't have that privilege, which is reserved for seniors, who are officers of the *folkthing*. Wenches go barefoot, too, except for sports, ceremonies, and duties, when tennis shoes and socks, or high heels, are appropriate. If you'd like to change, I'll take you for your tea – I believe you must do duty at the mistress's *vehmgericht*?'

Suze nodded, and Warsweide gave a little shiver, making her titties bounce.

'We all have to do that, when we first arrive,' she said. 'Throwing us in at the deep end, she calls it. It is much easier, with a good tea in your belly. There is strawberry jam, today.'

Suze let her sheet fall to the bed, stood up, and inspected her new clothes. As she riffled her dresses, she looked over her shoulder, to see the wench's eyes on her bare bottom, and Warsweide licking her teeth. She said that Suze possessed a fine, strong Saxon arse. Under the washtable stood an aluminium bucket, shiny and new, and Warsweide said it was a chamber pot, to be emptied daily in the stream, which flowed rapidly downhill, into the river Maroni, several kilometres away.

'There are plentiful toilet facilities,' she said in her clipped accent. 'The mistress believes in healthy bowels for all wenches.'

'I feel I need to go now,' Suze said.

'We do not want to be late for tea,' Warsweide said, shrugging, and gesturing at the bucket.

Hesitantly, Suze squatted just above the metal rim, and pissed loudly, her pee echoing inside the bucket as she spurted. Her slit and pubic forest were on full show, and Warsweide stared at the jet of pee, steaming from her cunt lips.

'A good flow,' she said, approvingly.

'Oops! There's more,' Suze gasped, blushing, and her piss continued, accompanied by a plopping of several hard dungs from her anus.

Warsweide observed that her firm stools also would please the mistress.

'You liked school,' she said.

'I suppose I must have. They punished us quite severely, and it's hard to separate like from dislike. But I think of St Ursula's a lot. The countryside was so beautiful.'

'Punishment? You mean the cane? That is the way of your English girls' schools.'

'Yes,' Suze admitted.

'On the bare?' said the wench.

'Mostly,' said Suze, with a shiver.

Warsweide sighed, then smiled at Suze, with wide white teeth.

'How I envy you island Saxons,' she said. 'Most of us here are old Saxons. I am from Hamburg, for example. We have not the seasoning of you islanders, which is why we come to Lady Saxworfa's.'

She frowned.

'I said "come to",' she added quickly, 'when I should have said "stay at". Most of us are rescued, or bought, from the horrid French prison. It is clear that the mistress will favour you – your bottom bears the marks of endurance. You have been flogged on the bare, recently.'

Suze pursed her lips.

'I have been chastised rather a lot,' she said, 'though I didn't deserve it at all! I don't really like to talk about it.'

'That is a wench's privilege,' smiled Warsweide, 'although you will find you want to.'

Before Suze chose her dress, she sponged herself down with a basin of cold water, which she threw into the runnel, leading under the hut wall, which ended a foot above the ground, allowing breeze and light into the room. Warsweide watched, as Suze moistened and cleansed the crevices of her body, opening her legs, to sponge her gash and anus. The wench said that the washroom proper was at the end of the block, in the clearing, and that wenches were permitted a shower every morning; otherwise, they might bathe in the rock pool as often as they pleased. As she spoke, Warsweide slipped her hand under her blouse, and began to stroke her bare breasts, her eyes fixed on Suze's wet nude body.

'*Masturbieren, das macht nichts?*' she murmured. 'You don't mind if I masturbate? I'm not a frigwench, you know, but you have such a tempting arse. It is good for a wench to keep herself at peak stimulation. I got all wet, the moment I saw your lovely bum welts.'

Suze gulped, and went crimson.

'It's OK,' she said.

'You have time, too, if you are quick,' Warsweide drawled, her free hand reaching under her skirt, and beginning to frig her naked cunt.

Suze shook her head.

'Dr Fredegund did you,' Warsweide said, sweeping her fist in broad strokes across her cunt, and Suze nodded, blushing furiously.

She threw up her slit, and parted her legs, allowing Suze to see her wet pubic jungle, and the wide pink oyster of her cunt, spuming oily come over her wanking fingers.

'Show me your bum,' she whispered, and, trembling, Suze obeyed, thrusting her buttocks, and parting her thighs, so that her soiled anus and dangling cunt hairs were in the masturbating girl's full view.

Her fingers penetrated her gushing slit, with a thumb prodding her erect nubbin.

'Ahh . . .' she gasped, 'that is so good. 'I shall soon come . . . yes . . . yes . . . ooh!'

The wench's belly heaved, as come spurted from her cunt, her legs shot straight in front of her, and her gash flaps twitched, in the intensity of her orgasm. Suze averted her gaze, but kept snatching a peek at the wide, heavy cunt basin, shivering and spuming juice, in the German girl's frigged ecstasy. After wiping clean her dung–slimed bum-hole, she dressed quickly, selecting a flowery top and skirtlet in bright yellow and orange, while Warsweide pissed in her bucket, and cleaned her own vulva with her hand.

'I don't mean to be personal,' Suze said, 'but you brought yourself off very quickly. I . . . I admit that I play with myself a lot, but it takes me longer to come.'

'Practice,' said the blond wench, tossing her mane.

'Question of knowing which fantasies to summon. With your bottom before my eyes, I needed no fantasy.'

On the way to tea in the refectory, Warsweide told Suze that Lady Saxworfa's had existed for three hundred years, its founder having been a sixteenth-century slave, fleeing her English buccaneer master, only to be reenslaved by the French. She escaped from that servitude, to found Saxworfa's as a refuge for Saxon girls, escaped from slavery, the definition of that word broadened to include any oppression which a modern girl had cause to resent.

'Saxworfa was an Anglo-Saxon, speaking the Saxon language,' she said. 'Your English history does not speak of the masses of Anglo-Saxons, who still spoke the old tongue of the shires, right up to the nineteenth century, and who were obliged to deliver their wenches as slaves of their Norman conquerors. Their slavery, like all slavery of females, was sexual. Saxon wenches were known for their fortitude. They could endure flogging on the bare buttocks or back, and took male penetration of their little holes as their appointed lot. That is the underside of your English history, about which the books are silent. Wenches crossed the ocean, to be free here. In particular, free of male oppression. Nowadays, with so much thoughtless travelling, girls are no less the victims of males. That is why the mistress sets so much store by artful and frequent masturbation. It is the way a wench frees herself of males, in body and spirit.'

'But . . . what about frigwenches?' Suze exclaimed, as they opened the door of the refectory. 'I thought . . . you know . . . excessive diddling was forbidden.'

'Excess of any kind is forbidden,' said Warsweide. 'Slavery to self-pleasuring is no different from enslavement by the male. Why, some sluts would do themselves at the meal table, if they were allowed. Happily, they receive thoughtful treatment from the mistress.'

Warsweide smiled, and slapped herself on the bottom several times, and Suze blushed again, gulping.

'Excessive diddling means a whipping?' she said, and Warsweide nodded. 'But how does a girl know what is excessive?'

183

'She doesn't,' said the Saxon wench.

Tea was a plentiful banquet of scones and sandwiches, with various fruits and tinned cream, and real English tea to drink. Service was by wenches clad in traditional maids' uniforms, like those worn by the filler models, on board Cordovan's yacht. They smiled dutifully, as they teetered among the tea tables, on high heels, despite the sweat beading their faces, and moistening their tight blouses and crisp black skirts, over clinging nylon fishnets. The maids, like the thirty-odd girls taking tea, were all shades of blond, and their costumes contrasted with the informal frillies, or flowery pastel skirts and tops, of the stockingless and barefoot diners. Several of the wenches had elaborate foot-paintings, or colourful displays of varnished toenails. Suze and Warsweide sat at a peripheral table, but the two tables in the centre drew most attention; each was dominated, or presided over, by a sultry, tanned blond wench, with her blouse knotted up around her breasts, baring her midriff; the serving wenches treated them with deference. The dominant pair had breasts, thighs and buttocks noticeably larger than the wenches who chattered around them, and both scowled at Suze, when she entered. Unlike the barelegged company, they wore high heels over their bare feet.

'That is Portia Poole, and that one, Gabi Hassler,' Warsweide said, her mouth dripping scone crumbs. 'You'll be seeing more of them, at the *vehmgericht*. A pair of proper madams, as you islanders say.'

Portia was tall, her ripe titties spilling from their flimsy covering, and the full nates clinging to the dress, as though to burst it. Gabi was more petite, with thrusting conic breasts, whipcord muscle, and her hair boyishly cropped; the two girls exchanged looks, at which Gabi bowed her head. Whatever her demeanour to other wenches, her bowed head and blushes indicated her submission to the sullen beauty of Portia.

'Gabi is Portia's spank slave,' said Warsweide, but refused to elaborate, saying that Suze would see soon enough, so that when she led Suze to the mistress's

184

quarters, shortly before five o'clock, Suze was quivering with curiosity.

Her quarters were a half-timbered chalet in the Saxon style, with a long, gently sloping roof. A wench, posted outside, stopped her, and asked her business. The wench wore socks and tennis shoes, and was stockinged in blue, with a short blue skirt, extending to mid-thigh, fastened by several pins, and a red blouse tightly buttoned over her large breasts, flattened against her chest by a clearly-outlined bra. She had golden shoulder flashes, and carried a short rubber quirt, of three thongs, two feet long. With this instrument, she waved Suze to enter the building. She found herself in a long hallway, panelled in dark wood, and with a stone floor. The slabs were cold, under her bare soles, as she stood, hopping from one foot to the other, not sure what to do. A wench approached from a doorway near the entrance. She too was blond, and in a short blue skirt, but her upper body was naked, and her firm breasts rippled bare over the tight waistband of her skirtlet. The pert melons of her rump, beneath the tightly-moulded croup of the skirt, were denuded of underthings. Her legs were bare, above fluffy white socks and tennis shoes, and her only instrument of correction was a small ornamental cane, less than two feet long, strapped to her waist.

'You are Suzette Shard?' she said, her naked titties quivering slightly, as she spoke.

Suze said she was.

'Remove your upper garment, please,' she ordered.

Suze's mouth opened, but she said nothing, and obeyed. She stripped off her blouse, folded it, and handed it to the wench, who tucked it under her arm. The air was cool against her naked teats, and her nipples hardened, with gooseflesh appearing on the golden skin of the breasts. The wench pursed her lips, as she stared at Suze's breasts, then nodded approvingly, before reaching suddenly, and lifting Suze's skirt above her waist. She nodded again.

'Bare bum. Good. I have to check, you understand, miss,' she said. 'Weren't you told to come wearing your gym shoes?'

'Why, no,' Suze replied. 'I'm a new wench.'

'Your roommate should have advised you,' she said.

'I haven't had the pleasure of meeting my roommate,' Suze explained.

The orderly disappeared into her cubby-hole, and came out with shoes and socks, like her own, then ordered Suze to put them on. Suze did so, bending to lace the shoes, and aware of the girl's eyes on her jutting titties.

'Follow me,' she ordered, when Suze was shod. 'The mistress will see you in her chambers.'

Suze followed the orderly, her long legs easily keeping up with the wench's rapid stride, and her bare breasts swaying, and slapping her ribcage as she walked.

'Why do I have to be ... you know, bare-titty?' she asked.

'Those are the regulations. Officers of the court must be at their ease, in case their services are required,' the wench explained.

'Then, why the shoes? It would surely be easier to remain barefoot. The mistress said I was to be a witness in the court case, that's all. She said I might have to witness bare-bum thrashing.'

'Witness!' exclaimed the orderly, leering at Suze. 'That certainly is not all. Girls at sport wear shoes, for athletic ease, don't they? With Gabi and Portia up for trial, you may be called on to serve. The mistress believes that caning must be as vigorous as possible, and as shaming as possible, so that a wench's humiliation is greater, when she is flogged bare bum, by her peers.'

'I must cane a girl on the bare?' Suze gasped.

The orderly turned, pinched Suze's erect nipples between her fingers, then pounced under her skirtlet, and jabbed her in the cunt, her fingers coming up wet with Suze's seeped come.

'Ow! Stop!' Suze cried.

'Beating excites you, slut,' the wench hissed. 'I know your type. Caning on the bare, whether watching it or taking it, makes your cooze wet. You want it so badly – how you long to have your bum reddened! – but if you

186

can't be thrashed yourself, you'll make a pretty whipper, striping another girl's arse out of spite. And as her bum reddens, you'll wank yourself off, to come after come.'

'No! I swear!' Suze blurted. 'That's cruel and horrid.'

'Why do you think the mistress chose you?' she said. 'The worst shame for a miscreant is to be caned by a frigwench.'

12

Buttered Bums

'Please sit down, Suzette,' said the mistress, without rising from her silk cushion. 'Don't be awed – a *vehmgericht* sounds forbidding, but I like to keep things more as a cosy chat, girls with girls. Portia and Gabi should be here any moment.'

She sighed, and shook her head.

'They are such imps.'

A uniformed orderly stood in attendance, bearing a quirt of four thongs, over her folded forearms. Suze perched herself on a high stool. Behind the mistress, in a glass case, hung several canes, straps, and other instruments of discipline, all polished and shining. Suze's eyes widened.

'You admire my collection,' said the mistress. 'It is mostly for show. My, how pretty your breasts are, dear. I so envy you wenches, strolling at your ease.'

She gestured to her tight costume and stockings.

'We seniors must keep up appearances. You understand. Your tea was satisfactory?'

'Oh, yes, mistress,' Suze blurted.

'Super. We hope you shall be very happy here,' said the mistress. 'You may consider this event as part of your learning process. I am familiar with your dossier, and know that you have suffered, from, ah, immoderate discipline. My aim is to help you come to terms with the thrashings to which you have been subjected, unfairly, no doubt. You will learn to accept *moderate* corporal punishment as a normal and desirable fact of life. It is healthy for wenches to atone for their peccadilloes with a sound beating on the bare buttocks – just as it is healthy for them to masturbate together, at least once a day, to cleanse their systems of harmful tension. Therefore we have a policy of wenches sharing rooms.'

'Dr Fredegund explained things a little, mistress,' Suze said.

'Your dossier describes you as a seasoned masturbatress,' said the mistress quietly. 'Is that true?'

'Oh,' Suze gasped, blushing furiously. 'That beastly MaBelle! She'd say anything. I wank myself off, of course, perhaps even a lot, but no more than other girls. In this heat, it is hard for a wench not to diddle.'

'It also says you are fond of the cane. Taking it, I mean.'

'That's not fair!' Suze exclaimed. 'How could I be fond of such horrid pain? I've been unlucky, that's all. I accept that caning in moderation is a necessary punishment, for naughty wenches, but I've . . . I've never done anything wrong!'

She wiped away a tear.

'I'm glad to hear it,' said the mistress, 'and this little chat with my two naughty wenches will let you show your moderation.'

The two girls were ushered in, by the orderly, and took their places, perching on uncushioned wooden stools, opposite Suze and the mistress. Each wench wore ceremonial costume: stiletto heels and sheer crimson stockings, an ankle-length crimson velvet skirt, slit to the waist, and revealing cream knickers and sussies, and a cream satin blouse, open to the third button, and showing ample bare breast, thrust upward by a tightly scalloped cream bra. Their waists were stick-thin; beneath their bras, they wore tight waspie corsets, matching the other undies, and visible through the gauzy blouse. The mistress picked up a document, and scrutinised it, then looked up at Portia and Gabi.

'Comfortable?' she said.

The girls looked nervously at each other, swallowed, and forced smiles, their haughty demeanour in the tea room quite vanished.

'My corset is very tight, mistress,' murmured Portia, and Gabi nodded.

'But it is so nice to wear proper lady's things,' she added, blushing.

'How tight were you corsed?' said the mistress.

Gabi said nineteen inches, and Portia, nineteen and a half. The mistress stroked her own pencil-thin belly, and said that she took a corset of eighteen inches, throughout the day.

'Well, ladies,' she said crisply, 'this is not the first time you have sat on the stools of penitence.'

'No, mistress,' muttered the two girls.

'Fighting', the mistress said, 'again!'

'This slut started it, mistress,' said Gabi.

'No, that lying bitch started it,' cried Portia. 'She threw mud at me.'

'That was to stop you cheating at netball,' retorted Gabi.

'And that inspired you to rip each other's garments off, and wrestle naked in the river mud, for half an hour? I think there is more to it,' said the mistress, pleasantly. 'Our purpose is to get at the truth, and devise treatment accordingly. I am told that you both share an affection for the wench Claudine Wulf?

Both wenches sullenly agreed that they were acquainted with Claudine.

'She is a known frigwench,' said the mistress, 'and has been punished many times for excessive masturbation. Neither of you could be ignorant of that, and yet you pursue her affection?'

'Claudine is a victim of misunderstanding, mistress,' pleaded Portia. 'We are special friends.'

'She's lying, the slut!' cried Gabi. 'Claudine is misunderstood all right, but this slut compounds it, by wanking her off immoderately. I'm her special friend. I understand her.'

'No, I really understand her,' protested Portia.

'And you are both suggesting that I do not?' hissed the mistress. 'That is contempt of court.'

Each wench put fingers to her mouth, as her eyes widened.

'Oh, mistress –'

'I didn't mean –'

'Silence, you impudent bitches. I had in mind a simple chastisement for misdemeanour, but now there is contempt to deal with. Miss Suzette is a witness. Aren't you, Suzette?'

Suze swallowed, pursed her lips, then nodded her agreement. The two wenches glared at her.

'I was prepared to decide which one of you should be caned, and leniently, but I think you'll agree that it must be both, and more than a token punishment. Don't you?'

The wenches nodded, red in the face, and with downcast eyes.

'I shall invite Miss Suzette to apply the cane to each of your bare croups,' the mistress continued, as the girls paled. 'Buttered bums.'

'Oh, mistress,' whimpered Portia, 'please, no . . .'

'A hundred lashes, prolonged until your butters melt,' continued the mistress.

'Oh, no, mistress,' wailed Gabi.

'Mistress,' Suze blurted, 'you know that I'm accustomed to taking punishment, but my dossier must also say that I have little practice in imposing it. I would not wish to let you down.'

'I don't think you shall,' purred the mistress. 'Take a look at your nipples, wench.'

Suze looked down at her naked breasts, and gasped. Each nipple was rock-hard in erection; she shifted in her skirtlet, squishy with ooze at her crotch. The mistress smiled.

'Her breasts are streaming with sweat, in this heat, yet her nips are stiff with excitement,' she said. 'The new entrant is quite keen to beat miscreant wenches on the bare. You may stand, ladies, and remove your garments.'

She rose, to open her case of disciplinary instruments.

'Please, mistress, wouldn't it be all right if we lifted skirts, and lowered our panties to our knees?' said Gabi. 'The full bare is so shameful, especially before a new wench.'

'That is exactly the point,' said the mistress. 'I am going to turn around, when I have selected the instrument of your punishment. If you are not braless, knickerless, and stripped to your stockings and suspenders, then you shall know the meaning of shame. You may retain your shoes, and your corsets.'

Her fingers played over the disciplinary tools, caressing their polished surfaces. Her lips creased in a shy smile and, at length, she selected a leather strap, studded with miniature silver *képis*, the hat of the foreign legion, and with its end split into two tongues. The other end was also split, and the tongues folded and sealed, to make a handle. The mistress explained that it was a genuine legionnaire's belt, adapted for disciplinary use. She handed it to Suze, who accepted it, her nostrils wide, and her hand trembling. She shifted in her seat, her buttocks squashing her moistening skirtlet, and shivered, as the leather strap brushed her erect nipples. Portia and Gabi peeled off their clothing, and stood, stripped to knickers, stockings and sussies. Their legs quivered on their high stiletto heels, and their corsets pinched their waists to pencils, thrusting out their bare bums, with their hands cupped at their knicker-less vulvas. The mistress ordered their stools placed together, at the far end of the room, and the orderly did so; then, she told the two wenches to take position over their stools. The two wenches teetered, heels clacking on the bare wooden floor, as they marched to their stools. Each placed a foot on either side of the stool, gripping its leg; then knifed her body in a fold, to grasp the seat with both hands, while presenting her naked buttocks high and spread. As they bent over, slivers of pinched belly flesh peeped over the rims of their corsets, revealing the livid bruises impressed on the skin by the tight waspies.

The orderly exited, and reappeared, bearing a bucket of ice cubes, in which lay two slabs of butter. Portia and Gabi moaned, as the butter slithered over their bare bums, until each girl's buttocks shone with a coating of grease. The orderly then wedged the slabs of butter into each buttock cleft, and the girls tightened their fesses, to hold it in place.

The mistress ordered Suze to take her stance for a good runup at the proffered bare fesses. She said the coating of butter was to make the strokes sting more, and holding the frozen slab between the nates, until the end of the beating, decreased the victim's ability to squirm and wriggle, in order to ease the pain of the strokes. Normally, a beating bent over stool permitted the wench to position her feet a good two feet behind, so that she took the strokes bent over at an angle, thus allowing the stool to absorb some of the jarring impact of the whip. Having their feet close up by the legs, meant that they could not use the stool as a prop or support, but had to take the full force of Suze's strap without moving. Suze ran her fingers along the leather strap, hard and pickled to the touch, and the silver studs sharp. The mistress ordered her to commence flogging; a stroke to each wench in turn: the beating to continue, until both slabs of butter were completely melted from the bum clefts.

'Mistress, I'm not sure . . .' Suze began.

'It's not as awful as it looks,' said the mistress. 'It's for show, really, to give these scamps a jolly good fright. Why, their butters will melt in no time. Now, lift your strap, and run towards your target, but aim your run a little past it, so that you deliver the stroke at an angle, with full force, while you still have momentum.'

Suze lifted the strap, and wiped sweat from her wet brow and breasts. On the mistress's signal, she began to run at Portia's bottom, her feet slapping the floor as she quickened her pace, and her arm straight up in the air. She aimed at a point just beyond the girl's head and, as she passed the upturned buttocks, brought the strap down as hard as she could. *Vap!*

'Oww!' shrilled Portia. 'Oh! Oh!'

Suze stopped, and turned back. She had caught the girl not on the bare bum, but on the fleshy top thighs, leaving a rip in her stocking. Portia's face was screwed in a grimace, and her body rocked, quivering, as she clung to her stool. She looked up, her face red, and moist with tears.

'You bitch,' she sobbed.

'Silence, slut!' hissed the mistress, and ordered Suze to try again, on Gabi.

Suze repeated her runup and whipped Gabi, with the same result: she swung too low, and lashed the girl across the stockinged thighs. Gabi howled, and her whipped legs quivered, with a shred of ripped stocking hanging loose; the slab of butter slid up and down between her clenching bum globes, with yellow drips starting to seep down her cleft, and over her trembling bare thighs. Again, the mistress ordered the wenches to take their beatings in total silence and, as Suze ran to deliver the next stroke to Portia's bare, the wench emitted no sound save an anguished snuffling, when the leather cracked once more against her stockinged thighs. Gabi took the same, then Portia, and for the next few strokes, Suze's aim did not improve: the stockings of both wenches were quickly in tatters, and their thighs striped with livid crimson welts, and imprinted with the shape of the *képi* studs. Suze's naked breasts bobbed up and down, as she sped towards her targets and, at her eighth stroke, she was lashing the exposed flesh of the buttocks. As she ran, dripping with sweat, her tennis shoes squelched on the floor. *Vap! Vap!*

'Uhh . . .' the girls gasped, their brows wrinkled in anguish.

Their buttocks rocked, at each lash from the studded strap, and the silver studs left raw imprints on the skin, now puffy and ridged with wide crimson weals. The width of the strap ensured that no inch of buttock meat was left unbruised, and Suze's pace quickened, as the bottoms turned from crimson to puce, with blackening at the edges of the welts. Butter from the arse cleft trickled down the girls' shredded stockings, wetting the ripped fabric, and puddled into their high-heeled shoes. *Vap! Vap!* Suze had her aim, and the girls shook, sobbing, as she targeted now the buttocks, and now, on purpose, the remains of the ripped stockings. The hose, soaked in melted butter, sagged and peeled from the naked flesh, which Suze whipped, until both wenches sported a purple dark mottling of bruises from top buttock, across the vividly wealed haunches, and down the thighs, as far as the backs of their knees. Suze's own thighs pumped as she ran, and a shiny trickle oozed from under her skirt, wetting her legs in her own come. She took the beating to forty, then fifty, and sixty lashes; behind her, the mistress sank in her fluffy cushions, her knuckles moving between her legs, as she stared at the welted girl flesh. The butter melted, between the wenches' buttocks, until their whole legs were slimed in yellow grease, yet, as their whimpers and sobs filled the room, and their buttocks continued to clench under Suze's strokes, both flogged wenches were juicing from their cunts.

'That must be a hundred, mistress,' Suze gasped, looking through sweat-blurred eyes at the reclining woman, her skirt up, and thighs apart. 'Shall I stop?'

The mistress shook her head.

'Only eighty-seven,' she said, hoarsely.

Suze let her gaze linger, and saw that the woman was blatantly masturbating, while the orderly, behind her, wore a sly smile, and a smear of come down her legs. She hoisted her strap for the next stroke, and ran to deliver it, to Portia's inflamed croup. When the *Vap!* of the stroke had ceased echoing, Suze placed her fingers under her skirt, and stroked her own come-slimed cunt. She gasped, as she touched her erect, throbbing clitty, and pinched it, as she jogged back for her next runup. Masturbating now, she ran, and continued to whip the livid bares, oblivious of the eyes of mistress or orderly. Come sluiced down the thighs of both girls, as their bare arse skin darkened and puffed out. Their bodies quivered like reeds, as the heavy strap rocked them. The mistress's fingers played at her open gash, festooned with a massive cunt fleece, and with her bikini panties pushed aside to show the swollen wet lips of her quim. She rubbed and pinched her huge, extruded clitty, shining red and raw, amid the gushing folds of her bare, slimed cunt. Suddenly, she opened her eyes wide, stared at Suze's vulva, and licked her teeth.

'Diddling, miss?' she murmured. 'It is permitted. We have courtroom privilege.'

The mistress continued her blatant wank, while the orderly imitated her, skirtlet up, and bare gushing quim exposed, and manipulated by deft fingers, with the clitty and slit pouring come over her thighs. Suze's fist delved right into her own slimy pouch, and she frigged herself, pushing her fingers to the hard wombneck, and reaming it, gasping, while her thumb pressed round and round on her throbbing clitty. She stood above the quivering bares, not bothering with a runup, but flogging the bares with backhand and forehand strokes, strapping each flaming bruised croup in turn, while masturbating harder. Gabi's nates were bruised dark; Portia's bare was aflame, wriggling under her lashes.

'Oh . . . no!' she wailed, as a stream of steaming piss spurted from her quivering gash.

Suze heard the mistress groan behind her, then burst into hiccupping little yelps, as she climaxed. Suze delivered the hundredth stroke to the flaming bare buttocks of the wenches, and whimpered, her cunt spurting come, as her belly convulsed in her own orgasm. She finished the beating with two valedictory strokes to the purpled thigh backs, and both girls screamed. Panting, Suze turned, and held her breasts, to stop them heaving.

'What, wanking off, frigwench?' the mistress said acidly.

Suze looked down, and gasped. Her masturbating hand still clutched her cunt.

'I beg pardon, mistress,' she blurted. 'I thought you said . . .'

'I said nothing,' snapped the mistress. 'What did I say, orderly?'

'Nothing, mistress,' replied the orderly, her own dress and legs soaked in her wanked come.

'Well, that is enough beating,' the mistress said. 'I feel like a canter. Bodwenna is not very frisky, these days – whinnies at the crop, for some reason. Saddle up the two sluts, orderly, and the new frigwench. Her bottom needs a taste of my horsewhip.'

'But . . . that's not fair,' Suze wailed.

'Silence, frigwench,' spat the mistress.

'Please, mistress?'

'What is it, Portia?'

'Permission for me and Gabi to wank off, before we are saddled? The whipping has made us hot.'

'Oh, please, mistress,' panted Gabi.

'Of course,' she said.

The mistress watched, while the two wenches frigged; Portia fucked Gabi's anus with two fingers, while Gabi crouched, bum up, so that she could tongue Portia's cunt, while wanking off her own clitoris. Portia pinched and rubbed her own nipples, which were stiffly erect. The mistress watched with arms folded, but a stain of come wetting her skirt at the crotch, as the two wenches masturbated swiftly to orgasm.

The orderly raised her quirt, and Suze followed the two dripping girls to the stable, a cosy barn, with a row of chariots, and the walls hung with saddles, crops and harnesses. They were ordered to strip off, and Portia and Gabi dropped their corsets, with sighs of relief. Nude, they were harnessed by the ostlers, coarsely jeering wenches dressed in rubber panties and bra, and thick rubber boots. Suze shivered, as leather snaked around her naked body, and her straps were tightened.

'Does it hurt, frigwench?' hissed Portia.

'Oh,' wailed Suze, 'it pinches awfully. I've never been so uncomfortable, as if it is designed to hurt.'

'As if *my* weals don't hurt?' hissed Gabi, flanking her. You're a ponywench now, so get used to it.'

Suze stood, stamping the ground, harnessed between the two girls, behind the mistress's two-wheeled jaunting car. Like Portia's and Gabi's, her nude body was wound in a harness of leather straps, binding her to the reins, held by the mistress. Her feet were shod with thick metal boots. Clamps pinned her nipples, and held back her cunt flaps, with both sets fastened to the harness, and causing excruciating pain, at each jerk of the reins. The mistress explained that flicks of the rein should be unnecessary, if the girls pulled properly, and the pain of clamped nipples and gash was to minimise her directions.

'I'm glad it hurts,' snarled Portia. 'You whipped me hard, you filthy cunt, on the thighs and everything, and spoiled my best hose. I'll get you, bitch. I'll do you, I promise.'

They were silenced with metal bits, wadded in their mouths, and the whip cracked, lashing all three naked backs. Suze winced, shuddering.

'Giddy-up!' cried the mistress.

The trio strained, and began to trot, pulling the cart out of its shed, towards the edge of Saxworfa's estate. Sweat poured from the three girls, their thighs pumping hard, to raise the heavy horseshoes, and the cart lurched forward, at a quickening pace. *Vap! Vap!* The mistress's long leather horsewhip sang in the air, lashing the girls on the bare. From time to time, she flicked the reins, and the trio wailed, or shrieked, as the clamps pulled their nipples and cunts. Even Portia's face was a mask of agony, as her gash lips were pulled raw, revealing the pink spongy mass of her cunt flesh. *Vap! Vap! Vap!* The flogged buttocks of Portia and Gabi, striped by Suze's strap, gleamed with the fresh welts laid by the horsewhip, and Suze's own buttocks blushed fiery pink with whipmarks, while her back was crisscrossed with weals. Their breath came in hoarse pants, as they neared the edge of the cliff, that was the limit of the mistress's domain, then veered left, and began to trot along the clifftop perimeter. Below them stretched a riverine panorama of jungle, stretching south into distant heat haze.

'That is Brazil, trollops,' said the mistress. 'You are fortunate that you shall never see it. Here with womenfolk, you are safe from vile and depraved males.'

She wore a wench's sporting costume, of short white skirt, fluffy socks and tennis shoes, with a halter top, that was a strip of thin white rubber, wound tightly around the bare breasts. After twenty minutes, she flicked the reins, and cried halt. The girls drew up at the clifftop, where the sun was beginning to set, its orange beams making their sweated bodies sparkle. The mistress leapt from her chariot.

'Exercise gives me an appetite,' she said, and stood, leaning back against her cart, with her legs parted, then lifted up the skirt, to show her massive pubic forest, and dripping wet cunt lips, nude of knickers. 'Portia, you go first.'

'The usual, mistress?' Portia murmured.

'Mm . . . yes.'

Portia thrust her fingers into the mistress's dripping bush, and began to masturbate her slit. The frigged woman groaned, and spread her arm on her chariot, while gazing at the sunset.

'Oh, that is so good,' she moaned, rubbing her nipples under her rubber top. 'Nature is so beautiful.'

Portia twitched and pinched at the extruded stiff clitoris, until come flowed over her wanking fingers. The mistress's belly undulated, fluttered, and, in a short time, she yelped repeatedly, her gash spurting come, as Portia's fingers brought her off. Gabi was next; she repeated Portia's caress, and brought the mistress to a second orgasm. Her thighs were dripping with come, by the time Suze, trembling, took her place. She extended her fingers to the swollen gash lips, and began to rub the nubbin, then got three fingers into the mistress's wet pouch, and began to fingerfuck her with hard jabs to the wombneck. The mistress gurgled, and moaned, and her thighs shuddered, as Suze, without withdrawing her fingers from the cunt, knelt, and began to tongue the throbbing clitty, while continuing to fist the gash.

'Oh . . . oh . . . yes . . . ah!' she shrieked, as Suze gamahuched her to climax. 'Oh, yes . . . I think this slut is qualified to give lessons in frottage class, even though a depraved frigwench.'

She used Suze's hair to mop her slimed gash and, when Suze rose, she had to sway her head, to wipe the mistress's titties of sweat. Trotting again, the three girls pulled the chariot, until dusk came and, illumined by the sun fading to the west, they arrived back at the stable. Ostler wenches stripped them of their harnesses, and sponged them of the muck adhering to their bodies. The three were permitted to remain nude for their visit to the tea room, for a cup of chocolate, before bedtime. All the girls took refreshment standing up, and discussing the stripes their bottoms had received during the day. Portia reverted to her normal self, of queening it over the others, and showing off her bruised nates, with spiteful glances at Suze, who stood drinking alone. The word 'frigwench' hovered in the air, and Suze quickly took her leave, making her way back to her hut, in the dark. She dunged in the bucket, then padded out to empty it. When she had sponged her slimed cunt and anus, she lay naked on the bed, sweat still dripping from her body in the hot, humid night air. She sighed, smiling, as she drifted into a doze, rubbing her welted skin, with the bruises from the mistress's whip beginning to crust. After a short while, the door opened, and a figure stood in the doorway, flanked by others.

'Who is – Portia?'

Suze sat up, but was quickly subdued, with a hand over her mouth. A posse of nude wenches secured her limbs, and one sat on her, crushing her to the bed under heavy bare buttocks. An oil lamp dimly illumined the bedroom.

'Hello, bitch,' said Portia. 'I'm your roommate.'

Gabi sat on her back, with two ostler wenches each securing a leg.

'Promise not to blab, and Gabi will take her hand off your mouth,' Portia said.

Suze nodded. Gabi withdrew her gagging palm, and Suze panted, regaining her breath.

'Why?' she gasped.

Portia showed her wealed bottom.

'This, bitch,' she snarled. 'You whipped me and shamed me. I've never taken a whipping like it. You made me piss myself, and wanked yourself off at my humiliance.'

The ostlers exchanged smiles, until Portia rounded on them, with a clenched fist.

'So now you're going to pay,' she said.

Portia was nude, like the others, save for a short ashplant cane, strapped on a rubber cord round her waist.

'Wait,' Suze pleaded. 'I was ordered to whip you, Portia. I meant nothing personal.'

'That is the worst kind,' murmured Gabi, and slapped Suze's face. 'This *is* personal, slut. We'll have some lovely wanks, as you shriek and squirm.'

A hand stroked Suze's wriggling bare.

'Her arse is so beautiful,' said an ostler girl. 'Under the welts, so smooth and firm and creamy.'

'Like scarred satin, all lovely and ripped and churned,' said the second ostler, holding fast to Suze's ankle. 'I'd like to eat those fesses. Take them in my mouth, and chew them and lick them and suck them.'

'Don't be soppy,' snarled Portia, unstrapping her ash-plant cane from her waist cord.

She brandished it in her left hand, and, with her right, unwound the rubber thong, folded it, and held it as a whipping strap.

'No . . .' Suze whimpered.

'Cheer up, slut. It'll be just like old times at St Ursula's,' Portia said. 'Hoity-toity bitch school that I wasn't good enough for. Isn't this what you girls got up to in your dorm? Wanking and spanking, eh? Only now, it's just the spanking. I've been wondering how to torture you.'

'Portia, I'm sorry I had to whip you,' Suze blurted.

'You enjoyed it, slut, as I'm going to enjoy this,' Portia replied.

Vip! Vip! The strap and cane descended together on Suze's exposed bare, tracing two vivid pink weals.

'Ooh! That hurts,' Suze gasped.

'Of course it hurts,' said Portia.

Vip! Vip! Suze's bare bum clenched.

'Ooh! Oh, stop, please, Portia,' Suze pleaded. 'I want to be your friend . . . your slave, even. Make me your slave, Portia, mistress, but don't whip me.'

'OK,' said Portia. 'You may submit, as my slave.'

Gabi glowered.

'But,' Portia added, 'a slave gets whopped at her mistress's whim.'

Vip! Vip!

'Uh . . .' Suze whimpered.

The wood and rubber cord laid adjacent red welts in the middle of Suze's quivering bare. Her naked fesses jerked at the strokes, squirming, yet helpless to move, in the ostler girls' grip. *Vip! Vip!*

'Uh . . .'

Vip! Vip! Portia's bare breasts bounced and swayed, as she doubly flogged her victim's naked buttocks, which turned cherry red, then darkened to puce. The big puffy ridges deepened, as the welts multiplied on her bare bum globes. *Vip! Vip!* Fists between their legs, the ostlers gleefully masturbated, trickles of come seeping from their juicing cunts, and slopping the backs of Suze's wriggling thighs.

'Oh! No it hurts so!' Suze squealed. 'Portia, I don't understand. Why are you doing this to me? I thought Saxworfa's was for nice girls, a refuge from men's terrible cruelty.'

Portia laughed.

'We are all girls together, bitch. If you do well in Miss Travemunde's class, you'll have plenty of wanking partners. No men here. You want cock up that fancy brown arsehole of yours? Thought you'd find some hunky legionnaires at Saxworfa's, like studs, to tool bitches when they're hot? No luck. Frigwenches think they can escape south to Brazil, and get to Sybaris, a girl's paradise of willing cocks. Some chance! Sybaris is a myth. There is no Sybaris in Brazil, just drooling legionnaires, with big cocks all right, but they take girls up the arse, the only way they fuck. They'll bugger your arse raw, then whip you and tie you up in the stables. Should suit you.'

Vip! Vip!

'No!' Suze yelped, her buttocks clenching and squirming. 'I'm not like that. Don't tell me about the legion. I never want to see any of those horrid brutes again.'

Vip! Vip!

'Oh! Please, no more,' she sobbed.

'You're a dirty frigwench, that's what,' sneered Portia. 'Can't go without wanking off, or a bugger's cock in your bumhole.'

202

She ordered Gabi to put her hand in Suze's cunt. Gabi obeyed, made a face, as she delved inside the wet slit, and brought her hand out, sopping with Suze's juice. Suze wailed and sobbed, as Gabi wiped her come over her face.

'Maybe it's true,' she panted. 'Maybe I am wicked. Go ahead, then, flog me.'

'Sybaris just can't be a myth,' said the first ostler girl, her thumb frigging her wet, stiff clitty, 'otherwise, we'd have nothing to dream off, when we wank off.'

'Hot, hard cock, up the bumhole,' murmured the second, masturbating vigorously, and licking her teeth. 'Any number of cocks, to service each girl.'

The ostler girls had thighs parted, and fingers greedily jabbing in their come-slimed cunts, with thumbs twitching at their hard nubbins. Their come flowed over Suze's legs, bathing her thighs and calves in the shiny cunt juice. Portia moved to the end of the bed, and ordered the ostlers to hold Suze's legs still. *Vip! Vip!* The strap and cane cracked in unison, on the soles of Suze's bare feet.

'Ahh,' Suze shrieked. 'No, no, no!'

Vip! Vip!

'Ahh . . . that's awful.'

Vip! Vip!

'Ah! Oh!'

Suze's naked soles pinked with vivid slashes from the rod and strap, applied alternately to each foot. Her toes wriggled, as the feet jerked, under each stroke to the naked underskin. *Vip! Vip!*

'Did you get the bastinado at St frigging Ursula's, wench?' hissed Portia.

'Noo,' Suze groaned.

Vip! Vip!

'Please, stop,' she wailed.

Vip! Vip!

'Ooh . . .'

Gabi thrust her fingers again between Suze's dripping cunt lips, and came up with a dripping wad of oily come, which she wiped on Suze's hair, then forced the sodden hank into Suze's mouth, and told her to suck. Suze's jaws

203

champed on her tresses, sucking and swallowing her own come.

'The bitch is juicing hard, mistress,' she said to Portia. 'You are exciting her.'

'Dreaming of Sybaris, no doubt,' panted Portia.

Vip! Vip!

'Ahh!' shrieked Suze, her striped crimson soles wriggling frantically.

'Sybaris exists, mistress,' said Gabi. 'It has to exist. Otherwise . . .'

'You soppy cow,' said Portia, and slapped Gabi hard with her rubber strap, across her breasts.

'Sybaris must exist,' said the ostler girls, in unison. 'You've a big mouth, Portia. Needs teaching a lesson.'

They snatched the implements from Portia's hands, then overpowered her. Gabi dragged Suze from the bed, and Portia was forced down, writhing, with her face in the spot soaked with Suze's oozed come.

'Gabi,' she squealed. 'Do something.'

Gabi took the cane.

'I'm going to do something, mistress,' she hissed. 'Something I should have done ages ago.

Vip! The cane seared a livid welt, on top of the bruises from Suze's strapping of Portia, and the bare arse convulsed.

'Ahh! You fucking slut,' Portia howled.

'Wait,' said Suze, staying Gabi's hand. 'It's not fair. She's been whipped enough today.'

'I've put up with the bitch for too long,' Gabi growled. 'Gabi, lick me, Gabi, bare your bum, Gabi, wank me off . . . who does she think she is?'

'Let Suze decide,' said one of the frigging ostler girls.

'Bugger her,' said the other. 'That should teach her a lesson.'

Suze gasped, as her fingers slipped between the dripping lips of her gash, and touched her erect clitty.

'Go on then, give her arse a . . . a good shafting,' she panted hoarsely. 'Why not?'

She began to masturbate, her cunt inches from the pinioned girl's face and, with come drooling her inner thighs, she dipped a finger in her slit, and pressed come to Portia's lips.

'Yes, bugger her,' she gasped.

'Please . . .' Portia moaned, 'please, no . . .'

The ostlers fetched a length of branch from outside, a good fifteen inches in length, and over three inches wide. They began to strap the tool around Suze's waist.

'*Me?*' Suze gasped. 'I don't know . . .'

'You, frigwench,' said Gabi.

Suze waggled her hips, and saw the tool standing stiff between her legs.

'I so want to be your friend, Portia,' she blurted.

Gabi rubbed Suze's cunt, and lubricated the tool with her come, then spread the cheeks of Portia's arse.

'Then give the cheeky madam a good hard seeing-to,' she said.

13

Spank Slave

Suze straddled Portia's squirming croup, and thrust the tool against her anal pucker. It opened slightly, and Suze penetrated, to a few inches. Portia squealed, her arse globes clenching, and Suze slammed her hips against the wriggling bare, getting the shaft further into the anus, until, with a final gasping thrust, she had the tool fully inside Portia's bumhole. She began to slap her belly against the girl's buttocks, slamming the tool in and out of the anus, and pushing it right to the rectum. Her bum jerked and waggled in the air, until Gabi lifted Portia's cane, and sliced it across Suze's bare. *Vip! Vip!*

'Ooh,' Suze cried, as her buggery of the squirming girl was driven faster by the cuts. 'Don't, Gabi . . .'

Vip! Vip! New livid weals striped Suze's pumping buttocks, as they drove the wooden tool into Portia's anus.

'Ah! That hurts,' she squealed.

'Bugger her harder, bitch.' snarled Gabi.

'No, no, please have mercy,' the buggered girl whimpered.

'It's for your own good, Portia,' gasped Suze. 'I have to teach you a lesson. You have to submit to this, so we can be friends.'

Suze's quim sprayed slimy come over her victim's bare arse globes, as she bum-fucked the girl. Portia was held tight, and despite her wriggling and threshing, was powerless to escape, or lessen the force of Suze's buggery. She groaned, as the tool slammed her rectum, but, beneath her quim, the bedlinen was soaking wet with her come. Portia pressed her cunt basin to the bed, and she churned, rubbing her clitty on the sheet. Her wails softened to sobs and yelps and moans, as her cunt juiced more and more copiously, and her croup sprang upwards at each buggering jab, to meet Suze's thrusts, and embrace her penetrating tool. As they held her down, the ostler wenches frigged their cunts, moistening Portia with their dripped come. *Vip! Vip!* Gabi's cane lashed Suze's bare.

'Ooh! I'm doing her as hard as I can,' she squealed. 'Don't cane me, it's not fair.'

Vip! Vip!

'Ow, that hurts,' Suze panted.

'Who needs Sybaris', Gabi said, 'when you have this, bitch?'

The masturbating ostler girls laughed, as Suze jerked under the caning, sliming Portia's buttocks in her sweat and come. *Vip! Vip!*

'Oh, please, please don't,' Suze moaned, her bottom striped red.

The jerking thrusts of her hips quickened, at each fresh weal to her arse globes, making her thighs stiffen rigid, and her fesses clench tight, as she slammed her tool into Portia's anus.

'She has too many fucking limbs for Sybaris,' said the first ostler, and the other laughed.

'Yes, they like a neater package down there,' she said. 'Ampies fetch a good price.'

Vip! Vip!

'Oh, Suzette, please stop,' Portia wailed, 'my bum is bursting, you're splitting me . . .'

Gabi's breasts bounced, as she caned Suze's churning bum, and she pressed the firm, fleshy cones back to her ribs, thumbing and pinching her nipples. Her gash was slimy with come, as her fingers flicked her clitty.

Vip! Vip!

'Oh!' Suze gasped. 'My bum smarts so. Please, don't.'

Vip! Vip!

'Ahh . . .' Suze grunted, her brow furrowed in pain. 'Wait! You mean, Sybaris does exist?'

Vip! Vip!

'Ooh! No . . .' she wailed.

'Everything exists out here,' said the first ostler. 'Doesn't mean it's nice.'

Vip! Vip!

'Ahh . . .' Suze and Portia whimpered in unison, as Suze's bare darkened with puffy blotched weals, and Portia's buggered anus squirmed, oozing arse grease, with her cunt, squashed against the bed, drooling come into the linen.

'Stop, stop,' Portia wailed. 'I can't take it up the arse.'

'Don't stop, Suze. You're going to bring the slut off,' said the ostler.

Suze continued the buggery, as Gabi's cane raised puffy dark welts on her own bare bum, and Portia's wails grew shriller, her cunt churning on the bed, until she gasped, in a long, staccato sob.

'Yes . . . yes . . . fuck me, do me,' she panted. 'I'm nearly there. Split my bumhole, fuck me harder, I need it, oh, yes . . .'

Come spurted from Portia's rubbed cunt, as she squealed in orgasm; after buggering her arse for a dozen more thrusts, Suze sank down, to straddle Portia's back. The cane continued to lash her bottom, with Gabi and the ostlers masturbating. Suze's fingers were in her juicing gash, rubbing her clit against Portia's arse cleft, and she masturbated vigorously, until her come bathed the girl's buttocks, and she panted in her own climax. The other wenches brought themselves off with firm strokes to the clitty, and Gabi's cane stilled. She thrust the cane handle into her cooze, and wanked herself to climax.

'Can we be friends, now, Portia?' Suze gasped.

'Yes, Suze,' Portia said hoarsely.

'I'll still be your slave, if you like.'

'No, that's not possible,' said Portia. 'You've whipped me and buggered me today. You have shown your power, and are my mistress. I must be *your* spank slave.'

Suze slept that night, lying on her belly; at morning tea, she found the deference, with which the wenches had formerly treated Portia, transferred to her own person. Even Warsweide curtsied to her. She got the crispest toast, and the freshest cup of tea. Portia was her spank slave, which meant that Gabi, remaining in Portia's thrall, was her secondary slave. Suze found it odd, that personal slavery was permitted.

'It is against the rules, of course, but everyone does it,' Portia explained, buttering a slice of toast for her mistress. 'Only the ostlers are not enslaved; they are too dirty and depraved.'

'And the frigwenches?' Suze asked, rather acidly.

Portia laughed.

'We all frig,' she said. 'A frigwench is what public opinion, or the mistress, deems. It is a handy label.'

'Why, I think the mistress masturbates more than any of us,' Suze murmured, and Portia put a finger of alarm over her lips.

Suze toyed with her breakfast.

'I wonder if I'm cut out to be a mistress,' she said. 'You know the things in my dossier, about being a sub, and craving cane and buggery. Well, people have said them so much, that I wonder if they aren't true.'

She told Portia about her relationship with the cruel Cpl Pette, and how, strangely, she missed the monopedal wench. Portia bit her lip.

'Those dirty wanking ostlers know things,' she said. 'They say Sybaris is a pleasure domain, whose overlord favours girl amputees – that girls who arrive with full limbs don't stay that way. It is the ultimate submission, to become no more than arse, titties and quim, for male pleasure.'

Suze shuddered.

'But tell me there is no shame in being a sub, Portia?' she blurted.

'There is every shame, mistress,' Portia replied, 'and that's what makes it so delicious. Every domina must bare her bottom to cane or tool, from time to time, and is all the fresher for it.'

'Even the mistress?' Suze asked.

'Perhaps not her,' Portia said pensively. 'She may wank off, but only for sport. I don't know what she does in private. You see, we live a good life here, and all we have to do is attend the occasional *folkmoot*. That's a ceremony of submission to Saxworfa's, where wenches must show total obedience. There hasn't been one, for a while.'

'And what happens, exactly?' Suze asked, to be rewarded with a paling of Portia's face, and a finger pressed once more to her lips, as she averted her gaze.

Over a few weeks at Saxworfa's, Suze accustomed herself to a life of leisured tranquillity. She played ball games, swam, and attended classes on needlepoint, flower arrangement, and deportment; the weals faded from her bottom, although she listened to the wenches gossiping about their punishments, at evening cocoa. She and Portia slept in separate beds, with Suze in frilly nightie or pyjamas, and Portia in the nude. Every morning, Suze gave her slave a vigorous hand-spanking on the bare, after which they wanked each other off, as approved by Dr Fredegund. She enjoyed the spectator sport of cart-racing, with seniors whipping on their naked pony wenches, to pull their chariots to victory, whose prize was a special cream tea. After tea, Portia knelt before her mistress, and tongued her to orgasm. Suze obtained a hula hoop, and obliged Portia and Gabi to perform, bare-breasted, for an hour each morning. Twice, Portia said she had been naughty, having beaten Gabi without Suze's permission, and deserved the strap; Suze duly thrashed her fifty on the bare, until Portia's cooze was dripping come, and she was permitted an extra diddle, with Suze watching, while she caned Gabi, for allowing Portia to beat her. Sometimes, if alone in her room, Suze took the strap to her own bare arse, and thrashed herself until the weals rose; on occasions, masturbating as she whipped herself. One day, Portia said it was time they showed up at Miss Travemunde's class.

It was early afternoon, as they trooped with the other wenches, into Miss Travemunde's classroom, and were handed the costumes into which they must change. Some wenches received white frilly underwear, of a cotton corset, knotted at the front with strings, and baring the breasts and torso to six inches, with panties, baring the cooze, and fastened by the same white strings, to show the full apparatus of the vulva and anus cleft. Portia was given one of those, while Suze got a nylon body stocking of wide black netting, ripped either on purpose or by neglect, so that the breasts poked entirely bare, through jagged holes, and most of the buttocks were also bare, while a huge slash at the crotch meant the entire cunt was on display, and warm air brushed her naked bum cleft. Warsweide, in a similar costume, gave Suze a nod and a smile.

Miss Travemunde greeted them crisply, and told them to take their places at the classroom desks, whose seats were covered with fluffy towels. Her classroom was spotless, with floor and furniture polished to a shine. She stood at her desk, on a platform raised a foot above the floorboards, with a large video screen behind her, and, beside the lectern, a gynaecologist's chair, with a high back, and splayed legs. Her blond hair was piled in a bun, and she wore a stern white blouse and black skirt, over black stockings and stilettos, the magisterial costume making her seem older than her twenty or twenty-one years. She brandished a long yellow cane, with a crook handle, and Suze whispered to Portia that she was reminded of St Ursula's. Her voice echoed more loudly than she had intended, and Miss Travemunde demanded the identity of the mischievous wench. Suze put up her hand.

'I'm awfully sorry, miss,' she said, 'I didn't mean –'

'*I'll* tell you what you meant, miss,' rapped Miss Travemunde, in a harsh Saxon accent. 'Get up here at once.'

There was an excited rustle of underthings among the wenches, as Suze, blushing furiously, strode to the front of the class, with her bare titties bouncing in front of her ripped costume. She ascended Miss Travemunde's dais, and stood meekly, with her back to the class, and head lowered.

'What are you waiting for?' barked the teacher. 'Oh, yes, you're the new English girl, aren't you? The frigwench.'

211

The class tittered, and Suze's blush deepened.

'I'm sorry –' she blurted.

'Take position, girl,' said Miss Travemunde, her face livid. 'I am going to cane you for insolence.'

'What, here, miss?' Suze gasped.

'Bend over and touch your toes at once, you slut, with your bottom facing the class,' said the teacher. 'For your extra insolence, you shall receive extra chastisement. I was going to cane you one dozen, but you shall now receive two.'

'On the bare, miss?' Suze quavered, as she bent down, with her bottom to the class, and grasped her stockinged toes, which were rather sweaty to the touch.

'My, the frigwench is intelligent,' said Miss Travemunde, her voice dripping sarcasm. 'Your costume scarcely permits otherwise. You may part your legs, miss.'

Suze shifted, until her legs and buttocks were well parted, and her pendant gash flaps and quim bush open to view, between her thighs. The German girl touched a switch, and a video camera began to whir.

'Your buttocks bear the imprint of healthy spanking,' she said, 'but you have not been caned recently.'

'No, miss,' Suze said, blushing, at the marks of her self-strapping, 'not since my first day.'

'Well, then,' said Miss Travemunde, to the class, as if deciding a point.

Vip!

'Ooh!'

The first stroke took Suze unawares, and rocked her on her feet, with her bum clenching furiously.

'Did that hurt?' asked the teacher.

'Oh, yes, miss,' Suze sobbed, tears moistening her eyes, and her gorge rising.

'Forgotten what it was like, I expect,' the teacher drawled. 'Nasty frigwench, playing with yourself.'

Vip!

'Ah . . .' she gasped.

Vip!

'Ooh!'

'Try to moderate your exclamations of distress,' Miss Travemunde ordered. 'They are unladylike.'

'Yes, miss. But you cane so hard. They really sting.'

'They should,' said her chastiser. 'I use an English cane.'

Vip!

'Uhh . . .'

Vip!

'Ohh . . .'

Suze's face, hanging between her legs, was crimson; her legs straightened rigid at each stroke, as her bare bum wriggled and clenched, but her yelps of agony stilled to a low, sobbing moan. Looking at the class, upside down, she saw faces bright and flushed with excitement, and both Portia and Warsweide licking their teeth, with their hands below their desktops. Each stroke made Suze shudder, with her buttocks clenching repeatedly between the cuts, and she clung desperately to her toes, to keep her balance, in her stockinged feet on the shiny floor. *Vip! Vip! Vip!* Three cuts in sharp succession sliced her on the bare, and she shrieked.

'Oh! I can't bear it, miss. Oh, please.'

'That is only thirteen strokes,' said the caner, but the beating paused.

There was silence in the classroom, and above the purr of the camera, echoed a steady plink-plink of dripping liquid. Miss Travemunde poked her cane tip between Suze's quim lips.

'Can't bear it?' she said. 'You are juicing, frigwench.'

'Oh . . .' Suze wailed, crimson with embarrassment.

She looked down at come, dripping from her cooze onto the floor.

'Mucky pup,' snapped Miss Travemunde.

Vip!

'Ah! Ah!' Suze howled, rocking on rigid legs; the cane had sliced her right between the cunt folds.

Vip!

'Oh, no, miss,' she gasped, as the next stroke took her in the bum cleft, the tip lashing her anus pucker.

Vip! The cane whipped across her top buttocks.

213

'Oh . . .'

Vip! Vip! A stroke to each purpling haunch.

'Ah . . .'

Suze sobbed, in a low, hoarse wail, as her beating continued, and she saw the drip of oil from her cooze turn to a flow, its dripping sound quickening, as it echoed through the classroom. *Vip! Vip!*

'How does it feel?' asked Miss Travemunde mildly.

'Oh, miss, my bum's on fire,' Suze whimpered.

'Worse than at your English school?'

'Much worse.' Suze blurted.

Vip! Vip!

'Ahh,' Suze gasped, repeatedly, as the beating continued.

'There. That is your two dozen,' said the caner. 'Now, you may kneel, and lick up your mess.'

'What?' Suze sobbed, rubbing the coruscated skin of her hot buttocks.

Miss Travemunde swished her cane, and Suze crouched.

'Hands off your bum,' cried the teacher. 'You may rub yourself when I say so.'

Groaning, Suze applied her face to the floor, and licked up every drop of her oozed come. When she had swallowed it all, she received permission to rub her bottom. As her hands stroked the deep ridged weals on her flesh, she sobbed louder. Her cooze was still juicing.

'It seems, class, that the new entrant is indeed a frigwench, and sexually stimulated by her bare-bottom caning,' said Miss Travemunde. 'So she will serve as our first model.'

She ordered Suze to climb into the surgical chair, with her legs up on the supporting arms, and her thighs spread wide, her open quim facing the class. Trembling, Suze obeyed, and lowered herself to the seat, made of rough horsehair.

'Sore on your bottom?' asked the teacher.

'Oh, yes, miss,' Suze wailed.

'Good. You will now masturbate for the class, taking your time, and using your favourite strokes. Your smarting bottom should help you juice.'

'I . . . I don't understand, miss,' she said.

'Why, my class is in masturbation technique,' replied the teacher.

The class was silent, expectant. Screwing her eyes tight, Suze put trembling fingers to her cooze. The lips were soaking wet, and dripping come. She touched her stiff, throbbing clitty, and moaned, as pleasure jolted her. Miss Travemunde touched a switch, and the video screen flared with a giant image of Suze's wet pink cunt, in close-up.

'Class, you will clasp your hands on the desks in front of you,' she said, without turning round.

Blushing, the wenches withdrew their hands from beneath their desks. Miss Travemunde took a wooden pointer, and indicated Suze's vulva on the screen.

'You will remember, from our last lesson, the importance of intimate knowledge of the female vulval apparatus, and its intricacies, and I trust you have done your homework during team frigging. Now, see how the subject skirts the opening of her pouch. A caress of the labium minus, and of the paraurethral duct. Ladies must never forget the sensitivity of their peeholes, when masturbating. Yes, the finger flitting between the labium majus and minus, and reaming the vestibular fossa beneath. This is very good. Note that the clitty remains untouched, save for a few brief, exploratory strokes, designed to titillate, before full stroking commences. Now, the clitoris, starting with the prepuce and frenulum, skirting the gland itself, always building the quim to a heightened sensitivity, before intense masturbation begins. Caress to the labial frenulum below, leading to the sensitive perineum, and touching the anus pucker. Fingernail inside, reaming the anus pucker, very good. Now, we get to the intimate touching, fingernails nipping the greater vestibular gland, the ragged rim of the pouch hole itself. Thumb on the clitty, squashing gently, and fingers probing the entrance to the slit, now fingers inside the vulval hole, with a double action, caressing the clitty. Reaming the clitty, round and round, with a jab at the nubbin, now nicely swollen. And look at the juice flowing from the vulval aperture. Quite copious, and enough to wet her fingers, for anal penetration. Good, the wench has got a finger well inside her bumhole, and is poking herself, while maintaining attention to the clitoris. Note how stiff the clitty has become, and very nicely extruded. Nubbin between thumb and forefinger – you can see from the squirming of the entire vulval apparatus, and the copious juicing from the quim, that the subject has reached the alpha stage of autostimulation, as we discussed last week.'

Suze's hips writhed, her buttocks grinding the horsehair seat, as she wanked off. Her wrist was dripping with her oozed come, and her cunt and clit squelchy beneath her poking fingers. She gasped, as she fucked her own arsehole with one, then two, fingers, using her other hand to stroke the quim, in double-handed masturbation. She twitched at her erect, throbbing clitty, pinching the hard nubbin, until come poured from her gash.

'I should say this wench is expert,' said Miss Travemunde. 'She has obviously attended masturbation class before. You will note how the exhibitionism of her performance helps to excite her. The knowledge that the vulva is on full view, and that other potential masturbat-resses are watching her exposed parts, is a great help to autoerotic fantasy. Girls are exhibitionists. We love to lose control – see the gush of her vulval juice – but we secretly like to be observed losing control, and thus gain approving sympathy. Very good, miss, continue masturbating.'

Suze's belly fluttered, as her come flowed faster and faster; her hand was a blur on her swollen clitty. Squirming, she got two fingers inside her anal shaft, and began to jab the root of her arse, her fingers filling her rectum, and she moaned, with little choked sobs, her face scarlet and dripping sweat.

'The subject is approaching orgasm,' said Miss Travemunde.

'Ohh . . . ohh . . .' Suze groaned.

She had three fingers inside her slit, their tips slamming the wombneck, as her thumb pressed, jabbed and pressed her erect clitty. Her come was a torrent, flowing from the pulsing swollen lips of her cunt. With her other hand, she buggered herself with three fingers inside her bumhole, poking hard, and emerging, slimed with arse grease. Her belly convulsed.

'Oh!' Suze shrieked, climaxing, 'Ah! Ah! Ahh . . .'

Miss Travemunde adjusted the video lens, and sat on her desk. She unpinned her skirtlet, and removed it, folding it neatly, and placing it on the desk beside her. Her lower body was nude, save for her stockings and sussies, and she coyly raised one leg, to cradle her knee under her chin. Her anal pucker, perineum, and cunt lips were exposed bare, with the fronds of her massive pubic bush draping the gash flesh and inner thighs.

'Class, those of you in frillies may now open your panties, and perform part one of the demonstration, that is, stimulation of the quim. You will masturbate by touch alone, and unseen, beneath your desks. Those in body stockings are already open. We shall leave advanced anal stimulation to the next lesson. For your guidance, I myself shall repeat the demonstration by our subject, who has proved herself –' she pointed to Suze's come-slimed thighs and cunt '– an accomplished frigwench, and an expert example. After masturbation, you shall deposit your wet towels in the laundry basket.'

The video screen focussed on the hairy swollen folds of Miss Travemunde's cunt. She placed the fingers of one hand on her perineum, and began to stroke, with occasional caresses to the outer lower labia. With her other hand, she fiddled at her thigh, and casually removed her right leg. It was a flesh-coloured artificial prosthesis, and she lifted it, to place it on top of her skirt. The class were busy with their hands between their hidden thighs, and evinced no surprise. Only Suze, gaping through sweat-blurred eyes, gasped: like Cpl Pette, the German girl was an *unijambiste*. Her naked stump twitched and writhed, as she masturbated, with drops of come wetting its silky golden hairs. The video screen pulsed with the motions of the teacher's frig, her fingers squashing the slimy cunt folds, and reaming her perineum, anus bud and clitoris.

'I expect you all to have reached orgasm within five minutes,' she panted. 'Next week's lesson shall include nipple touching. I shall again enlist the services of this excellent frigwench.'

Her fingers held open her slit, poking and rubbing, as she glanced at Suze, looking for acknowledgement. Suze did not respond; her eyes were fixed on the video screen, where the teacher's come-slimed quim folds writhed beside her twitching, silken-haired thigh stump, and she was masturbating afresh.

'Isn't Miss Travemunde a wonderful teacher?' said Portia, when class was dismissed, and the wenches were trooping to tea. 'I had the most marvellous wank. She is so inspirational.'

Exhausted from her own wanks, Suze nodded.

'I didn't know she was an amputee,' she said.

'What difference does that make?' said Portia. 'Unless you find it exciting? Reminding you of that cruel corporal, I suppose. She's probably having a good time, waggling her spanked stump, while the Brazilians bumfuck her.'

Suze blushed, and they entered the tearoom. On that occasion, and for weeks thereafter, she was treated with deference: as mistress of her friend Portia, and as the expert example to Miss Travemunde's class. She fell into an undemanding rhythm of life at Saxworfa's, becoming adept at vigorous ball-bouncing sports, as well as the womanly arts of needlecraft, cookery and deportment. Her model training served her well at the latter, where she was frequently required to catwalk in the nude, for the wenches to ogle her perfect carriage, and the ripe sway of her buttocks, which, the teacher advised, held the key to correct posture. She excelled at pulling the mistress's chariot, harnessed as a pony, and became her favourite pony wench. In truth, Suze strove to excel at the cruel entertainment, for that was the only way she could be sure of receiving the whipstrokes that made her bottom tingle, and which she now, blushingly, admitted she craved.

Her relations with her roomate grew more intimate, and she got Portia to agree that, as a slave, she must obey her

218

mistress's whim. She discovered a new joy in dominating the beautiful blond, and her secondary slave, Gabi: shaming her with mud baths, toe-lickings and spankings, and buggering either girl with the dildo, while the other was obliged to watch, masturbating. Even Portia and Gabi scowled, sometimes, at the extent of exhibitionism which Suze imposed: she discovered, for example, that both wenches were shy about their toilet, and took delight in making each girl dung and pee, while masturbating, under the other's gaze. She goaded them to the limit, with such humiliance, until Portia agreed, on occasions, to strip Suze naked, and administer a vigorous bare-bottom strapping, in revenge, as though Suze herself were the spank slave. After her strapping, Suze implied that her worst terror, far more than the searing welts on her thrashed bottom, was to feel the dildo cleaving her anus; there, too, Portia and Gabi were ready to lustfully oblige their mistress. Suze groaned with joy, through her tears, as her spanked arse writhed under buggery with the strap-on dildo.

She was not immune from everyday chastisement, usually for some minor peccadillo, thoughtlessly committed. The mistress thrashed her occasionally with a strap or holed paddle, deciding to exculpate her of several misdemeanours at once, with a single hard beating. Afterwards, tea was served, and Suze took it kneeling at the mistress's feet, while the mistress masturbated, sometimes inviting Suze to tongue her off, and swallow her come, between sips of tea. Wenches were required to have weekly checkups at surgery, with compulsory hot and cold enemas, and Suze's comportment, as the tubes were rammed up her anus, to spurt the freezing or searing liquid, was often less than satisfactory, on purpose: her squealing and shuddering frequently earned her a hand-spanking or strapping with a belt, or even the rubbers of a stethoscope, from nurse Aldwine. Dr Fredegund looked on approvingly, as Suze's bare, tubed bottom wriggled under Aldwine's strap, and spurted enema fluid.

'Subs are sneaky creatures, and will cheat abominably, to get what they want,' said the doctor, fingering her own bottom under her knickers. 'Suzette's superb sphincter control should cause her no enema problems. Right, wench?'

'Oh! No, doctor,' Suze gasped, her reddened bum squirming to the full. 'I have no control at all, I just cannot hold it in. Look.'

Dr Fredegund would smile approvingly, as a spray of anal fluid soaked the caning nurse.

Though the bumwelts of Suze's earlier imprisonments never disappeared, they faded to a regal purple, marbled under her skin, and lightly carried the pinks and crimsons of strapping, spanks and paddling. Dr Fredegund and her nurse used Suze's thrashing as an excuse to masturbate; the doctor said Suze's presence, and the glory of her fesses, had ushered in a new climate of liberation, where girls could admit to their secret desires, and masturbate as often, openly, and copiously as they wished, without having to endure the taunt of 'frigwench'. Some wenches had even experimented by trimming, or entirely shaving, their pubic hair, although the mistress drew the line at that desecration.

'We might as well admit what we do,' the doctor said, one day, as Suze, in the nude, panted under a sound strapping from the nurse, stripped to bra and panties. 'Aldwine has been attending your masturbation classes, and is thrilled by your techniques.'

The strap lashed Suze's bare bum, squirming, and reddened by over thirty strokes. *Vap! Vap!*

'Ooh!' she groaned. 'That's tight, nurse. They are not my classes, but Miss Travemunde's.'

'Come, come, everyone knows you are the expert, and Miss Travemunde prefers to sit to one side, mimicking your self-caresses,' Dr Fredegund said, herself frigging. 'You have quite a reputation, as a vigorous pony wench, as a hard and cruel mistress – Gabi is a chatterbox – and as a doyenne of the masturbatory arts. Such a wealth of experience, your tips on labial stimulation and perineum arousal are first class, and even the mistress has deigned to learn from you. I hear that you may be promoted to senior.'

Vap! Vap!

'I shouldn't like that, doctor. I'd have to beat girls all the time, without the chance to bare up, myself,' Suze said, grimacing, as the strap slapped her quivering bare nates.

The doctor laughed, and swivelled, showing her own scarred bottom to Suze.

'We seniors have our ways,' she said. 'We are all someone's spank slave.'

Vap! Vap! Suze bare squirmed, and darkened enema fluid spurted from her anus, while heavy come seeped from her cooze.

'Ooh!' she yelped. 'How many is that, please, nurse?'

'Forty-four,' said Aldwine. 'Shall I stop?'

'Please don't be deferential,' Suze gasped. 'No, don't stop. Can't you see I'm juicing?'

Vap! Vap! As she flogged, Aldwine masturbated her cunt, through her tight wet panties.

'Ahh . . . yes! Oh, yes, nurse, beat me, please.'

'You are a slut,' said the doctor, smiling.

'OK, I admit it. It has taken me such a long time to know myself and my body, and my cravings. Why was I blessed with such a big bottom? Now I think I know. I'm . . . truly a spank slave.'

'Your bottom is made for spanking,' the doctor said. 'For those fesses to be smooth of stripes would be a crime.'

Vap! Vap! Suze's clenching buttocks expelled her enema tube, and a jet of brown liquid splashed over the nurse's bra and belly. Her come spurted in torrents, down her thighs.

'You bitch,' hissed Aldwine.

Vap!

'Oww!' shrieked Suze, as the strap took her right on the slimed anus and cunt flaps. 'Oh, yes, please . . . doctor, permission to wank off?'

The doctor nodded, and moved her quim before Suze's face. Suze fingered her wet cunt, vigorously masturbating, as she tongued the doctor's swollen nubbin, and her bottom continued to quiver under Aldwine's lashes, as the nurse frigged. All three wenches brought themelves to orgasm.

221

'Oh, it's lovely,' gasped Suze, feeling her bare bum, as she looked at her strapwelts in the mirror. 'So many lovely wanks and beatings, I never want to leave here.'

'Some day, you must, Suze, when you have excelled in the ladylike arts,' sighed Fredegund. 'Our discipline and training, our instruction in the arts of frigging, lead us to pleasuring males. All this wanking … we are longing for cock to fill our quims and split our bums, aren't we? It is a fact that all females can think of is fucking. The things that interest us – cooking, beauty, clothes – are the preamble to fucking. And for self-esteem we need males, who treat us as things, and use our bodies as pleasure meat, thrilling us with their disdain.'

'Males!' Suze spat, grimacing. 'I've had enough of them. A girl knows best how to pleasure another girl, and how to thrash her properly. All men want is to hurt us and shame us, on their own revolting power trip.'

'Which is their way of showing affection,' retorted Fredegund. 'How I long for a hairy, sweaty male, to carry me off over his shoulder, for a proper thrashing, before he fucks me. Oh, to be the spank slave of a real, crude hunk! If a man likes you, he'll thrash and bumfuck you. Your humiliance and submission mean he wants to own you, and that shows he really cares. To make a wench his chattel, to bind her and whip her, totally humiliant and totally obedient, is the height of male devotion.'

'I cannot accept that,' murmured Suze.

'Of couse she can't,' sneered Aldwine, grimacing, as she wiped Suze's enema fluid from her titties, belly and panties. 'She's a lesbo, that's why. The dirty bitch fouled me on purpose.'

'What?' Suze flared.

'You heard, lesbo.'

Aldwine flicked a gobbet of muck at Suze, who ducked, allowing it to splatter Dr Fredegund. Suze lashed out, knocking Aldwine's hand away, and the nurse responded with a hard punch to Suze's titties, followed by a kick to her gash. Suze doubled up, and sank to the floor, clutching her belly, and groaning. Nurse Aldwine began to kick her in the titties and between the legs, and Suze wailed. Ordering the nurse to stop, Dr Fredegund whipped Aldwine between her thighs, on the wet crotch of her panties, and repeated the blow several times, until Aldwine shrieked and crouched.

'Oh, that hurts,' she whimpered. 'You whipped me right on my clitty. You're a lesbo too, you . . . you frigwench!'

The doctor blanched.

'You should not have said that before a witness, nurse,' she whispered. 'I shall have to report your scandalous behaviour and remarks to the mistress, and you know what that means. A public whipping, at the *folkmoot*.'

The nurse paled.

'Oh! I'm sorry, doctor . . . please, not that! You know I cannot bear pain.'

Dr Fredegund smiled.

'Exactly,' she said.

14

Robed and Ripped

In the pink light of early dawn, a quartet of fully-robed
seniors led the whimpering Aldwine, in her nurse's uniform, to the whipping post, in a clearing surrounded by a
glade of trees. Her hands were bound in front of her, on a
pole knotted to her hobble bar, causing her to stumble.
Her face was wet with tears, staining her stiff white nurse's
tunic, under a blue cape, and worn above white stockings,
stained by mud, for she was shoeless. Her white nurse's
bonnet perched coquettishly over her lush, but unkempt,
blond tresses.

'Oh . . . be merciful, mistress, I beg you,' she pleaded. 'I
haven't slept all night.'

'Were you merciful, when you insulted your superior, Dr
Fredegund, and the wench Suzette? I think not,' snorted
the mistress. 'Your only mitigation is providing your body,
as an offering at *folkmoot*.'

The wenches of Saxworfa watched, standing in rows
below the platform of chastisement, while, around the
whipping post, the seniors stood, robed in their uniforms
of rank: black rubber kneeboots and seamed black nylon
stockings, in a diamond mesh pattern, short pleated skirts
of black lace, and white blouses, with the breasts pumped
up beneath by black or pink brassieres, and the waists
narrowed to eighteen or nineteen inches, by pink corsets.
The blouses were open deep at the neck, baring breast
flesh. Dr Fredegund was among the seniors, wearing a
stethoscope round her neck, as symbol of her authority. A

pink morning sun illuminated the whipping post, in the form of a gallows, with a cross beam, festooned with pulleys and restraining straps, and the pole itself fitted with cuffs for the wrists and ankles of a victim. Of the two choices of restraint, the mistress opted for full suspension from the cross beam. Nurse Aldwine burst into frenzied sobbing.

'Oh, no, mistress!' she wailed. 'Please whip me at the crouch, or bind me to the pole!'

The mistress tore off Aldwine's cape.

'Strip her and hang her,' she rapped.

The senior girls peeled off Aldwine's garments, as she sobbed, stripping her to bra, knickers and stockings and sussies, then contemptuously ripping off those undergarments. They clawed the stockings to shreds, and tore her knickers and garter belt from her, breaking all of her sussie straps. She was released in the nude from her ropes and hobble, only to have two girls pinion her wrists behind her back, while two more crushed her feet with their rubber boots. Finally, her nurse's bonnet was knocked from her head by Fredegund, who stooped, to place her stethoscope between Aldwine's quivering bare titties. The breasts bounced and trembled, at Aldwine's choked sobbing, with drool trickling from the naked girl's mouth.

'I pronounce the prisoner fit to receive punishment,' Fredegund intoned.

The seniors replaced Aldwine's wrist binding, but with a long rope, much stouter than the cords before. It was looped through the pulley on the cross beam, and Aldwine was hoisted, wriggling and sobbing, with her feet dancing inches above the platform, and her toes just touching. Her legs were stretched wide apart, and each ankle tied by a rope to the platform's rim, so that her feet twitched in the air, several inches above the dais. Aldwine's back faced the assembly, and her buttocks were splayed to the full, with the slice of her gash, and her hairy pubic tuft, clearly visible, between her quivering bare thighs. Her wrenched back muscles rippled, as she writhed, her whole weight suspended from her straining arms. The senior girl, Elfina, scooped her roommate's torn panties, and slipped them on as a hood, tightly muffling the nurse's head, and obliging Aldwine to breath through her soiled crotch gusset. The panties' fabric heaved in and out, with Aldwine's frenzied gasps, and moistened rapidly from her tears. The mistress's bronze stockings shimmered, as she took position before the girl's buttocks, and lifted her three foot rattan cane. The crowd hushed. Suddenly, she smiled, and presented the cane to Fredegund.

'It is right that the aggrieved party should deliver the chastisement,' she said.

Fredegund curtsied, and shook her head.

'Begging your pardon, mistress,' she said, 'the truly wronged party is Miss Suzette. I suggest she should apply the strokes.'

The mistress summoned Suzette onto the platform, and asked her if she would do so.

'Fifty strokes to the bare buttocks,' she said.

'No ... no ...' Aldwine wailed. 'Not with rattan, mistress, please.'

Suzette sighed, and licked her lips.

'I'll do it, mistress,' she murmured.

'Then, you may strip naked,' said the mistress, 'for comfort and harmony. Nude should whip nude.'

Blushing, Suze stripped off her top and frilly skirt, and stood, nude, to receive the cane. The rising sun glowed pink on her bare breasts, and danced, glistening, in her moist pubic bush; already, in the growing morning heat, her body dripped with sweat. She flexed the rattan, and swished the thin, whippy rod in the air, with a loud whistling sound. The mistress ordered the watching girls to hold their hands behind their backs, then ordered Suze to begin. The suspended girl whimpered under her knickers hood, and her ankles shook her tethering ropes. Suze lifted her arm. *Vap!* The cane slashed the air, falling across Aldwine's ripe mid-fesses, and striping the buttock skin with a vivid pink weal. Aldwine gurgled and shook, her bare melons clenching. *Vip!* A second stroke took her slightly above the first. The flogged girl began to moan. *Vip!*

'Ah . . .' she whimpered, as the third stroke lashed the tender skin of her top buttocks.

Suze continued to cane the wench's bare, in hard, rhythmic strokes, at intervals of three seconds. She worked on the upper thighs, stroking the stretched flesh halfway down to the knees, and the haunches, which darkened the fastest, while returning to the darkly wealing meat of the central arse globes, at every fourth stroke. The caning rocked Aldwin's body back and forth, with her back muscles rippling, and her legs shooting rigid, under her clenching fesses. *Vip!*

'Ohh . . .'

Vip!

'Oh! No! No . . .'

Vip!

'*Ooh!*'

Aldwine's naked titties bounced, as her whole body shook, dripping with sweat, and with a trickle of come sprayed from her rocked cunt. Suze's own quim was moist and, as she pressed her thighs, the gash lips slithered in her cunt slime. The whipping platform was stained beneath Suze's dripping cooze, and there was a pool of juice below the loins of the flogged girl. The watching wenches had bright eyes and darting tongues, but kept their hands behind their backs, while wriggling to press their thighs together. *Vip!*

'Ah . . . no, please stop . . .'

Vip!

'*Ahh!*'

Aldwine's bare was stained bright crimson with caneweals, darkening to puffy ridges, and her haunches were a fiery dark blotch of purple welts. Choked sobs issued uncontrollably from beneath her panties hood. *Vip!*

'Oh . . . enough . . .'

A hissing gush of piss erupted from Aldwine's quim, splashing Suze's bare feet.

'You bitch,' Suze hissed.

Vip! Vip! Vip!

'*Ahh!*' screamed the pissing girl, as three hard cuts took her in one single welt, on mid-fesse, deepening it to an angry crimson trench.

Vip! Vip! Vip!

'Ohh!'

Three more lashes fell in the same welt; her buttocks jerked, clenching and squirming, as the whole nude body shook, straining against her ropes. A spray of dungs burst from her anus, plopping wetly on the wood beneath her bum. The mistress wrinkled her nose.

'Flog her ten extra for that disgusting display,' she ordered. 'I should have made the slut wear rubber caning pants; she can wear them for all of next week, and is forbidden use of the lavatory.'

Suze continued the beating to fifty-nine strokes, by which time Aldwine's wriggling had ebbed to a lifeless, mechanical jerking, and her hooded head hung low over her breasts. Her flogged bottom was black and purple with puffy ridged weals, which extended well down the backs of her thighs. *Vip!*

'Ahh!' Aldwine howled.

The final stroke brought her to life again, as Suze upended her cane, and sliced hard between her thighs, with the cane slapping her slimed cunt and anus bud. The mistress began to clap, and the applause was taken up by all the seniors, and the spectating wenches.

'It is you we applaud, Suzette,' she said, 'for you have at last earned your promotion to senior.'

Suze gasped, as Dr Fredegund unpacked garments from her medical bag, and the girls joined in robing Suze in the uniform of a senior: tight pink rubber corset, pink lacy bra and panties, a clinging white nylon blouse, and pleated black skirt, with pink sussies, and black stockings in real sheer nylon. The girls fastened her bra and corset tightly, and pulled her narrow thong panties up high, while touching her buttocks, breasts, and come-slopped quim.

'Let us see you, miss,' said the mistress. 'Isn't she lovely, my wenches? Show off, Suzette. Every girl likes to expose herself.'

Suze preened and twirled, as though on a models' catwalk; the girls cheered, as she flicked up her skirt to show her bum globes, left almost bare by the tight thong stretched in her arse cleft. She put her tongue out, and pirouetted, thrusting forward her bum and titties. The flogged nurse sobbed helplessly, still shuddering in her suspension, and with a trickle of pee dribbling from her cunt. To cheers, Suze performed a victory dance around the wench's bruised, blackened buttocks, still trembling, and with the weals from Suze's cane crusting into hard coruscated ridges. She opened her blouse, and scooped her breasts free of her bra, then thrust forward her rib cage, to make her bare breasts bounce and twirl, with the little castles of her stiff nipples gleaming strawberry red, in the rising shafts of dawn sunlight. Lifting her skirtlet, and lowering her panties to her knees, she thrust her naked bum at the assembly, clenching the fesses in and out, beneath her rolling hips, then turned, to part her thighs, and hold open her gash flaps, so that the girls could see her pink, juicing cooze meat. Her lips pouted in triumph, blowing kisses to the bright-eyed wenches. As Suze pranced, her face shining, and her dripping, pulsing cunt flaps wetting the tops of her nylon stockings, the mistress turned to the glade, and clapped once more.

'Seen enough, doctors?' she cried. 'I promised you this slut was prime beef, and worth every *sou*.'

Suze stopped still and her jaw dropped, as Drs Pance and Morue emerged from the thicket, leering at her nude body. Both men carried long, thick canes.

'Your merchandise is always of the best, Miss Gundersheim,' Morue said. 'I trust the men may taste, before they buy?'

'But of course,' said the mistress. 'Girls, you may place your hands in front of you, and lift your skirts. Remember, we are bound to obey the orders of our masters. The sacrifice you must make at *folkmoot* is for the survival of our community.'

Trembling, and with some sly smiles, the wenches bared their bums and quims, and placed their fingers at their gashes, parting their thighs, before rolling their cunt basins, and covering their coozes with their hands. Slow, sensuous frigging slimed their twitching fingers with oily come, glistening in the sunlight, as they exposed themselves. From the glade emerged a dozen males, unshaven and drooling, and carrying whips; as one, they made straight for Suze. They pinioned Suze, struggling and weeping, with her legs parted, and feet on the ground. Her breasts were pressed to the wooden punishment platform, and her buttocks were forced high and wide. They ripped off her brand new uniform, tearing the bra, panties, corset and stockings from her with loud slashing noises, and much grunting laughter, in which the mistress joined. They twanged Suze's bra and knicker elastic, and her rubber corset, against her teats and arse, leaving delicate pink marks on her skin, before shredding and ripping the garments, and contemptuously whipping her with her torn underthings. *Vip! Vip!* Suze wriggled, shrieking, as the whalebone stays of her ripped corset left jagged weals on her naked titties and bum. The men wore *képis*, and tattered white uniforms, that had once belonged to the French Foreign Legion. One by one, they dropped their shorts, revealing their erect cocks pointing at Suze's buttocks, forced wide. Dr Morue lifted his cane.

'I know this submissive bitch,' he said, 'and I know how to prepare her.'

He lifted his cane. *Vip! Vip!*

'*Ooh!* Stop! No!' Suze whimpered, a dozen hands pinioning her wriggling body, as her bare bum squirmed and reddened under two vicious strokes, leaving bright pink weals.

Warsweide darted forward, giggling, to hold Suze by the ankles, and squealed, as the men felt under her skirtlet, to paw her cooze, already wet, and sliming her thighs with come. Two legionnaires pinched Suze's nipples, mashing the teat flesh against her rib cage. Suze drooled, teeth bare in a rictus, and her trapped arse flesh writhing and quivering, in the cane's flickering shadow. *Vip! Vip! Vip!* Weals rose red on her skin.

'*Ahh . . .!*'

'The wench is gushing,' growled Pance, and thrust his fist into her pouch, withdrawing it, slopped with Suze's come.

He wiped it on her bare arse, and returned to the cooze, gathering several palmfuls of fluid, until her buttock meat shone oily bright with her own juice. The caning continued, wet bum. At length, Suze ceased struggling, and only her frantically twitching arse globes betrayed emotion, as they wealed and coloured. Warsweide's skirtlet was ripped off, and her own naked arse covered by the stroking palms of the men, with their fingers in her cleft, and between the lips of her gushing pouch.

'Oh, that's so nice,' Warsweide trilled. 'Gentlemen, forget this sorry bitch, and take me with you.'

'We can take whatever we want, slut,' snapped Dr Morue, slapping her face.

When Suze had taken over three dozen canestrokes on the writhing bare, she moaned, as a strong jet of piss steamed from her cunt, splashing Warsweide and her tormentors.

'Spank the bitch harder,' Warsweide cried.

Her own bare bum wriggled under a vigorous spanking, as the males in turn masturbated her. Come cascaded from the wet, dangling fronds of Warsweide's pubic forest.

'Oh . . . oh. Yes,' she panted.

As the men's fists frotted and poked her cunt, and her bum reddened under spanks, she too pissed, directing her spray of fluid over Suze's thighs and bottom. Suze wailed, sobbing, as the beating continued on her piss-soaked fesses, now deeply wealed with purple puffy welts, and the whole expanse of her buttocks a blotchy mass of inflamed skin. The cane whistled, flashing in the rising sun, as it stroked the girl's bare, and delivering its *Vip! Vip! Vip!* with a squelching sound, to the wet bum globes.

'No . . . no,' Suze cried. 'Please stop. Oh, anything but this.'

Vip! Vip! Vip!

'Oh . . . the shame, the shame,' she whimpered.

The beating stopped.

'Oh . . . oh . . . oh . . .' Suze sobbed. '*Ahh!*'

She screamed, as Morue's cock penetrated her anus, and drove into her rectum, to begin a vigorous bum-fucking.

The slapping of his hips on her buttocks echoed the spanking of the frigged Warsweide's nates, as she held onto Suze's left ankle, with the right leg flailing helplessly under the male invader. The man buggered her for five minutes, before he grunted, and a bubbling froth of sperm erupted from her anus. He climbed off, for his place to be taken by another legionnaire, who penetrated Suze's rectum in a single thrust of his engorged cockshaft, and began to bugger her. He, too, buggered her for several minutes, until he spurted, and Suze had scarcely a second to gulp, and shake the tears from her face, before another cock was inside her anal shaft.

'Please stop,' she whimpered. 'It hurts so dreadfully, oh, please stop.'

'Ah, yes,' cried Warsweide, her cries drowning Suze's bleats, as a legionnaire mounted her from the rear, and began to bugger her. She shook and squirmed, as he rammed her anus, and clawed Suze's leg with her finger-nails.

'Yes, bugger me, sir,' gasped Warsweide. 'My hole is tighter than the frigwench's.'

The legionnaire slapped her face several times, as he bum-fucked her, rocking her head back and forth.

'I judge the holes, you dirty little whore,' he growled.

One by one, the legionnaires took Suze in her anus, and the sun was high and hot, when the last had spermed between her jerking arse cheeks. Those who had buggered her inspected the ranks of exhibitionist wenches, feeling or frigging bums and cunts, and tasting the come that flowed from the masturbating wenches' open quims. Warsweide panted, as a second, then a third, bugger mounted her. Suze sobbed uncontrollably, panting hoarsely. Come and sperm drooled from her cunt basin, down her quivering thighs.

'Uh . . . uh . . .' she gasped.

Dr Morue laughed.

'The slut wants to come,' he said.

He thrust his hand into Suze's dripping cooze, and flicked her clitoris repeatedly with his thumbnail.

'Ah ... ah ... yes! Oh!' Suze shrilled, convulsing in orgasm, with a heavy spurt of come from her quivering cunt flaps.

The mistress beamed.

'I promised a real frigwench, and submissive slut, gentlemen,' she said. 'Please help yourself to wenches, by your folkright.'

The legionnaire buggering Warsweide snarled, as his spunk flowed, then kicked her, sobbing, to the ground. Besides Suze, the men selected Bodwenna, Claudia Wulf, and Warsweide, as their booty; the girls were forced to kneel, with their faces in the dirt, while anal plugs were inserted in their holes, and strapped around their loins with rubber girdles, then the plugs linked by a rope. Drs Morue and Pance exchanged glances.

'We'll take the flogged bitch, too,' growled Pance, gesturing to Aldwine in her bonds.

The mistress ordered the sobbing nurse cut down. Fredegund assisted in her release, and prompt addition to the rope of anally-plugged girls, crouching in the dirt.

'And that one, the doctor slut,' added Morue. 'She has a good arse.'

Dr Fredegund paled.

'But gentlemen,' said the mistress, 'Dr Fredegund is one of my senior staff, and invaluable.'

'Are you arguing with the legion, Gundersheim, you whore?' snarled Pance.

'Why, no, of course, not ...' she blurted.

'You are *deserters* from the legion,' spat Dr Fredegund. Morue leered at her.

'That earns you more than a flogging, when we get you back to base,' he murmured. 'We'll stripe your arse, then stake you out with honey smeared in your welts, and filling your gash, for the ants to feast on.'

Fredegund began to tremble.

'Be reasonable, gentlemen,' said the mistress.

'You forget who put you here, Gundersheim,' said Morue. 'We got you out of that women's prison, when there was a jail cell awaiting you in Cayenne for your crimes, because MaBelle is our creature. We send you choice morsels of cuntmeat, like this English whore, for your noxious lesbian pleasures. We take what we want.'

Leering, Pance raised Fredegund's skirtlet, and grasped her by the cunt, squeezing hard. Fredegund moaned, but parted her legs; her come began to ooze over the legionnaire's pumping fingers, as he masturbated her.

'No. I shan't allow it,' gasped the mistress.

'Forget the whore Fredegund. Give *her* a taste,' spat Morue, pointing at Miss Gundersheim. 'Hang the lesbo bitch.'

Wriggling and whimpering, the mistress, Miss Gundersheim, was stripped naked, and hung on the gibbet. Her feet and hands were bound, and Dr Morue lifted the cane, still warm from Suze's buttocks. Lighting a cigar, and holding it between his lips, he began to lash the squirming mistress's naked arse, with heavy strokes of the rod. She screamed and squirmed, as her bare nates clenched, reddening rapidly under the slices of the cane, and with her creamy bum flesh rapidly puffing to a welted, blotchy mass. At the twelfth canestroke, she pissed herself, spraying golden steaming pee over the platform, and thereafter, her cunt drooled pee, as she writhed under her flogging.

'No, gentlemen . . . Oh! Oh! It hurts so! Please stop! Enough! Oh, please . . .' she whimpered, as the cane striped her.

Dr Pance had Fredegund dancing on his fist, impaling her gash. Suze, groaning, was thrust face first in the dirt, and she yelped, as an anal plug penetrated her rectum, to be roped to the other girls in the chain. The plug slammed viciously at her anal root, and she looked round, her face twisted in anguish, to see the implement wielded by Portia, who jabbed her a few more times, then reamed her bumhole with the plug, before securing it to the tether rope.

'Every sacrifice day, the choicest cuntmeat gets sent away to sex slavery,' she laughed. 'How I envy you, slut . . .'

Suze looked to Warsweide, beside her.

'How could you be so cruel, Warsweide?' she moaned, as the glade rang with Miss Gundersheim's screams.

'You loved it, you dirty frigwench,' Warsweide hissed. 'Getting tooled in the bum by a dozen cocks made you come.'

'You said your bumhole was tighter than mine,' Suze whimpered. 'That's awful.'

Vip! Vip!

'Ahh . . .'

Miss Gundersheim's flogged bare wriggled frantically, as the cane striped her.

'No . . . no . . . please,' she gurgled.

Vip! Vip!

'Don't say that lesbo bitch has been kind to you,' hissed Warsweide. 'She deserves it, the cunt. Fattening us, and letting us preen, when all the time preparing us for slavery.'

Vip! Vip!

'Ahh! Enough, please. Oh, I can't take any more,' wailed Miss Gundersheim, her cunt drooling pee mingled with oily come.

Morue ordered her cut down, and her face pushed into the dirt, with her flogged bum in the air.

'Give the lesbo real meat, men,' he ordered.

'No,' begged Gundersheim. 'I cannot bear being arse-fucked. My anus is too sensitive. I'll do anything . . . please . . .'

All the legionnaires smiled, as their tools quivered to full erection. With Morue's foot on her neck, grinding her face in the dirt, Gundersheim took the same dozen cocks, buggering her, until sperm filled her bumhole, and dribbled down her thighs.

'Oh, no,' she wailed, as each new cock cleaved her anus. 'Not more . . .'

'You want it, bitch,' growled Pance. 'All you sluts want it. Whipped and arse-tooled, by real men – ask the English whore.'

'Suzette,' wailed Gundersheim, 'say it isn't true.'

Suze swallowed, and blushed.

'I can't tell a lie, mistress,' she said. 'We all want it. Some of us take time to learn.'

'You bitch,' hissed Bodwenna, 'We'll get you for that.'

'Whip her, and let me smear honey on her weals, and in her cunt,' whimpered Aldwine, through her sobs.

'We're going to a living hell,' said Bodwenna, 'because that is why Saxworfa's exists, to make offerings to these male brutes. But don't worry, we'll find ways to make it worse than hell for you, bitch.'

Suze shuddered.

'Ah! Ah!' squealed Gundersheim, as piss and come flowed from her cunt, under the ruthless buggery of the legionnaires. 'Oh . . .'

Her arse bucked, meeting their thrusts.

'Oh, yes . . .' she panted.

'The bitch is going to come,' said Morue.

'Ah . . . fuck my hole, split me, burst me, oh, yes!' gasped the buggered mistress, as a heavy flow of come spurted from her cunt. *'Yes . . .!'*

The roped girls stood, to form a cortege, with their hands tied behind their backs, while Miss Gundersheim was strung up from the scaffold, legs and arms bound, and bare arse exposed. Morue smeared honey over her arse weals, and plugged her anus with a honeycomb, then invited the wenches of Saxworfa's to do as they wished with their mistress. Portia seized the cane, and swished the air, as the legionnaires led their troop of girls out of the glade.

'Please, no, Portia,' gasped Gundersheim. 'Haven't I always been kind to you?'

Portia bared her teeth in a snarl, and knelt before the mistress's bared cunt. Her jaws opened, and she plunged her teeth into her extruded clit, gleaming in the sunlight. Her teeth fastened on the nubbin, and her jaws clamped.

'Ohh!' screamed the bound female, and her quim sprayed piss over her tormentress's face.

Portia rose, and licked her lips, dripping with the mistress's come and pee.

'You disgusting whore,' she murmured, lifting her cane over the quivering bare. 'You mucky, mucky pup.'

Vip! The cane lashed full across the bare buttocks, raising a livid pink weal.

'Ooh . . .'
Vip Vip!
'*Ahh . . .*'

Suze turned back to see the nude mistress, suspended from the scaffold, and twirling helplessly, as Portia's cane lashed her bare arse globes, rocking her body back and forth on its ropes, while Dr Fredegund, frigging herself, whipped her naked titties. Suze winced, as a legionnaire's belt lashed her thighs, making her buttocks clench, with the anal plug painfully tight inside her channel.

'Eyes front, you submissive slut,' he growled. 'What you had today is only a taste of what awaits you, *slave.*'

They reached the river, where the girls embarked on the same boat that had transported Suze to Saxworfa's.

'Dr Morue,' she gasped, 'please? I'm no troublemaker. I meant what I said . . . I recognise I am a submissive and a slut. When you brought me here, there was Cpl Pette – you remember, the amputee? Shall I meet her again?'

Smack!

'Oww!' Suze cried, as Dr Morue slapped her breasts.

'We keep no amputees at the base,' he snarled. 'No good as slaves.'

'Then where did you take her?' Suze persisted.

Smack! Smack!

'Ahh!'

He spanked her naked breasts, making them quiver, with pink bruises across her nipples. Dr Morue lit a cigar, and blew smoke into Suze's face.

'Maybe you'll find out, when the legion has no further use for your slave's arse,' he replied.

The slave girls remained roped, for their journey upriver. While the legionnaires drank wine, smoked, and played cards, the girls, hands and ankles bound, had to crawl, fetch and serve with their teeth. Suze had to learn how to pour wine from a bottle clenched between her jaws, as failure to do so meant an immediate bare-bottom caning. As playthings of their captors, the girls had to submit to every indecency and indignity, until, after several days' voyage, they no longer perceived them as indignities. Throughout, Suze had to listen to the whispers of her sister slaves vowing to make her suffer once they were unbound. The girls were not permitted the meanest scrap of clothing, but had to remain nude in their bonds even while sleeping, being released, only to pleasure a male. They became accustomed to the men shamelessly feeling their cunts and titties, often masturbating them to climax, in a contest between two or three legionnaires, to see who could bring his slave off the first; to summary thrashing on the bare arse or breasts, for no reason than the males' amusement, often with honey smeared in the caneweals; sometimes, a savage cunt-thrashing with a strap or cane, leaving the girl's vulva a mass of blistered welts. Listening to their conversation, Suze learned that they were destined for the hardest labour at the legion deserters' base, with a few lucky girls selected as arse slaves, whose duty was to sensuously pleasure the males.

Her cunt basin and arse ached with weals, most of the time, for the legionnaires liked to thrash and bugger her body the most, and she was in no doubt she was destined for an arse slave. Every morning and night, the girls' bodies were swabbed in healing ointment by the doctors, so that Suze's skin became sleek and silky, and the welts of her canings looked like fresh veinous marbling, glowing beneath her arse skin. The girls had to take a thrashing or a bum-fuck from one legionnaire, while kneeling, and tonguing the cock of another. The direst treatments, of which bare-bottom chastisement was a mere preamble, awaited a girl who allowed her licking and sucking of cock to falter, as her bottom squirmed under canestrokes, or the stiff cock impaling and ramming her anus. If teeth or tongue were used less than artfully on a swollen glans or cockshaft, she risked a ducking, bound and gagged, in the turbid waters of the Maroni; being strapped to the ship's funnel, with gash and teats pressed to the scorching metal; a whole day of bare-bum canings, every two hours, with her quim flaps clamped shut, and her anus blocked by putty. The girls were allowed to smoke cigarettes, but not with their mouths: they held the fumables in their cunt lips, sucking and blowing with their quims. Suze alone smoked cigarettes with her anus, and proudly puffed bigger billows than the other girls.

One day, Suze was bent over the deck rail, having been newly arse-fucked by three men, and taking the strap on her bare buttocks, from Dr Morue. Sperm and come glazed her quivering thighs, as the strap flogged her.

'Oh, doctor,' she blurted, 'why do men get pleasure from hurting us?'

'Because we are generous, slut,' he snarled, 'and it makes you sub sluts so happy. I've listened to what your girlfriends have in store for you, and hope the men choose you as an arse slave. You have my recommendation. I've never known an arse so tight for buggery, or to weal so well under whipping.'

His hand invaded her cunt, to emerge, dripping with her come, and then he thrust his fingers in her mouth, making her suck them.

'See? You juice under thrashing, bitch,' he said.

'I know,' Suze sobbed. 'To be beaten on the bare is . . . I don't know, it's not pleasure. It must be on the naked bum, because it is so shameful, and hurts so much.'

He began to rub her clit, in between strokes of his strap to her wriggling buttocks.

'Uhh . . . yes . . .' she groaned. 'Don't stop . . .'

'Personally,' he said, as her belly began to flutter, 'I don't care what those other sluts do to an English whore, except that it might be amusing to watch what tortures they inflict, and then punish them for torturing you. But I think you'll be a good arse slave, nothing but a female animal, naked and mucky, a pleasure tool, for males, who love to see girl flesh writhe under the whip; a mere arse for buggery. That shall be your life.'

'Oh, doctor,' Suze blurted, as she dripped cunt juice, 'yes . . . I'm coming . . .'

That night, the girls took her. They slept, roped to their bunks, in the foetid gloom of the ship's hold, but Aldwine managed to chew through her ropes, and liberated the others. They seized and gagged Suze, then bound her to a balsa plank, carrying her by moonlight up on deck.

'Sorry, frigwench,' said Warsweide, 'but it is the survival of the fittest. I heard you with Morue today. As an arse slave, you will be queen over us. There is no way we can compete against those fesses of yours. You won't drift for long, the current will take you to the shore, and if you can get free, why, you've a sporting chance, as you English say.'

The girls tittered. Warsweide bent, and bit Suze's bare buttocks, leaving a vivid impression of her canines, amid the bruises of Suze's recent strapping.

'Such a juicy bum,' she murmured. 'So hard to resist. Why is it that the bum is always the sweetest portion of a girl? Even a slut like you, Suze. That's why we must get rid of you. We are jealous of your complete submissiveness. Your bum says it. You are all girl, all arse, the perfect female animal.'

She bit again, hard, and then let her tongue lap the striated weals of Suze's whipped fesses, and the bruise of her own teethmark. One by one, the others, even the quivering Aldwine, did the same. Suze grunted and wriggled, to no avail: there was a splash, as her naked body, buoyed by her makeshift raft, slid into the water. She floated, sobbing under the moon, with fireflies lighting up her shiny naked flesh, as the boat dwindled upstream, and its lights disappeared into the blackness. Her ropes were soon soaked, and, by wriggling, she was able to loosen them. Her motions, and the eddies of the swirling river bobbed her closer and closer to the jungle shore. Her balsa raft foundered on mud, half sinking, until her body was submerged in the ooze. She managed to slither free of the ropes, then clambered stickily to the bank, where she grasped an overhanging branch, and hoisted herself to the safety of swampy moss and creepers. She sobbed for a while, before dozing off on the carpet of tendrils, awakening, when sunlight streaked her face, and humans stood over her, casting their shadows.

15

All Girl

'Well, what have we here?' said a girl's voice, in English. 'A trespasser . . .'

Suze blinked, rubbed her eyes, and looked up. Silhouetted above her stood a tall girl, carrying a long, thin stick, like a cane. Her comrades carried coiled whips. A blue trickle of French tobacco smoke flowed from the cigarette, drooping in the corner of the speaker's mouth, and Suze's nostrils opened wide, to smell it.

'I . . . I can explain,' she blurted. 'I am the victim of a dreadful misunderstanding. My name is –'

'I know what your name is, Suze,' said the girl.

Suze sat up, peering.

'Fiona?' she gasped.

'Quite so,' said Fiona Leatherhead, grabbing Suze's arm, and hoisting her.

Dried mud flaked from her body as she rose.

'My, you are a mucky pup,' Fiona said, spitting out her cigarette butt, so that it landed on Suze's mud-caked cooze.

'Fiona . . . what are you doing here? Who are these girls?'

Fiona wore a short uniform skirt of sacking, dyed khaki, that clung to her knickerless bottom and thighs, and clearly outlined the lush folds and heavy matting of her pubic forest. The top of her body was nude, her ripe breasts tan and swinging bare, like those of the others; all wore belts, knives and digging tools, strapped to their waists and torsos, and had thick rubber ankle-boots.

'They are my platoon,' said Fiona. 'We are scouts, looking for intruders. Of which it seems, I am afraid, that you are one.'

'Oh, Fiona!' blurted Suze, bursting into tears, and hugging her friend.

'Now, there's no need for soppy stuff,' retorted Fiona. 'You are among friends, if you play your cards right. Just be nice and submissive to the master, and you'll escape the penalty for trespass, if I put in a good word for you with Brunhilde.'

'Penalty? Trespass?' Suze cried. 'Fiona, what are you talking about? Can't you see I've been cast adrift, I'm the victim of unspeakable cruelty. Look at my body, I've been whipped and buggered, and . . . oh!'

She sobbed helplessly, as Fiona touched the welts on her bare.

'Well, the evidence of your bum supports you. You can say goodbye to your modelling career,' she said. 'But the master tends to think girls are guilty until proven innocent, and Brunhilde *knows* they are guilty – anything for a fresh sweet rump to cane. I'm afraid we'll have to truss you for the journey back to Sybaris. That is the way illegal aliens are dealt with. But we'll bind you lightly.'

'Sybaris?' Suze gasped.

'Of course,' snapped Fiona, as the girls began to rope Suze's unresisting body, wracked with sobs. 'Don't pretend you didn't know.'

'The girls spoke of Sybaris, a place of pleasure and comfort, but I thought it was just a myth,' Suze said.

'No myth,' Fiona replied. 'Well, giddy-up, girls. I imagine you won't object to being carried, Suze.'

Hogtied, Suze was carried through dense jungle, on the shoulders of the platoon, their path winding higher, until they emerged from the trees, onto a plateau of gently undulating hills. Grassland was studded with glades, hedges, streams and ornamental pools, in which naked girls swam, and in the middle stood a castle, girt with meadows of bright flowers.

'Oh, gasped Suze, 'it's lovely . . . it's a dream come true. It's just like home.'

In the distance, a group of nude girls were harnessed with ropes to a cart, which they pulled up a steep hill. A second cart was loaded with rocks by girls at the hill's base, and both groups were driven by the whips of bare-breasted, booted girls, in uniform skirts. When the first cart reached the summit, the team upended it, with whiplashes to their bare backs, and the rocks spilled out, to roll down the hill to their starting place. The girls turned, and drew the cart down the hill, where they were harnessed to the second cart, already filled with rocks, to recommence their ascent. Suze's guardians made for the castle, and, as they neared it, she gasped aloud.

'I've seen this place before,' she blurted to Fiona.

'Yes, you have,' Fiona replied.

'The master . . . Brunhilde . . . is she blond and German?'

'Yes, that is her. You do remember,' Fiona said. 'It was Brunhilde who cast you adrift from Cordovan's yacht.'

'Ouistreham castle, *here*,' Suze murmured, her face pale. 'And the master . . . Grobard Westerham.'

'The castle was founded by the voluptuary Capt Foulkes Westerham, when he pretended to disappear up the Orinoco, in 1923,' Fiona said. 'He created a playground of the instinct, where European females could fulfil their craving for strict corporal punishment and enslavement to the male, freed of western hypocrisies. Succeeding masters have improved and extended the structure. You see why the master was so willing to fund your precious film trip. He knew you would reach Sybaris, if you had the bottom for it. A true sub will always find her haven. Of course, the master has contact with useful perverts in the region, the legionnaires, and the French prison. He knows what girl meat is where.'

They entered the portals of the castle, where the platoon set Suze down, but left her in restraint. A tall young man, wearing a white suit and panama hat, with a pink orchid in his buttonhole, sauntered from the shaded vestibule. Beside him, and leaning on his elbow, hobbled Cpl Pette, nude, save for a rubber harness, binding her titties, arse cleft and cunt, and with her left prosthesis missing.

Her thigh stump shone with lush silky hairs, combed in a mane.

'Why, Miss Suzette Shard, the supermodel,' said Grobard Westerham. 'Such a pretty package. I am glad you have come to join us. Ladies, please untie Miss Shard, so that she may curtsy to her master.'

'What . . . ?' Suze blurted.

The girls untied her, and she stood, trembling in the nude, before the leering male.

'Curtsy,' hissed Fiona, 'or it will go ill for you.'

Trembling, Suze abased herself in a curtsy.

'I believe you know Cpl Pette, and of course, dear Fiona and you are old friends. You will want to get together for a good chinwag about your adventures, I'm sure, but first, there is the small matter of your formal induction.'

'My what?' Suze cried.

'On your departure from England, you had halfway proved your submission. By making your way here, guided by your bottom's yearning for correction, you have proved yourself wholly. There remains your welcome ceremony to our haven of female pleasure.'

Brunhilde, nude, save for black leather thigh boots, with spiked heels, emerged from the hallway, bearing an English school cane, perched on the stiffened nipples of her jutting bare breasts.

'You are invited to take a bare-bum thrashing,' he purred, 'in front of these friendly witnesses.'

'What?' Suze gasped, clutching her face. 'Oh, no . . . please! Fiona! What is this?'

Fiona had removed her skirtlet, and, nude, was bending over, fiddling at her right thigh. Her bottom melons shone in the shafts of sunlight streaking the shadow, illumining bright red canewelts.

'Oh, no, Fiona,' Suze moaned, 'a sub . . . *you*?'

Fiona stood up, holding her right prosthesis before her, and balancing on her left leg, until the master scooped her by the titties, and held her close to him, with Cpl Pette. Coyly, Fiona exposed her silken-haired right stump to her old school chum.

'Yes, me,' she murmured. 'We all have our destiny, Suze. Do you accept yours? You might as well, you have come far enough for it. I'm amputated, and I'm all girl. it's so lovely, to be helpless, and in thrall of men, the ultimate power trip. Like wearing white silk, forever. Don't worry, you'll need both those lovely legs for pulling the master's chariot, or the rock cart, if you are naughty. Soubise is here, and Michelle Cowley, and Doris Norton, remember? Even Dr Teidt, to give you your Gothic massage. There are other men, liege lords of the master, who may be permitted your favours and the use of your body. You are the only person who has no say in that use.'

'I can't believe this,' Suze blurted. 'They said Sybaris was a place of earthly delight . . .'

'So it is,' replied Fiona crisply. 'Here is a life of slavery and obedience to males, of constant flogging of your bare flesh, your bumhole sore from cock, and your bottom permanently crusted with smarting whip weals. You will abase yourself, masturbating publicly, or performing obscene acts with other girls, for the amusement of the master. Your humiliance shall be endless.'

'What if I refuse?' Suze whimpered.

'Why, there is London,' said Fiona. 'Pretty clothes, money, comfort and fame. You can take that life of ease, disillusion, and frustration, Suze, rubbing your smooth bottom every night, diddling yourself, yearning for a strong male to lash and humiliate you, as you crave to be humiliated. Do you want to go back to that life? This is your chance to be you, Suze. You don't have to live in denial any more.'

'I have responsibilities, my new line, the Laindoux people in Paris . . .' Suze moaned, helplessly.

'Suze, the master *owns* the Laindoux fashion house,' Fiona snapped. 'Do you really want to go back?'

'The choice is yours, Suzette,' said Grobard. 'Do you?'

'I . . . I don't know,' Suze bleated. 'I'm so confused. Fiona – I mean, master – may I please have a cigarette?'

Grobard laughed.

'Give the lady a smoke, Fiona,' he murmured.

Fiona did so, and lit her up. Suze sucked smoke, and shook her mane, smoothing it back from her forehead.

'Hold the cigarette in the corner of your mouth, and put your hands behind your back,' ordered the master.

Trembling, Suze did as he ordered.

'Now, feet apart,' he said.

She parted her legs. Smoke drooled from the cigarette, blurring her gaze. She took a strong drag, and held the smoke inside her, exhaling through her nose. She smiled.

'Doris Norton is here?' she said.

'In the flesh,' Fiona answered.

'I've a score to settle with that flesh,' Suze said, slowly.

'You may answer the question now,' said Grobard. 'Do you wish to return to your former life?'

'No,' whispered Suze.

'Louder, bitch!' cried Brunhilde,

Vip! She lashed her cane across Suze's bare breasts, and leaving an angry pink welt on her nipples.

'Oh!' Suze shrilled. 'N-no, master.'

'Louder, bitch!' spat the German girl.

Vip! Suze's caned titties wobbled violently, as did Brunhilde's bare breasts, in the ferocity of her canestroke.

'Oh! No, master!'

Grobard snapped his fingers, and Brunhilde, sweating, handed him the cane, which he flexed and examined, as though it were a new object.

'Do you willingly accept a bare-bum thrashing?' he said.

'I was strapped yesterday. My arse is very sore,' Suze blurted, her cigarette waggling at the corner of her mouth.

'Answer,' said Grobard.

'Yes, I do,' Suze whispered.

The cane slashed the air, beside Suze's cunt.

'Answer properly.'

'Yes, master,' she sobbed. 'You know I want it. Oh, don't play games, I beg you. Please . . . please cane me, on the bare.'

'Touch your toes, and part your buttocks well.'

Sobbing, Suze obeyed. *Vip! Vip! Vip!*

'Ah! Master . . .' she cried, dropping the wasted cigarette end from her lips as the cane laid three bright pink welts on her naked bumflesh.

Vip! Vip! Vip!

'Ooh . . .' she whimpered. 'Uhh . . .'

Suze's cheeks clenched repeatedly, as the beating continued, in sets of three strokes, and her legs stiffened and jerked stiff at each flurry of the cane, striping her naked buttocks deeper and darker, until she had taken over forty strokes. Her croup was a mosaic of welts; come dripped from her wet, writhing cooze.

'Is caning enough?' Grobard said.

'No, master,' she sobbed.

Vip! Vip! Vip!

'Ah!'

'Louder, bitch!

'No, master!'

'What more, then, slut?'

'Oh, master, you know. Must I answer? I am so ashamed . . .' Suze wailed.

'No,' said Grobard, 'you need not. Your wet gash answers for you. You are all girl, Suzette.'

Brunhilde opened the master's trousers, and freed his naked cock, massively erect. Fiona lit another cigarette, and placed it between Suze's lips. Hungrily, she sucked smoke, holding the cigarette at the corner of her mouth. Brunhilde parted the cheeks of Suze's arse, and pressed the glans of her master's stiff cock to the anus pucker. The cock penetrated her anus, plunging to the rectum, and he began to thrust.

'Oh, yes!' gasped the master. 'Oh, it's so good! Your arse is so tight! How do you do it?'

Suze panted hoarsely, without dropping her cigarette, and smiled, a pleased smile, as her master buggered her.

Nexus

NEXUS BACKLIST

This information is correct at time of printing. For up-to-date information, please visit our website at www.nexus-books.co.uk

All books are priced at £5.99 unless another price is given.

Nexus books with a contemporary setting

ACCIDENTS WILL HAPPEN	Lucy Golden ISBN 0 352 33596 3	☐
ANGEL	Lindsay Gordon ISBN 0 352 33590 4	☐
BARE BEHIND £6.99	Penny Birch ISBN 0 352 33721 4	☐
BEAST	Wendy Swanscombe ISBN 0 352 33649 8	☐
THE BLACK FLAME	Lisette Ashton ISBN 0 352 33668 4	☐
BROUGHT TO HEEL	Arabella Knight ISBN 0 352 33508 4	☐
CAGED!	Yolanda Celbridge ISBN 0 352 33650 1	☐
CANDY IN CAPTIVITY	Arabella Knight ISBN 0 352 33495 9	☐
CAPTIVES OF THE PRIVATE HOUSE	Esme Ombreux ISBN 0 352 33619 6	☐
CHERI CHASTISED £6.99	Yolanda Celbridge ISBN 0 352 33707 9	☐
DANCE OF SUBMISSION	Lisette Ashton ISBN 0 352 33450 9	☐
DIRTY LAUNDRY £6.99	Penny Birch ISBN 0 352 33680 3	☐
DISCIPLINED SKIN	Wendy Swanscombe ISBN 0 352 33541 6	☐

- - - - - - ✄ -

Please send me the books I have ticked above.

Name   ....

Address   ....

            ....

            ....

            .... Post code...................

Send to: **Cash Sales, Nexus Books, Thames Wharf Studios, Rainville Road, London W6 9HA**

US customers: for prices and details of how to order books for delivery by mail, call 1-800-343-4499.

Please enclose a cheque or postal order, made payable to **Nexus Books Ltd**, to the value of the books you have ordered plus postage and packing costs as follows:
UK and BFPO – £1.00 for the first book, 50p for each subsequent book.
Overseas (including Republic of Ireland) – £2.00 for the first book, £1.00 for each subsequent book.

If you would prefer to pay by VISA, ACCESS/MASTERCARD, AMEX, DINERS CLUB or SWITCH, please write your card number and expiry date here:

....

Please allow up to 28 days for delivery.

Signature ....

Our privacy policy

We will not disclose information you supply us to any other parties. We will not disclose any information which identifies you personally to any person without your express consent.

From time to time we may send out information about Nexus books and special offers. Please tick here if you do *not* wish to receive Nexus information.   ☐

- - - - - - ✄ -